DEAR DEPARTED

CYNTHIA HARROD-EAGLES

TIME WARNER
BOOKS

First published in Great Britain in 2004 by Time Warner Books
This paperback edition published in April 2005
Reprinted 2005, 2006

A CIP catalogue record for this book
is available from the British Library.

ISBN-13: 978-0-7515-3428-3
ISBN-10: 0-7515-3428-5

Printed and bound in Great Britain by
Clays Ltd, St Ives plc

Time Warner Books
An imprint of
Little, Brown Book Group
Brettenham House
Lancaster Place
London WC2E 7EN

A member of the Hachette Livre Group of Companies

www.littlebrown.co.uk

Cynthia Harrod-Eagles was born and educated in Shepherd's Bush, and had a variety of jobs in the commercial world, starting as a junior cashier at Woolworth's and working her way down to Pensions Officer at the BBC. She won the Young Writers' Award in 1973, and became a full-time writer in 1978. She is the author of over sixty successful novels to date, including twenty-seven volumes of the *Morland Dynasty* series.

Visit the author's website at www.cynthiaharrodeagles.com

Also by Cynthia Harrod-Eagles

The Bill Slider Mysteries

ORCHESTRATED DEATH
DEATH WATCH
NECROCHIP
DEAD END
BLOOD LINES
KILLING TIME
SHALLOW GRAVE
BLOOD SINISTER
GONE TOMORROW

The Dynasty Series

THE FOUNDING
THE DARK ROSE
THE PRINCELING
THE OAK APPLE
THE BLACK PEARL
THE LONG SHADOW
THE CHEVALIER
THE MAIDEN
THE FLOOD-TIDE
THE TANGLED THREAD
THE EMPEROR
THE VICTORY
THE REGENCY
THE CAMPAIGNERS
THE RECKONING
THE DEVIL'S HORSE
THE POISON TREE
THE ABYSS
THE HIDDEN SHORE
THE WINTER JOURNEY
THE OUTCAST
THE MIRAGE
THE CAUSE
THE HOMECOMING
THE QUESTION
THE DREAM KINGDOM
THE RESTLESS SEA
THE WHITE ROAD

In loving memory of Geoffrey Knighton –
Hero, reluctant soldier, teacher, writer,
critic and friend.

"Life's race well run, life's work well done."

1

open.guv.ok

There is nothing quite like knocking on a strange door for getting a policeman's adrenaline going. Slider stood in the hotel corridor, listening to the white noise of the air-conditioning and the interesting tattoo of his own heartbeat, and wondering if he was about to die.

His mouth was so dry he had to pause a moment and manufacture some spit. The kevlar vest under his shirt made him feel hot and awkward, and the tape holding the wire to his flesh was making him itch. He'd had to borrow a jacket from a larger colleague to conceal the fact that he was protected. He looked, and felt, over-weight and stupid.

In front of him was an ordinary, typical hotel door, and behind the door was an extraordinary, untypical man, who, moreover, might well be armed, and had amply proved his willingness to kill. Robert Bates, alias The Needle, was being brought to book at last. He had been the subject of ongoing investigations by various CO departments of Scotland Yard, not to mention – because nobody ever did – MI5 and MI6.

Slider's path had crossed with his during the

investigation of a murder, which, it turned out most disappointingly, Bates didn't do. However, Slider had turned up a number of things Bates did do, including the undoubted murder of a prostitute whom Bates had used, tortured, and then dispatched. Because of the involvement of higher authorities, Slider had been warned off Bates, but such disappointments were commonplace in a copper's life. Sooner or later, he had reasoned, The Needle would get his come-uppance. Then two days ago he had been summoned to the office of the area supremo, Commander Wetherspoon.

'Ah, Slider,' Wetherspoon said, tilting his head back so that he could look down his nose at him, 'someone here who wants to speak to you, Chief Superintendent Ormerod of the Serious Crime Group Liaison Team.'

Ormerod was a large and serious man, who towered over Slider and would have made two of him in bulk, and at least ten in conscious supremacy. He had a handsome, authoritative face, eyes like steel traps, and the smell of power came off him like an aura. This man was from the far, far end of policing, the place of hard deals done behind closed doors, of anonymous corridors, terse telephone calls, operations with code names and briefings with senior ministers where the senior ministers behaved quite meekly. It was as different from Slider's place on the street as the Cabinet Room of Number 10 was from the checkout at Tesco's. Slider felt faint just breathing Ormerod's aftershave; and when Ormerod smiled, it was even more frightening than when he didn't.

Ormerod smiled. 'Ah, Inspector Slider. Bill, isn't it? I'm glad to meet you. I won't waste time. Trevor Bates. You did some smart work on that case. I'm sorry you had to take a back seat, but very large things were at stake.'

'I understand, sir,' Slider said, since something seemed to be required.

'We've got to the point now where we're ready to arrest him, and we want you to be the one to do it.'

'Me, sir?' Slider couldn't help it, though it made him sound like Billy Bunter.

'Thought you'd like to be in on it,' Ormerod said. 'Sort of thanks for all your hard work.'

'Consolation prize,' Wetherspoon put in, and Slider was glad to see him quelled with a single look from Ormerod. Anyone who could quell Wetherspoon was a Big Monkey indeed.

'Also,' Ormerod said, 'we think you could be useful to us.'

Ormerod explained. Bates was a high-powered criminal, and as sharp and cunning as a lorry full of foxes. It would be impossible to arrest him in his home, which was better defended than Fort Knox, and pretty hard anywhere else if he saw them coming. Bates often went armed, and usually had armed bodyguards around him.

However, the day after tomorrow he was attending a business conference in a hotel in Birmingham, and staying overnight, and was unlikely to be armed in such a place, especially as they had taken pains to fall back from him over the past few weeks and let him relax. He would not be expecting trouble, and though he would have an 'assistant' with him, for which read bodyguard, he would probably not be taking very heavy precautions.

'All the same, we can't take him in any of the public rooms, in case his goon gets rattled and starts loosing off,' Ormerod said. 'So we have to arrest him in his room at the end of the day. But we don't want to go kicking the door in and provoking a shoot-out. We need someone to distract him. That's where you come in. He knows you, you've spoken to him before, and he's not afraid of you.'

With the rind taken off, what Ormerod was saying was that Bates thought Slider was a pathetic dickhead whom he'd already outsmarted once. He would therefore be more likely to open the door to him. Bates was also tricky, smart and strong, and had an unhealthy liking for torture, knives and needles. And guns. The words 'tethered' and 'goat' had wandered through Slider's mind, looking for something to link up with.

Which was why Slider now regarded that anonymous hotel door with trepidation. If Bates opened it at all, it might be simply to shoot him, and he didn't want to die. His pulse rate notched up another level as he raised his hand and rapped hard on it. The team was all behind him, he reminded himself. They had watched Bates to his room, watched the 'assistant' to his adjoining one, and were waiting just out of sight, listening to everything that came over Slider's wire, ready for his signal. He hoped the wire was still working. He hoped they weren't being deafened by his heartbeat.

He knocked again. Bates's voice – Slider recognised it, with a shiver - called out irritably from within. 'Who is it?'

Slider gulped. 'Detective Inspector Slider, sir, Shepherd's Bush. Could I have a word, do you think?'

'*What?*' Bates said incredulously. 'Slider, did you say?' His voice came again from just behind the door, and Slider guessed he was being examined through the peephole. He held up his brief. 'I know you,' Bates said. 'What are you doing here? What the hell do you want?'

'I'd like to have a word with you, sir,' Slider said stolidly, Mr Plod to the core. 'I'd like to ask you a few questions.'

There was a click and a rattle, and Slider's stomach

4

went over the edge of a cliff as the door was flung open and he waited for the hot flash and burn of a bullet or a knife in the guts. The kevlar was a comfort but it didn't cover everything.

But he didn't die. Bates stood there, lean, weirdly attractive, with his pale, translucent skin, clear grey eyes and backswept, shoulder-length fox red hair. He was still in his suit – three piece, exquisitely cut – but he had removed his tie and opened the top button of his shirt.

'What the *devil*?' he said, and looked Slider up and down with amused contempt. 'You came asking me questions once before about some pathetic trivia or other. A leather jacket, wasn't it?'

'It's a little bit more serious this time, sir, I'm sorry to say,' Slider plodded. 'Can I come in? I don't think you want to discuss your private business in the corridor.'

'I don't intend to discuss my private business with you at all,' he said. 'What the devil are you doing here anyway? Do your superiors know you've come bothering me?'

'I don't need permission from anyone when I'm following up a case,' Slider said, hoping he would take this to mean he was mavericking. Bates had not shut the door on him, apparently fascinated by the absurdity of this idiot policeman following him all the way to Birmingham. Ormerod had read him right: arrogance would be his downfall. Slider took the opportunity to walk past him into the room, noting with huge relief that there was no-one else in it. The goon was still in his adjoining room, the door of which was over to the left. One shout from Bates and he would come busting in, probably with a gun. Slider was not out of the woods yet.

'I didn't give you permission to come in,' Bates said, sounding annoyed now.

'This won't take long, sir,' Slider said. His voice shook

slightly, but it probably didn't matter. Bates would expect him to be nervous of a powerful man like him. 'And it is rather important.'

'More lost clothing? Or is it a lost dog this time?' Bates sneered; but he walked away from the door, and it swung closed with a soft click. Slider cleared his throat, which was the signal. Nearly there now. Just a few seconds more. The team would be creeping towards the two doors, pass keys in hand.

Slider turned towards Bates, so that Bates had his back to the door. Triumph was beginning to sing in his veins along with the adrenaline, a heady mixture. He felt drunk and reckless with it, and knew it was a dangerous state of mind.

'It's a bit more interesting than that,' he said, and the change of his tone brought alertness into the hard grey eyes. Slider saw the nostrils widen as though Bates were scenting like an animal for danger. 'It's to do with a certain prostitute called Susie Mabbot. I'm sure you remember her, even among your many conquests.'

'I don't know any prostitutes. How dare you suggest it?' Bates said, advancing grimly. Slider backed a step to encourage him.

'You used to know poor Susie, in the Biblical sense, anyway. Then one day you got carried away and killed her. Stuck her full of needles, had her, broke her neck, and chucked her in the Thames.'

'You're mad!' Bates said. Outside the team slipped the pass card into the magnetic lock and it gave a faint but unmistakable clunk. Bates's eyes flew wide as he realised the trap. He yelled, 'Norman!' and his small but rock hard fist shot out at Slider's face.

Without the adrenaline he'd have been felled, but all those flight–or–fight impulses he had been resisting in the last five minutes came to his aid now. He jerked his head aside so fast that he ricked his neck and the fist shot past his head, grazing his left ear. In the same motion, Slider ducked in low and flung himself at Bates, grabbing him round the middle, and Bates, thrown off balance by the missed punch, was just unstable enough to stagger backwards and go down, hitting the floor with Slider on top of him as the rest of the team burst in through the two doors simultaneously.

From the next room there was thumping, crashing and shouting as the bodyguard put up a vigorous resistance. For a moment Bates writhed viciously, but then he suddenly seemed to see the futility, or perhaps the indignity of it, and became still. With his teeth bared, he hissed at Slider, 'You'll regret this. I'll see you regret this, you pathetic moron. You don't know what you're meddling with. You're in over your depth. You're nobody!'

'Well, at least I'm not a murderer,' Slider said. He knew he ought not to provoke the man, but he couldn't help it. That fist had taken skin off his ear, and his neck hurt.

'You can't prove a thing against me,' Bates said, utterly assured.

'Oh yes I can,' Slider said blithely. 'Poor old Susie got washed up. We found her.'

It was impossible for Bates to pale, but his eyes widened slightly. 'You found her?'

'Yup. Got the body, got the semen, got the DNA. You're nicked, mate.'

A policeman's life, he thought afterwards, holds few moments so beautiful as seeing an arrogant, vicious, self-satisfied criminal crumple in the face of what he knows is the inevitable. Slider got to his feet, and as Bates began to struggle up, he began his victory chant.

'Trevor Bates, I arrest you for the murder of Susan

Mabbot. You do not have to say anything, but it may harm your defence . . .'

Bates wasn't listening. He stared at Slider as though burning his image into his brain. 'I'll get you for this,' he said.

'. . . anything you later rely on in court,' Slider finished. And suddenly he felt very tired, as all the adrenaline got bored with this part of the proceedings and went off somewhere else to look for a fight.

It is an immutable law, formulated by the eminent philosopher Professor Sod, that you will always wake up early on your day off. It was six a.m. when the alarm in Slider's head went off. He woke in his customary violent fashion, with a grunt. He rarely managed a controlled re-entry: usually he hit consciousness like a man being thrown out of a moving car.

Joanna wasn't there. He listened for a moment, then got up and padded into the kitchen. She was standing by the sink drinking water, staring out of the window into the small oblong of rough grass and blackberry brambles she called a garden. Since her pregnancy had begun to show, she had stopped wandering about in the nude. In an access of modesty she had taken to wearing a loose white muslin dress by way of a dressing-gown. As it was almost but not quite completely transparent, it was far more erotic than nakedness, but Slider hadn't told her that. He just hoped that she didn't answer the door in it when he wasn't there. The postman didn't look as though his heart would take it.

He slipped his arms round her from behind and rested his chin on her shoulder. 'All right?' he murmured.

'Hmm,' she confirmed.

'Couldn't sleep?'

'Not since half past four. Why are you up, anyway? We were going to lie in and cuddle.'

'Hard to do when you're in the kitchen,' he pointed out. 'Shall we go back to bed?'

He felt her hesitate, and knew what was coming.

'I'm hungry.'

'You're always hungry. It's just your hormones.'

'My hormones and I go everywhere together. Why don't the three of us have breakfast? It's such a beautiful morning, too good to waste lying in bed.'

He detached himself from her back. 'I thought pregnant women were supposed to feel extra sexy,' he complained.

'You've got to fuel the engine,' she said.

She fried bacon and tomatoes and made toast while he got a shave out of the way, and then they ate and talked.

'Fried tomatoes are definitely a seventh-day thing,' Slider said. Joanna had a theory that God had done all His very best creations on Sunday, when He was at leisure. A large amount of food seemed to get into her list: toasted cheese, raspberries, the smell of coffee.

'It's such a long time since we did this,' she said happily. 'I don't even remember when you last had a day off.'

He had only known since May that Joanna was pregnant. She had given up her job with the orchestra in Amsterdam and was back home permanently, looking for work for the next few months. With the baby due in November, she could work until about the end of September – if she could get the dates. She'd had no luck so far. Still, it gave her a chance to look for a place for them to live. Her tiny flat had one bedroom, one sitting room, a small kitchen and a breathe-by-numbers bathroom – adequate for them but tight for them plus baby.

Being an old-fashioned kind of a bloke, he was determined they should get married before the baby was born. And before they got married they had to announce everything to their respective families, something which work had made impossible for him. But now, with the debriefing and writing up of the Bates case done at last, he had two days off. Tomorrow he and Joanna were going to spend the day with his father – his only relly – and today they were going down to Eastbourne to see her parents. Slider had never yet met them, and was nervous.

'What if they don't like me?' he asked.

She was good at catching on. 'They'll like you. Why wouldn't they?'

'Debauching their daughter, for one. Getting you pregnant before marrying you.'

'My sister Alison was born only six months after the Aged Ps married.'

'Really?'

'Mum mellowed one night when Sophie and I took her out for a drink for her birthday, and confessed. She was a bit shocked the next day when she remembered. She swore us to secrecy, so don't say anything. Apparently the others don't know.'

'Except for Alison, presumably.'

'I wouldn't even be sure of that. She may not have put two and two together. She was always good at ignoring inconvenient facts.'

Slider reached for the marmalade. 'Tell me them again. I haven't got them straight.'

'Doesn't matter. You aren't going to meet them all.'

'You know me. I like to do my homework.'

'All right. Alison's the eldest, then the three boys, Peter, Tim and George.'

'They're in Australia?'

'No, only Tim and George. They all emigrated together but Peter came back.'

'Oh, yes, I remember now.'

'Then Louisa and Bobby, then me, then the twins that died, then Sophie.'

'What a crowd. It must have been nice, growing up with so many people around you.'

'I'm sure you got a lot more attention,' said Joanna.

'But you don't have much backup when you're an only child. No insurance. When Mum died there was only me and Dad, and when he goes . . .'

She reached across and squeezed his hand. 'You'll still have a wife, an ex-wife and at least three children.'

He began to smile. 'At least? What are you trying to tell me?'

She looked casual. 'Oh, well, I just thought if you're going to fork out all that money for a marriage licence, you might as well get your money's worth.'

He inspected her expression and was thinking they might go back to bed after all, when the phone rang. Joanna met his eyes. 'Oh, no,' she said, looking a question and a doubt.

He felt a foreboding. 'It couldn't be. They wouldn't. Not on my day off.' But he knew they could and would. Detective inspectors had to be available for duty at all times, and since they didn't get paid overtime it was easier on the budget to call them rather than someone who did.

He got up and trudged out to the narrow hall (Never get a pram in here, he thought distractedly) and picked up the phone. It was Nicholls, one of the uniformed sergeants at Shepherd's Bush police station. 'Are you up and dressed?'

'This had better be important,' Slider growled.

'Sorry, Bill. I know it's your day off and I hate to do it to you, but it's a murder.'

'Oh, for God's sake!'

'Came in on a 999 call. Female, stabbed to death in Paddenswick Park. Looks as though the Park Killer's struck again.'

'Why can't Carver's lot catch it?'

'They're knee deep in that drugs and prostitution ring. The boss says you're it. I'm sorry, mate.'

'Bloody Nora, can't people leave off killing each other for two minutes together?' Out of the corner of his eye he saw that Joanna had come out into the hall. At these words she turned away, and the cast of her shoulders was eloquent. 'All right, on my way.'

Joanna was in the bedroom. She looked up when he came in and forestalled his speech. 'I gathered.'

'I'm sorry,' he said.

'I know. Can't be helped.'

He could tell by her terseness that she was upset, and he didn't blame her. 'You'll explain to your parents?'

'Don't worry about it.'

'Will you still go?'

'No point. I'll call it off,' she said shortly, passing him in the doorway.

He rang Atherton – DS Jim Atherton, his bagman – and got him on his mobile at the scene.

'You don't need to hurry. Porson's got everything under control.'

'Hell's bells. What's he doing there?'

'He was in the office when I arrived at a quarter to eight. I don't think he'd been home.'

Porson, their det sup, had recently been widowed. Slider wondered whether he was finding home without his wife hard to cope with.

'The shout came in about a quarter past eight,' Atherton went on, 'and he grabbed the team and shot over here. He's already whistled up extra uniform to take statements, and the SOCO van's on the way.'

'So what does he need me for?' Slider asked resentfully.

'I expect it's lurve,' Atherton said. 'Gotta go – he's beckoning.'

So it was away with the cords and chambray shirt, hello workday suit and Teflon tie. Blast and damn, Slider thought. Any murder meant a period of intensive work and long hours, but a serial murderer could tie you down for months. If it was the Park Killer, there was no knowing when he'd get a day off again.

The traffic had built up by the time Slider left the house, and he had plenty of leisure to reflect as he crawled along Bath Road. The Park Killer had 'struck' – as the newspapers liked to put it – twice before, but not on Slider's ground. The first time had been in Gunnersbury Park, the second only a month ago in Acton Park. On that – admittedly meagre – basis it looked as though he was moving eastwards, which left room for a couple more possible incidents in Shepherd's Bush before he reached Holland Park and became Notting Hill's problem. Slider wondered what could be done to hasten that happy day. The very thought of a serial killer made him miserable. The idea that any human being could be so utterly self-absorbed that he would kill someone at random simply as a means of self-advertisement was deeply depressing.

It was part, he thought, as he inched forward towards a traffic light that only stayed green for thirty seconds every five minutes, of the modern cult of celebrity. To get on the telly, to get in the papers, was the ultimate ambition for a wide swathe of the deeply stupid. And the newspapers didn't help. This present bozo had killed two people, and already he had a media sobriquet. No wonder he had killed again so soon. He had a public to satisfy now. He was a performer.

To be a celebrity act, of course, you had to have a trademark, and the Park Killer's bag was to kill in broad daylight in a public place full of passers-by – people walking dogs, people going to work, people jogging, roller-blading, bicycling. The newspapers had been full of wonder (which the killer probably read as admiration) as to how he had managed not to be seen. Paddenswick Park fitted this MO. It lay between Goldhawk Road to the north and King Street to the south, and was not only a cut-through but was well used by the local population for matutinal exercise and dog-emptying. Morning rush hour was the PK's time of choice. If nothing else, Slider reflected, it slowed down the police trying to get to the scene.

By the time he reached the area, he had plumbed the depths. To add to the stupid senselessness of every murder, in this case there would be all the problems involved in liaising with the Ealing squad – how they would enjoy having to share with him the fact that they had got nowhere! – not to mention dealing with the inevitable media circus. It looked as though it would be a close-run thing whether he would get to marry Joanna or draw his pension first.

The park and a large section of Paddenswick Road, which ran down its east side, were cordoned off. Atherton was standing in the RV area behind the blue-and-white tape; he came over and moved it for Slider to drive through. Within the area were several marked police cars, Atherton's and the department wheels and the large white

14

van belonging to the scene-of-crime officers. Inside the park gates he could see that all the people who had been on the spot when the police arrived had been corralled, with a mixture of CID and uniform taking their basic details.

Though Slider kept a low media profile, some of the reporters recognised him and shouted out to him from where they were being kept at bay beyond the cordon. They only had one question, of course. 'Is it the Park Killer?' 'Do you think it's the Park Killer?' A nod from him and they'd dash off, click together their Lego stock phrases, and every paper and bulletin would have the same headline: PARK KILLER STRIKES AGAIN. Slider ignored them.

'What it is to be a star,' said Atherton.

'Me or him?' Slider asked suspiciously.

'Me, of course,' said Atherton. He was elegantly suited, as always, and his straight fair hair, which he wore cut short these days, had just the subtlest hint of a fashionable spikiness about it, making him look even more dangerous to women. That sort of subtlety you had to pay upwards of forty quid for. Slider, who had used the same back-street barber for twenty years and now paid a princely nine quid a go, felt shabby and rumpled beside him. With his height and slimness Atherton sometimes looked more like a male model than a policeman. He was also, however, looking distinctly underslept about the eyes.

'On the tiles again last night?' Slider enquired. 'Let me see, it was that new PC, wasn't it? Collins?'

'Yvonne. She's new to the area and doesn't know anybody,' Atherton said, with dignity. 'I was just making friends.'

'A wild night of friend-making really takes it out of you,' Slider said.

'Crabby this morning,' Atherton observed. 'Bad luck about your day off. McLaren's gone in search of coffee and bacon sarnies,' he added coaxingly.

'I had breakfast,' Slider said. 'I still don't know what I'm doing here, if Porson's in charge.'

'Looks as though you're about to find out,' said Atherton, gesturing with his head.

Slider turned and caught Detective Superintendent Fred 'The Syrup' Porson's eye on him across the little groups of coppers and witnesses. Porson was tall and bony and reared above the mass of humanity like a dolmen, his knobbly slap gleaming in the sun. It was still a shock to Slider to see old Syrup's bald pate. He had earned his sobriquet through years of wearing a deeply unconvincing wig, but he had abandoned it the day his wife died. Slider was forced to the unlikely conclusion that it was Betty Porson (who had been quite an elegant little person) who had encouraged the sporting of the rug. The nickname had been in existence too long to die; now it had to be applied ironically.

Slider liked Porson. He was a good policeman and a loyal senior, and if he used language like a man in boxing gloves trying to thread a needle, well, it was a small price to pay not to be commanded by a twenty-something career kangaroo with a degree in Applied Pillockry.

The Syrup was signalling something with his eyebrows. Porson's eyebrows were considerable growths. They could have declared UDI from the rest of his face and become a republic. Slider obeyed the summons.

'Sorry about your day off,' Porson said briefly. 'I've got things initialated for you, but you'll have to take over from here. I've got a Forward Strategy Planning Meeting at Hammersmith.' His tone revealed what he thought of strategic planning meetings. These days, holding meetings

16

seemed to be all the senior ranks did – hence, perhaps, old Syrup's eagerness to sniff the gunpowder this morning. 'Gallon was the first uniform on the spot – he'll fill you in on the commensurate part. I've got people taking statements from everyone who was still here when we got here, and SOCO's just gone in. All right?'

'Yes, sir,' Slider said. 'But—'

Porson raised a large, knuckly hand in anticipation of Slider's objection. 'A word in your shell-like,' he said, turning aside. Slider turned with him, and Porson resumed, in a lower voice: 'Look here, this might be the Park Killer or it might not. It could be, from the look of appearances, but I want it either way. The SCG's had to send most of its personal to help out the Anti-terrorist Squad, so Peter Judson's down to two men and a performing dog, and they're up to their navels.' The Serious Crime Group had first refusal of all murders. 'So it'll probably be left with us, at least for the present time being. If we can clear this one, it's going to do us a lot of *bon*. Definite flower in our caps.'

Slider wasn't sure he wanted anything in his cap. 'If it is a serial, there's Ealing to consider,' he said.

Porson looked triumphant. 'That's the beauty of it. They've not managed to get anywhere with it. We get the gen from them, and *we* clear it, see? Who's a pretty boy *then*?' Something of Slider's inner scepticism must have showed, because Porson lowered his voice even more, and practically climbed into his ear. 'Look here,' he said, 'I'm not trying to blow sunshine up your skirt. The bottom end is that I'm being considered for promotion. I've not got long to go. If I can retire a rank higher it makes a big difference to my pension.' His faded, red-rimmed eyes met Slider's without flinching. 'I've given my life to the Job. I think I deserve it.' Slider thought so too, but it wasn't his place to say so. 'But you know as well as I do what flavour goes down with the upper escalons these days,' Porson went on. 'We're not young and sexy. Dinosaurs, they call us, coppers like you and me. But a big-profile clear-up, that's just an incontroversial fact. They can't ignore that.'

Slider noted that Porson didn't say, 'Do this for me and I'll see you all right.' He had always been loyal to his troops and simply assumed that they knew it. Slider admired him for it. So he waved goodbye to his time off and did not sigh. 'I'll do my best, sir,' he said.

'I know you will, laddie. I know you will.' Porson was so moved he came within an inch of clapping Slider on the shoulder, changed the gesture at the last moment, tried to scratch his non-existent wig, and ended up rubbing his nose vigorously, clearing his throat with a percussive violence that would have stunned a starling at ten paces.

Slider decided to take advantage of the emotional moment. 'Any chance you can get me a replacement for Anderson, sir?' he asked. DC Anderson of Slider's team had been snatched by the National Crime Squad on a long-term secondment, leaving him a warm body short.

'I'll see what I can do,' Porson said, 'but don't hold your horses. You know what the situation is *vis-à-vis* recruitment.'

Slider returned to Atherton. 'All right,' he said, 'tell me about it. Where's the *corpus*, then?'

'In the bushes,' said Atherton.

On the Paddenswick Road side, the park was bounded by a low wall topped with spiked iron railings, the whole combination about nine feet high. An iron gate let on to a wide concreted path, which ran straight for twenty feet and then branched to give north–south and east–west walks, plus a curving circumference route round the northern end of the park that was popular with runners. The whole park was pleasantly landscaped, mostly grassy with a few large trees and one or two formal flower-beds beside the paths, filled now with the tidy summer bedders beloved of municipal gardeners – bright red ger-aniums, multicoloured pansies, edgings of blue and white lobelia and alyssum.

It was all open space, not at all murderer territory, except for a stretch of vigorous shrubbery of rhododen-drons, spotted laurels, winter viburnum and other such serviceable bushes, plus a few spindly trees of the birch and rowan sort. The shrubbery ran north to south, bordered on the east by the railings and on the west by the north–south path, which ran down to the gate oppo-site the tube station. And here, it seemed, among the sooty leaves, the murderer had lurked, and attacked.

PC Gallon, as promised, filled Slider in.

'It was a bloke walking his dog that found the body, sir, just after eight o'clock. A Mr Chapman, first name Michael, lives in Atwood Road?' Gallon was young enough to have the routine Estuary Query at the end of his sentences, but in this case he wanted to know if Slider knew where that was. Slider nodded.

'Well, he had his dog on one of those leads that reels out, and it went into the bushes there. He didn't notice till the dog starts barking and making a hell of a fuss. So he tries to reel it in, but it won't come, and he reckons the lead's caught up on the bushes or something, so he goes in after it, and there she is.'

'Was it him who phoned Emergency?'

'No, sir. Chapman comes out of the bushes and stops the first person he sees, bloke called David Hatherley who's walking through on his way to work, and he calls 999 on his mobile. Call was logged at eight twelve.'

'All right. Let's have a look,' Slider said.

Here, in this short stretch of path inside the gate and before the junction, the bushes grew close together, presenting an unbroken green wall of foliage. 'Here's where Chapman went in,' said Atherton. 'And presumably where the killer dragged the victim in.'

There were scuffmarks in the chipped bark mulch that had been spread under the shrubs to keep the weeds down. Some bark had spilled over onto the path, and there were two deep parallel grooves disappearing like tram lines into the shrubbery.

'You'd have thought there'd have been more damage to the bushes,' Slider complained. 'There's a few leaves on the ground, but no broken twigs or branches.'

'I suppose they just bent and whipped back,' Atherton said. 'There's better access for us round the other side. That's the way SOCO's gone in.'

They walked the few yards to the junction and turned left down the north–south path. On this side of the shrubbery the growth was less vigorous, and about twenty feet along there was a good two- to three-foot gap between two of the bushes. The crime-scene manager, Bob Bailey, met them there. He was a tall, lean man with wiry fair hair and a stiff moustache that Slider always thought must be hell on his wife. The scene-of-crime officers were civilians who worked out of headquarters at Hammersmith. In the course of things Slider and Bailey had a lot of contact and got on pretty well.

'The doc's been and gone, sir,' Bailey greeted him. 'Pronounced at eight twenty-nine.'

'Dr Prawalha? That was nippy.'

'Well, he only lives round the corner,' Bailey explained. 'We've nearly finished with the photographs and the measuring. Then you can come in and have a look.'

The modern trend was towards excluding even the senior investigating officer from the crime scene, and they were working on a 3D laser video camera that would create a digital version of the scene you could walk through on computer screen without ever getting near the real thing. But Slider had to see for himself. It was not self-glorification or thrill-seeking, it was just the way he was. There was so much he could glean from his own senses that he knew would not be the same in virtual reality. Bailey knew his preference, and since Slider was both polite and careful, he tolerated it. Not that he could do anything else, given that Slider seriously outranked him, but there was good grace and bad grace.

'There won't be much to be got from this bark,' Slider observed. 'No footmarks.'

'No, sir. And blood patterns will be hard to spot. It's either brown bark or dark green leaves. And everyone and his dog could have been in here. I hate outdoor scenes.'

'At least it's not raining,' Slider said, to comfort him. 'Well, let me know when I can come in. I'll go and talk to the witness.'

Michael Chapman didn't have much to add to the story as told by Gallon. His dog, a small, jolly-looking terrier, was lying down on the path now, chin on paws, thoroughly bored. Chapman was obviously still upset. He was in his late fifties, Slider guessed, well dressed and neatly coiffed, with a worn look to his face that seemed to predate the present shock. Early and reluctant retiree, perhaps?

'Yes, I do walk Buster here most mornings,' he said, in answer to Slider's question. 'I take him out later for two or three longer walks, but I generally do the first turn here. I only live just down the road, you see, so it's convenient.'

'So, as a regular park user, have you seen this girl before?'

'I'm not sure,' he said reluctantly. 'I might have. I can't really say. There are so many people exercising here in the mornings, jogging and so on. I don't really notice them. Anyway, I didn't really get much of a look at her in there,' he said, with a jerk of his head towards the bushes. 'Not to see her face.' A thought came to him, and his eyes widened in appeal. 'You won't make me go and look again?'

'No, sir,' Slider said reassuringly. 'You went in just there, I understand?'

'Yes, that's right. Between those two laurels.'

'Did you notice those marks in the ground?'

'Well, no. I didn't really notice anything, except that Buster was barking his head off and wouldn't come back.'

'Did you touch the body at all? To see if she was still alive?'

'No!' he said vehemently; and then looked worried. 'Should I have? As soon as I saw her I was sure she must be dead. I didn't want to go any nearer. I just wanted to get Buster out.'

'Did Buster touch the body?'

'Not to my knowledge. When I got in there he was jumping and barking but not actually touching her. She was lying on her back and her eyes were open and there was all that – all that blood – on her – on her T-shirt.' He swallowed hard, screwing up his eyes as if to force the vision away. 'I dragged Buster out the same way we went in, and then I saw that gentleman talking on his mobile phone and asked him to call the police.'

The phone owner, David Hatherley, was a different kettle of fish from the shocked and patient Chapman. He was a tall, vigorous, expensively suited young Turk, annoyed at being kept from his turkery by bumbling officialdom. He turned on Slider as he approached, scanned him for authority, and demanded hotly, 'Look here, how much longer am I going to be kept hanging around? Some of us have work to do, you know.'

'Yes, I do know, sir. We are doing our work at the moment,' Slider said.

The nostrils flared with exasperation. 'Well, I can't help you. I know nothing about it. I was just walking past when that idiot tried to grab my phone, and then started babbling about dead bodies. I had to interrupt a very important business call to dial 999.'

'It was very public-spirited of you, sir,' Slider said soothingly.

Hatherley seemed to suspect irony and snorted. 'So can I go now? Your man's taken down every damned detail from me, address, telephone, right down to my shoe size. You don't seem to realise, every minute I stand here I'm losing money.'

Slider had used those minutes to look over Hatherley's clothes, his face and hands, his manner. There was nothing there for them. 'Yes, you can go. Thank you very much for your help, Mr Hatherley. We might be contacting you again.'

When he had gone, Atherton said, 'He can't be our man, not in an Armani suit.'

'No,' Slider said. 'I think he just happened by at the wrong moment. Like Chapman. But with Chapman, he was actually on the scene, so we'd better get fingerprints and a buccal swab from him for elimination purposes.'

'What about the dog?' Atherton said merrily. 'Should we get his DNA as well?'

'I'm glad you're finding this entertaining,' Slider said.

The photographer was coming towards them. Old Sid had retired – not before time given his increasing misanthropy, which was ratcheted upwards by every scene he captured for posterity. The new man was David Archer, young, enthusiastic but with a nephew-like shy deference towards Slider and most of his team. He was a rather delicate-looking creature, so handsome he was almost pretty, and didn't look robust enough to cope with the things he had to photograph; but he was so passionate about his equipment and the wonderful things modern digital technology could do that Slider suspected the subject of his work didn't impinge much on him.

'Bob asked me to tell you you can go in now, sir,' he said to Slider.

'Finished your work?'

'Yes, I'm going back to the van to have a look at it, but I'll be on hand in case there's anything more when the forensic biologist arrives.'

'Do something for me,' Slider said. 'Take a long, slow pan around with your video camera at the crowd. All the onlookers. Try not to be obvious about it. Keep as far back as you can and do it on the zoom. Everyone who's hanging around the scene. I want their faces.'

'Yes, sir,' Archer said. He was too polite to ask, but there was a question in his eyes.

Slider took pity on him. 'I wouldn't be surprised if the murderer came back for a look. He'd want to see who found her, what their reaction was, how baffled we were. That'd be part of the fun. He might be here right now, enjoying himself watching us running round after him.'

'I'll get what you want, sir, don't worry,' Archer said. 'Would you like me to make a series of stills, so you can have them to study?'

'Good idea. Thanks.'

'He wouldn't hang about all covered in blood, surely?' Atherton said, when Archer had left them.

'No, but he probably wore a protective garment, which he might have discarded somewhere before coming back.'

'He might even live locally,' Atherton went along with it. 'Went home and changed and came back.'

'You do think of them,' Slider complained. They walked back to the gap in the shrubbery and clothed up, and then, conducted by Bailey, walked along the stepping boards that had been laid to make a safe path into the scene within the shrubbery.

The rhododendrons were massive specimens, some of them ten or fifteen feet high. They grew their leaves where the light reached them, so on the back side they presented bare trunks and branches. What looked from the path like dense vegetation was in fact a series of hollow caves. With the thick mulch of bark on the ground, there was nothing to mar the uniformity of dark brown except the odd piece of litter. Blown in by the wind? It didn't seem likely, inside the shrubbery. Left by kids playing, more like – or by someone hiding, lurking? Slider noted a cigarette packet (B&H), a torn strip of a Walker's crisps bag, and two wrappers from chocolate bars: one Picnic and one Double Decker.

'We'll have those,' he said to Bailey. 'There'll probably be some cigarette ends, as well.'

'There are,' Bailey confirmed. 'Quite a lot scattered about.'

'Take them all,' Slider said. Smokers were so used to throwing away the butt when they'd finished that they did it automatically, either not knowing, or forgetting, that DNA could be recovered from the saliva on them.

'Thank God there's no such thing as a non-smoking murderer,' said Atherton.

In the heart of all this brown, in a clear space, lay the body. It was a young woman, dressed for jogging in knee-length black Lycra shorts, a sleeveless white shirt, trainers and short white socks. She was slim and fit-looking, with lightly tanned skin, and shortish, tousled blonde hair that gave Slider an unpleasant tug because it reminded him of Joanna's. It was a shade lighter, though. Joanna's was more bronze. The sunlight filtering through the leaves touched it here and there and made it gleam like true coin.

She was lying on her back, one arm flung out, the other resting beside her body. Her face was very pretty, heart-shaped with a short, straight nose and full lips, parted to show good teeth. Her skin was smooth and lightly tanned, her hands well kept with short, unvarnished nails. She had small gold studs in her ears and a thin gold chain round her neck on which hung a gold disc – a St Christopher, he supposed. Around her waist was a sort of utility belt of elasticated webbing, on which was hung a plastic water-bottle on the right, a CD Walkman on the left, and a small zip purse in the middle. The headset was hanging round her neck, the cord loose, pulled out from the Walkman socket. He noted that the Walkman had been switched off.

The warmth of the day was lifting a pleasant, woody smell from the bark chippings and birds were singing near and far off in the park. Broken by the gently moving leaves of a birch tree, sunshine was dappling the ground and the girl. She might have stretched out for a rest to gaze up at the patch of clear blue sky above, except that her T-shirt was spatched and blotted with blood.

'Multiple stab wounds,' Atherton said, breaking the silence. 'Would that qualify as a "frenzied attack"?' It was what police reports and the media always called it, a cliché

26

there seemed no escaping. Atherton used it consciously, knowing Slider hated it.

The bark was scuffed in the immediate area, though not as much as Slider would have expected it to be. He hunkered down close to the victim, and now he could smell the clean odours of her shampoo and body lotion, and under them the reek of blood. There were defence cuts on her forearms and the palms of her hands, the blood resting in them, hardly smeared at all. There was definitely blood on the bark immediately around and under the body, but it was impossible to see how much, or to discern any spread patterns.

'Is there blood anywhere else?' he asked Bailey.

'We haven't found any so far, but it's impossible to be sure without close examination,' Bailey said. 'All I can say is that it looks as though all the action happened in this spot.'

Atherton, looking over Slider's shoulder, said, 'What's that grey mark on the T-shirt? Sort of greyish-brown, a smudge?'

'I think it's a footmark – or a toemark, at least,' Slider said. 'He turned her over with his foot. She was lying face down and he turned her over. It's the sort of dirty mark that could be left by a shoe.'

'I suppose he wanted to check she was dead.'

'We might possibly get a partial sole pattern from it,' Slider said.

'Yes, sir,' said Bailey. 'We have photographed it.'

Slider stood up and looked back towards the north side of the shrubbery. 'I don't understand why he dragged her in that way. Much easier the way we came in.'

On both his previous outings, the Park Killer had dragged his victim under cover, once into a shrubbery and once into a rose garden, stabbed her to death, and

27

escaped the scene without anyone's seeing or hearing anything. Speed had to have been of the essence. Probably that was why he had not robbed or molested either of his victims. It was getting away with murder that interested him, it seemed.

Atherton considered. 'The bushes give better cover on that side. If he'd lurked on the more open side, someone might have seen him.'

'I suppose,' Slider said. He looked around to fix the scene in his mind, and then again down at the body. She was out jogging, listening to her music, perhaps thinking about the rest of her day. He looked at her pretty face, all animation gone, her softly muddled hair, the yielding shape of her body against the earth, still warm and pliant, but pointlessly so now. He imagined the killer turning her over with his foot, thought how it would have felt, heavy and soft. In his country boyhood he had handled dead rabbits and knew that limpness. A dull anger filled him. Partly it was because she had reminded him fleetingly of Joanna, and he felt newly vulnerable about her. But the anger was for this girl as well, and especially. When she had got up and dressed in the morning, she had not planned to die this day.

The world was not safe. There were people in it who would do this hideous, hateful thing. Life, which was so strong and tenacious and filled you tight to the skin when you were young, could be taken from you so easily, slip away through a hole in you like a mist dissolving. The solid reality that you walked on was in fact no more than a thin sheet of ice, through which you might fall at any moment into the black water of oblivion beneath.

Everything this girl had, had been taken from her in the name of conceit. All Slider could do was to find the killer and hope to see him punished. He was glad now that Porson wanted it. It was his case now. He would find the killer. The really depressing thing was that even cornered, caught, accused, charged, tried and sentenced, the murderer would probably never really see the enormity of what he had done. What had they done to themselves as a society to have bred a person who would kill to get his name in the papers?

He pulled his mind back to the scene. 'I wonder why there's no blood on the footmark. You'd have thought with all this stabbing going on he'd have stepped in at least some of it, especially as he wouldn't have been able to see it.'

'Just lucky, I suppose,' Atherton said. 'Our first problem is going to be identifying her.'

'Yes,' Slider said. 'People don't go out jogging with their passport and driving licence in their pockets.'

'People don't go out jogging with pockets,' said Atherton.

2

Close Enough for Jazz

The CID room was quiet, with most of the troops still at the scene, helping with the search for blood, blood-stained clothing, and a murder weapon. Speed was of the essence. There was constant pressure on the police to reopen a cordoned-off area.

Slider was in his room making a start on the paper-work when the gorgeous DC Kathleen Swilley, always known as 'Norma' on account of her machismo in the field, came in. She was an expert in martial arts, could kick the eyebrows off a fly at five paces, and bring a man to his knees by use of just a forefinger and thumb. Or, indeed, without them, Slider reflected.

'Nothing so far, boss,' she said. 'Everyone in the park's had a preliminary interview and they're starting on the bystanders. And I've put in an enquiry to the traffic department about any parked car or MTI activity for this morning. The SOCOs are still going over the ground looking for more blood. The body's been taken away now.'

'Is that the deceased's effects?'

'Yeah. No help with her ID, though.' She put them down on the desk and went through them with him.

The little purse on the victim's belt contained nothing but a Kleenex tissue and a set of door keys – one Yale and one deadlock – on a ring whose tag was one of those articulated metal fish. That, and her gold medallion, were the only personal items they had to go on.

'We got some good lifts off the Walkman,' Swilley said. 'Presumably the victim's. We're waiting for her tenprint to compare. I've run them through records but there's no previous.'

The medallion turned out not to be St Christopher after all, but St Anthony. 'An unusual choice,' Slider commented. 'It may help to confirm her identity once we know it.'

'Ditto for the door keys,' said Swilley. 'So what's a St Anthony medal for, boss?'

'He's patron saint of the poor and afflicted, I think,' Slider said. 'And lost things. And travellers.'

'I thought that was St Christopher?'

'It's not exclusive. And some people think St Christopher didn't exist.'

'The things you know,' Swilley marvelled.

Slider sighed. 'What I don't know is how to ID our victim without trawling through the neighbourhood with a mugshot. And I really hate doing that when the only mugshot I've got is taken from the corpse.'

'It's early yet. Someone may miss her and come forward,' Swilley said. 'The report of the murder's going to be in all the noon bulletins. If someone hasn't turned up to work . . .'

While Slider was contemplating this slender possibility, Atherton came in, back from the scene. 'No clothes or knives as yet,' he reported. 'There were eight cigarette ends in that part of the shrubbery, but most of them are obviously not fresh.'

31

'He might have staked out the area beforehand,' Slider said. 'Keep them all until we see what else we get, before having them DNA tested.' There was always the budget to consider.

Atherton resumed. 'Mackay and McLaren are on their way back with the first stack of statements to go through, and the photographs have arrived. Hollis is putting them up on the whiteboard with the stuff we got from Ealing.' He looked at Slider's desk. 'Is that her Walkman?'

Slider smiled slightly. 'It would hardly be mine, now, would it? I'm a dinosaur, didn't you know?'

Atherton blinked, but let it pass. 'What was she listening to?' he asked.

'She wasn't listening to anything, if you remember. It was turned off and the headset was unplugged.'

'It probably came unplugged in the struggle,' Norma said.

'Yes, but it does seem odd to me—' Slider began, but Atherton interrupted him. He had picked up the evidence bag containing the CD.

'Ah, now, look at this! This isn't a commercial CD – it's a demo disc. This could be something. It might give us a lead on who she is.'

'How come?' Swilley asked.

Atherton was always glad of an opportunity to impress her. Since he had got his new haircut, he had shown a renewed interest in Swilley, even though she was now married to the man she had lived with for years. Atherton, who was not one to let logic spoil a good prejudice, insisted that the husband didn't exist – despite the fact that Slider had been at the wedding. He said nobody would really marry a man named Tony Allnutt. And anyway, even if he did exist, Norma would surely be regretting her folly by now, and be ready for Atherton's sophistication and non-joke surname.

'When a band makes a demo CD,' he said, 'they don't go on sale, they're distributed to the A and R people at record companies and to promoters and festival organisers and so on, which would cut down the field anyway. But this is even better. You see, the label's not printed, it's hand-written, and there's nothing on it but the band's name, the studio name and the recording date. That suggests that it's a master, or a band copy – something only a very few people would have. It would mean that our victim was closely connected with the band, or just possibly the recording team.'

'What's the date on it?' Slider asked.

'Monday,' said Atherton. 'That makes it even more likely that she was with the band. It's probably a first impression, given to them to approve before the final mixing. After mixing it would be a couple of weeks for the copies for distribution to be ready. This may be the master, or one of as few as half a dozen prints.'

'Well, that's good news,' Slider said. To have got a handle on the ID this early was a bonus. 'I thought we were going to have to house-to-house the whole of west London.'

'What band is it?' Swilley asked, trying to see over Atherton's shoulder.

'Baroque Solid,' Atherton said, passing it over to her.

She wrinkled her nose at the name. 'Never heard of them.'

But Slider looked enlightened. 'I've heard Joanna talk about them. I think they were mentioned in the paper last week, weren't they?'

'Only in the arts section,' Atherton said. 'They're new and hot and they do fusion music – classical meets jazz.

I saw them doing a foyer performance at the National Theatre – Satie and Stockhausen and a bit of Bartók. I thought they were pretty good, but it's an unusual taste, and without the right breaks that sort of thing can die the death. But they did a Purcell Room concert last week and got good reviews, so it looks as though they might be taking off.'

'Fusion music? It sounds dire,' Swilley said.

'It takes a bit of listening to. I expect you like Abba and Fleetwood Mac,' Atherton said kindly.

'Anyway, it's a stupid name,' she retaliated. 'If they mess up, everyone'll be calling them Baroque Bottom.'

Atherton's eyes gleamed. 'Now, I've always thought *you* had a—'

Slider intervened hastily. 'How do we get in contact with these people?'

'There's bound to be a website address for the band. Let's have a look.'

They went through into the CID room, where the computer sat in a corner, its screen-saver trekking through an endless brick maze, turning left and right at the dead ends with the strangely fluid jerk of a goldfish. Slider brought up the search engine and tapped in the band's name, but as soon as the site began to load Atherton was breathing down his neck in his eagerness. 'She's probably one of the musicians,' he said. 'I seem to remember there was a pretty female amongst them.'

She wasn't, though, and Slider was faintly and ridiculously relieved, as though it would have been a threat to Joanna if she had been. There were photographs of the eight members of Baroque Solid on the website, and though they were all in the right age group and four of them were female, none of the four sufficiently resembled the victim even to be worth wondering about.

'So what now?' Slider asked. Atherton was much more *au fait* with the music world than he was, in spite of Joanna.

'Go and see them. The victim must be closely involved with the band. There's the snail-mail address at the bottom. It's only just down the road in Barons Court.'

'Don't beg. You've got the job,' Slider said, handing him the disc.

'Everyone hates a volunteer,' Swilley said coolly, as Atherton bounded away.

Joanna came in to the office just before six, bringing two jam doughnuts in a bag from the good baker in Shepherd's Bush Road.

'Peace offering,' she said.

'Peace offering for what?'

'I think I was less than gracious this morning.'

'You were disappointed,' he excused her.

'So were you.'

'I'm used to it by now.'

'Well, I'd better get used to it too, if I'm going to be a policeman's wife. With the emphasis on "if".'

'Oh, Jo, I'm sorr—'

'Joke,' she assured him. 'Officers' wives for the use of. And talking of officers' wives, where's Jim?'

'Did you have doughnuts for him, too?' Slider asked innocently.

'Absolutely not,' she said grimly. 'I was talking to Sue today.'

'It's not his fault she changed her mind about marrying him,' Slider said.

'Isn't it?' Sue Caversham, Joanna's friend and colleague, had been Atherton's girlfriend, putting up with a great deal from him while he adjusted to the alien idea of monogamy. It was hard for a lifelong hound to give up the chase. On the very evening Slider discovered that Joanna was pregnant and proposed to her, Atherton was proposing to Sue. Slider couldn't have been more surprised – or thought he couldn't, until a month later Sue changed her mind. She had said she couldn't marry Atherton after all, a row ensued, and they had broken up.

'She was naturally doubtful about the leopard's changing his spots,' Joanna went on. 'All she needed was a bit of reassurance, and everything would have been all right. But what does he do? Bawls her out and then rushes off and starts dating other women like an amphetamine James Bond.'

The door between Slider's room and the CID room was open, as usual, and he felt this was not the place for this discussion. He turned her gracefully by saying, 'It looks as though the victim might have had something to do with that band you were talking about the other week, Baroque Solid.'

She allowed herself to be turned. 'Oh, no, don't say one of them's been killed! They're so talented.'

Would that make it worse? Slider wondered. From the outside, perhaps – talent being a rarity. But from the inside – everyone's life is precious to them. He said, 'No, she wasn't one of the musicians. We had a look at the website and there were photos of them. But she must have been close to them in some way.' A thought crossed his mind. Classical music was a small world and everybody tended to know everybody else. 'Would you be willing to have a look at the mugshot, to see if perhaps you know her? It would save a lot of time if you could give us a name.'

'You don't know who she is?' Joanna said, and then, mind working rapidly, she got it. 'Of course, she was out jogging and didn't have a handbag or anything with her.

All right, I'll have a look.' She put out her hand, but then a thought came to her and she faltered. 'It's not – she's not—?'

'No,' he said, 'not disfigured or anything.'

'Only dead,' Joanna finished wryly. She took the photo, looked carefully, and passed it back. 'No, I don't know her. Poor girl, she's so young and pretty. What a monstrous thing to do.'

Monstrous, Slider thought. Yes, that was a good word for it.

'Well,' Joanna said, 'I'd better not disturb you any longer. I suppose you'll be late tonight?'

'I'm afraid so,' said Slider. 'They're doing the post mortem at seven and I want to go to that.'

'The fun you have!'

He came round the desk to kiss her goodbye and escort her out. 'Did you have a proper lunch?'

'Yes, Mother. I had a very nice tomatoey pasta and a salad in Pizza Express, in between estate agents. I bet you didn't have anything.'

'I've got two doughnuts now,' Slider said.

She eyed him with sympathy. 'I'm going to go home and make a casserole that won't spoil for long, slow cooking. So whatever time you get home—'

'I'll try not to be too late.'

The murder made the BBC's *Six o'Clock News*, though there was so much else going on it only got a short mention. Slider and Hollis went along to Ron Carver's room to watch – Carver, fortunately, having gone home. There had always been rivalry between Slider's firm and Carver's, though Slider did all he could to discourage it. But DI Carver had been born with a grudge and was never happy unless he was nurturing some fancied slight to himself. The fact was that he always had the best of everything, more men, more overtime allowance, more consideration. Even a television. The overlords having decided that the department ought to have a TV set, it was put in Carver's room as a matter of course; and when Slider asked for one as well he was told that there was no sense in having two – one for everybody was quite sufficient. Of course, Carver was a mason, everybody knew that. Atherton said that was just paranoia on Slider's part, but as Slider said, *you*'d be paranoid if everyone was plotting against you.

The murder came in fourth, behind the oil crisis, the Middle East peace talks, and the prime minister's visit to Washington.

'A young woman was stabbed to death in a park in west London this morning, in what appears to be another attack by the so-called Park Killer,' said the studio announcer.

There followed a quick resumé of the previous cases, with background footage of the other two parks involved, and then a brief moving camera shot of the Paddenswick scene from earlier in the day: the blue and white tape, the policemen on guard duty, and a shot of a SOCO on hands and knees examining the bark at the edge of the shrubbery. Then it jumped straight into the next item, about a riot in an asylum seekers' camp in Australia's Northern Territory.

'Short and not sweet,' Slider said.

'They'll probably do a bit more on the local news,' said Hollis, and they settled in to wait.

The local news had it as lead item.

'Nothing like a murder on your own patch,' said Hollis. 'Local boy makes good sort o' thing. Or local girl makes corpse.'

The bulletin had almost identical film to the main news, but obviously taken from a minutely different camera angle. 'Good use of the licence fee money,' said Slider. 'Send two complete teams from different offices in the same building.'

'Everyone knows local telly's a job creation scheme,' Hollis said. 'I mean, look at the presenter bird. Who else'd employ her?'

London News also billed it as the Park Killer Strikes Again and précis'd the two previous outings, but they varied the approach with some of their beloved on-the-scene vox pops. There were short clips of local residents saying it was shocking, and you didn't feel safe on your own streets any more. Then one young woman said she would never walk through Paddenswick Park again, and another said she always walked through the park and saw no reason to change now.

Finally the reporter, who looked about fifteen, faced camera and, with lavish hand gestures, said, 'Police are asking anyone who may have seen anything unusual to come forward. They are pertickerly asking anyone who was in the park between seven forty-five a.m. and eight fifteen a.m. this morning to come forward and identify themselves so that they can be eliminated from enquiries.' And then it was back to the studio.

'Did you ask for that?' said Hollis, his pale green eyes bulging alarmingly.

'Not me,' Slider said. 'Someone did, though.' He did not need to say more. The press liaison unit was at headquarters at Hammersmith, close to the source of godhead. It took its orders straight from the fount, and it would not occur to anyone to let the blokes at the sharp end know what was decided.

'We'll have to man the phones tonight,' Hollis observed.

'And I've got a post to go to,' said Slider.

'I'll get on it, guv,' Hollis said kindly. 'We probably won't need more than a couple. I don't expect there'll be many calls tonight anyway.'

'You mean, because the Beeb didn't feature it prominently?'

Hollis looked pitying at his ignorance. 'No, guv. Because there's a footy match on tonight. World Cup. England v. East Moldavia. Nobody's going to miss the one tie we might win.'

The address for Baroque Solid was Gunterstone Road, a ground-floor flat in one of those big three-storeys-plus-basement terrace houses that abound all over Hammersmith and North Kensington. A new sticker had been put above the bell saying, 'Baroque Solid – Music Fusion'. This was the strapline from the website, too, and Atherton thought it neat and punchy. It was not until his third visit at half past seven that he got a reply to his ring.

The door was opened by a young woman in jeans, black T-shirt and a loose chambray shirt worn open.

'Is this the office for Baroque Solid?' he asked, glimpsing behind her what was obviously a residential and not a business space.

'Well, yes, it is,' she said, as though there were a good deal of doubt about it. He showed his warrant card, and she relaxed a little – a novel reaction in Atherton's experience. Most people tensed up when they realised their visitor was Lily Law. She said, 'You see, it's where I and Joni and Tab live, but it's also the band's headquarters. At the moment, anyway. Until we get really, really famous.' And she laughed to avert the hubris. 'Would you like to come in?'

She led him into the big front room on the left of the

40

entrance passage. At the far end with the bay window, there were bare floorboards, a semi-circle of hard chairs and music stands set on some kind of specialised rubber mat, and against the wall an impressive bank of sound equipment. At this, the door end, there was an office desk, a filing cabinet, a computer on a stand, and a table covered with papers.

'This is the beating heart of the operation,' she said, with an ironic wave of the hand. 'We're really just getting started. But we had our first proper concert last week, on the South Bank.'

'Yes, I know,' Atherton said. 'In the Purcell Room.'

'Oh, were you there?' she asked, with about equal parts of surprise and pleasure.

'No, but I read the reviews. And I've heard you before, in a foyer performance.'

'Are you into music?'

It was an expression he loathed, but it was sweetened a little for coming from her lips. When she had opened the door to him, he had thought her quite plain, with her straight brown hair and unmade-up face. But now at closer quarters and inspection, he was finding her unnervingly attractive. The hair, for instance — brushed straight back and cut about shoulder length — was a silky waterfall, and the word 'brown' didn't begin to cover the fabulous complexity of natural tints in it, from shining chestnut to amber and toffee, shot through with gleams of ink and pure set-on-fire copper. Her eyes were large and expressive and hazel, and makeup, he thought, would only have diminished their luminosity. Her mouth was wide and generous, and when she smiled she showed teeth so beautiful he wanted to kiss them. To find someone's teeth erotic must mean he was in a bad way; but so 'twas. He couldn't take his eyes from her.

'I love music,' he answered her belatedly. 'But I'm afraid that's not why I'm here.'

'Oh dear, I hope we're not in trouble,' she said. 'I'm sorry, I didn't catch your name.'

'Atherton. Detective Sergeant Atherton, Shepherd's Bush.' And then, to his own surprise, he added, 'Jim,' and held out his hand.

She took it. Hers was warm and dry and strong. A hand of ability. He wondered if she was a violinist. 'I'm Marion,' she said. 'Marion Davies.'

It was an oddly old-fashioned name, Marion. He wondered if she had older parents. But its plainness appealed to him. It suddenly seemed the essence of femininity.

'I play second fiddle,' she went on.

The words 'second fiddle' immediately brought Sue to his mind; one of those instant and uncontrollable associations. She lurked in his mind all the time anyway, though he kept his mental eyes firmly turned away from her.

'You haven't got a mark,' he said to Marion Davies, looking at her neck.

From the background of his thoughts of Sue, he had spoken too intimately. She blushed, and her skin was so delicate and clear he could actually see the blood racing up the corpuscles like BMW drivers up the M1. 'I've been lucky. But I've always used a pad,' she said.

He pulled himself together, and said, 'The reason I'm here is that we have come by one of your demo discs in unusual circumstances, and I wondered if you could give me an idea of who was likely to have had one.' He handed over the disc in its bag, and she took it, looking a little bewildered.

'Unusual circumstances?' she said. And then, 'I can't think how you got hold of this. We haven't sent them out yet. I mean, this isn't even a finished disc. We're going back to the studio on Friday to do the mixing.'

'I was hoping that was the case,' Atherton said. 'So how many other copies like this were there and who had them?'

'Well, it was just us in the band. Eight of us. Though I don't know if they made any for the studio people. It's a small independent studio in Goldhawk Mews,' she added, looking up at him.

'Yes, I know.' They must have longed to call themselves Goldhawk Studios, but as that name was already taken, they had gone with Mews Studios, which was a bit like chewing rubber.

'There's Mike, Mike Ardeel. He owns the studio. And there's Tony and Phil, the sound engineers.'

'And that's all? No-one else you can think of who might have had one.'

'No,' she said; and then, 'Oh, of course Chattie had one.'

'Chattie?'

'It's short for Charlotte.' She smiled. 'How cool is that? I love it! Chattie Cornfeld. She's our PR person, and – well, she does all sorts of things for us.'

'Can you describe her to me?'

'She's not in trouble, is she?' Marion asked, looking concerned, but only as worried as a speeding fine, perhaps, or a parking ticket. Atherton didn't speak, only gave her a stolid silence into which to insert her answer. 'Well,' said Marion, 'she's about my height, short blonde hair – very pretty.' She looked at him enquiringly, to see if that was enough.

'Does she wear a gold medallion round her neck?'

Now, belatedly, real worry entered. 'Yes, it's a St Anthony medal. She got it in Tuscany last year. She loves it. Why?

What's happened?' She looked down at the disc in its transparent evidence bag. 'Why have you got it all wrapped up like this?'

Atherton said, 'I'm going to ask you to look at a picture and tell me if you think it's her.'

She could tell from the kindly way he said it. 'Oh, my God, what's happened? She's been hurt.'

Atherton said nothing, only offered her the mugshot. She looked at it for a moment, and then nodded. He saw her throat move as she tried to swallow. 'She's dead, isn't she?' she managed to say.

'I'm sorry,' said Atherton. He was having to restrain himself from clasping her to the manly booz. She might have some irritating verbal habits, but she was as cute as all-get-out.

'What happened? Was it an accident?'

'No,' he said. 'I'm sorry. It wasn't an accident.'

Her eyes widened. 'You don't mean – she was *murdered*?'

'Yes, I'm afraid so.'

She had paled, and her lips moved soundlessly a few times before she was able to say, 'But who did it? Who would do such a thing?'

'I'm afraid from early appearances it seems to have been a random killing.'

'Oh, my God,' she said again. She swayed a little, and Atherton put out a hand to catch her elbow, and used it to guide her to a seat. 'When?' she asked.

'Early this morning. She was attacked while she was out jogging.'

'Oh, my God,' she said again. 'I can't believe it. Not Chattie.'

Normally Atherton felt restless while this sort of thing was going on, but this time he waited patiently, allowing her to cope with the shock and disbelief. After a bit he said, 'I'm sorry, but I need to ask you a few questions about her. You see, as she was out jogging when it happened, there was no form of identification on her, apart from this disc. That's why we had to come to you. You obviously knew her quite well.'

She straightened her shoulders to do her duty, though her eyes were still unfocused with shock. 'Well, yes. She's been involved with the band practically from the beginning.'

'Is she a musician?'

'Oh, no. Well, she studied music but she doesn't play. She has this really cool company called Solutions. She does all sorts of office-consultancy services to small businesses, the sort of things they haven't got the time or the skills to do for themselves. Like, for us she does the PR and advertising, and she advises us about everything, even pensions and what we can claim off tax. She knows *everything*, honestly. She's so clever. And she does all the IT stuff. She designed our website, and she found the guy to do the actual build.'

'Was she the one who designed the strapline – the one you have over your doorbell?'

'Do you like it?' She was brightening as she talked, the fact of the death slipping out of her mind with the ease of self-defence. Humankind cannot bear too much reality. Unconsciously she slipped into the present tense again. 'She's really brilliant at things like that. I mean, words are really her thing. It was her that thought up our name, Baroque Solid. I mean, cool, or what? Because that's what jazz fans used to say about really cool jazz in the old days, in the fifties or whatever. They used to say it was "solid". So it's a kind of cute name, don't you think?'

Atherton did think, had thought a long time back, and

rather wished that this divine creature had some of the dear departed's skill with words. 'Was she actually at the recording session on Monday?' he asked.

'She wouldn't have missed it. It was her idea. She set it up and booked the studio and everything. She was going to do all the PR for it, and she'd already worked out the list of people to send the demo disc to. I dropped the band copy round to her yesterday evening so that she could listen to it before the mixing session on Friday. We couldn't have that without her. She was always our best critic.' Reality came back and smacked her round the ear. Her lips trembled. 'But she won't be there now, will she? I can't believe she's dead. I only saw her yesterday.'

'You saw her yesterday?' Atherton asked. 'What time would that be?'

'Well, I picked up the copies of the disc from the studio at about six o'clock and took one round to her house straight away, because she lives nearest. Then I dropped the boys' and Trish's off, and brought the others back here for Joni and Tab and me.'

'You actually saw her when you called at her house?'

'Oh, yes. Well, she'd just got in. She was still in the hall in her business suit sorting the mail when I rang the bell, hadn't even put her briefcase away. We had a bit of a chat but she seemed in a hurry, and she said she had to get changed to go out, so I said, "See you on Friday," and that was that.'

'So you left at what time?'

'Half past six, maybe. I wasn't there long.'

'And did you see her later? Or speak to her?'

'Well, no.' There were tears in her eyes now.

'Do you know where she was going that evening?'

'No, she didn't say and I didn't ask. She seemed a bit – well, preoccupied.'

'I don't suppose it matters,' Atherton said. He had asked out of habit. If she was the victim of a random killing it didn't matter where she had been or with whom. 'Well, you've been very helpful in identifying her for us. It's saved us a lot of time. And now I wonder if you could give me her address?'

'Oh, yes, of course,' she said, rather hopelessly, and then pulled herself together. 'I've got one of her invoices here. She worked from home.'

Across the top of the invoice in large, heavy, raised type was the name 'SOLUTIONS' in caps. Under it in slightly smaller caps it said, 'OFFICE CONSULTANCY FOR SMALL BUSINESS AND SELF-EMPLOYED'. And under that, in yet smaller type, in italics, upper and lower, '*PR and IT Solutions and Much More*'.

The address was Wingate Road, a two-minute walk, if that, from the park gates.

Marion Davies showed him out, and at the door he turned back and said, 'By the way, just one more question.'

'Yes?' She raised her large, tear-polished eyes to him.

'Are you doing anything tonight?'

3

Pas de Lieu, Rhône, Que Nous

Slider always felt that Freddie Cameron, the forensic pathologist, was out of place against the backdrop of the mortuary of a modern steel-glass-and-concrete hospital. There was something quintessentially old-fashioned and gentlemanly about him, with his good suit, bow-tie and polished brogues (he always changed from black shoes to brown at the beginning of Henley week). He belonged with Victorian architecture and solid values. He was marble, not corian; leather, not plastic; solid mahogany, not veneered furniture board.

He was also looking seriously overworked. His eyes were red-rimmed and dark-bagged.

'Been making a night of it?' Slider enquired politely.

'You might say. Hannah had her baby last night – or, rather, early this morning – and since Andy's abroad, Martha and I stayed with her all through. It was a harrowing experience, I can tell you.'

'Why couldn't Andy get leave?' Freddie's son-in-law was a high-earning oil-rig engineer.

'The baby's three weeks early. He's on his way now, but he was in some God-forsaken backwater of

Kazakhstan, and it'll take him twenty-four hours to get home.' He sighed a profoundly weary sigh. 'I'm at the age when I need my zeds. To be fair, Martha did say at one point I should go home and leave it to her, but I couldn't do that.'

'Of course not.' Slider knew that Hannah was Freddie's favourite daughter.

Cameron met his eyes. 'It looked a bit touch-and-go at one point,' he said, and the starkness of his expression underlined the English understatement of the words.

'She's all right now?'

'Both all right. Another boy. They're going to call it Seth, poor little blighter. Mind you, if it had been a girl it would have been Daisy. Where do they get these names from? So I left Martha there at about half past six this morning, dashed home for a shower and a shave and was out doing my list at half past eight. It never seems to get any shorter. I could do without extras from you, thank you very much.'

'Sorry. Not my idea of fun either,' said Slider. 'It was good of you to fit me in.'

'Oh, I'd sooner get it out of the way. Don't want to be like a proctologist and get behind in my work.'

'Is this your last?'

'Yes, thank God. I might be home by nine with a bit of luck. I laugh at a mere twelve-hour day.'

The morgue attendants came in with the trolley and Cameron received the park corpse with the air of a long-haul passenger facing the fourth airline meal of the flight. 'What is it with you and parks anyway, dear boy?' he enquired of Slider. 'Some kind of symbiotic relationship?'

'I could do without it,' Slider said. 'And I hate a serial.'

'The Park Killer must have read what a good job you did on the Baxter case,' said Cameron. 'Deep down, they all want to be caught, you know. Subconscious desire for a father's discipline.'

'Are you qualified to practise psychiatry?' Slider asked coldly.

'Not me, old bean. I'm a corpse-cutter from way back. Got an ID on this one?'

'Atherton's working on it as we speak.'

'Good. I hate to think of a pretty young thing like this going unclaimed.' He stared a moment at the face. 'When you think what went into the making of this work of art, it makes me mad as hell that someone could destroy it so lightly. I think that's why I became a forensic pathologist.'

'You told me it was because dead men don't sue,' Slider objected.

'There is that,' Freddie agreed. 'Well, let's see what we've got.'

The TV image of the lonely pathologist toiling away in solitude was the stuff of fiction. What with Cameron's assistants, his students, the morgue attendants, the identifying officer, the photographer, the evidence officer, the investigating officer, his bagman, old Uncle Tom Cobbley and all, there was always a crowd around the table. With the new tables that constantly drew the fluids away from underneath, there was little or no smell. But Freddie handed round the Trebors out of old habit. With so many onlookers, the miasma of peppermint could have felled a horse.

Cameron pressed the recording pedal under the table with his foot whenever he murmured his commentary; in between he whistled softly, a habit he had developed in the early days to distract him from distress. The 'Songs for Swingin' Carvers' selection today was 'April in Paris'.

'Subject is female, aged about twenty-eight or -nine,

height five feet six, well nourished, appears fit and well muscled, no apparent signs of disease or drug dependency.'

McLaren, as evidence officer, received the clothes as they were removed and examined, and bagged them. Cameron examined the T-shirt, bent to look at the wounds, and at last said to Slider, 'Tell me, old chum, was there anything that struck you as odd about our friend here?'

'I did think there wasn't as much blood as I'd have expected,' Slider said tentatively.

'Give that man a coconut. For a frenzied attack . . .' Everyone says it, Slider thought resignedly '. . . there doesn't seem to be very much damage. One, two three, four, five wounds in front and one in the back, but all except one are quite superficial. You see here, and here, the blade has hardly penetrated at all. This is the only deep wound, this one in the back. You can see from the pattern of flow on the skin and the T-shirt that most of the blood comes from here.'

'Perhaps he couldn't get near enough,' Slider said, but immediately thought of the objection to that. The Park Killer had to be quick. His victim had to be grabbed, overpowered and killed within seconds. He couldn't afford a lot of dancing about and light wounding, with her screaming her head off and passers by coming to investigate.

'Another thing,' Cameron said. 'Look at the way the blood has run from this wound in the back. Look at the flow pattern. What does it tell you?'

Slider saw it now. The lines of blood ran from the wound sideways around the victim's ribs towards the front. 'She was lying down.'

'Correct.'

'So he knocked her down first and stabbed her when she was prone?'

'Cowardly,' Freddie acknowledged.

After the wounds had been photographed, Cameron took a blood sample from the femoral artery, and then began his delicate butchery, laying open the body from chin to pubic bone. Slider found an excuse to turn his head away at the first stroke of the scalpel. From this morning's sweet domesticity to the ugliness and stupidity of murder was too large a stride all at once. This young body and pretty face had so recently housed a hopeful life that he didn't like to see it mutilated, even though it was now surplus to requirements. Once the first cut had been made, however, experience and professionalism took over. Laid open, it was not a person any more. He was always all right once the first cut had been made.

'You see,' Cameron said to Slider, 'even the one deep wound doesn't touch any of the important organs. I wouldn't have thought it would be a fatal blow.'

'You mean she bled to death? Or died of shock?'

Cameron shook his head doubtfully. 'It wasn't exsanguination. And shock? Unless there's any congenital heart defect . . .'

He removed the heart to a separate table and cut it open carefully. 'A nice, clean, healthy heart — just what you'd hope for in a young jogger. No sign of disease. No infarction. Let's have a look at the brain.'

It was the part Slider disliked most. He hummed inside his head as Cameron deployed the electric saw, breathing shallowly not to smell the barbecue reek of burning bone. Cameron removed the top of the skull, then ligated and lifted out the brain, which he sliced like a large, pallid loaf. 'No sign of anything here. I'll take a section to examine under the microscope, but it all looks nice and normal. I think we can rule out heart disease or stroke.'

'So what killed her, then?'

Cameron turned a frank if rather bistred gaze on him. 'You tell me, chum.'

'Only if you hand over your pay packet.'

'Fat chance,' Freddie grinned. A forensic pathologist earned about three times what a detective inspector did. 'All right, then, let's see. She didn't put up much of a struggle. No broken fingernails, no skin or blood under them – she didn't scratch her assailant. Also – now, look here. Sandra, do you mind if I borrow your body for a moment?'

His assistant, used to these demonstrations, stood back from the table and waited. He walked behind her, put his left arm round her shoulders and positioned his left hand in front of her mouth, but without actually touching it, of course. 'I grab my victim from behind, covering her mouth to stop her screaming. Probably use my right hand, like this, to get her by the upper arm. And I drag her backwards by her arm and jaw—'

'Into the bushes, right,' Slider finished for him.

'But,' Cameron said, 'there's no bruising to the face or arms. No bruising anywhere on the body.'

'Well, that's – odd,' said Slider.

'There's more. Thank you, Sandra.' Freddie released her and continued. 'I knock her down without leaving a mark. Well, I suppose that's possible, if I caught her off-balance, or simply threw her down. I stab her in the back – the first wound, deep, but not disabling. But she doesn't scrabble away from me on hands and knees, or try to get up, she just lies there.'

'Too shocked, too frightened to move?'

'Perhaps,' Freddie allowed, though without great belief.

'Then he turned her over with his foot – or with the help of his foot,' Slider said, 'and stabbed her in the front.'

'Very lightly,' Freddie amended. 'Restrained, wouldn't you say?'

'Not much like the Park Killer on his other outings.'

'And when did she get the defence wounds on her arms and hands?' said Cameron. Sandra was about to speak but he silenced her with a glance.

Slider thought. 'I can't work it out.'

'I'll tell you when she got them,' said Cameron, with an actor's timing. 'After death. The cuts on the arms and hands are all post-mortem wounds.'

'You're sure?' Slider said – but surprise makes you say foolish things.

'Of course,' Freddie said. 'They aren't even very convincing – in the wrong place and at the wrong angles. I've seen enough of the real thing to know. So what we have here, old chum, is . . . ?' He paused invitingly.

Slider filled in the space. 'A set-up.'

'*Exactement*,' said Freddie. 'It was only meant to look like a frenzied attack.'

'Someone killed her and tried to made it look like the Park Killer's work?'

'Not terribly like. It was someone either not very bright or not very *au fait* with our methods, if they thought it would fool us for more than a few hours.'

'I knew there was something wrong with it from the start,' Slider said resentfully. 'The marks on the ground: there were two long grooves going into the bushes, but if you were dragged in still on your feet, there'd be a lot of scuffing and digging as you tried to get a toehold and resist. This looked like the heelmarks of a corpse being dragged.'

'Done afterwards, you think, to add verisimilitude . . .'

'. . . to an otherwise unconvincing narrative,' Slider finished. 'But if she wasn't stabbed to death and didn't bleed to death, what killed her?'

'Well, it is just possible that she died of fright, but it's a very outside possibility. In an old, frail person it might be plausible, but a fit young person tends to be more tenacious of life. I think, old boy, that we may have to wander down the primrose paths of toxicology,' Cameron concluded, with a sigh. 'She looks a little cyanotic to me – wouldn't you say, Sandra? And the lungs are too dark and show some congestion. I think she may have died of respiratory collapse due to an overdose of a depressant drug.'

'You mean – he poisoned her, and then when she was dead stabbed her for effect?'

'No, only the defence wounds were post-mortem. Certainly the main wound in the back was pre-mortem. Those in front have bled so little they might almost be *syn*-mortem, if such an expression were allowable. Of course, the killer might well have thought she *was* dead by then. She was probably so deep down, she was hardly breathing.'

Slider shook his head at the scenario that was opening up. 'So what was the poison?'

'Ah, that I can't tell you,' said Freddie. 'I'll send off a blood sample to the toxicology lab, but you know what they're like.'

'Yes, four to six weeks to get a result. You'll have to help me out, Freddie.'

'Well, there are the antidepressant drugs. Many of the tricyclic and tetracyclic drugs have an anticholinergic action that depresses the brainstem, which would lead to respiratory failure, but the trouble there would be that you'd need a pretty high dose. The sedatives, the benzodiazepines, are more likely culprits, and they leave no particular post-mortem appearances – though you might expect convulsions with a severe overdose, and there's no sign she convulsed. And then,' he added, with a faintly reluctant air, 'there are the barbiturates, though they're harder for the layman to come by. A high dose of one of the short-acting or ultra-short-acting barbiturates like thiopentone or hexobarbitone would produce rapid unconsciousness and death within ten or fifteen minutes.'

Slider met Cameron's eyes, and saw in them the memory of an old case of some years back, the Anne-Marie Austin case, where such a drug had been used. It had come at a bad time for Slider and had almost tipped him over into a breakdown, as Cameron knew very well. First another body in the park, now another death by short-acting barbiturate? Was he to be forced to relive his past like a police version of *Groundhog Day*? On the good side, he'd get to meet Joanna again; on the bad side, he'd keep finding himself still married to Irene. He brought his errant mind back to the problem in hand.

'But,' he said, 'if you want to poison somebody, you do it privately indoors. Why would you do it out in a public park in broad daylight with all the likelihood of being interrupted? And how do you get someone out jogging in the park to take poison anyway?'

'That,' said Cameron, 'I gladly leave to you.'

He rang Joanna to tell her he was on his way home.

'What do you think about James?' she asked, as soon as she heard his voice.

To his credit, he caught on. 'Do all women do that?'

'Do what?'

'Think about babies' names all the time.'

56

'I don't do it all the time. Anyway, you ought to know.'
He'd had two children with his ex-wife Irene.

'Too long ago,' he said. 'Don't remember.'

'Well? What about James?'

'It might not be a boy.'

'Of course it will be. First time out – you want the teapot *with* the spout, don't you?'

'If you say so. But James Slider sounds like badly fitting false teeth.'

She sighed. 'True.'

'Freddie Cameron's new grandson is called Seth.'

'Flaming Nora,' Joanna said. 'Seth Slider's even worse.'

'I wasn't suggesting it.'

'No votes for anything with an *s* in it. When will you be home?'

'Before you can say psephologically sesquipedalian.'

At least he had missed the evening rush hour. Traffic on the Uxbridge Road was down to tolerable levels, mostly people going out for the evening, pottering between traffic light and traffic light, off to the pub, to restaurants, to visit friends, to pick up a takeaway. Real life. None of them had spent the day pondering over a corpse.

Atherton phoned him with the identification when he was at the East Acton Lane lights. 'Did your witness give you a next of kin?' he asked.

'No, she didn't know. But she's sure deceased wasn't married and didn't live with anyone, and I tried the home telephone number and there was an answering machine on. I tried her mobile number, too, but it was switched off.'

'Odd that she didn't have it with her,' Slider said. 'Young businesspeople are usually wedded to them.'

'Maybe she wanted a bit of peace and quiet,' Atherton said. 'Or maybe the killer nicked it. How was the post?'

'Interesting,' Slider said. He told Atherton Cameron's findings.

'Oh,' said Atherton. 'Well, that's – interesting.'

'Is that the best you can come up with?'

'I'm trying. It puts a whole new complexion on things. If it wasn't a random killing, we're back with the who-saw-her-last and what-enemies-did-she-have routines.'

'Did you get any of that from your Marion Davies type?'

'I didn't ask, not knowing it was needed. She did say she saw the victim yesterday at around six p.m. and she was all right then. Just about to go out for the evening.'

'With whom?'

'As I said, I didn't ask. But I've arranged to see her again, so I can ask then.'

'See her again? What for?'

'What for?' Atherton repeated derisively. 'She's a bit of a sort, that's what for.'

'Oh,' said Slider. The lights changed and he moved off and turned left down Stanley Gardens, which perhaps prevented him saying something he'd later regret.

'Well, I've got the victim's address, anyway,' Atherton said. 'Do you want to look at the house tonight?'

'No. If she lived alone, tomorrow will do. Just put someone on the door. The media are still putting it out as the Park Killer, so the real villain will think he's getting away with it. And I'm less than five minutes from home.'

'Lucky man.'

Slider thought he sounded a little wistful, and said, 'Joanna's made a casserole. Do you want to—?'

'Thanks, but no. I've got a date,' Atherton said breezily.

'Fine. Well, don't let me keep you.'

He rang off, reflecting that it was just as well Atherton had refused, given that he was not Joanna's favourite person at the moment. Besides, he really wanted to be alone with her this evening, to enjoy the peace and comfort of her company and whatever was simmering in the slow oven. Plus a bottle of good, hearty red. He wondered who Atherton had a date with, but as he was turning the last corner before home he didn't wonder very much. There's no place like home, he thought, because in fact home isn't a place, it's people. There is no place, only us. And a bottle of Saint-Joseph.

Porson was there when Slider arrived in the morning, as if he had never been home. He was stamping about his room like a man looking for a cat to kick. Top-brass meetings at Hammersmith always did nasty things to his blood pressure. Under the harsh neon light of his room his head had a strangely bumpy look, like a bag full of knuckles. Bubbles of frustration trying to escape, perhaps?

'You were off pretty sharpish last night,' he snapped at Slider.

'I went to the post mortem. Cameron put it on the end of his list.'

'Oh. You could have let me know.'

'I left a message on your voice-mail, sir.'

'Oh,' said Porson again. 'I always forget about that bloody thing. Whatever happened to a piece of paper on your desk?'

Before he could think of anything else to complain about, Slider told him of the discoveries of the day before. His pacing slowed as he listened.

'Not bad for a start,' he said grudgingly, when Slider had finished. And then, 'Good thought of Atherton's to get the ID that way. He's a smart lad.' That was not always a compliment in the Job, but this time Porson meant it.

'Yes, sir,' said Slider. 'I presume we'll be keeping the ID under wraps for the time being?'

'Until we've informed the next of kin, at any rate.'

'Also,' Slider added, 'it might help us to let the villain think we've bought the Park Killer scenario?'

Porson frowned. 'Yes, that's a bit of a queer thing, isn't it, what Cameron's saying?'

'Of course,' Slider said, 'we don't know whether the drugging was meant to kill her, or only subdue her so she'd be easier to stab.'

Porson pondered. 'Doesn't make much difference, does it? Whoever gave her the drug was the killer, one way or the other. But you're sure in your own mind it wasn't the Park Killer?'

'It isn't his MO,' Slider said. 'As far as we can be sure from only two previous cases.'

'Right. He could have changed his pattern, I suppose.'

'But I think it's unlikely. The stab wounds were mostly superficial and not given with any force.'

'Not a frenzied attack, then.'

'No, sir. A slow and deliberate attack.'

'Well,' said Porson, gripping and bending a plastic ruler between his large hands, 'that's good news in its way.'

'Yes, sir. I hate a serial.'

'We all do, laddie, we all do. But what I meant was, while I was over at Hammersmith yesterday, I took the chance to have a talk with Mr Palfreyman about this.' Palfreyman was head of the Homicide Advice Team, the demigod with the power to say who would investigate any particular murder. 'As we know, the SCG's lost most of its men and they're struggling under a backlash of work. So there wasn't much chance of them taking on the case. On the other hand, Mr Palfreyman wasn't happy about leaving us to pedal our own Canute, so his idea was to form a new temporary dedicated Park Killer squad with some of us and some of Ealing's boys and girls, under his own personal regis.'

Slider looked his horror at the idea. Porson was so moved at the thought of it that he bent the ruler too far and one end slipped from his grasp. It flew whirling across the room like a rogue helicopter blade, hit the wall and fell with a clatter. Porson hardly flinched.

'Yes,' he said, 'so it's not bad at all if we can tell him convincively that it *wasn't* the Park Killer, you see.'

Slider saw. The special squad was a mind-watering idea, and given that it was Palfreyman's brainchild, which he had presumably seen as a path to glory, he wasn't going to be happy about giving it up.

'I'm satisfied in my own mind it wasn't,' he said firmly.

'So am I,' said Porson. 'The Park Killer's a stab-and-go raging nutter. He's not going to pussyfoot about with narcrotics, hang about having a fag while he waits for his victim to lie down for a kip. You can't teach an old leopard new stripes. So I think you can take it as read that we'll be keeping this one at home, Slider. I'll say what needs to be said to Mr Palfreyman.'

'Yes, sir,' Slider said. And, 'Thank you.'

Porson raised his eyebrows, and his deeply sunken eyes took the opportunity to flash fire. 'I don't know what you're thanking me for. You don't know yet what sort of a case this is going to be. It could turn out to be a sticker, and all eyes are going to be on you now to pull the chestnuts out of the fan in double-quick time.'

'All eyes' meaning Mr Palfreyman's, Slider thought. Well, he'd been threatened with top-brass disapproval all his career. 'I can live with that, sir,' he said. 'By the way, did you have a chance to ask about extra help?'

'Yes, I did. They're sending someone over this morning

who's been on a roving brief, so they're more or less spare.'

'Roving brief?'

'Some diversity programme follow-up survey,' Porson said, with an absolute absence of expression. These were dangerous waters, Watson.

'Oh,' said Slider.

'Only one body,' Porson went on, 'but it's better than nothing.'

'Right, sir,' said Slider. He hoped it would prove so. Some young go-getter who'd stepped straight from Hendon into a political-statistical job might well prove to be more of a liability than otherwise.

'So we have a whole new game on, boys and girls,' Slider addressed the troops, who were slumped over their tables in attitudes that would have made a chiropractor weep. Hollis was removing relevant stuff, now become irrelevant, about the Park Killer from the whiteboard. Atherton was writing up his report on the information he'd got from Marion Davies. Swilley was in a corner talking quietly to the coroner's officer, a new man who'd never met her before, who looked as though he couldn't believe his luck and was right about that. McLaren was bracing himself for the rigours of the day by eating Toast Topper straight from the tin with a plastic spoon, using his left hand to alternate mouthfuls from a small box of microwave chips. Slider wished he could get rid of that microwave oven, but its use was probably guaranteed under the Geneva Convention, not to say EU employment law.

He continued. 'It's back to basics, find out everything we can about deceased, who had a grudge against her, who had a reason to kill her.'

'It still could be a random killing, though, couldn't it?' Mackay called.

'It could,' Slider said fairly, 'but I think it's unlikely.'

'Only, it's a funny sort of way to off someone if you know them,' he persisted. 'I mean, if you wanted to poison them, you'd put something in their food or drink at home, wouldn't you? Where you could make sure she was dead, and clear up after yourself, without being interrupted.'

McLaren did a hasty swallow that would have challenged a boa constrictor and said, 'Yeah, I'm with Andy on that, guv. Most likely to me is that it's a copy-cat Park Killer, only he's not got the balls just to grab and stab, he's got to drug her first.' He looked round defensively. 'Well, I can see that. That makes sense.'

'Only to you and a moron,' said Swilley, who had sent her disappointed swain away and rejoined the group. 'Honestly, Maurice, if brains were money you'd need a mortgage for a cup of tea. How's a complete stranger clutching a big knife going to get her to swallow drugs while she's out jogging and then hang around until she feels sleepy?'

'Well, whoever did it's got to get over that problem,' Mackay said.

'Yeah, why's she going to do that for anyone?' McLaren put in resentfully.

'Guv, do we know how the drug was administered?' Hollis asked, like a breath of sanity.

'Doc Cameron says for the quickest reaction it should have been injected. I left him going over the skin with a magnifying glass. If it was administered orally, it would take quicker effect in liquid than solid form. Something may emerge from the stomach contents.'

'God, I hope not,' Atherton said.

'Maybe the murderer put something in her water-bottle,' said Mackay.

'He'd have had to have access to her house to do that,' Slider said. 'But we'll have the contents checked anyway.'

'How quickly would it take effect?' Swilley asked.

'We won't know that until we know what it was and how it was given. But for the method to work at all it would have to be pretty quick. Meanwhile, whether it was a murder by someone who had a grudge against her – '

'Or whether we go with the dim bulbs' theory,' Swilley inserted under her breath.

'– or it was a random killing,' Slider went on, 'much of the work is still the same. We carry on searching for a weapon, for blood marks, for clothing. Get her telephone statements and check all the numbers she rang, see if there was anything untoward going on. Ask the neighbours about any comings and goings or people hanging about. Follow up anything on the statements we've already taken. Start doorstepping the street, anyone who overlooks the park, the shops along Paddenswick Road, the streets on the other side of the park too.'

'What about the pub, guv?' Mackay asked.

This was the Wellington, which years ago had been called the George and Two Dragons, because it was run by a little man called George Benson who was henpecked by both his wife and mother-in-law. It was on Paddenswick Road and opposite the park railings, hardly more than a few yards from the park gate.

'Yes, good point. Someone had better call in there today.'

'I could go. I know the landlord pretty well,' Mackay said.

'All right.'

'And there's a different crowd in at night from lunch-time,' Mackay added quickly.

'True,' said Slider. 'All right, you can do an evening visit as well. You'd better have some help.' McLaren perked up no end at that, sat up straight and tried to look reliable. 'See if one of the uniforms is willing. Plain clothes, of course.' He thought. 'Not Renker: he'd still look like a copper if he was stark naked. Willans has got his hands full. See if D'Arblay's up for it. He's a nice, confiding lad. People open up for him.'

'Right-oh, guv.'

Swilley spoke up. 'There's the tube station, boss. The killer might have made his getaway that way. We ought to have someone on there at the same time of the morning. And maybe some leaflets to hand out.'

'Good thought. You can arrange that,' said Slider. 'All right, anything to follow up in the statements so far?' There were negatives all round. 'Anything come in on the telephone last night?'

'Just the usual attention-seekers and Daft Dorises,' Hollis said. 'Apparently there were strange lights in the sky over the park Tuesday night.'

'There are strange lights in the sky over the park every night,' Slider said. 'It's on the flight path to Heathrow.'

Wingate Road, where the victim had lived, was just off the main road, but surprisingly was a little haven of quiet. It was a short street with a pub at one end, a nice, small, old-fashioned-looking hostelry called the Anchor. It was obvious from the state of the pub and the houses that the street had been gentrified. Everything was in a condition of cherished middle-class repair, and the parked cars were rust-free and mostly under three years old.

The terraced houses dated from the 1850s, earlier than adjacent streets: two storeys plus semi-basement, square stuccoed fronts, the pitch of the roof hidden by a ruled-off parapet, the age given away only by the lovely proportion of the tall sash windows, each divided into nine small panes. At some point all the residents had been seized by a common urge to paint their stucco in a dusty pastel shade. The effect was delightful, like a tube of Refreshers.

'That's it,' Atherton said, indicating a house of pale hyacinth blue. 'Gloriosky! There's a parking space. I wonder if one of these is her car?'

'Didn't you ask what's-her-name – Marion Davies? You were there long enough.'

'She wouldn't have known, anyway,' Atherton said. 'Women never cease to amaze me. When you think of the hours they spend rabbiting to each other about shopping and hairdressers, and they don't even know what sort of car each other drives.'

Slider parked the car, pulled two pairs of gloves from the box in the dash compartment, and got out.

'Did you bring the key?' Atherton demanded.

'Yes, dear,' Slider said patiently.

Inside the house, the long hall was cool and dim, a pleasure after the heat of the day, and it smelt beautifully clean, with an undertone of furniture polish. The staircase rose up straight ahead, the handrail a shining snake of wood, smoothed and rubbed to a rich patina by a hundred and fifty years of hands. Though the house looked small from the street, it went back a long way, and the ceilings were lofty, eleven or twelve feet high, Slider thought. It was a wonderful house, built with the fine proportions and attention to detail that were characteristic of the age: the skirtings, the panelled doors and brass door-furniture, the decorated cornices and ceiling roses, the handsome fireplaces.

'Looks as if she made a decent living from this company of hers,' Atherton said.

'Or maybe she just had good taste,' Slider said. There was nothing expensive about the furnishings, but the simplicity with which everything was arranged made it look good. The floors had been stripped and polished, and there were a few rugs here and there for comfort; modern furniture, plain walls and curtains, and no clutter.

There were two rooms on this floor. At the front, with the bay window, was the drawing-room. The sofa and two armchairs were in coarse off-white material, grouped round a heavy glass coffee-table. Against the walls were hi-fi equipment, television and video, and a range of book-shelves. There were no pictures on the walls, just two four-foot-by-two framed posters. One was a movie poster for *Casablanca*. 'That must be worth a bit,' Atherton remarked. The other advertised a Festival Hall concert by the London Symphony Orchestra, with a date from the 1950s. Boult and Curzon, Slider noticed. Frivolity was limited to a number of large plants in big floor pots, their leaves glossily polished. The room was so big it was a little too bare for Slider's taste, but there was no deny-ing it was stylish.

The rear room was slightly smaller, square and fitted out as an office, with the usual equipment. Here, too, everything was neat, tidy, clean and dusted. There was a big engagements diary and a red address book on the desk, which Slider noted for removal; and a small pile of unopened mail. Postmarks suggested it was yesterday's. Presumably, then, it had arrived before she had gone out for her morning jog. She had picked it up and put it in here to be looked at when she got back. But she never got back.

'Everything in here will have to be gone through,' Slider said, with a wave that included the filing cabinets and the contents of the in- and out-trays. 'We need to know what sort of business she was doing, and with whom.'

This floor of the house was slightly above ground level, and stairs at the back of the hall led down to the semi-basement, with a landing half-way down with a lavatory and a door to the garden. The basement had been knocked into one long, large room with the original stone-flagged floor, fitted out as kitchen and eating area.

'Nice-looking kitchen,' Atherton said. 'All that slate and black granite must have cost a bob or two. She didn't stint herself.'

They went back up to the hall, intending to take a quick look round upstairs before getting down to a proper search, but as they were walking towards the front door, a shadow appeared behind its glass and the bell rang.

'Now what?' Atherton said.

Slider was ahead of him so he was the one to open the door. There, grinning engagingly, stood a very pretty young black woman in a bottle green trouser suit, with her hair plaited in windrows and tipped with green beads.

''Allo, guv,' she chirped. 'I was told to report to you.'

4

Brother, Can You
Spare Me a Paradigm?

Slider stared like a man who'd just been hit on the head with a large fish. 'Hart?' he said.

'Hollis fought you might need help. S'prised to see me?'

'Surprised doesn't begin to cover it,' Slider said. 'Don't tell me you're the extra body Mr Porson wangled?'

DC Tony Hart nodded. Slider stepped back to let her in. Behind him, he heard Atherton say, 'Extra body's the *mot juste*.'

'I ain't 'alf glad to be 'ere, I can tell you,' Hart went on. 'I'm sick of being the token black, token woman on all these special squads. I mean, it's all bollocks, innit? I told Mr Wevverspoon I wanted to get back operational, but he said I was too valuable to waste on police work.' She opened her eyes wide. 'I mean, straight, guv, can you believe it?'

'I believe six worse things than that every day before breakfast,' Slider said.

'I've been on this Diversity Advice Follow-up Team for three months now, wiv this bunch o' total tossers who've never been on the street in their lives. The acronym says it all. Honestly, not one of 'em noticed what it was.'

'Well, I'm glad to have you with us, Hart,' Slider said, skipping over that bit. Of all the firms in all the cop shops in all the Met, he thought, she had to walk into his. The last time she had worked with them, she had had a torrid fling with Atherton. Joanna, however, had opined that Hart had actually only chased Atherton because she really fancied him, Slider – a deeply unsettling thought. Whichever way round it was, complications like those he didn't need, especially given Atherton's currently over-stimulated state. Hart was too juicy by half to expose him to.

Hart turned her attention to Atherton now, and said lightly, 'Wotcher, Jim. I like the barnet. Cool or what?'

'Best not to encourage him,' Slider said kindly. 'He's on the loose again.'

'I can take care'v meself,' Hart said.

'Has Hollis filled you in on the story so far?'

'Sort of. The vic was drugged and stabbed in the park, to make it look like the Park Killer struck again.'

'Don't call her the vic. She's not a theatre.'

'All right,' Hart said agreeably. 'So what we doin'?'

'Looking round the house. What we need immediately is a photograph of the victim we can use with the public, and any information about next of kin. There'll be a full team in later to do the serious search. Of course you needn't ignore anything interesting or unusual if it jumps up and bites you. You'd better come upstairs with me and have a look at the bedrooms. Atherton, you can start going through the office.'

Upstairs, on the next floor, there were two bedrooms and a large bathroom, which, given the age of the house, must have originally been another bedroom. The floors were stripped and varnished all through, and echoed to their footsteps.

'Bit chilly,' Hart remarked. 'I like a nice bit o' Wilton meself.'

Slider thought it would be unwelcoming in winter, though at the moment it was pleasantly cool. The bathroom was done in a retro style, with a free-standing claw-footed bath, high-level cistern and old-fashioned pedestal basin. An odd place to make a stand for heritage. Of all rooms, surely the bathroom was the one in which you most wanted clinical modernity.

Of the bedrooms, the one at the back was the smaller. It was unfurnished, and being used for storage. There were several removers' cartons, still sealed up, presumably never having been unpacked since she moved in. There were also a number of ordinary cardboard boxes containing a variety of odds and ends – clothes, shoes, board games and jigsaw puzzles, sports equipment, ornaments, crockery, and one full of dolls and soft toys.

'It's like she brought everyfing wiv her when she left home,' Hart said. 'Look, there's pairs o' bally shoes in here, must be all of 'em goin' back to when she was five. An' about a thousand china horses. This is the sort o' stuff you leave cluttering up your mum and dad's house until they get mad and chuck it out.'

Yes, Slider thought, she was right. It was a good insight. 'Hell of a lot of sorting through to do,' he said.

'Oh, I dunno, guv,' Hart said comfortingly. 'If she's never unpacked it, it prob'ly never had anything to do with her present life. I wonder why she brought it wiv her, though.'

'Maybe her parents divorced and the family house was sold,' Slider suggested.

Hart grinned. 'Yeah, but most of us would still make

our mums take all this crap to her new house. There's people all over the country've got their cupboards stuffed full of their grown-up kids' junk, while their kids swank about bein' all minimalist in warehouse conversions wiv no storage.'

The larger, front room was evidently her bedroom. A king-size bed, neatly made; an extensive range of built-in wardrobes; an oak chest, probably Jacobean, under the window; a beautiful secretaire, probably Regency.

Hart had a look in the wardrobes. '*Well* nice,' she said, in emphatic understatement. 'Some top gear in here. Gucci and Karen Millen. Manolo shoes, even. Oh, and look at this pink suede skirt! Viv Westwood. I'm drooling, boss.'

'Just don't get DNA on the goods,' Slider warned. 'She did keep everything tidy, didn't she?'

'It's like one of them adverts for fitted bedrooms,' Hart said. 'Or that makeover programme – you know – where they turn out your messiest room and make you chuck stuff away. It looks about like this when they let the people back in. I've always thought they should do a revisit a week later. Nobody keeps their clothes like this. What was she, an alien from another planet?'

Slider headed for the secretaire. 'This is for us. This'll be where she kept her personal papers.'

'An' there's a photo,' Hart said. It was framed and standing on top of the secretaire, next to a small vase containing a single rose, whose petals were beginning to fall.

Slider picked up the photo and turned it to the light. The girl in the picture was smiling with radiant happiness, her face sharing the space inside the frame with that of a very nice bay horse.

Hart came close and looked too. 'Pretty. Nice face.'

'The girl's not bad, either.'

Hart slung a sideways glance at him. 'Bally an' horses.

She was someone's little princess, wasn't she? Will it do?'

'We could screen out the horse,' Slider said, 'but she was in her late twenties, and she only looks about seventeen or eighteen in this.' He looked round. 'Strange that this is the only photo. Most people have scads of them.'

'The only one on display,' Hart corrected.

The top part of the secretaire held lots of documents and letters. 'We'll have to take all this stuff back to the office and go through it,' Slider said.

In the drawer, along with various unremarkable odds and ends, was a number of Boots' developer's envelopes full of photographs. Slider and Hart looked through them, spread some out on the bed. There were holiday pictures and snaps of parties, outings, picnics, weddings and christenings. Young, good-looking faces were everywhere, laughing, mugging, drinking, having a good time. There was nothing that looked like a family shot – all the principals were young. Chattie herself appeared in very few of them – she must have been the one holding the camera – but when she did appear she seemed generally to have a champagne glass in her hand and her arm draped round a young man, and she was always laughing. Those fine, well-kept teeth shone out, the eyes disappeared into slits of hilarity, and everyone seemed to be looking at her, crowding round her as if she were the life of the group.

'Definitely a princess,' Hart observed, and it did not seem an entirely complimentary judgement.

Slider, though, was fascinated by her face. 'I'd like to have known her.'

'You'd nevera kept up, guv. She liked to 'ave it large, by the look of her,' Hart said. 'Any of these any good for us?'

'We'll take them back and have a look. She seems to

73

be laughing too much in most of them,' Slider said, with a hint of sadness. 'Let's look upstairs.'

There was another staircase, much plainer and narrower, going up into the roof space, into what must originally have been the servant's bedroom. Given that one of the main bedrooms was being used for storage, Slider would have expected more boxes up there, but it was furnished with a divan, fitted dressing-table and wardrobe and a tiny shower-room-and-loo carved out of a corner. It was also, in contrast to the rest of the house, perilously untidy, with clothes and shoes and bags spread over every surface, used mugs and plates on the floor, apple cores in the fireplace. A vast array of makeup and face and body unguents in clogged and dribbling bottles choked the dressing-table, smeared tissues lying where they had been thrown at the wastepaper basket and missed. Where any bare surface showed it was thick with dust, and there was a stale smell in the room, which was being baked to well-risen perfection by the heat under the roof.

'Oh, I love what she's done up here,' said Hart. 'Very post-modern.'

'Interesting,' said Slider. 'A complete personality change when you come up these stairs.'

'This is the attic she had in her picture,' Hart said.

'Eh?'

'Oscar Wilde. I knew there was something wrong wiv a person who kept her wardrobe that tidy. This is where her evil alter-ego had its 'orrible outlet.'

'Or,' Slider said, throwing cold water, 'she had a lodger.'

'Oh, yeah,' said Hart. 'There is that possibility.'

But apart from clothes and shoes and toiletries, there were no personal effects or documents in the drawers and cupboards. 'Not a permanent lodger, then,' Slider concluded.

'Maybe a friend who lived out of town and needed a place to crash during the week,' Hart suggested.

They descended again. Hearing their footsteps Atherton came out into the hall and said, 'I've found a safe.'

Hart assumed a breathless excitement. 'Hidden be'ind an ancestral portrait?'

Atherton gave her a quelling look. 'One of us doing that sort of thing is enough. No, it's sunk into the floor under the desk well. There's a ring in the floorboards that lifts up a square section and the door to the safe is underneath.'

Slider went and looked. 'Nice. Just hidden enough—'

'But not too tasty,' Hart concluded. ''Ow we gonna get in?'

'Manufacturer,' Slider said, and regarded her expression. 'Did you think we were going to blow it open with *plastique*? You really have got out of touch with reality.'

'I'm desperate for excitement,' she admitted. 'I feel as if I've been in a meeting for two years.'

'Meanwhile,' Atherton said patiently, 'I've found one or two things. Her passport – nothing much there, a few trips to the States, well spaced, probably holidays. Of course, European trips don't get stamped now, more's the pity.'

'We found holiday snaps upstairs,' said Hart. 'She liked to par-*tay*.'

'And I've found her bank statements. She had two accounts, one with a local NatWest for the business. Her personal account – this is the interesting bit – is with Coutts.'

'Coutts?' Hart said. 'That's the nobby bank, in't it? The Queen's got one of them.'

'That's right,' Atherton said. 'But you don't have to be

a nob. Anyone can have a Coutts account – anyone with assets of a quarter of a million.'

Hart's eyes widened satisfactorily. 'Is that straight?'

'So what are you suggesting?' Slider asked.

'I wasn't suggesting anything. I was just making observations,' Atherton said.

'No, you weren't,' said Slider.

'All right, then. I'm suggesting she must have had some other form of income than this business of hers, because the amounts going in and out of *that* account wouldn't buy her one of Coutts's paperclips.'

'This house must be worth a bit,' Slider said.

'I agree, but that doesn't change the question, does it? Where did she get the money to buy the house?'

'Is there a mortgage?'

'There's a monthly direct debit to Cheltenham and Gloucester, but working back from the amount it could only cover a mortgage of around a hundred thousand, which is about the most the business would support. This house must be worth four times that.'

'Inherited wealth, then, or rich parents?' Slider said. He thought of the photograph with the horse; he thought of the taste of the furnishings and decoration; he thought of the whole look of the body, the good skin, glossy hair, fine teeth. Someone's little princess, as Hart had said. 'If there was inherited wealth it might have something to do with the murder.'

'That's what I was thinking,' Atherton said. 'Given that all murders come down to sex or money. But the other possibility is that she had some kind of more lucrative sideline we haven't come across.'

'I don't like what you're suggesting,' Slider said uneasily.

'I don't either,' Atherton replied airily.

* * *

The Wellington was doing a roaring trade. Not only was it the closest the public could get to the goings-on in the park, but you could actually see quite a lot from the windows. The landlord had made the best of the situation. His 'pub grub' sign now sported a hand-written addition: 'We make KILLER sarnies!'

'You got to make a quid where you can, haven't you?' he excused himself, without shame, to Mackay. He added, with convoluted logic, 'I mean, if my pub had been a couple o' yards closer to the park gates, you lot would've closed me down for the duration, wouldn't you?'

Mackay wouldn't be drawn. 'Have a look at these, will you?'

'Is that her – the victim?' The landlord shook his head over the pictures – they were using cropped versions of the horse photo and a wedding snap where Chattie was in the line-up. 'No, I can't say I know her. Doesn't ring any bells.' He handed them back. 'We don't get the young crowd in here much. It's an old-fashioned kind of a pub. We get nice, steady regulars, local people, and the sandwich trade at lunch-time. Nothing here for youngsters. They mostly go down the Crown, now it's been done up and made all modern.'

Mackay reflected wryly that they, Slider's firm, had stopped going there for the very same reason.

Everyone was talking about the murder; everyone had something to say about the Park Killer. You couldn't chuck a brick in there without hitting an expert forensic psychologist. D'Arblay, with his nice wholesome face and gentle manner, was talking to some of the older customers, who clucked and ooohed in slow horror over the murder like broody hens, and found a perverse thrill in contemplation of the photos. 'That nice young thing!' 'Who could do a thing like that to such a pretty girl?'

The star of the show, however, was an old man who, it turned out, had actually spoken to the victim. He recognised her at once from the photos and said, 'It's that girl I see in the mornings when I'm walking the dog!'

He lived in Dalling Road, up the Brackenbury end, and mornings he took the old dog out, just round the streets, down Dalling, up Wingate, along Goldhawk as far as Brackenbury and back round. He used to take the dog to the park, but he was getting on now, the dog was, and round the streets was enough for him with his hips. Had Arthur Itis in his hips, the dog had. Well, oo 'adn't? He never knew dogs could get it, though. Got a lot of yuman diseases, dogs did. What come of living with yumans, he supposed. Anyway, quite often he'd see this young lady setting off in her PT gear, and she'd smile and say hello.

'Normally they wouldn't give you the time o' day, young people,' he said, with a sniff. 'Look at you as if you was dirt – if they don't barge right through you just as if you wasn't there. Never think we fought two world wars for the likes of them.'

D'Arblay guessed his age to be about sixty-five, which meant he wouldn't have fought in one war, never mind two, but he listened patiently. You never knew what you might find out if you kept your ears open and your mouth shut – that was what Mr Slider (something of a hero to D'Arblay) said.

'What time of day would that be?' he asked.

'Ooh, lessee, about a quart' past seven, give or take, time I get round there. We don't walk fast, the dog an' me. And she'd be coming out, down her steps, or I'd pass her going down the street. I see her most days, and she always give me a "good morning", and she'd say "nice day" or something like that. She walked nice, with her head up, not slouching along like some of 'em. Always smiling. Lovely smile, she had,' he said sentimentally, as though she had been a childhood sweetheart. 'Sort that makes you feel good to be alive, know what I mean? I can't believe anyone would kill her.' He sighed, drained off his pint, and smacked his lips hopefully, with a sideways glance at D'Arblay. D'Arblay only looked blank. The old man sighed again and said, 'Not a bit like that other one. Nasty piece of work, she was. Wouldn't give you the drippings off her nose, that one, never mind a smile.'

'What other one is that?' D'Arblay asked.

The old man feigned deafness, staring into his empty glass. D'Arblay fetched him another pint, and the old man perked up at once.

'Very nice of you. Very civil. Cheers!' He drank off half the bounty, wiped his lips, and said, 'That other one, I seen her going in and out now and then, different times o' day. Sometimes with my young lady, but sometimes not. 'Ad 'er own key.'

'What did she look like?' D'Arblay asked. They had all been briefed about the top-floor room. If he could get a lead on the lodger, or whatever she was, it would please Slider.

'Scrawny,' said the old man. 'Bag o' bones. Dyed hair – black – cut all messy, you know the way they do. Studs everywhere. She looked like she'd been up'olstered. And that 'orrible makeup, like Drackerler's mother, and black nail varnish. Skirts up to 'ere, no brassière and them thin little tops so you could see all she'd got.' He shook his head in condemnation. 'The other one was a lady, but this bit, well, she looked like a tart, there's no other word for it. And never a smile. You know the way they look, girls like that. Sullen, I'd call it. Like everyone was out to do 'em down. Most of 'em don't know what 'ardship is. And we fought a war for the likes of them.'

79

D'Arblay asked him a few more questions, but he didn't seem to have anything more to add, and D'Arblay left him to it, telling his story again to a fresh group who gathered round to marvel at someone who had actually Known The Victim.

The description of the Sinister Lodger went down well back at the factory.

'And it gives us a handle on her morning routine,' Slider said. 'The jog was evidently her usual daily round, so the killer may have known about it.'

Swilley had gained a small piece of information at the tube station. The paper-seller there had recognised the photo of Chattie and said that he saw her every morning. The station entrance, where he had his stand, was opposite the south gate of the park and he would see her come out of the park, 'in her tracksuit or whatever', and cross the road to buy the *Guardian* and the *Telegraph*. Round about eight o'clock, that'd be. Then she'd stick one under her arm, open the other, and start reading it as she walked back the way she'd come. He, too, described her as a 'really nice young woman, always ready with a smile and a bit of chat; friendly, you know? Not like some of them, just throw the money at you.'

'But she didn't have the newspapers with her,' Atherton said. 'It looks as though she was killed before she went down to the station, so a little before eight o'clock.'

'Unless the killer took the papers away with him,' Swilley said.

'Why would he do that?'

'Suppose they got covered with blood?'

'Well, that wouldn't matter, as long as it was her blood,' Atherton pointed out.

'If the murderer was bright enough to realise that.'

'So,' Slider said, 'she leaves home about a quarter past seven, runs around the park for half an hour or so, then on her way to the station to buy her paper meets the murderer.'

Of the incoming reports following the appeal, the most promising were of a man running out of the Paddenswick gate, and of a man on a bicycle riding very fast out of the King Street gate. The latter had almost knocked down the informant, a Mrs Beryl Rose, who was walking to the tube station on her way to work. He hadn't even looked round to see if he'd hurt her, though she'd shouted at him angrily. He'd just pedalled straight into the traffic, nearly causing an accident, weaving wildly round the cars and vans and shooting off down King Street towards Chiswick. This report was corroborated by two people, one of whom had stopped to ask Mrs Rose if she was all right, and exchanged a few words with her about the menace of people who rode bikes on the pavement, and why didn't They do something about it. The time given was variously just after eight, five past eight and ten past eight. The man was described as young, white, probably tall, probably fair, wearing black skin-tight cycling shorts, a lightweight blue windcheater jacket and a cycling helmet.

'Why would he be wearing a jacket on a hot day?' Hart asked, and answered herself, 'To cover up bloodstains maybe?'

The most promising thing about the description was that Mrs Rose said he had a sports bag strapped to the carrier behind the saddle. A bag of some kind would seem to be an essential for removing the weapon and any bloodstained clothing from the scene. On the other hand, the other two witnesses to Bicycle Man had not noticed the bag, so it was only Mrs Rose's word.

Running Man had also been fingered by three people, independently of each other. He was young, black, wearing baggy fawn chino pants, a loose grey hooded jacket over a black T-shirt, and trainers. He had raced 'like the wind' out of the park gate and up Paddenswick Road towards the Seven Stars. A further witness had seen him 'run madly' across the road at the Seven Stars, dodging the traffic filtering round the double roundabout there, and disappear up Askew Road. The time given was about eight o'clock, just before eight o'clock, and five or ten to eight. Against Running Man was the fact that none of the witnesses said he'd been carrying a bag, though one witness thought he had been carrying a mobile phone.

Probably they would turn out to be nothing, but both Running Man and Bicycle Man would have to be looked into. A media appeal was planned, asking them to come forward and get themselves eliminated from the inquiry. If Bicycle Man were innocent, there was good hope that he would turn up; but young black men in gangsta gear were generally suspicious of the police, and Slider was afraid that he would continue a thorn in their side for some time.

Porson got back from Hammersmith and scooped up Slider on his way upstairs. Slider scurried in his wake, feeling like Alice. Porson's legs were long, and he moved at a terrific rate, like an ostrich, his summer coat flapping around and behind him like shabby plumage. In the winter he wore a tent-like green ex-army overcoat, but his summer tegument was a beige mac. It had once been expensive, and had flaps and capes and pockets and buttons everywhere.

Reaching his room he barked, 'Close the door,' over his shoulder, shucked off his coat, threw it at the old-fashioned elk stand in the corner, and seemed slightly soothed when it caught and stayed. 'Well,' he said, 'I've done it. It wasn't easy. Mr Palfreyman wasn't best pleased, and I had to do a bit of fancy footwork, but I've got us the case *and* the budget. But we've got to get on with it. We can only have the extra uniform for a week. Have you got anything yet?'

Slider told him about Running Man and Bicycle Man. 'Of course, they may not turn out to be anything. What we really need to do is find people who saw the victim in the park that morning, but we're hampered because we can't issue a mugshot through the media until we've informed the next of kin.'

'And you don't know who they are?'

'We're going through her papers now, hoping to find out. It's a vicious circle, really – if we could publish her picture, we'd have all sorts of friends and family coming forward.'

Porson looked gloomy. 'Got to respect the susceptivities of the great GP,' he said, without conviction. 'If someone finds out about it the wrong way, they'll start screaming bloody murder.' Then his frustration burst forth. 'Everyone wants to sue these days. Nation of crybabies, that's what we are now. Everything you do, you have to look over your shoulder all the time in case a writ's coming flying at you.'

Slider murmured something sympathetic, and Porson stared at him, flame-eyed, working up to something.

'Fact is, I'm sick of all this pussyfooting PC malarkey. They tie both your hands, won't let you talk to anyone in case it upsets them, and then wonder why your clear-up rate's down. I'm thinking of pulling the plug after this case, promotion or not.'

'Oh, no, sir, don't do that,' Slider said.

Porson snorted. 'Miss me, would you?' he enquired ironically.

'Yes,' Slider said sturdily. 'We all would. A good super is hard to come by, more especially these days. Everybody admires and respects you, sir.'

Porson looked surprised. Then he turned away to stare out of his window and spoke with his back to Slider. 'Fact is,' he said again, and with the awkwardness of one unused to making personal confessions, 'I'm afraid of losing my edge.'

'No, sir,' Slider protested, but Porson held up his hand in his traffic-stopping gesture.

'It's true. When Betty died . . .' A long pause. 'When you suffer a bereavement, you run the gambit of emotions. I expected that. Says it in all the books. Denial, anger and so forth, blah-de-blah.' He waved away the psychotalk with a large hand gesture. 'But now I'm through all that, I just feel tired. As if I can't be bothered.'

Slider said, 'That's one of them. One of the reactions. You'll come through that, too.'

Porson said nothing. He cleared his throat thunderously, then fumbled a handkerchief out of his trouser pocket and blew his nose. He began to turn and Slider was afraid of what he was going to see – the trace of tears? A tremulous, confiding Syrup? He wasn't sure he could handle that.

Porson showed him a face like a badly hewn statue, and eyes that gleamed like steel rivets under scowling brows.

'So bloody well get on with it, then! Thirty-six hours on and you haven't even got a next of kin? I've stuck my neck out to get this case, and if you make me look like dick over it, I may be leaving, but you can kiss your bollocks goodbye, clear?'

'Yes, sir,' said Slider. He almost smiled with relief. Abuse from above made him feel more comfortable. It was his normal medium.

Atherton and Hart were seated at one desk, heads close together, going through the victim's diary and address book, cross checking them with each other and with other documents taken from the filing cabinet.

'The trouble is,' Atherton said, when Slider delivered Porson's gee-up, 'though she tends to write in business appointments with proper names, with the personal ones she uses a lot of initials and codes.'

'How do you know those are the personal ones?'

'Well, I'm guessing, of course, but it tends to be the evening engagements. There's one on Tuesday night – "JS 8pm". Her business engagements check out against the clients on file, and she keeps a time sheet for each, showing when and for how long she either worked for them or was with them on their premises. Expenses too. All very businesslike.'

'But then there's all this "DC 10 TFQ" stuff,' Hart put in. 'That's in here for Tuesday. I'm trying to run down the initials through the address book, but I'm not having much luck. There's definitely no-one under Q. DC 10's an aeroplane, and TFQ sounds like an airport terminal. Maybe she was meeting someone off a plane – ha ha.'

'If she was, she was spending the afternoon with them. There are two business appointments for the afternoon, both crossed out. We checked, and she cancelled them on Monday. So Tuesday is a mystery,' Atherton said. 'Apart from Marion saying she saw her at a quarter past six, we can't place her at all for that last day.'

'Marion!' Hart snorted, but very quietly.

'What about next of kin?' Slider pressed his own urgent need.

'People don't put their mums and dads in their address book,' Hart said. 'I mean, they know *their* addresses, don't they? There's nothing under Cornfeld, anyway. I tell you what, though, guv,' she added, lifting a confiding face, 'there's a lot of blokes' addresses in here, and quite a lot of just blokes' names and telephone numbers. I reckon she had a right merry old time on the quiet. Out most nights by the look of it.'

'The credit-card statements bear that out,' Atherton said. 'Quite a few donations to charities – I'm making a list of them. But lots of jollies, too – restaurants, theatres, cinema tickets, big food and drink bills. She didn't stint on enjoying herself.'

'Well, she was a good-looking bird, why not?' Hart said. 'If she had a lot o' boyfriends, what of it? This is the twenty-first century. Women are just as entitled to enjoy themselves as men.'

She had turned her head as she said that last bit, and she and Atherton looked into each other's eyes.

'I hate to interrupt this episode of *Oprah*,' Slider said, 'but could you concentrate on the problem in hand? Have you looked for a birth certificate?'

'Yes, but we haven't found one,' Atherton said. 'It's possible it's in the safe. Any word on when that's going to be opened?'

Slider shook his head. 'Some time tomorrow is the best I can get out of them.'

The phone on Atherton's desk rang and he answered it. 'No, he's here.' He handed it over. 'For you, the front shop.'

It was Sergeant Paxman, who was manning the front desk. 'Someone here to see you, about the Cornfeld case.'

'On my way,' said Slider.

5

Get Thee to a Mummery

The public access to the police station was a square room with the big, high desk across one side and a bench running round the other three. On the bench were two rather hopeless-looking young males with chronic sniffs and terminally baggy trousers, and, sitting as far away from them as possible, a middle-aged woman, neatly dressed though in cheap clothes, with a large shopping bag on her knee. She had grey hair with a few blonde highlights, done in the eternal short, rollered perm of the Decent Working Classes, and her face was tidily made up with blue eyeshadow and pink lipstick. She and her kind were the backbone of the country and Slider hoped it was her he was down here to see, and not one of the sullen youths.

Paxman pointed her out discreetly. 'Says she knows Cornfeld.'

'How did she know the name? We haven't released it yet.'

'She didn't. She says she thinks she knows deceased, wants to be sure.'

'What's her name?'

'Hammick. Maureen. Mrs,' said Paxman.

Slider resisted the urge to say, 'Lot. A. Thanks,' and went out to accost the woman. 'Mrs Hammick? I'm Detective Inspector Slider. I believe you wanted to talk to me.' She lifted suffering eyes, and he said, 'Would you like to come somewhere a bit more private?' and led her through into one of the interview rooms. He chose No. 1, which was marginally less repulsive than No. 2. They both smelt of sweaty feet, but someone had thrown up in No. 2 yesterday and it took time for the vomit stink to fade completely.

As soon as the door closed behind them she said, 'It's about Chattie – Chattie Cornfeld. Someone said – they said she was – that she's been murdered. Is it true?'

'Where did you hear that?' he asked neutrally.

'A neighbour of mine was in the Wellington lunchtime and she said there were policemen there showing a picture of Chattie and asking if anyone knew her. She recognised her because she's been with me when I've met Chattie in the street. But I thought maybe she'd made a mistake. I mean, she doesn't know her well. So I thought I'd – but it *isn't* her, is it?'

She looked at him with appeal, but not much hope. Silently Slider held out the photos. The woman took them, and her hand began to tremble. 'You took this one from her bedroom,' she said, as if that clinched it. 'You've been to the house.' She looked up at him. 'She's dead, then? She's the one – the Park Killer's latest victim?'

Slider nodded, reflecting how even at times of great emotion people couldn't help talking like the tabloids. 'Would you like to sit down?' he asked gently. He pulled out the chair from under the table and she sat, blindly, her eyes fixed on the empty air, her hands moving in slow distress, massaging the handle of her shopping basket. Slider took the seat opposite, and was glad to see that, though deeply affected, she was not crying or heading for hysterics. A sensible, level-headed woman – could be a good witness, if she had anything to tell.

'How do you know her?' he asked, after a respectful moment.

'I clean for her,' said Mrs Hammick.

Well, that accounted for the immaculateness of the house, anyway, Slider thought, because if this woman wasn't a thorough cleaner he'd eat his feather duster.

'I work for Merry Maids agency in Brook Green. They'll give you a reference, if you want. But we're more like friends now, really, and I do other bits of things for her as well, not through the agency – pick up her dry-cleaning, wait in for the plumber, that sort of thing. Well, I've got the key anyway, and I only live in Greenside Road, just across the road from Wingate.'

'So you know her quite well?'

'We're *friends*,' she said, with a little, desperate emphasis, as though that would change things, make the bad news not to be. 'It's not like with my other clients. I hardly see them, and most of them I wouldn't care if I never saw. But she works from home, so from the beginning she was often there when I came to do my work, and she's such a nice, friendly, cheery person we got on right away. She'd come up when I was half-way through my time and say, "Come on, Maureen, come and have a cup of tea and a good old chinwag,' and down I'd go to the kitchen and we'd have a chat over a cuppa. After a bit, I never both-ered about how much time I spent there. I just did what-ever she wanted doing, and if it took me over my time the agency was paying me, well, so be it. But she was a real lady, she always gave me a Christmas present and some-thing on my birthday – "For all the little extras you do for me, Maureen," she'd say. And I'd tell her, "You don't have to give me anything for that, I'm your friend. But she did, anyway. There's nothing I wouldn't do for her.'

Slider felt there was more and waited in silence. She looked down at her hands, and said, 'Last year when I had my divorce, I wouldn't have got through it if it hadn't been for her. I mean, just someone to talk to, yes, and she always had time for me; but apart from that she gave me advice, helped me with the papers and made phone calls for me. I mean, she was a person that just knew what to *do* about things, you know what I mean? I don't know what I'd have done without her.'

'How long have you known her?' Slider asked.

'I've been cleaning for her for three years, ever since she moved into that house. But it feels like a lot longer.' She looked up. 'She was a lovely person, ever so kind. Just last week, Friday, when I came in, she had this visitor, a poor lad with terrible acne. I could hardly look at him, poor soul, but the way she was looking at him and listening to him, giving him all her attention, you'd think there was nothing wrong with him at all. And then there's an old lady down the street she visits, spends hours down there talking to her – not a relative or anything, just to cheer her up. She was always cheerful, always smiling, full of jokes. And she worked so hard at that business of hers, all the hours God sent. She said, "Maureen, I'm going to make good, and it's going to be all on my own efforts." I admire that, people who do that. I can't stand freeloaders, people who expect you to carry them – like that sister of hers.'

'Sister?'

Mrs Hammick's mouth turned down in disapproval. 'That Jassy. You couldn't want a bigger contrast between two people.' She looked at him questioningly. 'You've been to the house? You've seen that room of hers?'

Slider was enlightened. 'The top-floor room.'

'That's it.'

'The sister lives there?'

'No, not now. She'd like to, but Chattie put her foot down – which is rare enough, because she's *too* kind, if anything, and people take advantage. Jassy walks all over her, and she'd have the shirt off Chattie's back if she could, in a minute. She lived with Chattie for about six months and it nearly drove her mad. Never cleaned up after herself, wore Chattie's clothes and spoiled 'em, brought people home without asking – not nice people. She was supposed to be putting up just for a week or two until she got her own place, but it was weeks and then months and I thought she was going to be a permanent fixture, only Chattie finally had enough and told her she had to go. But Jassy still regards that room as hers, and she's got a key to the house, so she comes and goes and sleeps there when she feels like it – when she has a row with her boyfriend, I expect. Or she wants to cadge money off her sister.'

'I gather you don't like her.'

'Jassy? She's one of them that thinks the world owes them a living. Never done an honest day's work in her life, lives on the dole and doesn't even try to get a job. Borrows money and never pays it back, takes Chattie's things without asking, and then complains that Chattie doesn't do enough for her. *And* she hangs around with a nasty rough lot. That boyfriend of hers – well, if he's not a criminal, I don't know! He's a coloured, you know.' She looked at Slider to see his reaction. 'I've got nothing against them as such, but I'm sure as I stand here that Darren's up to no good. He's got a shifty look in his eye, and once when Jassy brought him back to the house I found him snooping about where he'd no business. Casing the joint, that's what you call it, isn't it?'

91

'Did anything go missing?'

'Not that I heard, but that doesn't mean he wasn't thinking about it. I wouldn't put it past Jassy either. Just this Monday I caught her sneaking around the house. I'd just popped in with some croissants for Chattie – I get them at a bakery near a lady I do on a Monday afternoon, and Chattie likes them specially, so I often get her some and drop them round for her Tuesday breakfast. I was just walking down the hall when Jassy pops up the stairs from the kitchen, and as soon as she sees me she looks guilty. Gives a little jump, you know, and says, "Oh, it's you, what are you doing here?" or something like that. I said, "Chattie knows I'm here. I wonder if the same could be said for you," and she said, "I was just passing and I thought I'd drop in and see my sister. I just went down to the kitchen to make myself a coffee." And I thought, Yes, very likely, but I didn't say anything. I just stood there, and she sort of sulked off. I had a good look round, I can tell you, but I never saw anything missing. Interrupted her in time, that's what I think.'

'Did you say anything to Chattie about it?'

'No, Chattie's too soft-hearted. It wouldn't have done any good. She's so honest herself, she can't believe anyone else is different – though she did see through that Darren in the end and told Jassy not to bring him any more. But Jassy – well, you've seen that room of hers. I said to Chattie, in the end, I said, "I'm sorry, but I'm just not going to clean up in there any more. I'll do anything for you," I said, "but I'm not cleaning up after that little madam." And Chattie said she didn't blame me and she'd tell Jassy to clean it herself. But of course she never did. I always say, you can tell a lot about a person from the way they leave their house, and that Jassy's room is filthy and nasty, just like her.'

'Is she thin, black hair, lots of studs?'

'You've seen her, then?'

'No, someone described her. Said she had makeup like Dracula's mother.'

Mrs Hammick gave a grim sort of smile. 'That's good! Dracula's mother. Yes, black lipstick and purple eyeshadow and stuff like that. She's pretty enough underneath, though not a candle to Chattie in my opinion, but she makes herself look as ugly as she can. It's like she's spitting in your eye, you know?'

'Do you know her full name, and where she lives?'

'Her name's Jasmine – she hates it, that's why she calls herself Jassy – and her surname's different from Chattie's. Her mum and dad got divorced and her mum got remarried. She's called Jassy Whitelaw, and she lives somewhere down south of the river, Clapham, I think. Her address'll be in Chattie's book – the red address book on her desk.'

'Yes, we have that. Do you know Darren's surname and address?'

'Well, the address is same as Jassy's – they live together. But his surname . . .' She thought a moment, shaking her head slowly. 'I think it might be Brown. Darren Brown. Or Biggs? Or Bates? No, Brown,' she said firmly; then paused. 'Or was it Barnes? Yes, I think that was it. Darren Barnes.'

'And would you know who Chattie's next of kin would be?'

'Ooh, I'm not sure. I suppose it would be her mother, with her being divorced as well. Chattie's never mentioned her father to me, so I don't know whether she still sees him or anything, but she talked a lot about her mum. She's a writer – quite a famous one. Stella Smart – have you heard of her?'

The name was vaguely familiar to Slider, as something

seen in passing, on a shelf in Smith's. 'I think so. She writes romances, doesn't she?'

Mrs Hammick looked quite stern. 'Not romances, they're ever so much better than that. They're like those Aga sagas of Joanna Trollope's – good, long books you can get your teeth into, about real people. I've read quite a few of them now, from the library, and they're ever so good. Anyway, Chattie goes to see her and her mum phones her up, so I know *they* get on all right, so I should think she'd be her next of kin,' she concluded, as though it were something elective. 'But as to her address – well, I know it's in Hertfordshire somewhere, near Hemel Hempstead I think she said, but I don't know exactly.'

'I'm sure we can find it out, now we know who she is. If it isn't in the address book, the publishers will be able to tell us.'

'Yes, that's right,' said Mrs Hammick, looking despondent now, as her elation left her and she remembered why she was there in the first place. 'It'll be a terrible shock to her, poor lady. What a shocking, dreadful thing to happen to someone like Chattie. If it was Jassy, now, you could understand it, the sort of people she mixes with. I've often said she'd come to a bad end one day.'

'You've been very helpful,' Slider said. 'One more thing perhaps you can tell me – did Chattie have a boyfriend?'

Mrs Hammick pursed her lips. 'Well, she had a lot of menfriends, but not what you'd call a boyfriend, not one special person. She was always going out, meals and things, and it was generally with a man, but it was all casual, if you know what I mean. It seemed to suit her that way,' she added sadly. 'I sometimes said to her, wouldn't she like to get married and settle down, but she always said she was happy as she was. "I haven't got room in my life for another man," she said. "I'm too busy making my way in the world," she said. I said she didn't want to leave it too late, if she wanted to have kiddies, but she said she wasn't interested in that. I think maybe it was to do with her mum and dad getting divorced. It was a real pity, but I always thought she'd meet someone one day and then she'd change her mind pretty quick. I used to say to her, "You won't feel that way when you meet the right man." But now she never will, of course,' she remembered, and had to fumble in her handbag for a handkerchief.

'Did you ever meet any of them?' Slider asked. 'Did they come to the house?'

'Oh, yes, sometimes. She had them to stay over sometimes. Well, she was a healthy girl with normal urges,' Mrs Hammick defended her. 'I met one once, when he was still in the kitchen when I arrived to do my cleaning. Very nice young man he seemed, but I didn't linger, only to say hello, because he wasn't dressed yet which made it awkward. But usually they were gone by the time I got there. Well, people go off to work so early these days, don't they?'

'Can you remember any of their names? Was there one she was seeing more of recently?'

'I don't know,' she said thoughtfully. 'She did talk to me about her menfriends, told me funny stories about them. But I can't remember her mentioning anyone special, not lately.'

'Did she seem unhappy recently?'

'Oh, no, she was just like usual. But now you mention it, the last few days she might have been a bit more – I don't know – thoughtful than before. I mean, she was always cheerful when she spoke to me, but I caught her now and then with a frown on her face, when she didn't know I was looking.'

'She was worried about something?'

'I wouldn't say worried, exactly. More as if she was thinking something out. Just – well, thoughtful.' She came back to the word by default.

Slider took her contact details and thanked her for coming forward, and warned her that the house was now off limits and that she shouldn't try to go in. 'In fact, if you have the keys with you, it would be better to let me have them, for safety's sake.'

'They're in my purse,' Mrs Hammick said, rummaged it out of her bag and handed over the Yale and deadlock keys on an unmarked ring. At the last moment her hand lingered on them before she dropped them into Slider's waiting palm. It seemed to have struck her all at once. 'I suppose I shan't ever need them again. I can't believe she's dead. I just can't believe it.' She shook her head slowly.

Like the man who fell off the Cairo ferry, Slider thought, she was in denial.

When he got back to his office, Atherton came in and said, 'Mr Porson wants you urgently.'

'Is there another way?' Slider said wearily.

'What did your witness want?'

'She wasn't a witness, just the victim's cleaner.' He gave him a brief outline of the interview. 'Said Chattie was a really nice person, the sort who'd do anything for you.'

'Helpful.'

'Also that she had lots of boyfriends, but not one special one.'

'We sort of deduced that from her diary and address book.'

'Got any further with her Tuesday meetings?'

'No, we've pretty well drawn a blank. DC 10, TFQ and JS remain mysteries. We can't place her at all that day.'

'I wonder if that's significant?'

'Anything could be, and hardly anything ever is,' Atherton said. 'I was thinking of going home now, if you don't mind. See what a little R and R can do for the deductive powers. Or in my case, a lot of R and R.'

'Going out tonight?' Slider said, and then, hating himself for it, 'Hart, is it?'

'Hart?'

'You seemed to be getting on rather well.'

'She's just a colleague,' Atherton said. 'No, I'm seeing Marion Davies again.'

'Two nights running sounds serious. And boffing a witness? I'm surprised at you.'

'Considering that's how you met Joanna,' Atherton said, and didn't need to finish the sentence. 'Anyway, she's not a witness. Just a friend, like your cleaner.'

'You don't know that.'

Atherton smiled delicately. 'Then I'm going the best way about finding out.'

Slider got up from his desk and waved him away. 'Go. I've got Mr Porson waiting for me.'

'I won't offer to swap,' said Atherton.

Porson wasted no words. 'Right, I hear from Hemel police they've informed the mother.'

'What about the father?'

'The mother says the victim had no contact with him, and she doesn't know where he is. So we can go on air with the photo. They've sent us over a studio portrait the mother came up with, better quality than what we've got, so we'll go with that.'

Slider looked at his watch. 'It's too late to get it on the *Six o'Clock News*.'

'Time you entered the twenty-first century,' Porson

admonished. 'Hemel sent the photo electronically to the Beeb at the same time as us, and they're going on with that, and a plain studio statement. "Police have named the victim" blah-de-blah. But they want a live body for the ten o'clock, so you've got to go and record something.'

Slider's heart sank. 'Me, sir?' He hated being on screen.

'The camera loves you, Slider,' Porson said, straight-faced. 'They'll be filming it in the publicity suite. Get yourself over to Hammersmith quick as you like. You know what to say?'

'We're still sticking with the Park Killer?'

'We'll leave it run a bit longer,' Porson said. 'Don't say it was him, just that first impressions point that way, you know the score. Noncommittal. The publicity woman, Amanda Odell, will run through it with you. Ask for witnesses to come forward. And for anyone who was in the park to get himself crossed off the list.'

'Especially Bicycle Man and Running Man,' Slider said.

'Right.'

'What about manning the phones tonight?'

'I'll see to that. You get yourself to Hammersmith. Go. They're waiting for you.'

Get thee to a mummery, thought Slider, trudging away.

'You're early,' Joanna said, when he let himself in.

'It's nearly nine o'clock,' Slider said. 'You call that early?'

'I wasn't really expecting you until later.'

'Does that mean there's nothing to eat?'

'We can go out if you like,' she said, and then, seeing from his face how well that went down, 'or I could pop out and get some fish and chips.'

'Now you're talking,' he said, brightening. 'But what about you – haven't you eaten?'

'Only a snack. I could find space for fish and chips,' she said. 'Anyway, we're celebrating.'

'We are?'

'I've got some good news. Really good news. I had a phone call today.'

'Huh, that's nothing. I get those every day.'

'Stop clowning, this is important. I've been booked for some sessions.'

'Oh. Good for you. What sessions?'

'It's the soundtrack for the new James Bond film. Nine sessions, at Watford, tomorrow, Saturday and Sunday.'

'Tomorrow? That's short notice.'

'Well, obviously I wasn't the first choice,' she said. 'I'm subbing for some poor sap who's fallen ill and who's going to miss out on all the goodies. She'll be kicking herself, because film sessions pay top dollar, and it doesn't end there. They're going to make a CD of the music later, which will be more sessions; and Ronnie said there's some talk of taking it on the road as a concert promotion.'

'Ronnie?'

'Ronnie Barrett, the fixer. The soundtrack and the CD will all be on the one contract, so it'll be the same people for both, but he likes me so he says he'll try and get me the concerts as well.' She beamed. 'Lots of lovely work and lots of lovely money. Aren't you pleased?'

'Of course I am. Delighted for you. But – three lots of three sessions? On consecutive days? Isn't that too much for you, in—'

'"In my delicate condition"? My dear Inspector, you can't say things like that any more,' she laughed. He saw that it was not so much the money she was so happy

99

about as the work. She had missed being in the loop, missed the company, the music and the sense of importance it gave her, the shape it gave to her life. How would she cope when the baby came? And if, after her maternity absence, she couldn't get any more work at all, what then?

'Borrowing trouble are your two middle names,' as his mother would have said. Deal with that when and if it arose.

'I just want you to take care of yourself,' he said at last.

She stepped closer and put her arms round his waist. 'I will. I'll be sitting down all the time, remember.' She kissed him. 'I promise I'll eat proper meals and rest in the breaks. And I won't even have to drive. Pete Thomas lives in Hammersmith and he's going to pick me up, and we'll share petrol money.'

'Okay.' He felt the hardness of her belly pressing against him. 'I love you,' he said.

'I love you, too.' She kissed him again. 'I'll go and get the fish and chips now, shall I, while you change?'

'All right. We can eat them in front of the telly and you can criticise my performance.'

'You're on the telly again? My dear, this house is just full of artistes!'

The day dawned sunny, but the sunshine and the blue sky both had a watery, unstable look. Slider shoved his mac into the car, returned to kiss Joanna again – she was practising, from a book of 'studies' that looked like black hairy caterpillars crawling up and down the staves – and set off for Hemel Hempstead. Before he was within striking distance, loose, wet grey clouds came up, and sharp rain began to hit the windscreen.

Stella Smart's address was Owl Cottage, The Dene, and it was just outside the town – he had got directions from the Hemel police. He imagined a country lane and a cob cottage with a crooked roof and small, deep windows burdened with creeper. And Stella Smart he thought would either be artistic-Bohemian with pre-Raphaelite dresses, gypsy hair and clashing bangles, or celebrity-glamorous with lots of makeup and gold costume jewellery.

He stopped in Hemel on his way to buy one of her books in Smith's. He picked up *Long Summer Days*, which seemed to be the most recent paperback – there were lots of copies of it, anyway – and pulled into a lay-by to thumb through it. It seemed to be about a nice vicar's wife of the jam-making, sensible-shoe kind, who thought her husband was being unfaithful to her. There was a lot of villagey stuff about WI meetings and cricket clubs, and a lot of drinking went on – people seemed to be always propping up the bar in the village pub, or downing G-and-Ts in each other's kitchens. He was about to throw it aside and drive on when the word 'nipple' caught his eye and he found himself in the middle of a torrid love scene between Mrs Vicar and a young man, an artist and newcomer to the village. So, he thought, what would you call that, then? An Aga-bonker? A surplice-ripper? The Bohemian image of Stella Smart now seemed the more appropriate.

It was a surprise all ways up, therefore, when The Dene turned out to be a road on a dinky new estate of little Lego houses of yellow brick, with pink-tiled roofs that looked mysteriously as if they were made of Plasticine. To an eye used to London's Victorian stock, they looked impossibly small, as if they had been built to house the garden gnomes that decorated so many of the front gardens. Owl Cottage was a corner house, just as new, boxy and Legoland as the rest, and the door was opened to him by a small, neat woman in a plain dark blue linen suit over a white blouse, with tidy hair and makeup, who might have been just off to work in a solicitor's or estate agent's office.

'Mrs Smart?' he asked, though he knew it was her from the blind look of grief that had settled into her face. Perhaps he ought to have said Miss Smart, if it was her writing name. He wasn't sure of the etiquette. If she hadn't remarried she was probably Mrs Cornfeld. 'I'm Inspector Slider.' He proffered his brief, but she didn't look at it.

'They said you were coming,' she said; and then, with an air of pulling herself together, 'You'd better come in. You're getting wet.'

She backed off to let him into the hall – necessary because it was only as wide as the door and hardly any longer. She held out her hand for his mac. He struggled out of it, elbows bumping the walls, and she hung it on top of the others on the coat pegs. 'Come in,' she said, and led him through a glass-panelled door which gave directly onto a through-lounge-cum-dining-room ending in french windows onto the garden. The room was not, to begin with, spacious in this gnome-sized house; but the cramped effect was heightened by the fact that all the furniture in it had been made for a different class of house altogether. Old, fine and lovingly polished, it crowded the narrow space: a huge bookcase to the right, giving the impression of having to duck its head under the low ceiling, a lovely chiffonier on the left, a large brocade chesterfield and two Queen Anne armchairs beyond, lamps and wine tables forced in somehow, and in the dining-room section a mahogany table with William

IV chairs and a wonderful high Edwardian sideboard, which between them meant holding your breath and sidling if you wanted to get past to the garden. There were paintings on the wall, a mixture of watercolours and small oils, and on the surfaces delicate pieces of porcelain and two lovely clocks. Presumably some necessity had brought Stella Smart to this inappropriate setting.

'You'd like some coffee,' she said, and it was hardly a question, so he didn't answer it. 'Do sit down.'

She waved him to the chesterfield and went out through a door between the two sections of the room, which presumably led to the kitchen and stairs. The smell of fresh coffee sneaked in before the door closed again, relieving him of the fear that he might have to drink instant. Evidently she had everything ready for him, for before his look-round had had a chance to do more than note the similar-looking row of hardbacks in the bookcase, which were presumably her own, and no photographs anywhere (a family trait?) she came back in with a tray. She was keeping up standards: delicately embroidered tray-cloth, bone china decorated with tiny forget-me-nots, coffee in a china jug to match, and a plate of what looked like home-made shortcake.

She took an armchair catty-corner to him and put the tray down on the small table between them. 'How do you take it?'

'Black, please. No sugar.'

She poured, passed, handed him the shortcake, and he waited in silence while she did these things. She was marking her territory, giving herself the upper hand by these small rituals, which was as it should be. He studied her as she poured her own coffee. She was in her fifties, he thought, and well preserved rather than young for her age. Her hair was fair-going-grey; she was small and slight — thin, almost — with a bony nose and sharp chin. He could not see much resemblance in her to Chattie. He would not have called her pretty or even handsome, though there was something in the direct look of her brown eyes when she lifted them at last that was attractive. They were pinkish now, and the lids still swollen from crying, but at other times he thought she would have been able to do things with them that would have fetched most men.

She sat back now with her cup and sipped, looking at him steadily, not initiating anything. He gave it time, trying his coffee — very good — and the biscuit.

'Good shortcake,' he commented. 'Did you make it yourself?'

'Yes,' she said.

He waited, but she offered nothing more. He set down his cup and said, 'I am very sorry for your loss.'

'Thank you,' she said.

'And I'm sorry to have to bother you at a time like this, but I would like to talk to you about your daughter.'

'Why?' she said.

He had not expected that. 'Because I need to know as much about her as possible,' he said.

'But if she was murdered by the Park Killer,' said Stella Smart, 'he would have picked her simply because she was there, not for any other reason. How can knowing about her help you find him?' The eyes were like policeman's eyes, he saw now: they not only looked, but saw. He had never met an author before. He supposed that noticing and deducing would be part of a writer's trade too. An interesting new thought to come back to.

'You're very quick,' he said. 'I had better tell you at once that we don't think she was one of the Park Killer's victims.'

'Why not?'

'There were discrepancies in the method. I don't want to go into that with you. But we think the murderer was trying to make it look like the Park Killer's work.'

'I saw the news last night. It gave the impression—'

'Yes. We thought it might help us to let the murderer think we were fooled. But I believe she was killed by someone who knew her.'

She examined his face. 'You must have ruled me out, if you're telling me this.'

He had, in the first few moments. 'I can see what she meant to you.'

Now she moved her eyes away, breaking contact. She could observe other people, but could not have her own feelings observed. 'She was everything to me. She was all I had.'

'What about . . . ?' He glanced towards the bookcase.

'My work?' she said, with a sour twist of her mouth. 'Yes, I used to think it mattered a great deal. But that was while I still had Chattie. Now I can see it's just a handful of dust.'

'Tell me about her,' he invited.

Her eyes became remote as she looked into the past. She sipped at her coffee. He saw as she put the cup back in the saucer that there was a slight tremor in her hands, and now he looked more closely, there were broken veins in the cheeks and on the nose that the careful makeup only just didn't conceal. He wondered if she was a drinker.

She said, 'She was a happy baby, with a wonderful chuckle. She walked and talked very early, and then she was running about and chattering all day long. That was when we nicknamed her Chattie. Everyone loved her. And she was clever, too, and musical. Did well at school, won a scholarship at eleven, sang in all the school choirs, took up the cello. After school she went to the Royal College, and I thought she'd be a musician, but she didn't feel she had sufficient talent, though I thought she was wrong about that. Anyway, when she finished college she got a job instead. She worked for Regina Stein, the big music agency, for two years, and for a record company for another year, and then she decided to set up on her own.'

'Solutions,' Slider suggested.

Stella Smart's mouth turned down a little. 'Yes, that's what she called it. I said she should have called it Dogsbodies.'

'You didn't approve?'

'It wasn't a matter of not approving. I thought she was wasting her talents and that she would never make a living out of it.'

'Did you quarrel about it?'

'No,' she said. 'We never quarrelled. You couldn't quarrel with Chattie. She was too good-tempered.'

'How did the idea of Solutions come to her?'

'Oh, it was something she came across in America, and she liked the idea of the variety it would give her. She never wanted to do a routine nine-to-five job. She helped a couple of musician friends to set up websites, and taught herself about that side of the business that way. She thought she'd have all sorts of clients, but with her background a lot of them have turned out to be musicians and, of course, they never seem to have any money. She has a struggle to get them to pay. And much of what she does is menial office work. It's been four years, and she's still only scratching a living. All that intelligence and energy and talent, and she's doing people's filing and writing their letters.'

She sounded angry and frustrated. Definitely a *casus belli* here, Slider thought.

'How has she managed for money, these four years?' Slider asked. 'Did she have any other job, or source of income?'

'How could she?' she said sharply. 'It took up all her time.'

'Was there family money?'

'No,' Stella Smart snapped. 'Apart from some furniture and things left to me by my mother, I have only what I earn from my books, and that, believe me, is no fortune. You see,' with a gesture of the hand, 'what I am reduced to.'

'Did you help her out with money?'

'She wanted to do it all herself, with no help from anybody.'

'What about her father?'

'Chattie has nothing to do with her father. She feels the same way about him as I do. She hasn't seen him for years.'

'It's just that she seemed to live quite a lavish lifestyle,' Slider said delicately. 'Lots of restaurants and theatres, nice holidays and so on.'

She looked at him with a faint, triumphant smile. 'A woman can always enjoy those things without having money, if she knows how to attract men. Chattie never lacked for male company.'

'Did you ever visit her house?' he asked.

'She lived in some ghastly slum in Hammersmith – all she could afford. She never invited me there and I never wanted to go. We met in Town, or she came here.'

Slider wondered now whether the mother had really known anything about her daughter's life. Chattie might have had lots of dates, but she spent her own money as well; and the house was no slum. Either the mother was dissembling for some reason, or Chattie had kept secrets from her. He tried another tack. 'She was your only child?'

'Yes.'

'I thought there was a sister, or step–sister?'

The face became stony. 'Half-sister. Jassy is not my child, and I have nothing to do with her.' Slider kept looking at her expectantly, and after a pause she sighed and said, 'I had better tell you the story, or you won't leave it alone. I met Chattie's father at some ghastly party or other. We had an affair. He divorced his first wife for me. Later he met Jassy's mother and had an affair with her, and left me for her. So I suppose you could say I was served right.' Slider wouldn't have dared. 'There was a child from the first wife, too, another daughter, Ruth. So there are three half-sisters; but none of them grew up together.'

'Presumably Chattie had some contact with them?'

'None, as far as I know, with Ruth. She's a lot older, a different generation. They had nothing in common. And Chattie never liked Jassy. She disapproved of her.'

'But from what I've heard, Jassy lived with her for a while.'

'Chattie's too soft a touch. She never says no to anyone. Jassy leeched off her. The girl is a slut with no morals – just like her mother. Mother and daughter, they're like those ghastly underwater things with suckers that simply attach themselves and live by draining the victim's blood. I've never been beholden to anyone, and I'm proud of Chattie for making her own way and owing nothing to anyone.'

There was a great deal of food for thought here, and a lot of seething emotions under this Noddy roof, but he wasn't sure where it was getting him.

'I have to ask you this,' he said. 'Do you know of

anyone who would have wanted to harm your daughter?'

'No,' she said decidedly. 'Everyone loved her. She hadn't an enemy in the world.'

'What about jealousy as a motive?'

'Lovers, you mean? I don't believe that. She had a light touch. Yes, she always had men around her, but I don't think she ever cared deeply for any of them. It was just fun – on both sides. She knew how to handle them. She learned that from me.'

'Do you know of anything she might have been mixed up in, any business interests she had other than Solutions, any money troubles?'

'No, not at all.' She looked at him shrewdly. 'I take it that not everyone agrees with your assessment that it was not the Park Killer?'

Slider was startled. 'I'm sorry?'

'At first, when you came in, you said "we" all along, but then you said, "*I* believe she was killed by someone who knew her."'

'That's very observant of you,' he said.

'People are my livelihood – how they look and what they say. If I did not observe, I couldn't write.' She looked around her, with the air of someone suddenly waking up; the animation drained from her face, and the blind, grieving look returned. Talking with him, she had forgotten, deep down where it counted, that they were talking about her daughter's murder. Now she had reminded herself. 'What does it matter, anyway?' she said dully. 'Find her killer, don't find him. She's dead, and she won't be coming back.'

He took his leave. As he struggled into his mac, the book fell out of his pocket, and he picked it up and hesitated a moment, wondering whether it would please her if he asked her to sign it. But she looked at it, and when she met his eyes he saw that it would not be a good idea.

'What did you bring that for? *Long Summer Days*. My latest success,' she said, with bitter irony. 'It's waste paper. Throw it in the nearest bin. My daughter's dead, my lovely, smiling daughter. It makes me sick to think I ever cared about anything else.'

6

Summer Daze

The rain had cleared away, and the pavements were steaming in a Bangkok sort of way as Slider parked the car. His wet mac was making the car smell like old dogs, so he carried it in with him to dry out indoors. It must be hell on the tubes today, he reflected.

Stuff had bred on his desk in his absence, as usual. There was the preliminary report from Bob Bailey, and he pulled it out to read it first. There was nothing new. They had not found any blood other than that in the immediate vicinity of the body, which suggested the killing had taken place at that spot and without a struggle – but he already knew that. It also meant that the killer had not tracked the blood around and probably did not have much on his clothes; but Slider pinned his faith on a belief that you could not stab someone without getting blood on you somewhere. Blood from the bark next to the body had been sent off for DNA profiling and to be tested against the victim's. Sweet wrappers and cigarette ends were being held pending instructions.

On another piece of paper was a message asking him to call Freddie Cameron. He dialled, and just as Cameron answered Atherton appeared in his doorway with a question on his lips. Slider held up a hand. 'Freddie. What's new?'

'Ah, back from the jungle so soon? They told me you were in the wilds of Herefordshire this morning.'

'Hertfordshire.'

'A distinction without a difference. Well, old chum, I thought you'd like to know my official findings in advance of the written copy. It's pretty much what we discussed at the post. In my opinion death was due to respiratory collapse, caused by a toxic substance at present unknown.'

'So the stabbing had nothing to do with it?'

'The wounds aren't severe enough to cause death, and in any case wouldn't account for the cyanosis and congestion. If she was conscious when it was going on, it might have contributed to shock, but she would have died anyway.' He heard Slider's silence and added, 'My view, considering the blood patterns, is that she was probably unconscious when the blows were struck.'

'Thanks,' said Slider

'Does it occur to you,' Cameron said kindly, 'that you're too sensitive for this job?'

'Pots and kettles, Freddie. What else?'

'I found no puncture wound such as would be left by injection, and the stomach contents revealed no solid matter.'

'Jogging on an empty stomach? Not the recommended way.'

'What I meant was there were no tablet or capsule residues. But yes, you're right, no eggs and B, no toast, no porage. Just a quantity of liquid. I've sent a sample off to the tox lab, along with blood, kidney, liver and vitreous humour –'

'Sounds like a mixed grill.'

'– but from here on we just have to wait. Those tox boys are in a different time zone from the rest of us.'

'So she drank the poison?'

'It would seem so.'

'But how would she be induced to take it?' Slider mused.

'Not my province, thank God,' said Freddie.

'That never stops you having an opinion,' Slider said. 'How quickly would she lose consciousness?'

'Depends what the drug was and how much was administered. But liquid would pass quickly into the small intestine and be rapidly absorbed from there. With one of the ultra-short-acting barbiturates she could be unconscious within a few minutes and dead minutes after that. And,' he added, 'it would have had to be quick, wouldn't it, from the murderer's point of view? Anything taking longer than a few minutes to induce unconsciousness would risk the victim calling for help or running away.'

'It's a good job she was stabbed, otherwise it could be suicide and we'd be even more hampered. I wonder the killer didn't think of that.'

'This strikes me as a very stupid killer.'

'We'll have to have the contents of the water-bottle tested, just to be sure.'

'Done and done.'

'All right, assuming she was drugged with a short-acting barbiturate, where would the murderer get the stuff?'

'It's not prescribed in this country and you can't buy it legally. But there are lots of illegal pharmaceutical drugs about if you know where to go. You can buy them on the Internet these days. Or you can smuggle them in from places like Mexico or Hong Kong where they are prescribed. Or steal them from a hospital or warehouse.

The field of possibilities' – Slider imagined him waving a hand – 'is enormous.'

'Thank you so much,' he said drily.

'Don't mention it,' Freddie assured him. 'As to the weapon, I'd say it was a very sharp, narrow, single-edged blade about seven inches long, with a cross-guard only on the cutting edge. So it could be a combat knife or a kitchen knife. I've drawn you a picture of the sort of profile. You'll have the written report later today, when I've checked it for spelling mistakes. The man who invented the spellchecker should be shot. I'll send it over in the bag.'

'Thanks, Freddie.'

Slider rang off, and turned to Atherton.

'She drank it?' Atherton said.

'Apparently.'

'In a bottle marked "Poison", I suppose. Very Alice in Wonderland.'

'Someone might have spiked her water-bottle.'

'But that would mean access to her house that morning. I can't believe she'd fill her water-bottle up in advance, the day before. What did you get from the mater?'

'Not much, except a ferment of emotions revolving round the daughter and the divorce, which was obviously acrimonious. And that there was no family money or private income. But,' he added, with slight reluctance, because he could see this moving in a direction he didn't like, 'she evidently thought Chattie was living hand-to-mouth on the shaky proceeds of her business. She'd never seen the house, for a start. They always met elsewhere. She thought it was a slum and Chattie was ashamed of it.'

'Sounds as if our Chattie had something to hide from Mummy,' Atherton said. 'I wonder what?'

Slider said, to distract him, 'And there's another half-sister somewhere. Stella Smart was the second wife of three. But apparently there wasn't any contact between them. I suppose we'll have to talk to her, but it's not priority.'

'Always nice to have more things to check up on,' Atherton said. 'In the mean time, there was quite a response from last night's appeal. About a dozen people who were in the park and want to be crossed off. One or two possible sightings that are worth following up. And a man who says he saw Chattie on Tuesday evening in the Anchor – that's the pub at the end of her road.'

'Good! Get on to that one.'

'I was going to do it myself,' Atherton said, with a slight question mark.

'Yes, go. What else?'

'Oddly, a lot of people phoned up just to say they knew her and liked her. I've never known anything like that before. It was a bit Jill Dando-ish.'

'So – what then? There's an undertone in your voice.'

'I suppose I'm just being perverse, but when everyone says a person is an angel, I can't help wondering if there's a con going on. And given that she had a lifestyle above her station, and concealed it from her mum, I'm wondering more than ever what she was up to.'

'You're thinking drugs,' Slider said flatly.

'Well, they always do jump to mind,' Atherton said, not watching his feet. 'Or, given the prevalence of the man-motif, high-priced prostitution.'

'We've no reason to think either of those things,' Slider snapped. 'Let's not jump to conclusions, shall we?'

Atherton raised his eyebrows. 'Sorry. Have I stepped on a corn?'

Slider drew a deep breath. The image of her, softly

limp like a dead hare, and her rough-cut gold hair, so like Joanna's, called to him for pity and vengeance. He said, managing a fair imitation of lightness, 'It's your mental health I'm worried about. This job makes you too cynical if you're not careful.'

'I shall try to nurture a rosy outlook,' Atherton said, but he gave Slider an odd look as he left. Or Slider thought he did. Maybe it was just his paranoia again.

Joanna phoned. 'Just breaking for lunch.'

'It's not that time already, is it?'

'Half past twelve, ol' guv of mine.'

'Flaming Nora, where does the time go? How was the session?'

'Oh, brill. Lots of old friends. It's basically a scratch Royal London Philharmonia, like the one we used to cobble together for concerts in Croydon in the dear distant days of double booking.'

'Good. So you've someone to lunch with?'

'Lots of someones. God, it's good to be back!' The words burst out of her, and he understood the depth of the feelings she had been hiding from him. She needed her work, as he needed his.

'What's the music like?'

'Oh, you know. You've seen the films. Bang, crash, wallop, car chase, speedboat chase – dum-diddle-um-dum, dum-dum-dum. Lots of dots for us. It's hard work, but it's great being with real professionals. All these guys could do it standing on their heads – or, at least, they let you think they could. That's showmanship. What do you think of Charlie?'

He had to be quick on his feet for that one. 'Charles Slider? It sounds like a senior officer in the Salvation Army.'

'That's odd – you know, it does,' she said wonderingly. 'But I didn't say Charles, I said Charlie.'

'You can't christen a child Charlie. You have to start with Charles – and we said nothing with an *s* in it.'

'Sebastian,' she said. 'Septimus. It's like something out of Monty Python – six seditious Sadducees from Caesarea.'

'Keep thinking, Butch,' he advised. 'That's what you're good at.'

'Gotta go. The guys are waiting.'

'See they keep waiting,' he warned, and she was gone.

As he replaced the handset, McLaren came in with a cup of tea for him – or, rather, half a cup of tea and half a saucer of tea. 'Sorry, guv, I slopped a bit,' he said. Slider hastily cleared a space for him to set it down.

'How's it going?' Slider asked. It was rare to find McLaren with his mouth empty and it seemed a shame to waste the opportunity.

'Not bad,' he said. 'We're getting through 'em. Funny lot of calls we've had, from people saying they liked her. Like if they said what a nice person she was, we'd let her off being dead.'

'Character references,' Slider said, charmed not so much by the flight of fancy, but that McLaren had had it. 'Atherton told me.'

'We've had two people say they saw her jogging, both sound all right. But no help on the murder. She was just jogging round the track, the circular one, with a few other people.'

'With them?'

'Not with them, as such. Just, there were a few going round.'

'Nobody saw her near the shrubbery?'

'Not yet. But,' McLaren went on, 'it's looking good for my idea, the copycat murder.' His head took on a defiant tilt as he said it. 'We've had another four reports about Running Man. A lot of people saw him legging it out of the park, and three of them reckon he was clutching a mobile phone in his germans. And given that the vic's is missing, I reckon that makes him tasty.'

'Don't call her the vic. This is not America,' said Slider, fighting another losing battle.

'All right,' McLaren said equably. 'So whajjer reckon, guv? Shall I follow it up? We know he went off up Askew Road. We could start canvassing up there, see who else saw him, spread the search area, see if he dumped anything.'

Slider considered. He had to be flexible enough to consider that McLaren might be right, even though he was McLaren. 'I need you here for the moment. See how it goes today. If it's still looking good later we may put out a specific appeal on him tonight. Have you got a good description?'

'Yeah, as to height and clothes and probable age. We haven't got a witness who saw his face close up – yet.' He gave Slider a hopeful look, like a dog in the presence of chocolate.

'All right, well, keep on the follow-up for now, but you can ask specifically about him. And you can recontact anyone who was in the park at the right time. If you find anyone who saw his face, get 'em in and try for a photofit. But – McLaren!' He called him back as he swung happily away. 'Don't push. Don't put ideas into people's heads.'

McLaren looked wounded. 'Guv!' he protested. 'It's me!'

'That's why I said it.'

PC Yvonne Collins stuck her head round Slider's door. 'Sir, there's a man in Lycra shorts downstairs for you.'

'Funny, I didn't order one of those,' Slider said.

118

She sniggered. It was a point up to her that she had a sense of humour; and she wasn't a bad-looking young woman, but there was the hardness in her face that women police always developed, which made Slider wonder why Atherton had gone after her – unless it was purely instinctive, like a dog chasing rabbits.

'It's the bloke you appealed for on the telly, sir, the bloke on the bike.'

'Oh, right. I'll come down.'

Her duty done, she allowed herself a personal question. 'Is Jim Atherton around, sir?'

It sounded rather wistful. Slider felt he ought to warn her off, but what could he say? Anyway, he didn't want to get caught in the fall-out from Atherton's trouser department.

'No, he's out interviewing a witness.'

'Oh,' she said, and seemed not to know what to do with the information. Well, she wasn't his problem, he thought gratefully, as he brushed past her and went off down the corridor, leaving her standing there like a spare dinner at a conference banquet. Which, sadly, was pretty much what she was, he reflected.

'I'm Phil Yerbury,' said Bicycle Man. He was dressed in the skin-tight Lycra shorts and matching vest, and was carrying his helmet, one of the sporty ones with the point to the back and a lightning flash design on the side. He was tall and fair, but tanned, so that his body hair showed up white against his brown skin. A tuft of it poked out shyly from each armpit like a chinchilla rabbit scenting the air. He was very lean and his legs were admirably muscled, the tendons behind the knee standing out sharply like freshly chiselled relief, the calf muscles seeming to squirm impatiently under the tight skin, as if they would go off on their own and get cycling again if their owner stood there talking for much longer.

A wave of heat and a smell of sweat came off him, but it was fresh sweat and not absolutely unpleasant. His face was lean and firm and missed being handsome by so little that you might not notice it in all that healthy tannedness.

'I think I may be the person you were appealing for on the telly last night,' he said, 'but if I am, I don't know why. I haven't done anything.' And in what looked like a nervous movement he pulled the water-bottle from its holster on his belt, and slugged back a good gulp.

'You did the right thing by coming in,' Slider said, putting warmth into his voice. 'Would you like to sit down?'

'I hope this isn't going to take long,' he said. 'I'm working, and I don't want to get behind schedule.'

'Can't you call it your lunch-hour?'

'I don't take a lunch-break,' he said with barely suppressed scorn. 'I'm self-employed. There's terrific competition in the bicycle-courier world, you know. You can't afford to slack.'

He still hadn't sat down, so Slider perched on the edge of the table. 'It shouldn't take long,' he said. 'Were you in Paddenswick Park on Wednesday morning at around eight o'clock?'

'Yes. Well, I cut through it, because the traffic was slow on Paddenswick Road. But I don't know anything about this woman who was murdered. I've never met her or even heard of her in my life.' The eyes were wide and nervous.

'Witnesses say you rode very fast out of the park into King Street, so fast you almost knocked a woman over, and dashed into the traffic without looking, almost causing an accident.'

Relief and annoyance chased each other across his face. 'Is that what it's about? I didn't nearly knock her over, I didn't touch her. I'm an excellent cyclist. I know exactly how narrow a gap I can get through. She only had to stand still. And of course I didn't join the traffic without looking. I wouldn't last a day in this job if I did things like that. There was no near accident. I knew exactly what I was doing.'

His professional pride had been touched, Slider saw, and it was so important to him that he had forgotten there was a murder in the background. This, he thought, was not their man – unless he was a fabulously good actor.

'Why were you in such a hurry?' he asked.

'I was working. I told you, there's huge competition—'

'At that time of day?'

Yerbury looked scornful. 'I start at seven. It's the busiest time, seven thirty to eight thirty. Modern business doesn't slouch in at half past nine any more, not if it wants to survive. It's a competitive world out there.'

'I see. Well, Mr Yerbury, if you'd like to write down your name, address and telephone number for me—'

'But what do you want them for? You can't think I had anything to do with it. You can't think I'm the Park Killer?'

'Actually,' Slider said, 'I've just been thinking that being a bicycle courier would be a wonderful way for the Park Killer to get about and cover his tracks.'

Yerbury's eyes bulged in horror. 'But I—' His mouth remained open, but no further words got out.

'Just sit down here and write your name and address,' Slider said kindly. 'It's routine, that's all. We have to check everything and everyone, you must see that. And write where you were immediately before and immediately after your ride through the park. I presume you were in transit from one firm to another. If they can vouch for you, I don't expect we'll need to bother you again.'

He sat, and took up the biro laid waiting for him, and applied himself to the pad. His hand shook at first, but writing calmed him down. 'I was delivering to a printing firm in King Street,' he said. 'I don't know their phone number off hand, but you can get it from Directory Enquiries.'

'You have a bag of some sort on your bicycle, I suppose?'

'Not a bag, a box. A plastic carrier – like a cooler box, only with a locking lid,' he said, not pausing in his writing. So much for the witness's accuracy. It was amazing how much people got wrong. Or perhaps what was amazing was how much the layman expected them to get right. If juries only knew.

Yerbury finished writing and looked up at Slider. 'Am I done now?'

'Yes, you're done. Unless there's anything you can tell me that might help with the investigation. A young woman was brutally stabbed to death in the park just about the time you rode through. Did you see anything, anyone, unusual?'

'I was riding fast,' he said, but apologetically now. 'I mean, I pass people in a flash. Obviously I didn't see anyone killing anybody. Whereabouts in the park did it happen?'

'In the shrubbery.'

'Well, I wouldn't be able to see in there.'

'You rode past it,' Slider said, not making it a question or a challenge.

His eyes went past Slider's as he thought back. 'There were a couple of people on the path by the shrubbery, standing talking. I had to dodge round them. I don't suppose that was anything?'

'Anything might be anything. What were they like?'

'I don't know. I was past in a flash, I only got an impression. Just two joggers stopped for a chat, I suppose.'

'Why did you think they were joggers?'

He screwed up his face in effort, but said, 'I really don't know. It was just a flash as I went past. I think one of them had one of those hooded tops that joggers wear.'

'Colour?'

'I really don't know.'

'Was it red?'

'I don't think so. A neutral colour or a dark colour perhaps. I don't think it was anything obvious like red.'

'Hood up or down?'

'Well, up,' he said after a fractional pause, 'otherwise I wouldn't have known it was hooded, would I?'

'Were they male or female?'

'I think the one facing my way was a woman. Maybe with fair hair? The one with the hood was taller, so I suppose it was a man. But I can't say anything for sure. It's just an impression. I was going too fast, and thinking about other things.'

'And whereabouts were they standing?'

'On the path by the shrubbery, the path that goes down to the station and King's Road.'

'So you came in at the Paddenswick Gate, turned left at the junction of the path, and *then* you saw them?'

'That's right.'

That was on the side of the shrubbery where the SOCOs had gone in, not on the side where Mr Chapman's dog had disappeared. If the people Yerbury had seen were Chattie and the killer, it was more suggestion that the grooves in the bark were faked.

'All right,' Slider said. 'Thank you. You've been most co-operative. And if anything else occurs to you that might help us, or you find you can remember more about the people you saw, you will contact me at once?'

'Well, yes,' he said, rising and exuding relief along with the sweat, 'but really, I don't think there's anything more I can tell you. I just happened to be there at the time. I didn't even know the woman.'

Slider saw him out, and went back to his room, pondering. Yerbury's story held together, and Slider did not feel he was their man. A policeman has to go on instinct a lot of the time, or the work would never get done. On the other hand, it was looking better for McLaren's copycat-killer theory. Running Man had been wearing a hooded sweat top – a hoodie, the young people called it. And if Yerbury had seen two people talking on the path by the shrubbery, someone else would have, too. At that time of day, with so many people around, someone would have.

A sunny afternoon was shaping up after the morning's rain. The air seemed washed, the trees moved about as if refreshed, and happy, trotting dogs had a whole lot of new scent-marking to do. The Anchor had its door set open, and a pleasant murmur of voices drifted out. Atherton went in and waited a moment for his eyes to adjust from the brightness outside. It was a nice, ordinary, old-fashioned pub, with no music, no games machines, no décor, and a fireplace in the corner that bore all the marks of having a real fire in the winter. People were sitting around tables eating, drinking and conversing – a nice mix of ages, but all responsible adults. The sight of decent English people not bothering each other was a lovely thing, he thought – a sort of poetry.

He went up to the bar, and the barman approached him with an expectant face, polishing a glass without looking. 'Help you, sir?'

'I'm looking for a Mr Fosdyke,' Atherton said.

'That's me. Reggie Fosdyke. I'm the landlord.' He was a round man with a round, red face. He was bald over the top of his head, and had a close-clipped white beard – got his head on upside-down, Atherton thought automatically. He was smiling genially but he had the cold and noticing eyes of a London licensee and they went over Atherton like a scanner. 'From the police?' he concluded.

'You rang saying you had information for us,' Atherton said.

'Right it is. Come up the end of the bar, bit of privacy,' said Fosdyke. 'Drink?'

'Not for me, thanks. I'm on duty.'

'Oh, come on! I know coppers. Anyway, it looks bad you sitting there without a drink. I'd as soon the rest of the bar didn't know you were the Bill. Nosy bastards, some of them – especially that lot up the end. What do you drink? Gin and tonic, is it?'

Atherton assumed this was a calculation rather than a wild guess. The man was good. 'Thanks.'

'On the house,' Fosdyke said. 'If anyone asks, you're my new accountant.'

He mixed the drink, excused himself to refill someone's pint, and came back to Atherton. 'Sorry about that. The girl's on her lunch.' At that moment a young woman came in from the back, wiping her lips, and he said to her sharply, 'Finished? About time. Look after the bar, will you? I'm having ten minutes talking business here. Right, then.' He settled himself, elbows on the bar, arms folded, head approached confidentially towards Atherton's. 'You wanted to know about Tuesday night?'

'Yes. I had a message that you had seen Miss Cornfeld in here.'

'Is that her name? Chattie, she was called, that's all I know. Nickname or something. She lives in this road. I dunno the number. But,' he caught himself up with a short laugh, 'you know that. Why am I telling you? You got the house sealed off and about a million coppers in and out. Searching it, are you? What you looking for?'

'You saw Chattie in here on Tuesday,' Atherton prompted evenly.

Fosdyke tapped the side of his nose and winked. 'Right. Fair enough. Well, she comes in a lot, does our Chattie. What a nice girl, eh? Always full of it, having a laugh – and jokes? She knew a million of 'em. Said it was hanging about with musicians – they're always telling jokes. Mind you,' he said sternly, as if Atherton had made an adverse suggestion, 'she was a nice girl. A real lady, if you know what I mean. She could tell a joke, right, that was, well, a bit blue – funny as hell – and it'd be just on the line, but she'd never cross it. She knew exactly how far to go, know what I mean?'

'Tuesday night?' Atherton suggested.

Fosdyke was offended. 'I'm just filling in the background for you. You in a hurry?'

'Not at all,' Atherton said soothingly. 'I'm enjoying my drink. Please go on.'

'Well, Tuesday night,' Fosdyke resumed, with a little huffiness, 'she came in about five past seven. The bloke was waiting for her. He came in about five to, so I reckon they'd arranged to meet at seven.'

But the diary entry was 'JS 8pm', Atherton thought.

'Can you describe the man?'

'Yeah. He was, what, about twenty-five or so – looked younger than her. Kind of roundish, babyish face. About medium height, had very dark hair, straight, kind of flopped in his eyes – kept pushing it back, you know?' He made a graphic gesture of swiping his forehead clear. 'I don't know how he could stand it. It'd drive me barmy, having hair in me eyes all the time.'

Atherton resisted the urge to glance at his bald top. 'You didn't catch a name, I suppose?'

'Well, I think it was Toby,' Fosdyke said. 'Only when she came in, she said, "Hello, Tobes." Or I think that was what she said.'

Toby, Atherton thought. One of the musicians in the band, the oboist, was called Toby Harkness; and from what he remembered from the photographs on the website, he had a young face and dark hair. It was not in the diary, so it was a casual meeting. He must have called her up – on the missing mobile, perhaps – and said meet me in the Anchor. Why hadn't he gone to the house, though? Maybe he'd rung from the pub – come on down for a drink.

'Did they seem on friendly terms?'

'Oh, yes. She got up on the stool next to him and kissed him hello.'

'On the cheek or the mouth?'

'On the cheek. And then she sort of ruffled his hair – a bit mumsy, like. As if he was her kid brother. He didn't like that – sort of jerked his head away. But they were friends all right. Known each other for ages, I'd've said.'

'How long did they stay?'

'Not long. Had a drink, then she up and leaves, about a quart' to eight, give or take.'

'He didn't leave with her?'

'No, he sits there looking a bit glum, and I goes up

127

and asks him if he wants another, and he sort of shakes himself and says, no, he's off. And he gets up and goes.'

'Did they quarrel?'

'Well, I wasn't hanging over 'em listening. I was serving, and it was a busy time – lot of office workers call in on their way home. Seven to eight's a busy time. But I don't think they quarrelled. I never saw anything of that. And when she goes, she seems friendly towards him, and, like, kisses him again. No, I wouldn't say they quarrelled. But,' he added, with the air of having saved this until last, 'they were talking seriously. You didn't often see Chattie without she was laughing, and I didn't see her laugh with this Toby bloke.'

'Had you seen her with him before?'

'Yeah, I reckon I had, once or twice, but not recently. Mind you, she often came in with a man and it wasn't often the same one twice.' He dropped a ghastly wink. 'Well, why not?' he asked broadly. 'Nice, pretty girl like that, full of beans, why shouldn't she play the field? I know I would, if I had her opportunities.' A thought seemed to strike him. He looked almost bewildered. 'Doesn't seem possible she's gone. What sort of a bastard would do that to a pretty girl? I know what I'd do to him if I caught him.'

'So Chattie left at about a quarter to eight? And you didn't see her again?'

'No,' he said, with a sentimental sigh. 'I never laid eyes on her again. If I'd known then what I know now . . .'

He left it hanging, and Atherton couldn't imagine how the sentence could be ended. More interesting was this serious talk with Toby, probably Toby Harkness, which she left for the date with JS. Had she told Toby whom she was going to meet? Had she told him what was on her mind? The cleaner had said she was thoughtful the last few days, now Fosdyke said she had a serious conversation for once in her life. If she'd had some business with JS that went wrong, was it possible that he had killed her the next day? He felt there was some investigating to be done around Baroque Solid's members, which was a happy thought for him.

7

A Tree Grew in Brixton

It was lucky for credibility that the call came in to someone other than McLaren. Witnesses were suggestible at the best of times, and his keenness had led him astray on previous occasions. But it was Hollis who came to Slider to say, 'We've had another witness, guv, who saw the victim talking to someone in a hoodie on that bit of path.'

'Let's be accurate. We don't know that it was the victim,' Slider said.

Hollis smirked under his appalling moustache. 'We do now. This bloke was walking past and saw her. He recognised her from the photo on the news.'

'How sure is he?'

'He sounds okay,' Hollis answered the question behind the question. 'Sensible enough. And he described her hair and clothes and general height and build, which I don't think he could have got from the telly.'

'Did he see the face of the man?'

'No, guv,' Hollis said regretfully. 'Bloke had his back to him. He says he had his hands in his pockets and the hood up and was sort of hunched. Looked furtive, witness says, made sure to keep his face hidden as he went past. But he says he was slim and a bit taller than the victim.'

'Wearing?'

'Well, the hoodie, like he said – grey, he thought. But he wasn't sure what else he was wearing. Thought it might be a tracksuit bottom and trainers.'

'Running Man was wearing chinos,' Slider reminded him. Hollis shrugged. 'Get him in and get a full statement from him. Try and test his memory about the victim, see if he remembers the CD Walkman or the water-bottle. Was she holding anything? Did he see her expression? Was she talking or listening? Anything to substantiate his identification of her.'

'Right you are,' said Hollis. 'He's on his way now. Pity he didn't see the man's face, but at least it fits with what Yerbury said. It was the same part of the path. So it looks as if we can chuck the random killing idea. I can't see a savvy bird like her going into the shrubbery with a stranger if she wasn't forced.'

'*If* the person she was talking to was the killer,' Slider said. 'He might just have been someone asking for a light.'

'No, guv,' Hollis said, 'there was more to it than that. This witness saw them standing together for more than a minute before he passed them. He was coming from the station end and he saw them when he came round the bend of the path. And when he turned right to go out the Paddenswick gate, he thinks they'd gone.'

'Both of them?'

Hollis's large, gooseberry eyes widened as he nodded to the implication. 'Both of them. So where could they have gone except into the shrubbery?'

On leaving the pub, Atherton decided to pop in at the house to see what was going on. It was only sense, as he was right there on the spot; nothing to do with the fact that Hart was among the searchers. PC Renker was on the door, and nodded to him as he trod up the steps.

'Sounds as though there's a bit of excitement down there, sir,' he said, gesturing with his head over his shoulder. 'I wouldn't be surprised if they hadn't found something.'

The raised voices were coming from the basement. Atherton went down the stairs and Hart turned as he entered, and said, 'Wotcha, Jim. Is that good timing or what?'

'Judging by your enormous grin, you've found something,' Atherton said. There were two other people there, a woman called Viv Preston, borrowed from the SOC team, and WPC Coffey, who was blonde, hard as an acid drop, and had had a sense-of-humour bypass when she joined the Job.

'First time I come down here,' said Hart, 'I said to myself, "Blimey! Top kitchen! I bet this cost a bob or two." And now I think I know where the bobs came from.'

She gestured to Coffey's position by the furthest cabinet. The door of the wall-mounted cupboard was open, and on the worktop below were some tins of tomatoes and soup evidently removed from it.

'Go on, 'ave a look,' Hart invited.

Atherton went across. Inside the cupboard a few tins still remained, and tucked behind them, peeking out coyly, was a ziplock plastic bag containing a white powder.

'Cocaine?' he said. It was the sort of thing to thrill a sad copper's heart. Everything suddenly became much more explicable when drugs entered the equation.

'And not just a single wrap, either,' Hart said happily. 'It's not even a party-sized bag. There must be something

132

like a hundred grams in there, enough to sell to a lot of friends for a nice profit.' She almost chortled. 'Little Princess Perfect turns out to be a naughty girl after all.'

'I did feel all along she was too good to be true,' Atherton said. 'But the boss won't be pleased. He's taken a shine to her.' He turned to Viv Preston. 'Can you take a photograph of its position?'

'I already have,' she said. 'You can take it out now.'

He gloved up, and carefully withdrew the package. 'Of course,' he said, holding it up by one corner and estimating the weight, 'we don't know until we test it. Might be bicarb for all we know.'

'Yeah,' said Hart ripely. 'And my arse is an apricot. Anyone want to bet it ain't charlie?' No-one did.

It was cocaine. They had field kits at the station for all the common drugs: a presumptive test and a confession could save a lot of time and money in possession cases.

'Well,' said Atherton, lounging against the door jamb of the CID room, 'it certainly helps to explain how she could afford the high life, and the house.'

Looking round the room, Slider saw how cheered everyone was by this find, which seemed likely to explain so much. He, on the other hand, felt his heart sink, and realised that he had become attached already to the pretty, clear-skinned girl called Chattie, the smiling, always cheerful girl, who was nice to old men and paper-sellers. Perhaps she wasn't Princess Perfect, as Hart had dubbed her, but an awful lot of people had liked her. He didn't want her to be a coke-head and a drug-dealer.

Atherton must have divined his thoughts, because he said, 'A lot of people don't regard cocaine as a dangerous drug, and don't think it ought to be illegal. To them, snorting it or even selling it wouldn't seem like a crime.'

'Yeah, celebs do it all the time,' Hart said, belatedly catching on. 'They talk about it openly, and they don't even get, whachercallit, *déclassés*.'

But she'd be *déclassée* with me, Slider thought. 'What about fingerprints?'

'There were a couple of nice ones on the plastic bag,' Atherton said. 'They're comparing them now with the victim's tenprint. Luckily people don't generally bother to glove up when they're handling their own little baggie of joy.'

'Boss,' said Hart, 'I've just thought: what if the killer was her supplier? That would make sense of why she went into the bushes with him. Say she was scoring a bit o' charlie to sell to her friends, she wouldn't want to do that in full view of the joggers and jigglers.'

'Yes,' said Slider, but uneasily. He could see the images, of the man in the hooded top talking to Chattie by the shrubbery, of the man in the hooded top running away 'like the wind' from the park; and in between he could construct a scenario of the two of them in the shrubbery talking, a quarrel – over money, perhaps; the flash of a knife, the urgent flight. What didn't sing to him was the notion of a drug-dealer calculatedly sedating his victim before stabbing her. 'If it was a real stabbing,' he said, 'it would play like panto. As it is – why would he drug her and then go in for a bit of light wounding?'

Swilley said, 'That's right. I can't see a drug-dealer being squeamish about putting the knife in.'

'With all due respect to Dr Cameron,' Atherton said, 'we don't know that she did die of a drug overdose. Not till the tox report comes back.'

Swilley looked at him pityingly. 'That's when you know you've got to get out more – when you start trying to make the evidence fit your theory.'

'It's not evidence, only the doc's opinion,' Atherton said.

'Freddie Cameron's opinion *is* evidence,' Slider said.

'Leaving aside the method of killing,' Hollis put in, 'her line of business would be ideal for dealing coke. She moved around a lot, met lots of musoes and showbiz types.'

'Yeah, she was giving 'em all sorts of services – why not that? And maybe a bit of the other an' all,' McLaren said, with relish.

Slider controlled himself. 'Well, let's remember that this is all conjecture. We've no evidence yet that she did anything untoward. What else have we got?'

'Still haven't found her mobile, guv,' Hart said. 'We found her handbag in her bedroom, but it wasn't in there, and we pretty well covered the house. I reckon she must have had it with her and the killer took it.'

'Which would fit with the drug-dealer idea,' Mackay said. 'If she was murdered for personal reasons, why would the killer have it away with her phone?'

'Well, we know it's switched off,' Slider said. 'We can put the provider company on alert and as soon as it's switched on again we can get a fix on it. So, we're actively looking for Running Man?'

'Yes, guv,' McLaren said. 'Asking everyone about him. Is there gonna be another TV appeal tonight?'

'On the local news only,' Slider said. 'The main news has lost interest. Too much else going on with the Middle East crisis and the cabinet split. And yes, I will make sure that they ask about Running Man. But let's remember we don't know that he has anything to do with it, or even that he is the same man who was seen talking to her.'

This caveat went down with the assembled troops like a barbed-wire sandwich.

'So let's consider the possibility that it was a murder for personal reasons,' he went on. He looked at Atherton. 'What about the man who saw her in the pub on Tuesday evening?'

Atherton told the tale. 'The description he gave fits Toby Harkness, who was one of the members of the band Baroque Solid, so I thought that would be a good place to start.'

'How come you didn't latch onto it before, Jim? You've been spending enough time with the band,' said Hart.

'Maybe if you'd had your mind on the job when you were on the job,' Swilley began dangerously.

Slider intervened. 'All right, Toby Harkness. Maybe there was some sort of history between them.'

'Or maybe she was just selling him charlie,' Hart said. 'It don't sound romantic. Ruffling a bloke's hair in public is a quick way to lose his interest. They hate that – don't they, Jim? Buggers up fifty quid's wurf of blow-drying.'

'But,' Hollis said, being the voice of sanity, 'I thought her date for Tuesday night was with a JS?'

'True,' Atherton said, 'and so I thought—'

'Wasn't one of the band called Jasper something?' McLaren asked. 'I remember thinking what a poncey name it was, just what you'd expect for a Beethoven freak.'

'That's right,' Hart said. 'There was a Jasper. What was his other name? I can't remember.'

'It was Stalybrass,' said Atherton. 'I thought I'd go and see him, and Toby.'

Hollis looked considering. 'If she was seeing both of them at the same time, that might cause jealousy—'

'And a motive for murder,' Hart finished for him. 'If they knew about each other.'

'Oddly enough,' Atherton said, 'that had occurred to me.'

'Well, you're the obvious man for the job,' Slider said, 'since you're so well in with the band. But can you see them separately without the other knowing? Don't they all live together?'

'No, Mark Falconer, the cellist, shares a flat with the clarinet, Chaz Barnes. But Jasper Stalybrass and Toby Harkness each have their own flats,' Atherton said.

'It woulda been hairy dating both of 'em if they'd lived together,' Hart observed. 'I'd a given the vic plus ten for balls.'

'I can tell you've never studied anatomy,' Atherton said kindly.

McLaren had been looking impatient, and now burst in with, 'All this love and jealousy guff makes me tired. We've got a bloody great bag of charlie out of her gaff, and she was a high spender. What more do you want?'

Slider could have told him, but at that moment the telephone in his room rang and he left them to it while he went and answered it. When he returned the discerning might have noticed a quiet smile of satisfaction on his face, but the discerning weren't looking.

'That was Viv Preston,' he said. 'She's run the fingerprints from the cocaine bag against the victim's tenprint. They don't match. Nothing like.'

'Oh, pants,' Hart said. 'Another good theory bites the dust.'

'No, hang on,' Mackay said. 'Just because there's someone else's prints on the bag, doesn't mean it wasn't still hers. I mean, what was the stuff doing there anyway? Look, maybe it was one of her boyfriends left it there for her – didn't that cleaner say she had a lot of people in and out? She had to get the stuff from somewhere. Someone might have dropped it there for her to pick up. Just because her prints weren't on it doesn't mean they weren't going to be, see what I mean?'

'Or maybe she was just careful,' McLaren said. 'Smart bird like her, she might always have used gloves.'

'So who was she meeting in the shrubbery, then, in your theory?' Slider asked.

'Someone she was selling to,' McLaren suggested shamelessly.

'Nice try,' Slider said. The mention of the cleaner had triggered something in his mind. 'But I think I've got a better theory. Mrs Hammick said she saw Chattie's sister Jassy in the house on Monday, coming up from the kitchen and looking furtive and guilty. She also said that Jassy mixed with a rough lot.'

'Yeah,' said Hart, 'I've seen the mess she made of her bedroom. Drugs do fit better with the stud-queen image than with Princess Perfect,' she admitted.

'I think perhaps it's time we had a talk with Jassy,' Slider said.

'Me for that,' Hart said. 'Remember, her boyfriend's black. She's more likely to trust me than one of you white boys. Where's she live, boss?'

'Clapham, I think. Ferndale Road,' Slider said, from memory. 'The number will be in the address book.'

Hart raised her eyebrows. 'Then you'd definitely better send me. Ferndale Road's not Clapham, it's Brixton.'

'There's a lot of fuss about Brixton,' Atherton said. 'It's just Shepherd's Bush having it large.'

'They'd be on you like a flock of piranhas,' Hart discouraged him. 'There's another thing, guv,' she went on. 'Jassy's boyfriend's black and Running Man was black.'

'There's more than one black person in Shepherd's Bush,' Slider mentioned.

'Yeah, but if she wasn't dragged into the shrubbery by

force, which we know she wasn't, it had to be someone she knew, di'nt it? This way, you've got the personal motive and the drugs motive together in one person.'

Slider sighed. 'Since I can't seem to stop you jumping to conclusions, I suppose I'd better go with you and keep a hand on the rein. What?' he answered her look. 'You didn't think I was going to let you go there alone, did you?'

'I'm a big girl,' Hart complained.

'That's why I'm going with you,' said Slider.

Atherton was right, there was a lot of fuss over nothing made about Brixton. Though there was a greater preponderance of black faces, white people still lived there perfectly peacefully and went about unmolested. Nobody even glanced sideways at Slider as he walked with Hart from the throbbing heart of Brixton down Ferndale Road. As with most communities, the vast majority of people of all shades just wanted to get on with their lives without bothering or being bothered by their neighbours, and the small element that did want to cause trouble was as disliked by the majority as anything else that made their environment unpleasant.

Still, there was a certain healthy tension in Slider's muscles, because they had looked up Jassy's boyfriend before they left. Darren Barnes – as it had turned out to be – was well known to the police, having been pulled in numerous times for possession, possession with intent, social-security fraud, once for affray (that was a brawl outside a pub) and once for malicious wounding. He was not one of the big racketeers, just a small-time distributor of recreational substances, and Mick Dangerfield at Brixton nick had told Slider that he seemed to try to avoid trouble on the whole, and lived a reasonably comfortable lifestyle on the proceeds of his dealing and multiple claims on the state's purse, plus, probably, other minor scams they hadn't caught up with yet. But, Dangerfield had warned, he was also known to go tooled up, and apart from the malicious wounding charge was thought to have used a blade on other occasions when the victim had not been willing to tell his side of the story to the police. Barnes was also inclined to be political, which made him more trouble than it was worth to take all the way, and accounted for his numerous warnings rather than charges. He had gone to court after the malicious wounding, but the judge had decided there was probably equal fault on both sides and had given him a suspended. The other time he had made an appearance before the beak was for the social-security fraud, where the sentence was generally community service. Barnes had been sent to help out at a youth club for black youngsters in Clapham which, Dangerfield said wryly, had proved right up his particular boulevard as it enabled him to extend his customer base clear into the next borough.

So, thought Slider, the drugs and the knife were all present and correct, which was one up – two up – to McLaren; and while it was comforting to think that Darren usually tried to avoid trouble, there was always danger when you cornered a fox in its own lair. And if Darren Barnes had been both Running Man and Talking-to-Chattie Man, there might be enough at stake to make him reckless.

There was a beautiful London plane growing outside the house, which was the only nice thing about it. The house itself was tall and run down, and obviously divided into flats or rooms. The front door stood open, and the steps up to it were cracked and chipped and had lost their handrail. Inside the door was a passage floored with worn and dirty brown linoleum, the walls painted brown up to dado-level and cream above. The usual litter of electricity bills addressed to long-departed tenants, hand-bills and junk mail lay on the floor beside and behind the door. From somewhere above the relentless beat of rap music shook the air, which was cold inside the dark hall and smelt of feet, sweat, junk food and the rich undertone of ganja.

'Just like home,' Hart said, straight-faced, noticing Slider's nostrils twitch. 'So, which flat is it?'

'Number six,' Slider said. There were two doors off the hall, and stairs straight ahead. 'Let's assume these are flats one and two.'

'Let's,' Hart humoured him.

On the next floor there were three doors, behind one of which a baby was crying monotonously. The stairs that went on up were much narrower, and the thumping music came from the door at the top.

'That's gotta be six,' Hart said.

'No worries about creeping up on them,' Slider said.

They went on up. It was quite dark at the top, and the sheer volume of the music seemed somehow threat-ening. Slider began to feel vulnerable. With only a small landing and the steep narrow stairs behind them, they would be an easy target for whoever opened the door. If they opened it. He glanced at Hart, who seemed cheer-ingly unperturbed, took a deep breath and thumped long and hard with the side of his fist on the door. He was so sure there would be no answer that he almost fell back down the stairs in surprise when the door was flung open and someone said, 'Dow?'

Despite the crepuscular gloom, Slider recognised Jassy Whitelaw at once from the descriptions. She evidently

141

recognised the Bill when she saw it, too, for alarm widened her eyes, and she said, 'Shit!' and tried to slam the door. Hart inserted her body and Slider his foot in the path of it, and between them they forced it, and her, back.

'Iss all right, girlfrien', it ain't grief for you,' Hart said soothingly. 'We jus' wanna talk.' She was exaggerating her accent for purposes of winning trust. Slider still had no idea whether it was deliberate or instinctive.

'Better let us in, Jassy, so we can talk where it's private,' he said. 'You don't want to talk out here where anyone can see you.' They inched her backwards until Slider could close the door behind them, preventing her from trying to bolt. 'He's not here, then, your boyfriend?' he deduced. When Jassy had said, 'Dow?' she had not been offering Slider a glass of port. It was the Londoner's pronunciation of 'Dal', which was the Londoner's abbreviation of 'Darren'. She had been expecting him back, otherwise she might not have opened the door at all.

Her way forward blocked, Jassy turned and ran. The short, dark hall led into a large, lighter room with a sash window straight ahead and the shadow of an old-fashioned iron fire escape outside. They caught her while she was still trying to heave the part-open window further up. Like most old sashes it had not only warped but had been so often and so badly painted that there was no chance of it gliding effortlessly as it had been originally designed to do.

'Don't be daft, girl,' Hart said, pulling her round. 'You jus' makin' trouble for yo'self. We gotta talk to you some time. No sense puttin' it off. You wanna sit here and talk nice, or you wan' us to take you down the station? 'Sup to you.'

Seeing she had the situation under control, Slider sought out the source of the brain-pulping beat and turned it off. Hart was coaxing Jassy backwards towards a sofa, and he had his first good look at her. She was thin – not just slim but last-chicken-in-the-shop bony – and it was emphasised by the skimpy dress she wore, sleeveless, low-necked and nearly backless, which left her collarbones, shoulder-blades and spine sticking out and clearly visible under her sallow skin. There was clearly no room under the dress for anything by way of underwear, and her hip bones and ribs and nipples were outlined seamlessly by the clinging pink knitted cotton. The skirt was short, above her bony knees; her feet were bare, with matching pink varnish on the nails; her bony arms ended in nervous hands with bitten fingernails.

But it was above the neck that she was truly remarkable. Her hair was coke-black and cut in haphazard spikes. She looked like a cartoon character who has touched a live wire, except that the spikes were not symmetrical. Her face was very white, her eyeshadow and lipstick a very dark near-black red, her eyes a mass of thick, black mascara. She had four rings around the rim of one ear and three round the other and black shiny studs in the lobes, a stud in her nose and one between her lower lip and her chin, two rings in one eyebrow and a row of studs in the other.

She had done everything she could to make herself look disagreeable; but someone else – presumably the absent Darren – had still done more. Her eyes were red with crying and her mascara had smeared clownishly below them. Under the white foundation her face had a bumpy look with which Slider, like other policemen, was sadly all too familiar. She had a large bruise on her right cheekbone, a cut on the left side of her mouth, which was swollen, and a bruise on her left cheekbone, which had spread round the eye. Three blows, he thought,

143

with sad expertise. A right-handed assailant: hit the left side first, then a backhander to the right (the cut was probably caused by a ring), then the left again. It was the carelessly callous assault of accustomedness. And yet still she expected him back and opened the door to him.

'Did Darren do this to you?' Slider asked, injecting fatherly tenderness into his voice.

'None of your bloody business,' she muttered.

'You don't have to take that, you know, Jassy. No-one's got the right to hit you.'

'What do you want?' she asked irritably, but with a shade of weariness, as if she'd heard it all before.

'Just to talk to you.'

'I've got nothing to say. Not to Fascist lackeys like you.' She glanced at Hart. 'What're *you* doing this job for? You're the worst sort, sucking up to the enemy. Haven't you got any loyalty?'

'Just sit down, Jassy,' Slider said firmly, 'and let's get this over with.'

'Who d'you think you're talking to? You can't order me about in my own home. Get out of here and leave me alone. I'm not talking.'

'I'm trying to make this friendly,' Slider said, 'but I'm not going to waste my time. Either you talk to us here, or I'll arrest you and you can talk at the station. It's up to you.'

'Arrest me?' she said, with a fair attempt at lip-curling contempt. 'What for?'

Hart took it up. 'We got some very nice lifts off that bag o' charlie hidden in Chattie's house. We gonna find out they're yours soon as we print you.' Jassy's face registered dismay for a telling moment. 'You know how it goes, girl. Own up and you get some credit. Make us work for it and you don' get nuffin'. Plus, this is your

144

chance to tell your side o' the story. What's it gonna be?'

Slider thought she was overdoing it a little, but it played like vaudeville with Jassy, in her, presumably, overwrought state.

'Bastard,' she said, but it didn't seem to be directed towards either of them. She sat down heavily on the sofa, and tears began to well up in her eyes. She tried to sniff them back, and said, in an unsteady voice, 'You got any fags? He cleaned me out, the bastard.'

Silently, Hart produced a pack and handed one over, and Jassy reached across to the coffee table for a box of matches. While she was lighting it, Slider took a quick and covert glance round at the room. It was sparsely furnished, but in a way that suggested this was a style choice rather than lack of money. The stereo system racked along one wall would have cost thousands, and there was a large, new plasma-screen TV on an expensive corner unit. The floor was stripped and polished – which must make life miserable for the people underneath, he thought, given the kind and volume of the music Jassy seemed to prefer – and the black leather sofa and chairs were top of the range, and still smelt new. Whatever Jassy was doing here in Brixton, it wasn't slumming – unless of the cultural sort. Though her language was not elegant, her accent was out of its place.

'So where's Darren?' Slider asked at last.

She shrugged, without looking at him.

'He hit you, and then he took off?' Another shrug. 'What did he hit you for?' No answer. 'Was it about the cocaine in Chattie's house?'

She fidgeted a bit, but didn't answer. One arm was folded across her waist, the elbow of the other resting on it so that her hand was by her face, handy for concealing it, and for smoking and nail-biting which she did alternately. She stared away from them, out of the window, which, being at the back of the house, had no view of the lovely tree, only the no-escape fire escape and the backs of other buildings.

Slider tried again. 'Did you know that your sister Chattie was dead?' he said, hoping that either way it might shock a response out of her.

It worked, though it was not the reaction he had expected. She looked at him balefully for an instant. 'Oh, for Christ's sake, what d'you think this is all about?' There was a breath of a pause, and then resentment burst the banks. 'It's all her fault, stupid cow! She always had everything she wanted, always, and I never had anything!' And then she cried – not tears of grief and mourning, but what, in Slider's experience, were always the most sincere and heartfelt of all, the tears of self-pity.

8

Snow White and the Severn Dork

There was a residual reluctance to overcome, but Hart worked on Jassy with sympathy and sisterly solidarity. 'Look at your face. I wu'nt take that from no-one, girl. He ain't got the right to knock you aroun'.'

'We had a row,' Jassy confessed, wiping tears and kohl from under her eyes with a Kleenex.

'About the bag o' white at yo' sister's house, was it?' Jassy did not answer this. Hart leaned forward a little and said earnestly, 'Listen, grassing up a mate's one fing, I know that, but this is different. This is serious. You don't want to do time for that bastard, do you? After what he did? He ain't wurf it, girl. I mean, that's yo' fingerprints on the bag, ennit, an' we know you was there. We got a witness.'

'That cow of a cleaner, Maureen or whatever her name is,' Jassy said viciously. 'Always poking her nose in. Who does she think she is?'

Hart tossed Slider a quick look, and he took up the thread. 'Jassy, I want you to understand this is something much more serious and important than the bag of cocaine. Now, if you help us by telling us everything you know, you won't get into trouble for that. But if you won't help us, then we'll have no option but to arrest you. That was a very large quantity of snow in that bag. It's not just possession. We're talking jail here.'

She stared at his stern face, and then at Hart's sympathetic one, and sighed. 'I never wanted to do it in the first place,' she said. 'I mean, that's Darren's business. I didn't want to know.'

Happy to live off the proceeds, though, weren't you? Slider could see the thought in Hart's eyes, but fortunately Jassy didn't.

'So he made you hide the bag in Chattie's house? Why was that?'

'*I* don't know.'

Slider looked at Hart. 'I don't think this qualifies as co-operation. I think we'd better continue this down at the station.'

'Yeah,' said Hart. 'You can't be nice to some people.'

Jassy stirred indignantly. 'Look, I don't know. He just said to take it there and put it in the cupboard behind the tins of tomatoes. I thought he needed a safe place to stash it, that's all. I know some of your lot have had their eye on him. Maybe he had a tip-off or something that he was going to get turned over.'

'He didn't give a reason and you didn't ask for one? You just hid a bloody great bag o' white in your sister's house, no questions asked?'

She gave a sulky shrug. 'Why should I care about her? She's never done anything for me.'

'But Darren obviously knew his way about her kitchen all right, if he knew what was in that cupboard,' said Slider. 'How well did he know your sister?'

'Look, if you're suggesting there was something going on between them—'

'I didn't suggest anything, but it's interesting that you jump to that conclusion,' said Slider, with an air of intellectual enquiry.

Hart lowered the tone judiciously. 'Was he bonking her, love?'

'No!'

'So it was a business relationship?'

'I don't know, and I don't care,' Jassy said. 'I hid the charlie for him, that's all. Then Wednesday night he tells me to go and get it. But when I get to the house there's a copper on the door.'

Atherton got that done just in time, Slider thought.

'So I came home and told Darren and he was furious. He just went off at me, as if it was my fault. I told him it was nothing to do with me, but he said the coke must have been found and I couldn't have hidden it properly, and he shouted at me and then he hit me and then he took off and I haven't seen him since.' She drew a breath, and added, 'I don't care if I never see him again, either, the bastard. It wasn't my fault. I put it where he told me to. He'd got no right to hit me.'

'You're right there,' Hart said warmly. Jassy turned minutely towards her and away from Slider, responding, he saw, to female sympathy. Hart was good, he thought. 'So where was Dow Wensday morning, Jass? Did he go out early?'

'I don't know,' she said. 'I wasn't here. I went to see my mum Tuesday night and stayed over. But he wasn't here either. He went up to Manchester to see some mates on Tuesday. That's why I went to see Mum. He didn't get home until about eight o'clock Wednesday night, and then he told me to go over to Chattie's and get the coke.'

'How come he's got mates in Manchester?' Hart asked.

'He went to college there. Not for long – they chucked

him out for selling weed.' She smiled slightly as she said it – a proud smile for the rebel without a cause.

'D'you think that's where he's gone now?'

'I don't know. It might be.'

'You haven't tried to find him? Rung round your friends?'

'Why should I, after what he did? I never want to see him again. I hope he rots in hell, the bastard.'

'Can you give us the name and address of these mates?'

She came down off her high horse, belatedly alarmed. 'What d'you want that for?'

'We'd like a word with him about that charlie – and we can do him for assault on you at the same time, if you like,' said Hart.

But Jassy looked uneasy. 'He's got some funny mates up there, hard men. I don't want to get mixed up with it. I mean, they'd be pissed off if they thought I'd put the coppers on their tail. They could be serious trouble.'

'We won't tell them it was you told us,' Hart said. 'There's lots of ways we could've found it out.' Jassy still looked uncertain, and Hart allowed a little toughness to creep into her voice. 'In return for a bit of leeway on your prints being on that bag of coke.'

'I've told you about that. It wasn't mine.'

'Yeah, but he's put you right in it. You don't wanna go down, just protectin' him. Do yo'self a favour. You don't owe him nuffin'. Give us a name, girlfrien'. No-one won't know you said anyfing. 'At's a promise.'

Jassy sighed, and said, 'I know one of 'em's Dave O'Brien. I don't know his address but his phone number's around somewhere. Will that do?'

'Yeah, that's good, girl,' Hart said. 'You get that for us, an' that's a lot o' Brownie points for you.'

Jassy got up and said, 'If you find Darren, make sure

150

he falls down a flight of stairs or something.' She found the number on a pad by the telephone and handed it to Hart with an air of having finished all transactions.

But Slider said, 'So when did you find out your sister was dead?'

She turned to him, wariness creeping into her expression and posture. 'Eh?'

'When you went to her house on Wednesday night and saw the policeman on duty, you didn't know then she was dead?'

'Well, of course I didn't. I thought it was to do with the coke. That's why I had the fight with Darren.' She said it with the exaggerated exasperation of the age.

'So when did you find out?'

Jassy sat down. 'If you must know, my mum phoned me up about it last night. She saw it on the telly, on the news.'

'Don't you watch the news on television?'

'No, why should I? It's a load of rubbish. Capitalist indoctrination. All those TV companies are tools of the establishment.'

'That's a big TV set you've got,' Hart remarked.

'It's Darren's. He watches the sport on it.' It was said with a roll of the eyes.

'You don't seem very sorry that she's dead.'

Resentment flared. 'Why should I be? She was only my half-sister. Anyway, she wouldn't care if it was me. She always thought she was a cut above everyone else. Her mum is a stuck-up bitch. She called my mum all the names under the sun for stealing my dad from her, but she'd done just the same, so who was she to give herself airs? The first time I went to her house for tea when I was a kid, she went on and on about table manners and had I washed my hands and was I allowed to eat like that at home. I wasn't good enough for her. I mean, I was just a little kid! You don't take it out on a little kid like that, do you? And Chattie was just like her – thought she was oh-so-posh, looked down on me and my friends, all holier-than-thou every time I wanted to do a line of charlie or a couple of tabs of E or whatever. The fuss she made when I smoked a bit of weed in her precious house! You'd have thought I'd been spraying anthrax around. I said to her, everybody does it, and she said, I don't, and I said, well, that doesn't surprise me because you're just bloody perfect, everybody knows that. Her and her stupid little piddling business, and all that crap about doing it on her own and not taking anything from anybody! That was aimed at me, that charming little remark. All very well for someone who's always had everything they wanted, all very fine and nice. She made me sick, she was so bloody pious, sitting in her ivory tower and telling me I had no right to draw social security, as if it was a crime. I said to her, I know my rights, and she made some smart-mouth remark about not knowing my duty. Duty! Yeah, duty to the forces of global capitalism, I said. Never mind the third-world poor, grind them in the dust, as long as you've got your share! She was such a hypocrite. I mean, she only had that house in the first place because our dad gave her the money for it. So much for not taking anything from anybody.'

'Is your dad well off?'

She shrugged again. 'All I know is, he's never given me anything.'

'Are he and your mum still together?

'You've got to be joking!' she said, with a toss of her head. 'He scarpered the moment I turned up. Cleared off and left Mum to it. I was just glad he'd done the same to Chattie and her snobby mum. Her and her stupid

152

books! My mum got one out of the library once. She said it was rubbish.'

'Sounds like you've really got some issues wiv your sister,' Hart said sympathetically.

'She always had everything,' Jassy cried, with a fresh burst of self-pity. 'She's pretty, she's brainy, and everybody always takes her side, because she sucks up to them. Everything she does turns out right, she always had tons of boyfriends, and now she's got that house and she hangs around with celebs in that potty job of hers, and her life's just bloody perfect! All I've got is this crummy place, and Darren. And now,' she reached the peak and tumbled over, 'Darren's hit me and gone off and I don't know where he is or when he's coming back!'

She began to cry again, and Hart handed her another Kleenex and met Slider's eye over her bent head. The resentment was fresh and hot and there was plenty of material here for motive. And the absent Darren, Hart's look said as clearly as words, was more than a bit tasty.

Baroque Solid were not playing together on Friday evening. Marion and Trish had outside work, playing at Milton Keynes, and the others were about their normal social rounds – or normal-ish, considering the shock they had all sustained. Atherton eventually tracked Jasper Stalybrass down in a pub in Islington, which was filled with well-scrubbed, well-dressed young people spending large amounts of money on designer beers (the men), which they drank out of the bottle, and bizarre cocktails (the women) that came laden with fruity bits and twisty glass straws. Stalybrass was tall and handsome and was evidently being the life and soul of the group of laughing people he was in company with. It was a delicate manoeuvre to cut him out from his adoring fans.

Atherton's experience, backed up by what he had learned from Joanna and Sue, was that horn-players were often men with enormous charm and cold, cold hearts, so he started off with a mild prejudice against him, especially as he had found him telling jokes and laughing heartily. But once he had him alone in a quiet corner, he fell victim himself to the charm, especially as it was allied to a sharp mind, a straightforward delivery, and an obviously genuine shock and sadness about Chattie.

'God, it's hard to believe,' he said. 'I keep forgetting for a time, and then remembering all over again. It was a hell of a blow, I can tell you. I mean, everybody liked Chattie. Who in the world would want to kill her?' He put his hand up to scratch his eyebrow in an almost boyish gesture of hiding his tears. He cleared his throat, and then said, 'But I was forgetting – it was this Park Killer, wasn't it? So that means he picked her at random. God, what a terrible, awful chance. You never think it could happen to anyone you know, do you?'

'I imagine the whole band is very upset,' Atherton said neutrally.

'Upset? That doesn't come near it. We were back at the studio today to do the final mix on our CD, but we all just sat around and talked about Chattie. We hadn't got the heart to get on with it. Mike Ardeel – the studio boss? – he was really cut up. He said in the circumstances he'd give us another session and wouldn't charge us for the wasted one, and usually he's red hot on money – has to be, in a small operation – so that shows you. But really, none of us could think about doing it right then. It would have been too weird. The last time most of us saw her was in that studio on Monday. The girls were all in tears. I nearly was myself.'

'You knew her quite well,' Atherton said, as a statement rather than a question.

'Yes,' Stalybrass said. He eyed Atherton for an instant, as if working out how much he already knew, and then said, 'Well, I suppose it doesn't matter if it comes out now. She and I were very close. We'd been having a thing for about a year.'

'You were lovers?'

'Yes,' he said. 'But I don't want you to get the wrong idea about it. We weren't in love or planning to live together or anything like that. It was all very light-hearted. We liked each other very much but we were just good friends, with sex added, that was all. Chattie was a great girl – a real pal, if you know what I mean. One of those rare women who can meet men on their own terms and be proper friends without dragging in all that female baggage and emotional trappings. We met when we felt like it, made love when we felt like it, lived our own lives and had no obligations to each other beyond having a lot of fun.'

'Was that the way she was in general?'

'Well, I can't speak for every corner of her life, but from what she said to me it was. She liked men and she enjoyed sex but I don't think she'd ever felt seriously about anyone. She told me that she'd never been in love, and never expected to be. She said to me more than once, "There's no room in my life for another man."'

Atherton noted that, the same words she had used to Mrs Hammick. Another man? So who was the first? 'Had she had a bad love affair and been hurt, or something?'

'Not that I ever heard. She just liked to keep emotions at a distance,' Stalybrass went on. 'Well, it suited me, because I've been through a bad divorce, and it suited her, and it was nobody's business but ours, was it?'

'So she may have been seeing other men as well as you?'

Atherton was amused to notice that he didn't like that question. For all his vaunted independence, he didn't want to think of Chattie in someone else's bed. 'She may have been,' he said lightly. 'I suppose I ought even to say that it was likely. She was very attractive and she liked men, so why wouldn't she? But I would never have asked her, and if I had, she certainly wouldn't have answered. She was quite a private person in many ways.' He smiled faintly. 'I've seen her and Marion having those girls' heart-to-hearts they all go in for and, believe me, it was Marion doing the telling and Chattie doing the listening. She would never have given away *her* inmost secrets.'

Touché, thought Atherton. So it was all round the band, then, that he had seen Marion two nights running? He had managed not to come face to face with Marion's flatmates yet, by bedding her at his place and leaving her at her door afterwards, but evidently there were no secrets kept within the group. Or, perhaps, not within the female half of it.

Down to business. 'Did you have a date with her on Tuesday night?' he asked.

'Yes. How did you know that?'

'It was in her diary. "JS 8pm". It seemed likely that JS was Jasper Stalybrass.'

'JS could have been anyone, but in fact it was me. I've nothing to hide. We went to see the new Woody Allen film, and then we went back to my place, but she didn't stay long. She said she had a lot to do the next day and wanted to get up early.'

'Did she usually stay the night?'

'More often than not, but not invariably. Sometimes we went back to her place instead, and then I generally stayed the night, unless I had something early the next day.'

'Did she say what it was she had to do?'

'No, we didn't talk about business. But she did seem a bit preoccupied — not as forthcoming as usual.'

'Was she worried about something?'

'I wouldn't say worried exactly. She just seemed to have her mind on other things. She was perfectly cheerful when she did talk, and she laughed her head off at the film. No, not worried or unhappy, just busy, I think.'

'Do you know what she had been doing earlier that day?'

'No. She'd been working, I presume, but she didn't say and I didn't ask.'

'It didn't come up in the course of conversation?'

'No, we mostly talked about the band and the CD and music in general. She never did speak much about her other clients, unless they were friends of ours. And even then — well, she was discreet, I suppose. Which was quite right.'

'Of course,' Atherton said. 'It's just that there was an entry in her diary for that day which we haven't been able to work out. It said, "DC 10 TFQ". Does that mean anything to you?'

He shook his head slowly. 'No, I'm afraid not. I've no idea what that means.'

Atherton tried another angle. 'You said about your relationship with her, "It doesn't matter if it comes out now." Were you keeping it a secret?'

'It wasn't really a relationship in the sense—'

'Okay, take that as read, but was it a secret you were seeing each other?'

'Yes, it was — but not for any sinister reason,' Stalybrass said, and he gave a charming, confiding smile which

Atherton tried to resist, but with difficulty. 'You see, though Chattie never took any relationship seriously, it didn't always follow from the other side, if you get what I mean. She'd been out a couple of time with Toby – Toby Harkness, our oboe-player – and he'd fallen desperately in love with her. He just couldn't understand that she didn't feel the same. Poor old Toby's a bit intense, and he had a sheltered upbringing – in Bristol, to make it worse. To him, the fact that she'd been to bed with him meant she loved him and they were going to get married. Once she found he wasn't singing from the same hymn sheet she tried to disengage from him but it was difficult. In the normal course of events she would just have refused to see him or talk to him any more. But, of course, with Tobe she couldn't do that, because of everything she was doing for the band. She'd be seeing him in the course of things several times a week, so she had to try to let him down gently. And part of that was not letting on to anyone that she and I were seeing each other, because it would just about have killed old Tobes, and if any of the others had known it would have got back to him. So I'd be grateful if you didn't let on about this to anyone.'

Atherton promised nothing. 'Did you know she saw Toby on Tuesday evening, before she met you?'

He raised an eyebrow, but didn't look unduly concerned. 'No, I didn't. Where was that?'

'In the pub at the end of her road.'

'The Anchor? Oh, well, I expect he was just trying to get her to go back with him, and she was telling him kindly it was no go.'

'So she was still sleeping with him?' Atherton tried. He had to wonder whether Chattie had not been a manipulative little minx.

'Oh, no, it had only been a couple of times, and it was all over as far as she was concerned. But I'm not altogether sure she was right about handling him with kid gloves,' he added thoughtfully. 'I mean, I know Toby's an emotional sort, and all oboe players are a bit mad anyway, but he just wasn't capable of believing there'd been nothing in it, and a short, sharp shock might have been better for him in the long run.' His expression changed and he said bleakly, 'Well, he's had that now, hasn't he? Couldn't be any shorter or sharper. I suppose old Tobes will be able to go to his grave believing she loved him really. Oh, God, I just can't believe – I mean, I was making love to her on Tuesday night and just a few hours later—' He chewed his lip, staring away from Atherton while he tried to keep control.

Much as Atherton would have liked to resist, he felt honesty in this man, and real affection for the dear departed. Whatever he was, he didn't think he was First Murderer.

'You said, "All oboe-players are a bit mad"?' he queried.

'Well, it's playing with a double reed, you see – causes huge pressure on the frontal lobes. They all go a bit barmy in the end.' Stalybrass smiled and added, 'It's a musicians' joke, that's all. Well, some of them are peculiar but, then, to a horn-player, anyone who wants to play any other instrument seems peculiar.'

Atherton had heard about oboists being mad from another source – well, from Sue, not to mince matters. He shied away from the thought of her. 'How has Toby reacted to Chattie's death?'

'Well, he was devastated, like the rest of us. Maybe a bit more so, given that he thought she was the one true love of his life. And he tends to be a bit intense anyway, does Tobe. Artistic temperament. He was just sunk in depression at the studio this morning – hardly said a word to anyone.'

'Is he the jealous kind?' Atherton asked. 'Did you keep your affair with Chattie secret from him not to hurt his feelings, or from fear of what he might do?'

'Fear of what he might do?' Stalybrass looked puzzled.

'You see, we aren't making this public at the moment, but we don't think it was the Park Killer who did it. We think it was someone who knew her.'

Now Stalybrass looked alarmed. 'Oh, good Lord, you aren't thinking Toby did it? He would never do anything like that. Not old Tobes. He's a bit emotional and, as I said, he's had a rather sheltered upbringing, so he didn't understand Chattie the way we would.'

Atherton liked the touch of the little slipped-in 'we' – men of the world like you and me, he meant.

'But he would never hurt a fly. Wouldn't have the guts, apart from anything else. I mean, if you knew the man – well, it's laughable to think of him stabbing anyone. He's really a bit of a dork. And he's soft – even lets wasps out of the window rather than killing them. He's just not capable of murder.'

He stopped talking and looked pleadingly at Atherton. Atherton said nothing for a moment. In the eyes opposite he had seen a flash of knowledge, the sudden realisation that the unthinkable was possible. 'A bit emotional'? Toby had been 'desperately in love' and now the woman he wanted would not see him. Atherton thought of the kiss on the cheek and the hair-ruffling at the last interview. A man in that situation might decide that if he couldn't have her, no-one else should. A man rejected and humiliated and not taken seriously might find that a mixture of anger in with his grief was enough to stiffen the sinews and summon up the blood.

After a moment, Stalybrass said thoughtfully, 'Killed by someone who knew her, eh?'

Atherton nodded. 'So, you see, we need to find out all we can about her and her life.'

Stalybrass seemed relieved by this, as though it were letting Toby off the hook. 'Well, I'll tell you everything I know. I was pretty close to her.'

'Let me get you another drink,' said Atherton.

It was late by the time Slider got back to the office, but an enquiry at the desk told him that Porson was still on the premises. O'Flaherty, the uniformed sergeant who passed on the news, did it with a sad shake of the head. 'Got no home to go to,' he said. 'Or, at least, not one he wants to be in, wit' the missus gone. I wouldn't be surprised if he was headin' for a crack-up.'

Slider climbed up to the eyrie, remembering, unwelcomely, a previous boss, Det. Sup. Barrington, who had killed himself shortly after Slider had refused an invitation to dinner with him. In the fridge there had been the dinner for two he would have cooked, and nothing else. The loneliness of Barrington's life as revealed had haunted Slider – not that the Syrup was strictly comparable, for Barrington had had no family and was, in any case, seriously bonkers; but if Porson had asked Slider back, he probably would have gone.

Fortunately there was no chance of that. Porson was reading and taking notes at his desk when Slider tapped politely on the open door, and he looked up with work- and insomnia-reddened eyes, keeping his finger on his place to indicate he was busy and this should be kept short. Slider dredged up his précis lessons from school and gave Porson a short version of what they had learned from Jassy Whitelaw.

'So you want to alert the Manchester police and get them to go and give this O'Brien a tug, see if Barnes is there?'

'We've got the phone number. We can get the address from that. And we've got a photograph of Barnes from his flat we can send them.'

Porson considered. 'But you don't know that that's where he's gone. It was only because the girlfriend said that was where he was on Tuesday and Wednesday.' Give the old boy credit, he could fillet a story at the first telling. 'You don't even know that's where he was on Wednesday, either,' Porson continued. 'It's only what he told her. I don't suppose their relationship was based on trust and veracitude.'

'It didn't seem that way,' Slider agreed.

'In fact, he could be anywhere in the country. Or out of it.'

'Yes, sir. But the only lead we've got is this friend in Manchester, and I'd like to get hold of Darren Barnes before the trail gets cold.'

'I don't doubt you would, but when it comes down to it we've no evidence that Barnes had anything to do with the murder.'

'No, sir, but we've got the cocaine against him, and it's a large amount.'

'Fair enough,' Porson acknowledged. 'On that basis you can ask Manchester nicely in the morning and they'll do it when they've got a minute. But you can't go getting them out of bed and telling them to drop everything. Nor,' he anticipated Slider's next appeal, 'can you flash Barnes's picture round the country with a request to apprehend if seen. I'm sorry, Slider, but until you get a bit more to link him to the murder, it's softly softly. Check with his known associates and family, if any, ask Brixton

162

for help, but you can't go demanding favours of other forces without a bit more to go on.'

'I understand, sir.'

Porson raised an eyebrow. 'It's late,' he said. 'Get off home to your woman, laddie. Leave burning the oil at both ends to the likes of me, without one.'

Slider took himself away before he did the unforgivable and offered sympathy. He went back down to his own room to collect his mac (was it really only this morning that he stood outside Stella Smart's door in the rain?) and rang Joanna's mobile. She answered him at once, to the background sound of a car's engine and radio.

'I'm on my way home,' she said defensively. 'We didn't even stop for a drink.'

'I was just going to say that to you. Have you eaten?'

'Before the last session. What about you?'

'Some time last year, I think,' he said. 'I'll stop at that all-night deli in Turnham Green and pick up something.'

'Get enough for two,' she said. 'I'll join you in a spot of supper. I'm hungry again.'

'You're always hungry.'

'This is where we came in,' Joanna said. 'See you soon.'

He had only just got down to his car when she phoned him back.

'I've just had Jim call me,' she said. 'He said he didn't want to call you in case you were still with a witness.'

'You sound as though you didn't believe him.'

'He sounded weasely. He sort of invited himself to supper.'

'How did that happen? I thought you hated him.'

'No, I don't hate him. I'm very sad about him and Sue. Besides, I can't kick his behind unless we're face to face, can I?'

'Perhaps not even then.'

'You know what I mean. Anyway, he said he had something to tell you and he sounded excited, and I was about to say can't it wait for the morning when he asked if we'd had supper and I – sort of – found myself saying come and join us.'

Slider sighed. 'I can't take these late nights like you youngsters. I need my sleep.'

'Better get used to going without,' she warned.

'Don't remind me,' he shuddered. 'So, I'm getting enough supper for three now, am I?'

'Yes, but Jim said he'd bring wine.'

'Small mercies, I suppose,' said Slider.

It was an odd sensation to have the door of Joanna's flat opened to him by Atherton. 'I've just got here,' he said. 'Joanna's getting the plates and glasses out. Is that the nosh?'

He held out his hand for the paper sack in which the deli, aiming for an American look, had taken to packing its wares. In the background there was a clashing sound from the kitchen. Slider handed over the bag and said, 'What was so important it couldn't wait for tomorrow, anyway?'

Atherton raised an eyebrow. 'Am I unwelcome? I didn't think I needed an excuse to have supper with my oldest friend.'

'Oldest is how I feel,' Slider said, but he left the question unanswered. 'Can you two manage between you? I want to wash my hands and face and take my tie off.'

When Slider joined them in the sitting room, they were chatting in what seemed a perfectly friendly way, so he assumed that whatever bones Joanna had had to pick with Atherton, she had buried them for the time being. The food had been laid out on the gate-leg table. There was French bread, two kinds of pâté, a thoroughly degenerate piece of Brie that really ought to have been wearing a corset, a large bunch of red grapes, and three slices of the deli's own cheesecake. Atherton's hand was visible in the fact that the lettuce, green pepper and vine tomatoes he had bought had been assembled in one dish as a salad, with dressing: Joanna would have dumped them on the table separate and undressed for picking at. And the wine Atherton had brought was two bottles of beaujolais – Regnié, one Slider didn't know.

'So, what was the news you were so excited about?' Slider asked, as they began. The French bread had been warmed, he discovered – Atherton again.

'Did you tell him I was excited?' Atherton asked.

'Get on with it,' said Joanna. 'Spinning it out like that.'

'All right, here it is – I know who Chattie's father is. Ever heard of Cornfeld Chemicals?'

'I thought it was Cornfield,' Slider said. 'There's that logo of theirs—'

'Oh, yes, I know it,' Joanna said. 'I saw something in the paper about them a couple of weeks ago – didn't read it, because I wasn't interested, but I noticed the logo: the oval thingy with the picture of a field of waving corn on it.'

'That's the one,' said Slider. 'Always reminded me of Ovaltine. I could never fathom what it had to do with chemicals.'

'*I* always read it as "Cornfed Chemicals",' Joanna said. 'You know, like "cornfed beef".'

'You see a picture of a cornfield and read the word underneath and naturally you think the name is Cornfield,' Slider reasoned.

'Oy,' said Atherton. 'You're spoiling my effect. When I

165

say, "Ever heard of Cornfeld Chemicals?" you're supposed to gasp in wonder, not witter on about etymology.'

'What's insects got to do with it?' Joanna said.

'No, that's lepidometry,' Slider said.

'I'll take my ball away and go home,' Atherton warned.

'All right,' Slider said kindly. 'Are you telling us that Chattie Cornfeld had something to do with Cornfeld Chemicals?'

'I'm telling you,' Atherton said with dignity, 'that her father *is* Cornfeld Chemicals. He owns the thing. He started it, he runs it, he is the chairman and chief exec rolled into one.' He used his hands as a balance. 'Dad – Cornfeld Chemicals. Cornfeld Chemicals – Dad. Am I getting the idea across now?'

'You mean,' Joanna said gravely, 'she was *that* Cornfeld.'

'At last,' Atherton sighed, and topped up the glasses. 'Well, at least I've established that we've all heard of the company, even if we didn't pronounce its name right.'

'Heard of it, yes,' said Joanna. 'It's not exactly a household name but one comes across it. One knows it exists.'

'Those of us who are able to read further through the paper than the health and beauty hints,' said Atherton, risking his life, 'are aware that it is a small company, which nevertheless does some important research in its pharmaceutical division and has come up with some cracking new drugs from time to time. Coprylon, for one, which is used to treat epilepsy. And Nuskin, a sterile artificial skin used post-operatively.'

'But Chattie's mother said she didn't have anything to do with her father,' Slider said. 'How did his owning a chemicals company affect her?'

'I shall tell you,' said Atherton, magnificently. 'I had a very interesting talk with Jasper Stalybrass, who knew her pretty well.'

'The horn-player?' Joanna said. 'I know him. I've played with him on gigs over the years.'

'What did you think of him?' Atherton asked.

'A bit full of himself, like most horn-players, but okay. A good player. And good company.' She caught Atherton's look and realised what was wanted. 'I think he's all right, for what my opinion's worth. He came across as an honest bloke and I've never heard anything against him.'

'That's what I thought,' Atherton said. 'Anyway, he's been having a sort of affair with Chattie.'

'"Sort of"?' Slider queried, spreading duck pâté thickly over buttered bread. 'How can you sort of have an affair?'

'Be accurate, I said having a sort of affair.'

'All right, what's a "sort of" affair when it's at home?'

'He said it was like being good friends with sex added, but with no intention of getting any further entangled than they were.'

'You needn't say it as if it sounds like heaven,' Joanna said, with an edge.

Slider flung her a silencing glance and said, 'Okay, go on.'

'Well, over that time, they exchanged life stories, and he knew quite a bit about the Cornfeld ménage. Bolstered by a few dates out of *Who's Who*, I'm now in a position to give you . . .' He paused and then announced in American movie tones '. . . The Cornfeld Story: The Early Years.'

'Get on with it,' said Slider.

'Our story opens,' Atherton obliged, but in the same voice, 'in the small Midwest town of Enfield, Middlesex, England.'

9

Toby or Not Toby?

Chattie's father had been christened Heinrich. His parents had come over from Germany in 1936 when he was a year old and, having decided to settle permanently in England, they had changed his name to Henry.

The Cornfelds didn't have much money, but Henry was a bright child and ambitious, and he had supplemented his basic education with self-help and library books. His bent and his passion were both for the sciences. When he left school at fifteen he got a job as a laboratory assistant in a private school where, although the pay was poor, he could continue to breathe the fumes, so to speak. When he was twenty his father died, and his mother gave him the proceeds of the life assurance policy so that he could set up his own business.

'I got all this out of a morgue article – one of a series about self-made men,' Atherton said. 'Henry started in a small way with what he knew, supplying chemicals to school labs, and built up from there. Soon he was supplying university and hospital labs too, as a middle man, and then he started the manufacturing side. The thing really took off in the sixties, and he branched out into pharmaceuticals, where the rewards are so much greater.'

'The risks, too,' said Slider.

'Right. But he had the core business to fall back on, to fund the experimental stuff. Anyway, by the time he met Chattie's mother he was well entrenched and pretty well off.'

'So there was family money after all. But what about wife number one?' Slider asked, prompted by his tidy mind.

'I only got the bare facts about her from *Who's Who*. Name, Mary Rogers. He married her in 1960 when he was twenty-five and struggling, but by the time he divorced her he was rich and important and being invited places, so one can deduce that she didn't fit in any more.'

'So he ditched her,' Joanna said indignantly. It was amazing, Slider thought, how they always take the woman's part, even when it's a strange woman they've never met and never will.

'Presumably,' said Atherton. 'There was one daughter from the marriage, a girl called Ruth, born in 1962. He married Stella Smart in 1974. Chattie told Stalybrass that her father gave the first Mrs C the family semi in Enfield while he moved to a more upscale place in Hemel Hempstead with Mrs C number two, which was where Chattie was born in 1975.'

'And the third wife?'

'Ah, that's where all the acid creeps in. Apparently Stella Smart discovered that he was bonking his secretary and went completely spare. Considering she'd snatched him from wife number one, she shouldn't have been too surprised, but – according to Jasper, who gathered it from Chattie, who must have gathered it from her mother – she couldn't stand being superseded by a mere secretary. It was a cliché too far for her, and humiliating to have her husband prefer a common typist. So she confronted him, forced the issue and insisted on a divorce.'

'Now, why do you find that incredible?' Joanna asked. 'I can tell from your voice you think she ought to have kept her mouth shut and put up with it.'

'What I think or don't think has nothing to do with it,' Atherton said. 'But I suppose most women would want to hold on to the meal ticket, if he wasn't agitating to leave.'

'Most women? You really are a—'

'Can we get back to the story, please,' Slider said quickly. 'You two can fight later. I want to hear the end before I fall asleep.'

Atherton resumed. 'So, acrimonious divorce, and Daddy Cornfeld flew the coop and married the secretary. But it seems he was very attached to Chattie, who was a bright child and very clever, and he kept contact with her, and had her to stay in the even smarter house in High Wycombe he could now afford. And in spite of everything that Stella could do to turn her against him, Chattie remained very fond of her father, and was – so Jasper says – intensely proud of him. She was especially proud that he had started with nothing and worked his way up through his own efforts.'

'Ah,' said Slider, 'I'm beginning to understand something Jassy said.'

'About Chattie wanting to succeed in her business without help?' Atherton asked. 'Yes, I got that from Jasper, too. It was a bit of a theme with our Chattie. He said she was so keen to do it alone like him that she never told people whose daughter she was. Afraid people might do her favours on his account. It was a bit of a pillow-confession to Jasper, and she made him swear secrecy.'

170

'Yes, Mrs Hammick said she never talked about her father,' Slider remembered.

'She might also have been afraid people would tap her for money if they knew she had a rich dad,' Atherton said.

'Don't be cynical. But, look here,' Slider said, 'Jassy called Chattie a hypocrite because in fact she *did* receive money from her father. She said that Chattie was given lots of things while she, Jassy, got nothing.'

Atherton nodded. 'Yes, Jassy came up quite a bit in the conversation. Jasper had no time for her – called her a self-pitying little parasite and an inveterate ligger. He had a brush or two with her at Chattie's house. She was always borrowing, and when that wasn't enough she stole. Found her going through his wallet one day. He said Chattie was far too lenient with her. As to Chattie having everything and Jassy nothing, it seems that the bone of contention from Jassy's point of view was that Daddy Cornfeld gave each of them a lump sum when she reached seventeen. Chattie used hers to buy a one-bedroom flat in an up-and-coming part of Shepherd's Bush, which she sold in 1998 for a big profit. A very smart buy – it tripled in value. This happened to be just the time when Jassy was given her lump sum, so to start with she got it into her head that she hadn't been given as much as Chattie.'

'But—' Joanna began indignantly.

'I know,' Atherton anticipated, 'but with a chip as large as Jassy's, there's no room for logic or common sense. Anyway, Jassy blued her lump sum on a fancy sports car, which she wrapped round a lamp-post soon afterwards, having omitted to get insurance for it. Daddy sorted out the fine for driving without, but he was so furious with her he wouldn't give her the money to replace it, so Jassy was left with nothing but a feeling of resentment and a determination to get as much out of teacher's-pet Chattie as she could.'

There was a silence when he stopped talking. Joanna refilled the wine glasses and took some grapes. 'So,' she said at last, 'it explains how she got the house.'

'But not how she funded the lifestyle,' Atherton said. 'The income from her business wasn't enough. So we come back to the question: where did she get the rest of the money from? Did she deal coke? Did she accept "presents" from her many menfriends?'

'Code language for prostitution, I gather,' said Joanna.

'There are numerous other possibilities we haven't uncovered yet,' Slider said. 'It's all very interesting, but I'm not sure it gets us much further forrard. The question we come back to is who killed her, and why?'

Atherton called on Toby Harkness early on Saturday morning, to be sure of catching him in. He had a flat in Aynhoe Road, just off Brook Green, one of six in a small block that had been put up where a large house had been demolished in the council-vandalism days of the seventies. The block was showing its age, with cracks in the concrete facing, several slipped tiles on the roof and the windows in dire need of replacement. It was often a problem with such places, that they tended to be occupied either by the young or the old, neither of which groups was ever keen on spending money on communal upkeep.

There was an entry-phone, and Atherton buzzed long and hard, then waited, listening to a blackbird in a nearby plane tree trying to pretend this was countryside. He was about to ring again when there was a click and a rusty voice said, 'Who is it?'

'I'm Detective Sergeant Atherton from Shepherd's

Bush police station. I'd like to have a little chat with you about Miss Cornfeld. Would you let me in, please, sir?'

There was a pause, and then the voice said, 'I don't—' and broke off in a bout of coughing.

'Press the buzzer, please, sir,' Atherton said. 'I can't discuss things through the intercom like this.'

There were some amplified clicks and bumps, and then the buzzer went off, and Atherton pushed the door. There were three flats to a floor, and Harkness's was upstairs. When he reached the top of the flight Atherton saw him at the door to his flat, holding it open. He was naked from the waist up, showing a rather undeveloped white torso, with a few dark, flat moles scattered here and there, and a hairless chest, hunched round at the moment as if its owner was feeling the cold. Below the waist he was crammed into a pair of tight jeans that looked rather the worse for wear, as if he hadn't been out of them for a few days. His feet were bare, his toenails dirty, and he stood on one leg and used the right foot to scratch the top of the left. His face was unshaven and bleary, his eyes red, his dark hair standing up in a mad bush, and even from the distance of six feet Atherton could smell the booze coming off him in waves.

'Mr Harkness?' Atherton said, not because he was in any doubt, but to get things moving.

'Yes,' he said. 'But I don't—' He broke off, and a sweat suddenly sheened his face, which had turned greenish white. 'Oh, God,' he said, hunching, and put his hand up to his mouth.

'Bathroom, quick,' Atherton barked, and caught the door as Harkness turned and fled. Atherton stepped in and shut the door behind him as the sounds of retching came from somewhere out of sight. The door opened straight into the living room, with the kitchen immediately on the right, and the bedroom and bathroom presumably down a small passage that led off beyond the kitchen. There was parquet flooring in the area just inside the door, which disappeared under fawn carpeting in the living-room area, but it was neglected, very scratched and bereft of polish, yea, these many years, if Atherton was any expert. The air smelt stale, even leaving aside the fact that Harkness was evidently a smoker. A quick glance into the kitchen revealed a chaos of young epic proportions, with used plates and mugs piled everywhere along with fragments of food and empty takeaway cartons, some of which looked as though they needed carbon dating. The tiles on the floor were stained with food and grease and liberally sprinkled with crumbs, and the peel of a satsuma and a lone chip lay near the gas stove, mutely begging lenience.

The living-room was likewise a mess of clothes, books and papers, used crockery and more empty food cartons, empty beer cans and overflowing ashtrays. The curtains were still drawn over the window, but inefficiently, so that sunlight was streaming in through a foot-wide gap and heating up the composite smells towards combustion point. Atherton went across, drew them back and fought the window open – the metal frame had warped – before he expired from lack of oxygen.

In the bathroom the sounds of vomiting had been superseded by a lengthy micturition, then flushing, and now the trickle and splash of water being, he hoped, dashed on the face. Harkness reappeared at last, wiping his mouth, the hair round his face damp, missed drops and dribbles running down his chest.

'Sorry about that,' he croaked. He coughed long and hard, then resumed in a sort of gruff mumble, his eyes never meeting Atherton's, 'Bit of a heavy night last night. You know. Trying to cope. Not doing very well,' he added, with a deprecatory half-smile, which did not seem to know what to do with itself and wandered off his face as he looked around the room as if searching for something. 'Time is it?'

'It's a quarter to nine,' Atherton said. 'I'm sorry to call on you so early but I wanted to catch you before you went out. I wasn't sure if you were working today.'

'Not today,' Harkness mumbled. 'Maybe never work again.' He wandered into the living-room and slumped on the sofa, his hands hanging uselessly between his legs.

Fried to the tonsils last night, Atherton thought. Slept on the sofa – passed out, rather – and still not fully sober. 'If I make you some coffee, do you think you'll keep it down?'

'Yeah. Thanks,' Harkness said, staring at the floor.

Atherton left him, and went, reluctantly, into the festering kitchen, where he unearthed and filled the kettle and switched it on. While he waited for it to boil, he tried to calculate from the debris how many days were represented by it. Chattie had been killed on Wednesday morning and Harkness would have heard about it, at the earliest, on Wednesday evening, if Marion had rung round straight away, or Thursday morning if not. Two and a half days at most. But the plates, mugs and cardboard cartons had been accumulating here for a lot longer than that. Either Harkness was congenitally untidy, or he had had something serious and depressing on his mind for the best part of two weeks. Atherton knew which option he'd like to go for.

He found instant coffee in a cupboard, washed a mug and spoon and, finding no tea towel he'd be willing to touch without protective clothing, sighed and dried them on his clean handkerchief. In the fridge there were horrors beyond description. Bung a fork of lightning through that lot, he thought, and you could start evolution all over again. There was a cardboard carton of milk but the contents were completely solid to the external touch so he didn't even bother to open it. Black would be better for him, anyway.

When he returned to the living-room, Harkness was sitting in the same position but had recovered enough to light a cigarette, and the smoke was curling up into the bars of sunlight and wavering when it hit the air from the window.

'Coffee,' Atherton said, putting the mug down on the edge of the coffee-table in front of him.

'Thanks,' Harkness said. 'I'm sorry about . . .' He waved his hand, presumably to indicate the vomiting. 'Had a load on last night.'

'Just drink, was it?'

'Eh?'

'Or did you mix it? Speed, charlie, any little recreational helpers?'

'Drugs, you mean? No, I don't do drugs,' he said, and the indifference of his voice convinced. If Chattie had been selling, it was not to Toby Harkness.

'You've been depressed,' Atherton suggested, moving out of the way of the smoke, which always seemed to seek him out like a friendly cat when he was in the vicinity of a smoker.

'Yeah,' said Harkness, sinking lower in his seat, his chin slumping towards his chest. 'Well, you know. Christ, she's dead. What d'you think?'

'You were depressed before that, though. You've been unhappy for quite a while.'

Even this minimal sympathy brought tears to Harkness's

eyes. God, he was young, Atherton thought. The slight chubbiness of his face was a boy's, his self-obsession was a student's. He had no curiosity about Atherton or why he was here; he was thinking about his own sorrows, and as he thought, the tears oozed out and down his unshaven cheeks.

'I loved her. I would have died for her, she knew that.' He had a very slight Bristol accent, a rolling over of the vowels, which made him sound even younger than he was. 'But she kept pushing me away. And then she said she wouldn't see me again, except for business. How could I live like that, seeing her but never being allowed to touch her?'

'You and Chattie had an affair, didn't you?' Atherton said, as kindly as he could, given that everything about this young man irritated him. Harkness stubbed out his cigarette and, still breathing out the last mouthful of smoke, reached for another one and put it between his lips. Atherton watched him in amazement. How could he smoke when he depended on his lungs for his livelihood?

'It wasn't an affair. We were in love,' Harkness said. 'The first time I saw her, the first time I played with Baroque, I knew then. She was so lovely. The most beautiful girl I'd ever seen. I didn't believe at first anything could happen. I mean, not with me. I've never been very good with girls. I didn't dare ask her for ages. But I could see she was attracted to me. She always came over and talked to me. When we were in a group, she always sat by me, and was nice to me and made me laugh.'

Sorry for you, Atherton thought. Saw you were shy and tried to bring you out of yourself. He remembered Slider saying once that it was funny how often shy people turned out to be terribly conceited underneath. Harkness saw Chattie's kindness and took it for appreciation of his own fine worth.

'Then it sort of happened one day. We were doing a gig down in Hastings, at the White Rock, and we all stayed overnight, at this weird bed-and-breakfast place – all except Jasper, who stayed with a friend. Well, we had some drinks in Trish's room, and then went to bed. Chattie's room and mine were both on the top floor, and we went up the stairs together. We got to the top landing. She was laughing and suddenly it came over me in a wave and I just grabbed her and kissed her. And she kissed me back. And then, I don't know, we were, like, swept away by passion. We went into her room and—'

He stopped, gazing down a long corridor at memory, his lips parting in remembered rapture.

'It was wonderful,' he resumed at last. 'And the next day, when we went back to London, I went to her house and we made love all night. I told her I loved her. We talked about marriage. I told her I wanted to spend the rest of my life with her.'

I bet she was pleased to hear that, Atherton thought.

'It was wonderful at first. I didn't get to see as much of her as I wanted, because she was often working, and I was too, and it was hard to get our schedules together. But when we did get together it was wonderful. Only she wanted me to keep it a secret. She said it would upset the band if anyone knew about us. I didn't see that. But she said there was a, like, dynamic, about the group, and her and me being together would disturb it. So I went along with it. Well, I thought, they'll know all right when we get married.' He stopped and drew on his cigarette.

'Did she say she would marry you?' Atherton asked.

He scowled. 'Yes, she did,' he said defiantly. 'Afterwards she said she never had, but I know what I know. I just don't know what went wrong. I wanted to see her more often, that's all. She said she couldn't manage it. She was busy. I said why didn't we move in together, and then we could see each other all the time? But she said no, and then she got cross with me for asking. I said, I love you, and she said, I never asked you to. I mean, what sort of a thing is that to say?'

'Terrible,' Atherton said, shaking his head sympathetically.

'I said, "I know you love me, why are you treating me like this?" She said she couldn't see me any more. She said I was too intense. "Well," I said, "if you love someone, you are intense, aren't you?" I started to think she was seeing someone else, but she said she wasn't — and, anyway, if she was too busy to see me, how could she have had time for anyone else?'

What a plonker, Atherton thought with amazement.

'I told her I'd kill myself if she refused to see me again. She got angry about that, and said it was blackmail, and I said it wasn't, it was just that I loved her. How can love be blackmail? Anyway, she said it would be a wicked waste of my talent if I were to kill myself. She said I was the best oboist she'd ever known. That's how I knew she still did love me, really. She wouldn't have said that if she didn't. I just don't understand why she broke it off.' He paused, smoking hard and slowly. His face darkened as he stared through the smoke at nothing. 'At the end, the last time I saw her, she said if I didn't leave her alone, she wouldn't see me or talk to me at all, not even at the band. She said she'd stop coming to any of the band things.' The tears that had subsided welled up again.

'This was in the pub, the Anchor, on Tuesday night?'

'Yeah,' he said, not interested in how Atherton knew. 'I'd been phoning her all day, but she was out, and when I tried her mobile it was on voice-mail. She always answered her mobile normally, so I knew she was avoiding me. So I sat in my car at the end of her road where I could see the house, so I'd know when she got home. And when she did, I rang her again and said I had to see her. I said I'd meet her in the Anchor. I told her if she wouldn't see me I'd cut my throat.'

'What did she say when you said that?'

'She just said, "No, you won't." But she sounded worried. Anyway, she said she'd see me for five minutes, at seven o'clock. When she came in, she was all smiling and lovely and so nice to me, just like she used to be, and I thought we could patch things up. She'd said five minutes but it was at least half an hour, so she must have been enjoying my company, mustn't she? But then she said this was the last time she'd see me alone, that she was serious, that there could be nothing more between us, that I must really leave her alone or she'd drop the band altogether and it'd be my fault. I couldn't believe it. So then I asked her, is there somebody else? And she looked surprised a bit, and then she said there was, and she laughed. She *laughed*!' He choked on his smoke. 'I almost hated her then.'

'Almost?' Atherton urged, but gently. This was promising stuff. But Harkness said no more. He smoked and brooded. 'Do you know who it was she was seeing?' he asked at last.

'Yeah,' said Harkness, his voice so low it almost went off the scale. 'I didn't then, but I found out. After she left the pub, I went back to my car, but I didn't drive away. I stayed watching her house. I was thinking I'd maybe give her time to calm down and then I'd go and talk to her again. But then after a bit I saw him arrive. He knocked at the door and she let him in and a minute later they both came out and walked off together. Arm in arm. And when she let him in, she kissed him. So then I knew.'

'Who was it?'

'*Jasper.*' It was almost a sob. 'How could she prefer him to me? I mean, he's nothing. He's just a horn-player. And he's never serious about anything. He wouldn't marry her. He was always having different girls, one-night stands. I knew he'd only end up hurting her. He'd break her heart. I couldn't stand that.'

Atherton almost held his breath. 'You couldn't stand to let her get hurt. So what did you do?'

'What *could* I do?' he said.

'Yes, what? A brave man would want to save her from that, at any price. Even if it meant—' He left a tempting space but Harkness did not respond. 'The thought of her having her heart broken by someone like Jasper – well, if it was me, I don't know what I'd do. It would be the worst thing of all. Worse even than—'

This time it worked. 'Yeah,' Harkness said. 'I thought that, too. I thought even death would be better than that.' He sighed tremulously, wiped his nose on the back of his hand, reached for another cigarette.

'So what did you do?' Atherton urged.

'I waited for ages, but they didn't come back. So I went home and got drunk.' He looked around him incuriously. 'I've been drunk pretty well ever since.'

'The next morning,' Atherton said, 'what did you do?'

'Do?' he said vaguely.

'You'd had all night to think it over, about you and Chattie and that man. You decided you had to do something – something drastic to save her.'

181

Now Harkness looked at him, his eyes widening slightly. 'What do you mean?'

'You thought it would be better, if you couldn't have her, that no-one should have her. You knew she went running in the park every day. You thought it would be the best thing for her as well as for you if she was at peace.'

He had cottoned on now. 'You think I killed her?'

'You had such good reason,' Atherton said soothingly.

'It was the Park Killer,' he said. 'It was in all the papers. It was a frenzied attack, like the other ones, those other girls he killed.'

'And where were you at eight o'clock that morning?'

'I was here, at home. I was in bed asleep. I didn't get up until nearly ten. I didn't know anything about it until Marion phoned me that night. How could you think I'd kill her? I loved her.'

'Love is sometimes the strongest reason. And you did say just now you thought death would be better.'

He stared a moment, and then said, 'No, I meant *my* death. I thought I'd sooner be dead than see her with Jasper.'

And yet, of course, Atherton thought, Chattie's death would yield the same result, with the added advantage of his being around to mourn her properly. And a man in bed, alone, has no witness to his alibi.

The CID room was full, with the firm at their desks and the extra bods from uniform they had been loaned lining the walls. Most people had plastic cups of coffee from the machine or styrofoam cups of something better from the sandwich shop by the market, and one or two had bacon rolls by way of breakfast from the same source. McLaren had two. Some were reading papers. The sun was shining away maddeningly outside the window, eager to remind everyone that it was Saturday, when ordinary mortals washed the car, had a pint down the local and watched the footy.

There was a low buzz of chat. Hart had pulled up a chair to Atherton's desk. 'So what happened about that bird you were dating, then?' she asked. 'Sue? I thought you two were serious. Some said you were gonna get married.'

'Which some was that?' Atherton asked, his nostrils flaring as he tried to work out what her perfume was.

'Oh, stuff gets around,' Hart said airily. 'So, what happened?'

'She dumped me,' Atherton said, going for the sympathy vote. He looked full into Hart's eyes with a tragic air. 'Hell of a shock to the system, I can tell you. First knock-back since I joined this firm, not counting Norma.'

'What are you saying about me?' Swilley said sharply, catching her name. She had been trying not to eavesdrop, but Atherton had meant her to hear that bit.

'He says you wouldn't have 'im, Norm,' Hart said cheerfully.

'I'd rather be the love-toy of a Greek army battalion,' said Swilley, going back to her paper.

'Actually,' Atherton said loftily, 'Ms Swilley doesn't have what I want in a woman.'

'What's that?' said Hart. 'Low standards?'

'God, you're funny,' Atherton said. 'So, what are you doing tonight?'

'Don't tell me you've got no date?'

'I thought I'd give you first refusal. How would you like to have rampant sex at my place?'

'Well, I dunno,' Hart said, pondering. 'I really ought to get home. I've got a banana going black. I shouldn't leave it alone for too long.'

McLaren called across, 'Oy, Jim, I should watch it if I was you. Yvonne Collins is after your blood.'

'I don't know how he's got the energy,' Mackay said wonderingly. 'I mean, he's not as young as he was. Must be the Viagra.'

'Here,' said McLaren, 'did you hear about the load of Viagra got nicked? They're looking for a hardened criminal.'

There were groans. 'Old one, Maurice!'

'Got whiskers on it.'

But McLaren looked round grinning anyway, pleased with himself.

'Who's Yvonne Collins?' Hart asked.

'Don't tell me you haven't heard about her?' Mackay said. 'She hadn't been here five minutes before—'

Slider walked in at that point. 'There's so much gossip in here, you should all have dryers on your heads,' he said. 'Can we settle down, please? There's a lot to get through.'

Quiet descended, and between them Slider and Atherton reported the new information gained from Jasper, Jassy and Toby.

At the end of it, Swilley said, 'So it looks as if we've got two possible directions. There's Darren Barnes and the coke connection, and there's Toby Harkness and the jealousy bit.'

'Harkness is barely a suspect,' Atherton said. 'All we've got against him is motive.'

'And no alibi,' Mackay reminded them.

'Most of the world's got no alibi,' Slider said. 'However, it is such a good motive that I think we ought to look into his background, in case he has any record of violence; and see if we can get a look round his house, to see if there are any bloodstained clothes or knives. But at the moment, Darren Barnes looks a lot more tasty.'

'Right,' said Mackay, 'and the drugs thing makes more sense. The way I see it, Barnes and the victim are in business together. He supplies her with a big bag of white. Gets his girlfriend to drop it at the house. Meets her on Wednesday to collect the cash. Only she's not got it for some reason, or she tries to stiff him, or they have a row about something else, I dunno. Anyway, he offs her and has it away on his tiny toes. Only he doesn't want to leave all that good charlie going to waste at the victim's house. So he goes back home that night and tells his girlfriend to go and see if it's still there – he can't go, you see, in case the place is being watched. She comes back saying it's no go, there's a copper on the door, and he takes fright, belts her one for good luck and scarpers, and he hasn't been seen since.'

He looked round for approval at the end of this narrative, and Slider could see there was plenty of assent in the faces round the wall. It was the sort of simple tale they could all appreciate. They had seen it a dozen times before – fallings out among drug-dealers were about the commonest cause of death on the streets.

'So, do you reckon his girlfriend was in on it?' McLaren asked Mackay.

'No, the way I reckon, he couldn't have got her to go back there if she'd known anything about it. When he got home he must have realised she didn't know her sister was dead yet, so it was worth a try to get the charlie back – especially if the reason he killed her was that she hadn't paid him for it.'

'But why wouldn't he have gone straight round there after killing her?' Hollis asked. 'That would have been the safest time. He could have taken her door keys and let himself in.'

'Maybe he had blood on him,' Mackay said.

'Or maybe he had to establish an alibi,' McLaren put in.

'Some alibi, that no-one knows about,' someone at the back muttered.

'Maybe he just didn't think of it,' Swilley said. 'He doesn't sound as if he was a practised killer. He probably couldn't think of anything but putting as much distance as possible between him and the park.'

'It's a nice scenario,' Slider said, 'but you're forgetting one thing.'

His eye caught that of Hart, and she continued for him, as if he had asked for suggestions. 'She wasn't stabbed to death.'

'In Doc Cameron's opinion,' Atherton said.

'And if she was drugged,' Hart continued, unchecked, 'then it was premeditated, not the result of a sudden quarrel.'

'Right,' said Slider.

'But, boss,' Hart went on, 'even if it was premeditated, it don't mean it couldn't've been Darren. Maybe he didn't trust her, or she was threatening to cut 'im out, or shop 'im. There could've been a stack o' reasons why he'd want her dead. Maybe even Jassy was in on it. We know she was wicked jealous of Chattie, plus she thought she'd been hard done by. She could've got Darren to kill Chattie for her.'

'Why would he agree?'

'Because he's on her side. And there'd be money to come, maybe.'

'Why did he hit her, then?' Swilley asked.

'To make it look as if she wasn't in on it,' Hart suggested. 'She's staying put, and the police are bound to come and interview her. It takes the suspicion off her.'

'And puts it smack on him. She was pretty quick to finger him, by all accounts,' said Swilley.

'Maybe she got scared,' Hart said.

'This is all very well,' Slider said, 'but if Darren did kill Chattie for whatever reason – and I admit he sounds stupid enough to try to fake the Park Killer MO and think it would fool us – where did he get the barbiturates from?'

They all seemed to think this was a foolish question. 'He's in the biz, boss,' Hart answered for them, at last. 'He'd know where to lay his hands on the right tackle. Blimey, you can get drugs, guns and explosives on the Internet wiv a credit card these days.'

'Hmm,' said Slider. 'Well, I agree with you at least that Darren is the best suspect we've got, and that efforts should be put into finding him.' He looked across at Hollis. 'Follow up the Manchester lead, and find out from Brixton who his associates were and get after them. I leave that to you. And the other thing we must keep on with,' he addressed the room at large, 'is identifying Running Man, and finding someone who saw the face of the man seen talking to Chattie by the shrubbery – we'll call him Standing Man. Also, if Chattie really was selling drugs, she must have had customers. Find them, if they exist. Follow up on Toby Harkness. What else?'

'Find out where Chattie was on Tuesday?' Swilley suggested.

'Yeah, and what this DC 10 malarkey is,' said Hart. 'That's bugging me.'

'Well, it may or may not be important where she was on Tuesday, but I agree we ought to know. Try her friends and contacts, see if it makes sense to any of them.'

'If only the killer would use her mobile,' Swilley said wistfully.

'If the wooden horse of Troy had foaled, horses today would be cheaper to feed,' Atherton said.

'Eh?' said Swilley.

'It's the epitome of pointless speculation.'

'I wish you came with sub-titles,' she complained.

10

Outrageous Fortune

As Slider was about to return to his own office, Porson appeared at its communicating door with the CID room, and beckoned. 'A word,' he said.

Slider gave him one. 'Sir.' Obedient to Porson's gesture, he shut the door behind him.

'I've had one Henry Cornfeld on the dog. The *grand fromage* of Cornfeld Chemicals. Business typhoon, baron of industry, what you will. VIP.'

'Ah,' said Slider.

'You didn't tell me the victim was one of *those* Cornfelds.'

'We've only just worked that out, sir. The mother was not entirely frank with us. She didn't let on who he was, and told us Chattie had nothing to do with her father. She said she didn't know where he was living.'

Porson waved all that away. 'He wasn't best pleased we hadn't told him.'

'*I'm* surprised he didn't contact us himself. He must have seen it on the news,' Slider countered.

'Ah, well, he's been out of the country for a week. Just back from the States this morning on the red-eye, and various members of his staff all thought one of the others had told him. Carpetings all round.'

'It's a bit much blaming us, then,' Slider complained.

'Oh, don't worry, I told him the circs, identification-wise, and he understood. He's not a raging ecomaniac out to see heads roll. Upset, more than anything, that he was out of the country. Says if he'd had any inclination anything would happen to her blah-di-blah. As if he could have stopped it – but that's a father's paternal feelings for you. Anyway, he wants someone to go and talk to him, and you're it.'

'Has he got anything useful to tell us?'

Porson rolled his eyes. 'I don't know. I didn't give him the first degree over the phone.'

'It's just that there's a lot to do and I don't want to waste time hand-holding. If that's all he wants, we can send him a PC. Preferably a female one.'

'No *bon*, Slider. You're the persona gratis,' Porson said. 'You don't have to be all day about it. Look on it as thinking time. Little trip out into the country, lovely weather for it. And you never know, he might have a tale to tell.'

Slider thought, on the contrary, that he did know. Henry Cornfeld didn't need to have a tale to tell. Like the congenial dustman, he had friends in high places.

It certainly was a lovely day, and as he headed out on the A41 Slider thought what a pity it was that Joanna was working. Her company in the car and a pub lunch – even if a snatched one – would make it all worth while. The Cornfeld mansion was in a village called Frithsden, not far from Hemel Hempstead. So Henry had returned to Stella Smart country in his ripe years, Slider thought.

He wondered at the magnate's coming down to the

country after an absence of a week rather than powering his way through his office finding dereliction on all sides. And, Slider reflected, he hadn't threatened Porson or thrown his weight around. He obviously hadn't been to the right school of tycoon paranoia.

The country round Frithsden was lovely: rolling hills, deep lanes, trees, hedges, beech woods. There were fields of green wheat and fields of brown cows – it somehow comforted Slider to see that farming still went on, even so close to London – and the froth of elder dripped petals onto the kex and moon daisies in the lush verges. God, England was beautiful! he thought. It took him three passes through the village (with a longing look at an ancient village pub with chairs and tables set outside) before he found the almost hidden entrance, because trailers of traveller's joy had hung down and roadside grasses, bartsia and mallow had grown up to cover the nameplate. But apart from this obscurity, there were no other security measures, no cameras and electronic gates but just an open, if narrow, driveway bending round some mature rhododendrons to the out-of-sight house.

The house turned out to be mid-Victorian church gothic, and charmingly appropriate, Slider thought, for a self-made mogul, given that it had probably originally been built for one such. An ancient yellow Labrador was lying in the sun outside the arched oak front door, and banged its tail on the gravel in welcome as Slider got out of the car, but indicated that it was far too fat and old to get up. Slider stooped and scratched its head, noting that the front door stood open, and wondering again at the lack of security. No-one was in sight, so he lifted and dropped the cast-iron knocker, which must have weighed ten pounds, then spotted a bell almost hidden by the wisteria and rang that.

A young woman appeared, clacking down the decorated tiles of the hall on impractical high heels. She had a fine figure well displayed by her tight toreador pants and sleeveless, low-cut top, dyed blonde hair and a lot of gold jewellery.

'Detective Inspector Slider?' she said. 'I'm Kylie, Mr Cornfeld's companion.'

At last, thought Slider, a cliché I can recognise. She even said, 'Would you like to come this way?' and walked off with a wiggling rump. Slider repressed the Carry On response and followed her into the cool, lofty hall.

'He's in the morning room,' she said, showing Slider through an open door. The room was large and light and airy, with a twelve-foot-high ceiling and fine pieces of furniture thoughtfully placed and gleaming with care. There was a vast Victorian-mediaeval stone fireplace, and in the hearth an arrangement of blue and white delphiniums in a Chinese vase was spitting petals onto the glazed tiles. Cornfeld was sitting at a small table by open french windows onto a garden, reading one of a stack of newspapers.

'Can I get you coffee or anything?' Kylie asked.

'No, thank you very much,' Slider said.

She beamed and withdrew, and Cornfeld stood up and came across to shake his hand. He was not a tall man, and though not fat he had an elderly thickness through his body – Slider had worked out that he was sixty-eight – but his movements were easy and alert, and there was firmness in the lines of his face and the grip of his hand. This was a man in his power, not ready yet to babble of green fields, even if he liked inhabiting them. His face was tanned, his white hair thick and elegantly cut. Despite being at home he was dressed in a suit of admirable cut and beautiful cloth, the style a nicely judged balance of modernity and dignity; but his tie was black, and he did not smile, though Slider guessed that charm would always have been one of his tools in securing his advantage in the world. And there was something in his eyes that Slider recognised, the blankness, the almost wandering look of shock.

'Thank you for coming,' said Cornfeld. 'I suppose you think it's a great nuisance, when you are so busy, to trek all the way out here just to see me. But I had to see you myself, and hear for myself what's been happening.' His voice was strong, the accent neutral, the delivery rather clipped, as though he expected words to do an efficient job like everyone else. But as he said the next word, his voice thickened and wavered, and Slider saw that he was close to tears. 'Chattie – was my favourite child. I know one isn't supposed to have favourites, but she was always the pick of the bunch. So bright, so quick, so clever. I need to know – I need very badly to know – who has done this thing.'

He drew Slider to a chair at the table, and sat himself, folding his hands and pointing his face and his attention straight at him. So, Slider thought resignedly, it is just hand-holding. There was a strong resemblance between Chattie and her father. He had only seen Chattie dead, of course, but the shape of the face was the same, the nose, the chin; there were the blue eyes, too, and he could imagine that the thick wavy hair had once been gold. In Cornfeld *père* he could see what Chattie might have had in life, the sharp intelligence, the firm resolve. He wished again, strongly, that he had known her, and resented less the time he was being forced to give to her progenitor.

Assembling his thoughts into order, he told Cornfeld about the manner of Chattie's death, and what they had found out so far. Only once did Cornfeld turn his face away and pass his hand over his eyes; otherwise he listened with an almost audible whirring of the mental motor. At the end of his exposition, Slider asked the usual question, 'Do you know of anyone who might have wanted to hurt your daughter?'

'No,' he said at once. 'I think she was universally beloved, or as nearly so as anyone ever is. She was a happy, friendly, funny girl, warm-hearted and generous. Too generous, at times. I can't think what grudge anyone could have against her. If it had been the work of a madman, a serial killer, it would have made more sense to me.'

'I'm sorry to ask this, but what about your business – rivals and so on? Could somebody have been striking at you through her?'

He shook his head slowly. 'Naturally, I've been thinking about that.' The idea seemed to agitate him and he became less coherent than before. 'But there's nothing – I can't imagine – there's no situation I can think of where this would make sense. And surely, if I were the real target, something would have been said – some note, phone call, threat? Why kill her to get at me, and then not be sure I knew? No, it doesn't make sense.' He passed his hand over his eyes again, and said, 'It is something I have thought about over the years. Not in terms of business rivalry, but simply money – kidnap, you know. But I am not so fabulously wealthy, and I've never indulged any of the children, or encouraged them to think they had expectations. I don't believe the younger two even spoke about being my daughters. The parting with their respective mothers,' he added, 'was not friendly. I suppose by now you know things like that?'

Slider nodded.

'Marriage has always been a toll on my time and energy, which I could ill spare from my business,' Cornfeld said. 'Thank God for modern times! Now I don't need to marry them. I can have all the female company I want without repercussions.'

At that moment they were interrupted by another female entering the room – a very different proposition, this one, from Kylie. She was a very elderly lady, with such a look of frailty Slider almost expected the light to shine through her: thin as a rail, a halo of silver-white hair like spindrift around her face, cheekbones you could cut yourself on. She was dressed in an expensive knitted two-piece of brown jersey over a white lace blouse, high-collared with a cameo brooch at the throat, and glossy brown court shoes. But despite the thinness and age, her eyes were bright and her gait steady.

Cornfeld rose at the sight of her. 'Inspector Slider, my mother,' he said.

Mrs Cornfeld inclined her head. 'Inspector.' And then, to her son, 'I came to tell you there is a telephone call from Brussels. Kylie is speaking on the other line.'

'Ah!' Cornfeld turned to Slider. 'I must take this. It's a very important call. I'm sorry.'

'I will entertain the inspector while you are away,' said Mrs Cornfeld. There was no German accent after all these years, only a certain precision about the consonants and a purity of the vowel sounds that might betray a foreign origin. 'Go, my dear. They are waiting on the line. Hurry.'

Slider thought, with an inward smile, that, like his own father, she had not got used to the cheapness of inter-national calls these days. Cornfeld went out, and Mrs Cornfeld walked across to the table by the window and allowed Slider to pull out a chair for her. When she was seated she waved him graciously to his own chair and said, 'It will be a long call. It is the European drugs regu-latory authority. We have something quite new coming out. When Henry went away to America he was so excited about it, he looked ten years younger. Now, today, he hardly cares. This has been a great blow to him, a great blow. I would not be surprised if he gave up and retired now, though a week ago he was fit to go on fifteen years more. But this has taken the heart out of him. I truly believe Chattie was the only thing he ever loved, apart from his business. He has always been a driven man; she was his one human weakness. It was I who gave her the nickname Chattie, did you know that?'

'No, I didn't.'

'Henry would not tell you that. Men never know any of the important things in life, only the serious ones.' She looked at him intently. 'I suppose *you* must be interested in minutiae, however, because of your job. It must make you a uniquely satisfying companion for a woman. Are you married?'

He disliked personal questions, but it was impossible to snub such a venerable lady. 'I am – engaged.'

'How nice. I hope you will be very happy. Henry has not been fortunate in his wives, but then, did he deserve to be? Now he does not think of marriage again. It is better as it is. You have seen Kylie?' The eyes were cataloguing him. 'I can see your thoughts. But, really, she is a dear creature. Like the hedgehog of legend, she knows one thing. I like her very much, and Henry cannot hurt her because she knows exactly what he wants her for.'

Slider could not think of anything to say, and cleared his throat noncommittally.

'Am I being indiscreet?' she said. 'But surely that must be a boon to you, when people tell you what they ought not.'

Slider would not look at his watch, but there was a clock on a table behind the old lady and he allowed his eyes to slip quickly there and back. Not so quickly, however, that she did not note his change of focus.

'You must be very busy,' she said coolly.

'I'm sorry. I didn't mean to be rude.'

'No, no, I understand. And you should be busy, trying to find out who killed my Chattie,' Mrs Cornfeld said, and a world of grief came into her face. 'At my age, one gets used to losing people. Almost everyone I ever cared for has died. But I don't think I can ever get over her death. Do you have any idea who killed her?'

'Not yet. We have some leads to follow, but nothing definite. We think it must have been someone who knew her.'

'Yes, I suppose that is the case with most murders.'

'Were you and Chattie very close?' Slider asked. Might as well make the best of it, he thought. 'Did you see her often?'

'Oh, yes. I loved her dearly and she was very attentive. Once a week at least. We had wonderful conversations. I truly believe she told me everything. She had an unhappy childhood in many ways, but I hope I was able to be an element of stability in it.'

'Tell me about that,' Slider invited.

She looked at him consideringly. 'I go a little way further back first. So that you understand Henry a little.'

Slider settled in for the long haul.

'First, Henry married Mary. She was the daughter of friends of ours in Enfield, a nice girl but plain, and five years older than him. She was thirty by then and "on the shelf" – that horrid phrase. This was – oh – 1960, I suppose. Girls then still did not have careers. They went to school, sometimes they had a little job for a year or two, and then they got married. So Mary was – what shall I say? – not useless, exactly, but surplus to requirements.'

'And Henry felt sorry for her?'

The almost transparent eyebrows shot up. 'Sorry for her? Certainly not. He was engaged in building up his business – going through a crucial stage, trying to set up the manufacturing side. It meant much work, long hours, many difficulties, living on his nerves. He had no time for feelings, for sentiment.'

'So why did he marry her?'

She looked faintly triumphant at having forced him to ask. 'He wanted a housekeeper. He was too busy to cook his own meals and wash his own clothes, and he was not making enough yet to be able to employ servants. The only practical solution was to marry. Also, if he married, he would be able to have sex when he wanted it, without payment and without risk. Do I shock you? No, of course not. You understand the world. So, Mary was available, with the added advantage that she wouldn't have to be wooed, Henry had no time then for wooing. All he had to do with Mary was to ask.'

'Didn't you try to dissuade him?'

'Good heavens, why should I? Mary was no worse off as his wife than living at home with her parents. She was probably happy at first, relieved not to be a spinster. But Henry was not home much, and when he was, I doubt he ever talked to her. She was thrilled when she found she was to have a baby. Henry was not. He was taken aback. It was nuisance and expense. His home comforts were disrupted. And then it turned out to be a girl, not even a son he could leave his business to.'

'That was Ruth?'

She nodded. 'Poor child, she had the misfortune to be just like her mother – plain and dull. Henry could never be interested in her. And as his business grew, he began to move in different circles. Mary was no longer

198

a suitable wife. He needed a hostess, someone who would sparkle in company. At a reception one day he met Stella, and thought how smart and clever she was. So he left Mary and married Stella.'

'And Ruth?'

'He did what he thought was right by her. He paid for her to go to a very good boarding school. He wanted her to have an education and the possibility of a career. And in case the career didn't work out, he thought it would give her polish so she could make a good marriage. But polish didn't take on her. It only taught her to be resentful, seeing what all the other girls had. For a dull girl, she has a surprising capacity for anger – the slow, smouldering sort. Henry left Mary enough to live on, and a perfectly good house, but Ruth saw the way he lived with Stella, the parties, the important guests, the clothes – Stella was always a clothes horse – and thought she and her mother had been hard done-by.'

'Did Ruth make a good marriage?'

'Better than she might have expected. Henry practically arranged it. A young man called David Cockerell who was up and coming in the company. Ruth thought he was the bee's knees – handsome, charming, bound to get ahead. Besides, she'd have done anything to get out of working for a living, which she thought degrading. She'd obeyed Henry's wishes and studied chemistry at school, but she hadn't the intellect to go far. She ended up as an assistant in a hospital pharmacy – couldn't pass the exams to become a pharmacist herself. So David came as a saviour to her. As for David, he thought Ruth would be a good handle on Henry's wealth. And Henry thought David might be a right-hand man for him, take the place of a son in the business. But he soon discovered David's limitations. He was handsome and charming, but nothing more – though he's done well enough for himself on charm alone. But he let Henry down very badly. I suppose he felt he wasn't being appreciated enough, or advancing in the company quckly enough, because he went off and joined GCC – the Global Chemical Company – where he could have a big desk and an expense account and a pension fund. Henry was furious and for a time he wouldn't have David in the house, which of course spoiled things as far as Ruth was concerned. I patched things up, for appearances' sake. God knows, at this distance, why we care about such things, but I did, though I don't think I ever made much difference to the way Ruth felt. To be fair to David, I think he really does admire Henry. They get on all right when David visits him on business. But Ruth only sees the difference in their lifestyle and Henry's. And so we come to Stella and Chattie,' she said, with a twinkling look at Slider. 'You see, you needed to know the state of play at the time.'

'You must tell the story in your own way,' Slider said neutrally.

'Be sure that I shall,' said Mrs Cornfeld. 'You are a good listener, young man, and I don't have many opportunities to talk without interruption.'

Slider had not been called 'young man' for a long time. 'Please continue,' he said.

'Well, Henry and Stella were happy at first, being very social together and having dinner parties and being important. Stella was happy when her picture was in the paper, and she thought all the new contacts she was making would advance her writing career. Have you read any of her books?'

'I flicked through one,' Slider said, not sure whether he was supposed to admire them or not.

Not, it turned out. 'That is all you need to do. All

200

surface and no substance – nothing of worth in them from beginning to end – like Stella herself. But they might have gone on being more or less contented if she had not found herself pregnant. Unlike Mary she was furious. She had never wanted children and it threatened to ruin her carefully planned life as well as her figure. Henry was moderately pleased, however. He thought he was fond of Stella, and he was more secure now, better off, so he didn't fear the financial consequences. He thought he might quite like to have a son to boast about to his business acquaintances. But of course it was another girl.' She sighed, but it was a sigh of pleasure this time.

'Chattie was a pure delight from the beginning. She seemed born to smile. Henry adored her, and almost forgot he had wanted a boy, especially when she turned out clever as well as pretty. She had a very masculine grasp of intellectual things – and quite a way with machinery too. He taught her to drive when she was only twelve, on a disused arifield. Anyway, things were very happy for a while. But the business was going through another expansion, and Henry was away from home a lot, and Stella didn't like being left behind. She was from an old county family, and she felt she had lifted Henry up to a better social class by marrying him. When she didn't get her share of the parties and being in the papers, she resented it. The last straw was when he went to a reception at 10 Downing Street as a Giant of Industry, or some such nonsense, and she found out that he could have taken her with him. Shortly after that she found that he was having an affair with his secretary and she threw him out; but that was only the excuse. It was Downing Street that did it. She never forgave him for that.'

'And he married the secretary?' Slider said, to get her along.

'Susan Hatter, her name was. He wouldn't have married her, except that she got herself pregnant and he was in the news quite a lot and he thought it would look bad. It was another daughter, of course – Jasmine. Oh, that girl!' She gave an exasperated roll of the eyes. 'He bought a house in High Wycombe and installed Susan there with the child, and by now he could afford staff so it didn't matter that Susan hadn't the first idea of how to run a house or host a dinner party.'

'And what about Stella and Chattie?'

'Stella kept the house – the houses Henry leaves scattered behind him! – and Henry paid her alimony, of course, so she ought to have been all right. But all right was not what Stella thought she was owed. She would have kept Chattie away from Henry if she could, to punish him, but he had visitation rights. And of course he was rich, and Stella loved money. So Chattie went to visit. She loved her father obsessively, and was heartbroken when he left. She'd have been about five or six. He had her to stay whenever he could, and visited her at school, and they were always the best of friends. He arranged her education, and as she grew up she became very like a son to him, with her cleverness and her masculine mind and her determination. They were very close.

'Well, the marriage to Susan was always a mistake and it didn't last, though he was away so much it didn't seem necessary for him to divorce her at once. When the time came, he took charge of everything. Susan didn't want a divorce at all, but she was a very weak-minded woman and easy to bamboozle. He sold the High Wycombe house and bought this one, and moved Susan and Jassy into a small house in St Albans, gave them enough to live on, and forgot about them.'

'And Chattie?'

'Oh, he went on seeing Chattie. When he bought this place I came to live here to run it for him, so it was easier, because we could pretend to Stella she was coming to see me rather than him. Once Chattie was eighteen she could do as she liked, though she pretended for her mother's sake she never saw Henry. Poor Stella fell on very hard times. She had always been fond of gambling, and after Henry went, she turned to it for solace, I suppose. She was a hard drinker, too, and she liked the high life, and expensive clothes, and when she found she couldn't afford it all, she had to attach herself to really very unsatisfactory men to make up the difference. In the end, Henry refused to pay her debts, so she had to sell the house and move into a horrid little box and pay them off. It's another thing she'll never forgive him for.'

'She told me she had always paid her own way in life,' Slider said.

Mrs Cornfeld chuckled. 'Yes, Stella would like everyone to believe she owed Henry nothing and he owed her everything. She's a woman who lives in a world of make-believe. What she wants to be true, is true.'

It explained a lot, Slider thought. 'And Chattie went to music college,' he said.

'Yes. That was a disappointment to Henry. He liked music but couldn't see it as a career. But when she finished college she decided she didn't have the talent to go to the top, and she didn't want to be second-rate – which was an attitude he *could* understand. So she did an apprenticeship in the commercial side of the music business, thinking she might be an agent. And then she had the idea for her own business.'

'Was he pleased about that?'

'Oh, yes, on the whole. He didn't see that it would ever amount to anything, but he thought the experience could be applied to some other field later on. He assumed she would not be content with a small business, though I think he may have misunderstood her there. Chattie cared about other things than money and success. Anyway, he encouraged her and believed in her. He was only sorry she wouldn't let him give her money to set it up. She said, "You built up your business from nothing, and so will I." I pointed out to her that in fact I had given Henry two thousand pounds to set up; and she said that he had given her a hundred thousand when she was seventeen, so it came to the same thing.'

'Did he never give anything to the other girls?'

'He gave Ruth a lump sum when she was married. And he gave Jassy money all the time. She's a bad lot, that one. The Lord knows how she gets through so much money. Apart from the car she ruined, I don't know what she spends it on. Drugs, I suppose. After the car, Henry told her no more, enough is enough. But I suspect that cheques get posted off every week or so, after one of her impassioned phone calls. The difference from Chattie could not be greater. She invested the money Henry gave her in property and shares and turned it to good account. He was so proud of her.'

'You mentioned drugs?'

The face became stern. 'Jassy turned up here one day very much the worse for wear. I was shocked. Young people getting drunk now and then is natural, I can understand it, but not this other thing. Thank God Henry wasn't here. I sent her away, told her never to come here like that again.'

'Does Chattie take drugs?'

'No,' Mrs Cornfeld said, shocked. 'She hates them as I do. She hardly even drinks, just wine with meals. She says she hates the feeling of not being in control.'

'We found a large quantity of cocaine in her house. More than one person would take. The sort of quantity a person might have if they were supplying it to others.'

She stared a moment, and then laughed. 'Oh, ludicrous! You thought my Chattie was a drug dealer? No, no, put it out of your head. If there were drugs in the house, it was Jassy or one of her friends who put them there. I know Chattie's mind on the subject. You see . . .' she hesitated, and then went on in a low voice '. . . You see, there was a time when Stella was smoking marijuana. I think she may have tried other things as well. It was when Chattie was, oh, fourteen or fifteen, and away at school. Sometimes she came home and found Stella the worse for wear, and it shocked her very much. But she never told Henry, so please do not you, either. Poor child, so many secrets she had to keep, holding her tongue when her mother abused her father, keeping her mother's exploits from her father. Chattie knew about the other men, you see, Stella's other men, and if Henry had found out, he could have stopped her alimony. So Chattie was caught between two hard places, poor child.'

'Did Chattie never want to get married?'

'It was the thing that made me most sad, that Chattie would never fall in love. I suppose, after her mother's behaviour, and seeing how her father had gone on, one wife after another and then all the women he has had since, she felt that marriage could never work. And she loved Henry so much. When Henry asked her if there was anyone, she always said, "Only you, Papa." She couldn't take young men seriously. They had to match up to her father and, of course, they never did. I think,' she added, with a world of sadness, 'she would have found someone one day, when she was older, maybe when Henry was dead. But now she never will have the chance. She was a girl with so much love to give, and no-one to give it to – not the right one, anyway. Maybe that's why she was so patient with Jassy. Too much love to keep to herself.' She turned her head away towards the garden, where birds were making cheerful noises in the bushes and trees. 'Who could kill such a girl? So much life, so much love, all gone. Snuffed out. It shouldn't be so easy.'

Slider left a small silence for her, and then said, 'There is one more thing I'd like to ask you, if you don't think it an impertinence.'

She sighed, and turned her head back, ready to do her duty. 'What is it? About money, I suppose?'

'Why do you think that?' Slider was intrigued.

'It is the obvious thing. Henry is a rich man. You want to know how he leaves his estate.'

'Well, yes. In case there might be a motive that way for removing Chattie.'

'Removing! Such a word! But Henry has never told anyone, not even me, who he means to leave things to. He says he doesn't want anyone to have reason to wish him dead.'

'Has he made a will?'

'I don't know. If he has, he keeps it secret.' She gave a snort of laughter. 'Perhaps all will go to Kylie.'

'I believe Cornfeld Chemicals is a public company. Do any of the family hold shares?'

'Oh, yes. When we floated, I and each of the children had ten per cent, and Henry kept twenty. That way the family kept overall control. That was before David left to join GCC, of course, otherwise he would never have given Ruth any. When that happened Henry bought another share, just to be on the safe side. Of course, I always let Henry exercise my vote. He knows what's best for the company. I would not think of anything else – unless it was a matter of principle, but since I brought him up, I should hope his principles are the same as mine.'

Slider smiled at her little joke, and at that moment the willowy Kylie reappeared, with a professional smile that was at war with her attempt to convey heartfelt regret.

'Oh, Inspector Slider, Mr Cornfeld is very sorry, but his call has taken longer than he expected, and now he has to go straight out to a meeting. He sends his regrets, and his thanks for your time in coming here.'

'Oh, really, how deplorable not to come himself. And I was just saying that I brought him up!' Mrs Cornfeld said lightly. 'Kylie dear, you must tell him when you see him that I am very cross with him. Now, Inspector, won't you stay for lunch with me, to make your long journey worth while?'

Slider was already on his feet. 'You are most kind, ma'am, but I really have to get back.'

'Yes, of course, what was I thinking? I have enjoyed so much talking to you that I was forgetting.' The light went out of her face and her eyes became bleak. 'You have important work to do. You must find who did this thing. I only wish that there was still capital punishment in this country. I am not a vindictive person, but I would like whoever did this to Chattie to die,' she said seriously. 'I would like very much that they should die.'

11

Barn to be Wild

'Exciting things have happened here while you've been away,' Atherton said, sitting catty-corner to Slider at the canteen table, his legs elegantly crossed, his fingers drumming lightly on the table top in a way that told Slider it was not random but the accompaniment to some music going on inside his head. Joanna did it too, on the dashboard, when he was driving. Atherton was one of those rare individuals blessed with perfect pitch. Joanna said perfect pitch was when you got the viola into the skip first throw.

Slider had given Atherton the précis of Mrs Cornfeld's exposition. Now he was forking in a hasty shepherd's pie and beans (no chips, no gravy) by way of lunch, and wondering what he would have got at the Cornfeld house. A delicate consommé, *foie gras*, roast duck and green peas? He sighed and swallowed. The meat in the shepherd's pie tasted of gravy browning and the potato had that slippery, embarrassed texture of instant mash that knows it isn't fooling anybody.

'Exciting things always happen in places where I'm not,' he said. 'I ought to hire myself out to bored people not to be anywhere near them.'

'I'm sure there's a flaw in your reasoning somewhere,' Atherton said. 'And how can you eat that stuff?'

'I've seen the alternatives. Get on with it – what happened?'

'Oh, right. A bloke came in, who not only had seen Running Man but had seen his face. Name of Alan Maltby. He was just about to turn in at the park gates on his way to the station – his usual route going to work – when Running Man shot out and he had to sidestep sharply not to get knocked down.'

'Why hasn't he come forward before?' Slider asked.

'I asked him that. He seemed quite indignant. Said he works on weekdays. Now it's Saturday he's come straight in to tell us and all he gets is abuse. He's got a good mind to turn round and walk right out again – which is about all the good mind he's got in my opinion.'

'You didn't tell him that?'

'What do you take me for? Anyway, for a brief but telling moment, Running Man's face is inches from his and he gets a really good goosy at the famous phizog – so good that he's prepared to sit in on a photofit.'

'Blimey, our luck has changed,' Slider said, pushing his plate aside. 'Shove my pud over, will you?'

'You're not serious?'

'What? I like jelly and blancmange.'

'You've got retarded tastebuds, that's your trouble. Anyway, you might not say that when you've heard all.'

'Might not say what?'

'That our luck has changed.'

'Oh, Nora, what now?'

'Well, friend Maltby had a good look at chummy's face, as I said. Said he was sweating, eyes popping, every sign of agitation, so we all got terribly excited. And he was holding a mobile phone, the same sort of Motorola as Chattie's, though Maltby didn't see any blood or a knife. But when he had okayed the photofit, we compared it with the photo of Darren we got from Jassy, and there was no resemblance. And when we showed the photo of Darren to Maltby, he was confident it wasn't the same man.'

'You had to tell me that. You had to spoil my afters. And it was pink blancmange as well – my favourite.'

'Look, it needn't be as bad as that. After all, Darren could still be the murderer. It could still have been him who was standing talking to Chattie. We don't know that that person and Running Man were the same.'

'I've been telling everyone that from the beginning,' Slider said, frustrated. 'Now you *want* them to be different?'

Atherton waved a large hand blandly. 'Or they could be the same and Running Man is the murderer and Darren's a red herring.'

'No luck with finding Darren yet, I suppose?'

'No. We're trawling around his usual haunts and associates, but no-one's admitting seeing him. Manchester actually sent someone round to the mate's house, Dave O'Brien—'

'That was quick.'

'But Darren wasn't there and they think he hasn't been. They believed O'Brien, and I suppose they ought to know,' Atherton said, with deep scepticism. 'They've promised to keep an eye out for him, but they didn't think we had a good enough case against him for them to make it a priority.'

'Nor have we,' Slider said. 'Oh, well, at least we've got a photofit of Running Man to work with. Get that circulated, will you, and I'll see what Porson says about banging it on the telly tonight.'

Hart appeared, weaving between the tables towards them.

210

'Boss, they've just rung from the house. The man's turned up to open the safe.'

'At last,' Atherton said. 'I'm sure we could have got someone out of the Scrubs to blow it for us quicker than this.'

'You live in a dream world,' Slider told him, getting to his feet. His lunch slipped about in his stomach, threatening to cause trouble.

'You're going over there?' Atherton asked.

'I wouldn't miss it. You coming?'

'Can I come, boss?' Hart asked.

'It's not a party. Go and get on with your work,' Slider said sternly, but she only grinned and shrugged.

'Wurf a try,' she said.

'You just can't intimidate some people,' Slider complained to Atherton as all three headed for the exit.

'When you've worked on the DAFT squad for three months, there's nuffing more they can do to you,' Hart chirped.

The man from Acme Safes ('How traditional,' Atherton had murmured) was waiting for them at the house, and fidgeting about being kept waiting.

'You kept us waiting long enough,' Atherton reminded him.

'There's a lot of calls on my time,' he said, with imperishable dignity. He was a small, rounded sort of man in very clean overalls with ACME over the pocket and very shiny shoes on his rather small feet, on which he teetered a little like a teacher at a 1950s prep school. His hair was so neat and shiny it looked painted on. 'By rights I shouldn't be here now,' he said sternly. 'This is supposed to be my Saturday off.'

'We are rather a special case,' Atherton said, though

Slider had flung him a look that said leave it alone.

'Oh, I know, I know,' Acme man sneered. 'You people think you're so important just because you go around investigating murders. Well, other people have important jobs too, you know. Opening safes is skilled work.'

Slider gave Atherton a slight kick to stop him retorting, and said, 'Please carry on, Mr – er.'

'Pickett's my name,' said the Acme man, and Slider could see now why he had need of so much dignity. PC Gallon, who was in attendance, made a snorting noise, but when they all looked at him his face was rigid and his eyes fixed on the distance, though his cheeks looked suspiciously hollow.

The safe contained one or two pieces of jewellery, chequebooks, birth certificate, house deeds and other documents, and a great quantity of share certificates. Atherton sat down at her desk with them and leafed through, his eyebrows going up and his lips pursed in a soundless whistle.

'This is quite a portfolio,' he said. 'I think we know now where she got the money from to support her lifestyle. I wonder if she did her own buying and selling or if she had an adviser?'

'Her grandmother says she was given a hundred thousand when she was seventeen, which she invested in shares and property,' Slider said.

'But only eighty thousand went on the flat she bought, according to Jasper.'

'So she presumably put twenty thousand into shares. Quite a lump sum.'

'Yes, and at the beginning of the biggest bull run in history. With the right transactions she could have increased that ten or twentyfold. I'd like to take these back to the office and work out what sort of an income they would generate. Enough to keep a girl in goodies, anyway.'

'A lot of them must be Cornfeld Chemicals,' Slider said. 'Granny said she was given ten per cent at the float.'

'Yes. I don't know what the shares are at at the moment. I'll have a look when we get back. I've got a paper in my desk.'

'Might be an idea to find out if there are any other big shareholders, outside the family,' Slider said.

Atherton gave him a sharp look. 'You think it could have been to do with money, or the business?'

'I don't know. But it never hurts to have a few facts to hand.' He was examining the rest of the papers. 'Ah,' he said, 'now here's something.' He held it up, a long, narrow envelope of the sort that only lawyers ever used.

'Her will?' Atherton said eagerly.

'It ain't chopped liver,' said Slider. 'Now we might find out who had a motive for her death.'

'Only if they knew about it,' Atherton said. 'It's usually you warning me not to jump to conclusions.' He waited impatiently while Slider read down the pages. 'Well?'

'Interesting,' said Slider. 'If her nearest and dearest did know about this, there'd have been a few who'd be pissed off with her, but whether it would make grounds for murder is debatable. She's left everything to charity.'

'Really?'

'A very conventional mixture of medical, educational, third world and environmental,' Slider said. 'Well, well. Unless our basic charities have got more ruthless chief execs than hitherto realised, I think we can rule out inheritance as a motive.'

Atherton's afternoon with the newspaper and a calculator resulted in the conclusion that her portfolio was worth about three quarters of a million, and averaging out the yields would have brought her an income of around thirty thousand a year. Not a fortune, but, as he said, enough as a supplementary income to buy nice clothes and theatre tickets and restaurant meals, and to support her generosity to various charities.

His call to Companies House brought further interesting news. 'I thought you said that Daddy Cornfeld gave each of the children ten per cent?' he said to Slider.

'That's what Granny said.'

'Jassy's name doesn't appear on the list.'

'Really? I suppose she must have sold them.'

'If she did, it must have been a while ago. I checked back five years.'

'I'm not surprised, though. Given what we know about her, I suspect Jassy would have sold anything that wasn't nailed down.'

'Yes,' said Atherton, 'and it's probably another cause of her resentment. She must be kicking herself. The Cornfeld shares have gone up a lot in recent years, and the current yield is five point two per cent. That's partly because of the recent slight downturn in share price, which has affected the whole sector – the whole market, in fact – but the yield–price ratio has always been good.'

'What did Horace say, Winnie?'

'The share has always produced good income as well as capital growth,' Atherton translated.

'It sounded better the other way. Well, I don't know that it gets us any further forward. Chattie certainly had money to leave, but if anyone knew about her will, they'd know they weren't going to get anything.'

'And if they didn't know – who might think they would benefit?'

'Jassy?' Slider hazarded.

'Possibly,' Atherton said. 'She'd been given enough by Chattie over the years. She might think big sis would have cut her in for something and she's selfish enough to be cold-hearted about it. And that brings us back to Darren.'

'The Absent.'

'And now that we know Running Man was not Darren,' Atherton said, 'either Darren was Standing Man and he did it, or Running Man did it – or,' he added, suddenly thinking of something, 'Running Man was a friend of Darren's and they were in it together.'

'Or,' Slider reminded him, 'it was someone else.'

'Yes, there is that,' Atherton said, subsiding. 'Well, I don't know. What now?'

'We carry on, what else?'

'I think I should keep an eye on Toby,' Atherton said. 'The band's playing tonight at the Jazz Barn, and I think I ought to go along and maybe have a word with him.'

Slider eyed him. 'Oh, you think that, do you? It wouldn't have anything to do with Marion Whatsername, would it?'

'Of course she'll be there,' Atherton said. 'Naturally. But I go there for the music anyway. It's a pretty hot scene.'

'Hot scene?' Slider wrinkled his nose at the expression.

'Hot scene – cool jazz,' said Atherton.

'And where is the Jazz Barn?'

'Newport Pagnell.'

Slider suppressed a smile. 'Oh, well, I definitely think you should go, then.'

'There's nothing wrong with Newport Pagnell,' Atherton said loftily. 'I'll have you know it's where they make Aston Martins.'

215

'Did I say anything?'

'I know the look.'

'I hope you don't expect me to write this up as overtime for you? You'll have to conduct your love life on your own time, like everybody else.'

'All right.' Atherton sighed. 'But if I have a pop at Toby afterwards?'

'Be my guest. But the answer's still no.'

'Oh, this is nice,' Slider said. He and Joanna were lying in bed spoonwise, her back to his front, his arms round her and his hands cupped over her bulge.

'Mmm,' she agreed.

'What a pity you have to go to work.'

'There are two ways to look at that.'

'I know, lots of nice money. But it is Sunday.'

'Extra fee, Sunday,' she said. She squirmed a little, to get even more comfortable, her buttocks nudging into his groin, which began to have thoughts of its own.

'You're enjoying working, aren't you?' he said.

'God, yes! It's wonderful to be back, after all those weeks with nothing. Though I suppose I'd better get used to idleness. There's no guarantee anything else is going to come in after this.'

'Mm. But if it does – well – you'll have to stop eventually, won't you?'

'When the baby comes, of course,' she said; and then, 'Is that what you're worried about? That I shan't be able to live without music when junior makes his appearance?'

'I didn't say I was worried about anything.'

'I know all your tones of voice by now.'

'It's pitiful to be so transparent.'

'No, it's not,' she said, kissing his arm, all she could reach of him. 'It's endearing.'

'I don't want to be endearing. I want to be exciting, challenging, dynamic and overwhelmingly sexy.'

She revolved eelishly in his arms to present her frontside to his body and her lips to his. 'Well, you're already all of those, honeybun.'

'*Honeybun?*'

'Tiger, then. God, it's hard work getting you to make love to me!'

'Oh, is that what? You only had to ask.'

A satisfactory period later, when she was lying damply in his arms with her head on his chest, he said, 'But seriously.'

'Seriously?'

'About this working business.'

'There's no deflecting you, is there?' she murmured. 'Seriously – I am fully cognised of the demands of the situation. And I'm pretty sure holding our child in my arms is going to come out tops over cradling a fiddle under my chin.'

'Only "pretty sure"?'

'I've never done it before, so how can I be certain? But the one is life and the other's a job. So be at peace, my love.'

'What a pity you've got to go to work,' he said, kissing the top of her head.

Ten minutes later she got up, and an hour after that she was gone. Slider felt at a loss. He had said he wasn't coming in, there being nothing on that someone else couldn't do, but he wasn't used to having time off. He finished the main section of the paper, and then telephoned Atherton.

The phone rang for a long time, and then a voice answered, 'Hello?' – a mumbling, sleepy and definitely female voice.

'Hello,' he said kindly. 'I was expecting a baritone, not a soprano.'

'Wha'?' the voice said, then coughed, and said, 'Did you want Jim? I think he's in the shower.'

'He'll be an hour or two, then,' Slider said. Atherton took washing very seriously. 'Can you ask him to ring—?'

'Hello?' It was Atherton's voice this time. He had evidently snatched the receiver from her.

'I see you didn't waste your efforts last night,' said Slider.

'Wait a minute, I'll take it in the kitchen.' The line went dead, and a moment later opened again. 'I forgot to tell her not to answer the phone. I wasn't expecting any calls. Why aren't you asleep at this time of a Sunday?'

'It's a quarter past nine,' Slider observed.

'Civilised people don't get up until eleven on Sunday.'

'Well, that accounts for it, then. Was that Marion Davies?'

'Yes,' said Atherton. He didn't say, 'if it's any of your business,' but the implication was there in his voice.

'So how did it go last night? The interview with Toby,' he added, when the silence warned him he had been misunderstood.

'We all went for a drink at the Sow and Pigs after the concert, but I managed to get him on his own for a bit, and put some pressure on him. I think there may be something there after all. He was definitely edgy, and a bit more leverage could get him to cough. If only we had any direct evidence. You can't lever someone effectively if all you've got is no alibi and a motive. I wonder if we could justify having a look round his flat? If we could find a hoodie or a bloodstain or a knife—'

'Yes, *if*. I don't think we could get a warrant on that

218

basis. See if he'll let you have a voluntary look round to begin with, and we'll go from there.'

'Okay. You're not coming in?'

'I'm going to have a day off if it kills me.'

'Pity Joanna's working.'

'Oddly enough, that sentiment had occurred to me.'

It was another lovely day. He improved the shining hour by telephoning his ex-wife Irene, had a shy chat with his son Matthew, mostly about football, and a long listen to his daughter Kate, who wanted to have her navel pierced – 'no' was about the only word he managed to get in – and after doing the washing up, balancing his chequebook, contemplating without enthusiasm washing some shirts and wondering fruitlessly about Atherton and Marion Davies, he finally settled down on a chair in the garden with the paper and a gin and tonic. Atavistic memories of a more leisured life asserted themselves, and he was beginning to relax and think that being alone for once in his life was rather pleasant, when the phone rang. It was Atherton, and he sounded disturbed, which was in itself disturbing.

'I think you'd better come,' he said. 'We've got trouble.'

When Marion had departed to her own devices, Atherton had decided that it would be a shame to let up the pressure on Toby Harkness now, when he had got him nicely simmering, and went round to his flat to have a little chat with him and see how amenable he was to having his place searched.

His ringing on the entryphone bell was not answered, but he could see Toby's car in its parking slot, so he rang and rang again. Probably dead drunk last night, Atherton thought, and still unconscious. Eventually there were footsteps on the stairs and a tall young woman appeared, dressed in leggings and a vast T-shirt and with her hair sleep-tangled. She mouthed something at Atherton from behind the glass doors and he held up his warrant card. At that, she fumbled the door open, and said, 'Is it Toby you want? I could hear you buzzing him. I live next door.'

'His car's here, so I assumed he was in,' said Atherton.

She looked at him from under her fringe. 'Only,' she said breathlessly, 'I think he might be in trouble. He's been a bit strange these last few days. I mean, usually he's ever so friendly but when I've seen him recently he's just brushed past me as if he didn't see me. And then last night—'

'Just a minute – your name?'

'It's Manda – Amanda Hare.'

'All right. What happened last night?'

'Oh, well, you see he came in late and I think he had someone with him because I could hear him talking. Those walls are ever so thin. And then he put music on, really loud, which is not like him, and I was trying to get to sleep so I banged on the wall, but it didn't stop. And then I heard something like furniture being moved about, sort of thumps and bangs, and a lot of shouting. And then the music stopped and it all went quiet. And since then, nothing.'

'Do you think he went out again?'

'I didn't hear him go out. Anyway, like you said, his car's there.'

'True,' said Atherton, and then something occurred to him. Toby hadn't had his car with him last night. Jasper had given him a lift both ways. He stepped back, looked up and down the road and spotted Jasper's Toyota MR2 parked a few yards away. Something cold walked up his spine. He had said that Toby was edgy last night, but perhaps 'on the edge' was a better description. What if Atherton's pressure had pushed him over?

'I think I'd better go up and see if he's all right. I don't suppose you have the key to his flat, by any chance?'

'No, sorry,' Manda said. 'Are you going to break the door in?' she asked hopefully.

Was he? Atherton pondered briefly the fact that he hadn't any justification for it, except the copper's instinct that was making the hair on the back of his neck stand up like someone in a crowd trying to see the parade. 'We'll see,' he said.

She followed him up the stairs. 'Stay behind me,' he said as he thumped on the door and called out. There was no response. 'Did you hear anything?' he asked sharply, turning to Miss Hare, who was wide-eyed with excitement.

'I don't know.'

'I thought I heard someone call out for help. Very faintly. There, again. Did you hear that?'

'Yeah, yeah, I think so,' she said, her eyes so wide now he was afraid they'd fall out of their sockets. Thank God for suggestible females, he thought, took a step back and kicked.

The Yale gave at the third blow – or, rather, the wood around the Yale, being of the normal standard used in modern building, crumbled like Madeira cake. The door swung back and hit the wall behind with a bang that made Manda Hare squeak. Atherton, adrenaline in place, took in the scene with a single scorching glance. The same mess and muddle, the same smell of frowst, tobacco and stale food, but with something else added that made his stomach sink and his adrenaline rise yet further – the smell of blood.

Toby was sitting on an upright chair at the far end of the living-room, naked to the waist, his hands dangling between his knees. The curtains were drawn and his pale face and body gleamed weirdly in the dimness. On the carpet in front of him was sprawled a male figure Atherton had no difficulty in identifying as Jasper, by the clothes he had been wearing last night. He was immobile, and there was a dark stain underneath and around him on the fawn carpet. The blood had evidently soaked through and had run along underneath because it had appeared in an interesting flow across the exposed parquet inside the door, dark, in the gloom, like oil.

Manda made a muffled sound. She had managed to cram the fingers of both her hands into her mouth and her eyes were fixed and bulging dangerously. Atherton moved slightly to block her view of the scene.

'Don't look,' he said. He spoke firmly but calmly. 'Go back to your own flat and dial 999. Tell them to send police and an ambulance. Go and do it now, there's a good girl. Go on. Hurry.'

She went, dragging her eyes away like pulling off a plaster. Atherton turned to the scene again. His nerves were singing with tension and played again and again the image of Toby leaping into sudden action, springing from the chair and across the room like a pale cat. Where was the knife? There must be a knife. It was so hard to see in this twilight. Yes, there it was, on the floor, half under Toby's chair where he must have dropped it. Could he get to it before Toby did? Make a rush for it, or try creeping up? The muscles of his stomach seemed to twitch with their own memory of harm. God, he hated knives!

The cautious approach, he decided, trying to breathe evenly. He spoke quietly and began to edge forward. 'Toby. Toby. Are you all right? Toby, can you hear me?'

There was no response. He reached into his pocket carefully for his handkerchief as he advanced. Though Toby's muscles seemed genuinely relaxed, a madman could feign this state of shock and leap into lethal action at the last moment. Atherton's adrenaline peaked as he stooped and secured the knife with the handkerchief, expecting the sudden violent movement; and then subsided with a rush as Toby remained motionless. Sweat was standing cold all down his back, and his legs were trembling. He drew a few deep breaths and backed off a step or two.

The next most important thing, having got the knife, was to check the status of the victim. Jasper was face down and limp, and Atherton thought he was probably dead, but on squatting (keeping his eyes on Toby) and applying two fingers to his neck, he found a faint pulse. Thank God for that! If he survived, he could be a witness to what happened, because Toby didn't look as if he would ever speak again.

But just as he thought that, Toby spoke. 'He defiled her,' he said. The sound of his voice coming out of that still figure made Atherton jump

'What?' he said involuntarily.

'That's why I killed her. I had to do it. And then I killed him. You can only wash away things like that in blood.'

Atherton almost held his breath. 'You killed her?'

'She's mine now,' Toby said, in that same dead, toneless voice. 'She's mine for ever.' And then he drew a great shuddering sigh, put his head into his hands, his elbows resting on his knees, and began to rock.

Slider met him at the hospital, at the entrance to the emergency unit. As they walked through, Atherton filled him in.

'They're both being looked at now. Toby still seems completely out of it. There was a lot of blood on him and plenty of it round the walls, so I don't know if it was a fight and they're both wounded, or all the blood is from Jasper. God, it's a mess,' he finished bitterly.

'It's not your fault,' Slider said.

'Well, maybe it is. I was pushing Toby last night, and Jasper had already told me he was unstable.'

'He only said all oboe-players are mad. And you know that's an orchestra joke, like viola-players being thick.'

'But I knew he was on the edge. That's the very reason I went after him.'

'Stop beating yourself up. It doesn't help. We've got a job to do and we do it.'

They sat on moulded chairs in the corridor until a young doctor with seventy-two-hour-week eyes came out to them.

'Right,' he said. 'Jasper Stalybrass is stable for the moment, but he's lost an awful lot of blood. There is some internal bleeding into the chest cavity and in the abdomen so we have to send him up to theatre to see what's going on.'

'Will he survive?' Slider asked.

'It depends on what we find up in theatre. From observations here I think a lung may have been punctured, but that's survivable. It depends where the rest of the bleeding is coming from. However, he's young and healthy so he ought to have a pretty good chance. He'll be very weak for some time, and there's always a danger of complications, but as long as we don't find anything too bad up there, he should make a full recovery.'

It was as near as you could get to an opinion from a doctor, these days. They were all so scared of being sued. 'What about Toby Harkness?'

'Ah, yes. Well, there was so much blood on him we thought he'd been wounded too, but when we cleaned him up we didn't find any injuries. The blood must have been all the other man's. So he's not physically hurt, but he's very disturbed. We had to sedate him in order to examine him, and we've got him under restraints at the moment, pending a psych consult.'

'Can I talk to either of them?'

'Well . . .' he hesitated '. . . I know it's important for you to know what happened. You can talk to Jasper Stalybrass very briefly before he goes up. Two minutes only. And you can see Toby Harkness, but I don't think you'll get much out of him. As I said, he's very disturbed – and, frankly, we don't want him made more so, so if he becomes agitated I'll have to ask you to leave.'

'I understand. I'll be careful. By the way – about the clothes?'

'Yes, it's all right, I know the drill. They're all being bagged and listed and you can take them away whenever you like.'

Jasper Stalybrass was lying on a trolley under a sheet than which he was not less white. His eyes were closed, the lids delicately blue, his skin with the transparent, waxy look of extreme blood loss. He barely seemed to be breathing. Slider warned Atherton back with a look, and said, 'Mr Stalybrass. Are you awake?'

He hardly expected a response, but the eyes slowly opened.

'I'm Detective Inspector Slider,' he said. 'Can you tell me what happened?'

Stalybrass tried to speak, licked his lips feebly, and then said, in a breath of a voice, 'I drove him home. Went in. For a drink. Sat down. He went – kitchen. Came back – stabbed me. In the back.'

He stopped, panting shallowly. Slider nodded, holding his eyes. 'I understand. Take your time.'

He resumed. 'He was raving. I tried – struggled – get the knife.'

He closed his eyes and Slider waited. The nurse, who had been standing back, came to his elbow. 'We've got to get him up to theatre,' she said quietly.

'I know. Just one minute more.'

Stalybrass opened his eyes again. 'He kept – stabbing me. Raving – about Chattie. Me and Chattie.'

He stopped again. The nurse said, 'Sir—'

Stalybrass held Slider's gaze with feeble urgency. 'There's more,' he said.

'Go on, I'm listening,' Slider said. 'What is it?'

'He said – said *he killed her*,' Stalybrass finished. 'Because of her and me.'

Slider nodded calmly. 'I understand. Well, don't worry about it now. We've got him safe. You just concentrate on getting well. We'll talk to you again later, when you've been taken care of.'

He stood back and Stalybrass was wheeled out. Slider met Atherton's eyes. 'So,' he said, 'your plan last night worked.'

'At a price,' said Atherton.

12

Absit, O Men

They saw Toby briefly in the emergency room where he was being guarded by a uniformed policeman – it was Ridpath, from Hammersmith, who looked at them curiously, but said only, 'He hasn't said anything, sir.' Toby was lying on the examination bed, his eyes closed, the restraint straps round his body. A nurse was also in attendance.

'Can we talk to him?' Slider asked her.

'You can try,' the nurse said, 'but I don't know if he'll answer. Try not to agitate him.'

Slider approached the bedside. 'Toby, can you hear me?'

The eyes opened. They looked unfocused, wandered a little like those of a new baby. Slider could feel Atherton's tension like heat radiation behind him. 'Toby, I'm Detective Inspector Slider. Can you tell me what happened?' No answer. 'Back at your flat. Jasper came in with you—'

A shudder ran visibly through Toby Harkness, through his body and up his face.

'Did you do something to him?'

'I couldn't bear it,' Toby said, and his face drew into an exaggerated mask of tragedy. '*He'd had her.* Defiled her.

I had to kill them both. Better that way.' And he began to cry, weak, tearless sobs, more like the whimpering of a puppy than any expression of humanity.

'Toby,' Slider said, ever more gently, 'are you saying that you killed Chattie?'

Toby moaned, and began rolling his head back and forth slowly on the flat pillow. The moans grew rhythmic, and louder.

The nurse touched Slider's arm. 'I think you'd better leave him alone now.'

Slider obeyed, seeing that he wouldn't get any more sense out of him anyway. He paused on the way out to say to Ridpath, 'Stay with him and write down anything he says. I'll arrange for you to be relieved by one of ours.'

'Thank you, sir.'

Outside in the corridor, Atherton said, 'Well, I don't think that would stand up as a confession, but he did say it to me *and* to Jasper. Assuming Jasper survives. But you heard Jasper say it. I wish he'd confessed to me in front of the neighbour, but I'd already sent her to call an ambulance, damnit.'

'Settle down,' Slider said. 'Toby's not going anywhere, not for a long time. And if he confessed to killing Chattie in a fit of remorse, he'll probably say it again, many times over.'

Atherton looked at him carefully. 'There's something in your tone of voice. A confession and a second attempted killing, what more do you want? With a similar sort of knife. It was a kitchen knife, which is what Doc Cameron thought Chattie was attacked with. A Sabatier, if you want to be picky. Might even be the same one. God, if we could get a bit of Chattie's DNA from it—'

'If,' said Slider. 'Don't get too excited. Confession is as confession does.'

'What does that mean?'

'Toby said he killed Chattie because Jasper had defiled her. Presumably in a rush of blood to the head. But he attacks Jasper *three days afterwards*.'

'That's not much of an objection,' said Atherton. 'He's a coward. Stabbing a female's one thing, stabbing a man taller than him's another. Took him time to get his bottle up.'

'False confessions aren't unknown,' Slider said. 'Especially from young men in emotional turmoil.'

'Going after Jasper had to wait until he was drunk enough and the opportunity presented itself.'

'It could be his way to make himself important to Chattie in retrospect, so to speak, when he knows he wasn't important to her in life.'

'If it was a false confession, then it was my fault for pushing him so hard last night,' Atherton said.

'Oh, we're back there, are we? All right, if you want to punish yourself, think of all the extra work it's going to cause us.'

'What does that matter, if it gets us our man?'

'Attaboy. You can go back to the scene and direct the search of the flat, see if you can find anything useful to back up your theory.'

'Ugh. The thought of searching that flat. You haven't seen it.'

'You've described it to me. I thought you wanted to be punished?' said Slider.

There was no point in thinking about a day off now. Slider went back to his office to begin the procedures surrounding this new event, the back of his mind occupied with wondering whether Atherton was culpable in any way, whether he could have known how close to snapping Toby Harkness was. But you have to trust your men. By all accounts Toby had been sinking further into the mire all on his own. Did he kill Chattie? Motive, no alibi, and now a confession. Slider would have been happier about it if she really had been stabbed to death. There was something about that drugging and fake stabbing that didn't fit with jealous rage. But, then, jealousy often did smoulder rather than blaze, sickening its host: the slow, brooding burn. And someone had said that Toby wouldn't hurt a fly. So maybe the only way he could kill her was to subdue her first. If the prime purpose in his mind was that she had to die, he might have plotted how reasonably he could do it. But where did he get the drug from? If he only knew about Chattie and Jasper on Tuesday night and killed her on Wednesday morning, he would either have had to have the drug to hand anyway (in which case, why?) or have put in an amazingly hard night's work between eight p.m. Tuesday and eight a.m. Wednesday.

Of course, they couldn't be sure he hadn't known about Chattie and Jasper for much longer. He said he had only found out that night, but he could have been lying. A lot would depend on what he said when they were finally able to interview him properly. And what, if anything, Atherton found at the flat. The time lapse between Chattie's murder and the search reduced the chance there would be anything to find; but blood was a persistent little chap, and, as the poet had it, would out.

The phone rang. He picked it up, and a female voice that sounded faintly familiar said, 'Oh. I wanted to speak to Jim. Jim Atherton. Is he there?'

'I'm afraid not. I'm Detective Inspector Slider. Can I help you?'

'Oh. Um. I'm not sure. You're his boss, aren't you?'

He had placed the voice now. A mental association with tousled hair and gummy eyes went with it. 'It's Marion Davies, isn't it?'

'Yes, that's right.' A pause, and then the words in a rush: 'I heard about Toby and Jasper. God, it's terrible! I mean, what's going on? What's happening to us?'

He assumed these were rhetorical questions. 'How did you hear about it?'

'Manda – Toby's next door neighbour – phoned and told me. I tried ringing the hospital but they wouldn't tell me anything. Is Jasper – is he— ?'

'He's not dead. The last I heard he was going up to surgery but there's a good chance he'll recover.'

'Oh, thank God for that. But did Toby really stab him? I mean – Toby! I always thought he was such a, you know, weakling. A mummy's boy. I can't imagine him stabbing anyone. And why Jasper? I always thought they were friends.'

'I'm sorry,' Slider said, 'I can't go into it with you at this stage.'

'I suppose not,' she said, and she sounded despondent. 'But it's so terrible. I can't see how the band can carry on after this. It's like a sort of curse on us, ever since Chattie . . .' Her voice trailed off.

'I'm sorry,' Slider said, who had a mass of work to do. 'But is there anything I can help you with?'

'Yeah,' said Marion, seeming to pull herself together. 'Would you give Jim a message from me? Would you tell him – well, not to come round any more?'

'Isn't that something you ought to tell him yourself?' Slider said, suppressing impatience.

'Oh, I know, but I really can't. I don't want to talk to him. I mean, he's a nice bloke and everything, and I don't want to hurt him, but, well, he's been sort of hanging around me, wanting to see me every night, and honestly, I can't. I mean, it's not going anywhere and, well, we haven't, like, got anything in common, have we? Apart from him looking into Chattie's murder and, well, that's not something you can build on. To be frank, it kind of gives me the willies now, especially with what's just happened to Tobe and Jasper. I mean, I know it's not Jim's fault, but he brings it all back to me, like he's a sort of jinx or something – well, I don't mean that, really, but seeing him again now would be, like, so *ghoulish*.'

Slider had made several efforts to stem this flow, and only his early indoctrination with good manners prevented him from putting the phone down on her. Now as she drew breath he got in quickly with, 'I really don't feel I can—'

But she was off again, and this time, though what she said was short, it was devastating. 'Apart from anything else, well, he's just too *old* for me.'

Slider reeled, but managed to pounce on the pause before it got away again. 'I'm sorry, but I really can't undertake to pass on personal messages of that sort. You'll have to talk to him yourself. Ring him at home tonight.'

She sighed. 'If I leave it that long he'll be round my flat again. Can't you just tell him I don't want to see him?'

'I'm sorry,' Slider said firmly. 'I have to go now, there's a call on the other line.' And he put the phone down. Now his head was occupied with unwelcome bits of knowledge like the worst sort of squatter. He didn't want to be on the inside of Atherton's love life, and it was a damn cheek of the girl to think he was going to be her go-between, especially as she was in bed with Atherton this very morning, and presumably they hadn't only been discussing counterpoint or fingering techniques. It was one thing to think she must be a flighty little madam to bed someone on such short acquaintance and then chuck him out equally quickly, but quite another to be forced to wonder whether Atherton had been making a fool of himself and whether it might have clouded his judgement about Harkness. And, oh dear, oh dear, too old? Atherton, the boy wonder, the serial bird-puller, the Peter Pan of sexual frolic, who was forced to fight the totty off to get a moment's peace – Atherton being knocked back because he was *too old*?

He hadn't got time to think about this, damnit! He shook his head violently, stood up, stretched until his muscles cracked, then sat down again and resumed his work.

The day wasn't over yet.

'It's a bit of a mess,' Porson said, quite mildly, considering.

Nicholls, ringing up to Slider from downstairs to say Porson had arrived, had reported the old boy seemed almost glad to be called in. 'Sundays are hell when you're on your own.' Perhaps that accounted for the mildness.

'Now we've got another two sets of doting parents breathing down our heels – and Harkness senior turns out to be a junior minister in the Arts Department, whatever it's called these days, whose wife is pally with the PM's wife. The last thing we need at this junction is political ramplications.'

Did he mean complications, ramifications or implications, Slider wondered. In any case, he certainly didn't want any of them. 'No, sir,' he said.

'He's busting everybody's guts wanting to know what his son's accused of and when he can move him to a private facility.'

'It looks as though Jasper Stalybrass is going to recover,' Slider offered his own small comfort.

'Yes, that brings it down to attempted murder, or GBH, assault with a deadly, depending on how hard Stalybrass or his parents want to press it. I wouldn't be surprised to learn *his* dad's best friends with the Attorney General and plays golf with the Lord Chief Justice. But what about this other thing? This confession?'

'We haven't been able to interview him yet. He's still under sedation and considered too unstable.'

'Yes, and his father's agitating to get a solicitor in there, which'll shove another spanner in the spokes,' Porson said gloomily. 'If we ask him anything it'll be "questioning while non compost mental", and the case'll collapse and we'll be hung up to dry. What did you think of it – the confession?' he asked abruptly.

'It makes sense, and Harkness hasn't got an alibi for the time in question, and he's certainly been behaving in a disturbed manner since the death.'

'But?' Porson asked sharply.

'It's just a gut feeling, sir. It doesn't feel right to me. But I have to admit I've nothing to base it on. On the other hand, we've no direct evidence against Harkness, apart from the confession.'

Porson sighed. 'Yes, and they won't go on that alone, these days. Mind you, if the lad's gone doo-lally, he'll probably be locked up anyway and that'll be that, though it won't help our clear-up figures. Well, keep an open mind. See if we can find anything to back it up. The knife gone off to the lab?'

'Yes, sir, and we've fast-tracked it. That should mean a result by tomorrow afternoon.'

'Right. Meanwhile, what to tell the press? I suppose we'll have to let them have the assault. It's public knowledge anyway by now. But given it was a stabbing they'll add two and two and make him the Park Killer and Daddy Harkness will never believe we didn't tell them he was. Then the Shah will really hit the Spam. We'll have top brass all over us and writs flying about like doodlebugs.'

'I can't see that we can help that, sir. Even if we don't tell them anything, there's bound to be speculation, given his relationship with the girl.'

'Yes, and the next thing I'll have Daddy Cornfeld round my neck as well. We'll just have to cover our arses and hope for the best. So we'll say Harkness is being questioned about the assault on Stalybrass, which they can't argue about, and so far we have no reason to believe – no, we can't say that, in case it goes the other way – no evidence that there is any connection with the Cornfeld murder.'

'Do you want me to do it?' Slider asked unwillingly.

'No,' Porson said, with a deeper sigh. 'I'd better do it myself. Having an MP involved raises the stakes. No offence, Slider, but we don't want them saying we sent the monkey when it should have been the organ grinder.'

Now how, Slider thought, as he trudged back to his office, could he think I'd take offence at that?

Slider got off the phone from the umpteenth trying conversation to find Hart hovering in the doorway.

'They called from downstairs, guv. There's a woman come in about the murder, something to do with Running Man. She was asking for you, but d'you want me to do it? I know you're busy.'

'No, I'll go,' said Slider. 'I don't suppose it's important, but anything to get away from this desk for ten minutes.'

'I bet you haven't had any lunch,' she said, eyeing him like a mother hen about to start clucking.

'You can't bet with me about that. I know the answer,' he said, heading for the door.

She was not so easily put off. 'D'you want me to get you something? A roll or something?'

He tried to ignore her and hurry on, but his stomach caught his foot by the scruff, so to speak, and he halted involuntarily. 'On a Sunday?' he said.

'There's that place under the railway arch the cabbies go to. That's always open.' She saw she had him by the hearts and minds, and added seductively, 'I could get you a sausage sarnie or a bacon sarnie.'

He practically salivated. 'Well, it's a thought. Do you mind?'

'Course not. Whatjer fancy?'

'Sausage, then.'

'Wiv tomato sauce?'

He capitulated. 'Of course. Two rounds.' Might as well go for broke. 'And make sure it's butter, not marge.'

'Yeah, I remember.'

'Thanks, Hart.'

She beamed as if he were doing her the favour, not vice versa.

Downstairs in the front shop there was only one person waiting: a young West Indian woman, in her late twenties, he calculated, with a plump, pretty face, plaited hair and a figure that strained at every seam of her tight Lycra mini-skirted dress. With bosoms and buttocks like those, he thought, she'd take a long time to pass you in the street. Her legs were bare and her knobbly feet, thrust into high-heeled strappy sandals, evidently resented it and were trying to escape through the gaps. She wore hoop earrings, bangles, and a multitude of gold chains round her neck, and she clutched on her lap an enormous shoulder-bag (why did young women these days all go around with these near-haversacks for handbags? What the heck did they need to carry with them all the time?) He noted with interest that she was sweating, despite its being reasonably cool in there, and was extremely nervous. Her brow was furrowed, her hands massaged nervously at her bag strap, she chewed at her lower lip.

When she saw Slider she did not wait for him to speak but got immediately to her feet, and said, 'Are you the man round here?'

'I'm Detective Inspector Slider. I'm in charge of the investigation. What can I do for you?'

'I got to talk to you,' she said. 'It's important.' She had a Shepherd's Bush accent with nothing of the West Indies in it other than the husky timbre. Born and bred, he concluded.

'What's your name?' he asked.

'Lizzie Proctor,' she said. Her eyes flitted about anxiously. 'Look, I can't talk here. You got somewhere we can go?'

Slider conducted her into the nearest interview room, and was interested to note that she looked about her as one to whom this was a new experience. 'It's a bit primitive, I'm afraid, but it's private,' he said. 'Would you like to sit down, Miss Proctor?'

She seemed pleased with the formality, and brushed her skirt under her as she sat down with a little fluttery movement of femininity.

'Now, what's it about?'

She paused a moment, evidently on the brink of some leap, and then said, 'It's about me bruvver. Look, you've not got to let on it was me told you. He'd just about kill me if he knew I was here. But I begged him and begged him to come. I said to him, if Dad was alive he'd make you. I mean, he's just making it worse, innee, making you

237

all look for him? But he never done nuffing,' she said, looking up urgently into Slider's face. 'He's a good boy, and I swear my Bible oaf he never done nuffing.'

'What's your brother's name?' Slider asked, hoping for enlightenment.

She hesitated. 'Look, I'll be straight wiv you. I mean, it don't matter me telling you because you'll find out anyway. He's got a record. That's partly why he won't come in. He's shit scared of the p'lice. But it's only little stuff, and he's going straight now. He's tried so hard, he really has, and me and Mum's so proud of him, and then this has to 'appen and spoil it all.' Her eyes filled with tears.

Slider tried again, patiently. 'Just tell me what he's done.'

'That's the 'ole fing, he's never done nuffing!' she cried, as if he were being wilfully stupid. 'He just happened to be there, that's all, just by chance, and he doesn't know nuffing about it. He's never even knew this woman, this Chattie Cornfield. You got to believe me.'

'Your brother was in the park at the time of the murder?' Slider said.

'That's what I've been *telling* you,' she said, wiping a tear from her eye with a forefinger. 'You been putting it out on the news about wanting to talk to him, and that was bad enough, but at least it could have been anybody. But then you put out a picture of him last night and that did it. He's gone into hiding now and he says he daren't go back to work on Monday, and if he loses that job I just know he'll turn bad. He thinks nobody trusts him.'

Running Man, Slider thought. So that was what it was all about. 'All right,' he said soothingly, 'just tell me from the beginning about — what's his name?'

'Dennis,' she said automatically, without noticing she'd given it away. 'You see, he was always a bit of a live wire, and when Dad died he sort of got into bad company at school, the way kids do, and he done a bit of shoplifting. We didn't know at first, Mum and me, but I was a bit worried because he was out all hours, and he didn't talk to me like he did before. I mean, he was a cheeky little devil, but him and me got on all right, you know what I mean? He told me things.'

She seemed to want a reply at this point so he said, 'Yes, I understand.'

'But now he was never home, and when he came in he'd just rush past wivout saying anyfing and go straight to his room an' shut the door. So I started to get worried. I mean, he was never a bad kid, but they dare each other and egg each other on, kids do. That's all it was to him, just a dare. But he got caught and warned, I don't know how many times, and the first we heard about it was when he was arrested proper, and that one went to court. Well, he only got a suspended, but that was enough. It broke me mum's heart. She always fought the world of Denny. She told him, she said if Dad was alive he'd beat you black and blue for it. And Denny promised he'd never do it again.'

'And did he?'

'He never shoplifted – I don't fink he did, anyway – but when he left school he got in wiv another lot and started smoking weed. Well, 'cause he was hanging about on the streets he got stopped and searched a few times by the – by policemen,' she corrected politely, 'and one time he had some weed on him and he got done for possession. When Mum found out about that one she burst into tears, and Denny was really frit then. He'd never seen Mum cry before. So then he said he really would turn over a new leaf if we'd help him. Well, me and Mum helped him get this job, and he really has been trying hard, only it's not easy. His mates are always on at him. But I said, Den, you stick to it. You're doin' great, and never mind what them bastards say, excuse my French. And then *this* has to 'appen!' She cried again, what seemed like tears of frustration, and fumbled in her bag for a tissue. 'He's been in such a state since you started asking on the telly for him, and I told him to come in and clear it up, but he wouldn't. He said you coppers have got it in for him, and that you hate blacks, and that you'd fit him up for something. I said, don't be daft, but he said you'd never believe him 'cause he was black an' he's got a record. And the longer he left it, the worse it was. And then that picture was on the telly last night, and now he finks everyone finks he's a murderer!'

'So what was he doing in the park?' Slider asked, trying to keep a grip on the thread.

'He was going to work, of course. He always goes frough the park, it's the quickest way. And the only reason he was running was he didn't wanner be late. I mean, he's a good boy, and just because he's running you make him out to be a murderer and ruin his life.'

'We only ever wanted him to come forward so that we could eliminate him from our enquiries,' Slider said soothingly.

'Well, that's what I *told* him, but he doesn't trust coppers. But it's all right now, in't it? You do believe me?

Slider believed her. Everything about her was patently honest, and she was trying to do her best by her brother. It did not, of course, mean that the brother had not lied to her.

'We'll have to check into it, just as a matter of routine. If you'd like to write down for me your name, address and telephone number, the time Dennis left home that morning, and the name and address of Dennis's employer, so that we can check with them what time he arrived that morning—'

'If you go asking his boss stuff about him like that,' she said bitterly, 'he'll lose his job and that'll be that.'

'I promise you we'll make it very clear we're just eliminating everyone who was in the park.'

She only shook her head slowly, her face profoundly troubled. 'Denny'll never forgive me. He'll find out I told you and he'll fink I shopped him.'

'I won't say anything about your visit here.' She was still unconvinced, and he didn't want to threaten her, so he said, 'You were right about one thing – the longer it went on the worse it looked for your brother. Now, if we can get this cleared up quickly everything can go back to normal. If you say he didn't know Chattie Cornfeld—'

'He *didn't*. I swear to you. He told me so and I know when he's lying and he wasn't lying then. He doesn't know any white birds.'

'Right. So all we have to do is check with his employer what time he got in that morning, and we're done.' He pushed the pad and pen at her temptingly. 'Sooner the better. Let's get it over with, eh?'

She sighed, reached for the pen, and began to write in an unpractised, loopy hand.

'Where is your brother now?' he asked.

'He's staying with a mate. He's scared to come home.'

'This friend he's staying with, it isn't Darren, is it, by any chance?' Slider said casually.

'No, it's Baz, I fink. Baz King,' she said, still writing. 'That's his best mate. I dunno where he lives, though. I fink it's somewhere in Acton but I dunno the address.'

'But he does know Darren? Darren Barnes?'

'I dunno,' she said. 'I don't fink so. I never heard him

talk about him. Who is he?' He showed her the photo of Darren. She looked carefully and shook her head. 'No, I don't know him. Why ju wanna know?' Then her eyes widened. 'He's somfing to do wiv the murder, innee? That's why you're asking did Denny know him. You still fink Denny's in on it.' Tears rose again to her eyes and her lips quivered with anger and self-pity. 'You said you believed me!'

'I do believe you,' Slider said. 'You must understand that we have to check everything and everyone, even those people we believe with all our hearts. It's just our job.'

The use of the word 'hearts' got to her, but she was not quite ready to give up her pique. 'Denny's a good boy. I wish I'd never come,' she said, in hurt tones.

'I'm very grateful to you that you did,' Slider said. 'The more quickly we can get these little things cleared up, the sooner we can get after the real villains.'

She sniffed back her tears and seemed mollified. When she had finished writing, Slider asked her if she had a photograph of Dennis, and she produced one from a little folder in her bag. 'Can I keep this, for the time being? I'll let you have it back in a day or two.'

He ushered her out with full old-fashioned gallantry. 'Thank you again,' he said at the door. 'Mind the steps, now. Good afternoon.'

He watched her descent to the street with amazement, hardly able to believe she could walk on those tiny spike heels. It was something like seeing a huge water-filled balloon balance on a golf tee. As he turned to go back in, Hart arrived at the foot of the steps with a paper bag in her hand, and watched the departing form with raised eyebrows.

'Blimey,' she said. 'I bet she'd make a cracking tight-rope walker.'

'Is that my sandwich?' Slider said, practically snatching it from her. He was so hungry he could have eaten straight through the paper. 'How much do I owe you?'

'You can pay next time,' she said airily.

He gave her a stern look. That sort of thing had to be nipped in the bud. 'How much do I owe you?'

'Oh, well, you can't blame me for trying,' she said. 'You're not married yet.' And she changed the subject quickly. 'Who was that lady I saw you with just now? That was the one who came in, was it?'

'It was Running Man's sister, and she says he didn't do it, but was too scared to come forward because he doesn't trust the police and he's got a minor record.'

'Just the way you predicted, guv,' she said. 'So, do we cross him off?'

'Not just yet,' he said. 'He's run away and gone into hiding with a friend, which might be excessive caution for a man who really hasn't done anything. And we don't know that he didn't know Darren. He used to smoke weed and got done once for possession, according to his sister, so he may have bought something from Darren at some point. We'll have to look into him a bit more closely before we eliminate him.' He passed over the sheet of paper. 'Check with his employer what time he arrived that morning, then we can work out if he had time to do anything between leaving home and getting to work other than getting there. Run his record, see if the sister's told us everything. See if you can find any connection between him and Darren. Show this photo to Mrs Hammick, see if she remembers him ever coming to the house. And try to find this Baz King he's supposed to be staying with, lives somewhere in Acton.'

'D'you want me to go round and roust him out when I've found it?'

'Definitely not. I don't want him flushed out and running. We'll leave him be until we find out whether there's anything in it.'

They reached his door and she eyed the greasy bag in his hand. 'Want me to get you a tea to go with that?'

He hesitated long enough to feel he ought to discourage her from mothering him, but the thought of tea won by a couple of lengths.

'Yes, thanks,' he said. He heard his phone begin to ring and with an inward sigh pushed into his office to answer it, wondering if he'd get to the sausage sandwiches before they grew hair.

13

The Silence of the Labs

Baz King also turned out to have a record – for possession, carrying an offensive weapon, shoplifting and a couple of TDAs – which made it easy to find out where he lived. So if it became necessary to collar Dennis Proctor they could be there in a jiffy. But it seemed less and less likely they would need to. The owner of the small printing shop on the corner of Becklow and Askew Roads, a Mr Badcock, who had the honour to be his employer, was not best pleased at first at being tracked down and bothered on a Sunday afternoon when there was an international on telly; but when he heard that the cause was eliminating Dennis from enquiries he straightened his shoulders and got down to it. Dennis was a good boy, he said, and he was glad to be helping him overcome his unfortunate beginnings. He firmly believed that Dennis had been influenced by a bad lot and that underneath he had the right instincts, inculcated by his late father (who had been a friend of Mr Badcock – they had worked together at one time at the Gillette works on the Great West Road) and upheld by his mother and sister who were decent people.

What time had Dennis arrived at work on Wednesday? Wednesday, Wednesday – oh, yes, wait a minute, that was the morning he was late. He'd been late once or twice before, and Mr Badcock had warned him very sternly about it, so that lad had really been making an effort. How late? Well, not by much. He'd arrived out of breath from running at five past, and Mr Badcock had forgiven him because he'd obviously run so hard to make it on time he couldn't speak for about five minutes. Mr Badcock had advised him to start out earlier in the morning, and set him to work. How did he seem that day? Oh, just his usual self: cheery – a bit cheeky, if you want to know, but that was youngsters, these days, and there was no harm in him. You'd to keep after them, none of them had an idea of hard work, but Dennis was no worse than the rest in that department, a bit better if truth be told because he was interested in the business. Had quite a little flair for setting things out – artistic, you might say. How had he been the rest of the week? Well, now you come to mention it, he was a bit absent-minded on Saturday, and he dashed off on the dot of five without tidying up, which Mr Badcock was going to have to talk to him about. But Wednesday, no, Wednesday he'd been fine.

'You've been a big help,' Hart said. 'There's just one more question – can you remember what he was wearing on Wednesday when he came in?'

'Well,' Mr Badcock said slowly as he thought, 'well, now – no, I can't say that I do. They all dress much the same, don't they, these lads, baggy pants and a T-shirt? Always clean, though, Dennis, I'll say that for him. Spotless, really. I expect that's his mother's influence. But I can't remember exactly what he had on, what colour or anything. I wouldn't really notice, you see.'

'Do you remember if he was wearing a grey top with a hood?'

'No, no, I'm sorry, I can't say. I believe he *has* worn one of those but whether it was Wednesday or any other day . . .' He laughed. 'I have a job to remember what I've got on without looking. Typical man, my wife says.'

'So you see, boss,' Hart said to Slider later, 'it looks as though Dennis may not be our man. For one thing, if he'd just done a murder he wouldn't've been likely to seem just like his usual cheery cheeky self – unless he's a total psychopath. Also, his mum says he left home for work on Wednesday at ten to eight. They live in the flats in Rivercourt Road and that's a mile as the crow flies, a bit more allowing for corners and that. Well, you can do a mile in fifteen minutes at a brisk walk, and he was running like the clappers, but even so—'

'Yes,' said Slider. 'Hardly time to fit in a murder on the way.'

'Unless they're all lying.'

'There's always that,' Slider said. 'But it seems more likely that he dawdled along with his head in the clouds and then realised he was going to be late and dashed the last bit.'

'Yeah,' said Hart. 'Also, McLaren took the photo of him round Mrs Hammick's, and she said she's never seen him. It don't prove Chattie didn't know him, but it's all on the same side. It's a pity the old geezer can't remember what he was wearing. If he didn't have the hoodie on, that'd mean he'd chucked it on the way, which would be a help, but—' She shrugged.

'Hmm,' said Slider, pondering. 'Well, I think we'd better go round to his friend's house and get him, ask him a few questions, get a voluntary buccal swab from him for elimination purposes, and then take him home. Tell him he's not wanted for anything and there's nothing to worry about. Make sure he believes that. If he really is innocent, I don't want to lose him his job and ruin his life; and if we find evidence against him later, it'll be easier to pick him up if he's going about his normal daily business than if he's on the run.'

'Yeah, boss, good one. Who's going?'

'I think you should do it – you look nice and unthreatening. Take McLaren with you in case he panics, but tell him to keep his mouth shut. We want to reassure this boy, not frighten him.'

'Understood. I'll make 'im stand behind me,' Hart said.

She turned to go, and in the doorway passed Atherton, just coming in. He answered her enquiring look with a shake of the head. To Slider he amplified, 'Nothing. No blood anywhere except in the living-room where he attacked Jasper. No traces on any clothes or shoes, nothing down the drains. No evidence at all. It's all on the knife, now. If they don't find Chattie's DNA on that, we've got nothing but his confession. Haven't you heard from them yet?'

'They only had it this morning, give them a chance.'

'God, is it still Sunday? It feels like a week. That flat! I don't know why we have prisons. Making someone live in that would be punishment enough.'

'To you, not to them,' Slider said. He could see Atherton was depressed. He said, 'The hospital phoned to say that Stalybrass is making progress. There were some internal injuries but nothing life-threatening, though they had to remove his spleen. They've got him patched up and it's a matter of rest and recuperation now.'

'That's not all it's a matter of,' Atherton said. 'Remember, I've been there.'

'Well, yes, of course, I know that—'

'But do you? You seem to be taking it very lightly.'

'I'm just trying to reassure you. Don't bite my head off.'

Atherton sighed and rubbed the back of his neck. 'Yes, sorry. I'm tired, that's all. I think I'll knock off now, if you've nothing else urgent for me.'

Slider nodded, and then, unwillingly – but compassion demanded he didn't let his friend walk into it unprepared, 'Have you got plans for tonight?'

Atherton clearly didn't know how to take it. Was he going to be quizzed on his love-life or was it an invitation to supper? 'Um, well, nothing definite.'

'Were you meaning to see Marion Davies?' Slider asked, hating it.

'Nothing planned, but I thought I might call in and see if she's all right. It must have been a big shock for her. Why?'

'So she hasn't phoned you?'

'No. What is all this about?'

'Have you checked your answer machine at home?'

'For God's sake!'

Slider gave in. 'She phoned here, asking for you, and when I said you were out she asked me to give you a message. I made it clear I don't do that sort of thing, but if she hasn't phoned you – well, I don't want you to . . .' He hesitated, looking for the right words.

'Make a fool of myself?' Atherton said, with a sour smile. 'What was the message? From your face I gather it was thanks but no thanks.'

'She doesn't want to see you again. I'm sorry,' Slider added awkwardly. 'I didn't want to get in the middle of this.'

'No, it's all right. I'm sorry you got let in for it.' Atherton wandered across the room and sat down on the windowsill. He stared at his feet, still kneading his neck muscles. The angled sunlight picked out the planes of his face and Slider realised the boy wonder was showing signs of wear.

Atherton looked up suddenly, and gave Slider a rueful smile. 'Can I tell you something? I find I'm actually not too disappointed. I think I went a bit off the rails with her.'

Slider nodded, not to indicate agreement, which would have been tactless, though true, but to show he was listening.

'She's a gorgeous girl, and I couldn't resist her. But – God, she's so young! I mean, not so much in years but – her *mind*. She doesn't know *anything*! How can someone educated be so ignorant? History, geography, literature, current events – all closed books to her. Half of what I said to her went straight over her head. And she wasn't even curious; she didn't care, she didn't even seem to *know* how ignorant she was.' He paused. 'And I hated the way she talked. All that "you know" and "sort of" and "like". All we had together was bed.'

'Well, that's always been enough for you in the past,' Slider couldn't help saying.

'Mm,' said Atherton; and then, 'Can I tell you something else?'

'Is it going to hurt?'

'Eh?'

'Don't tell me anything that's got body fluids in it. I'm squeamish.'

Atherton acknowledged the hit with a movement of his hand and a tired smile. 'I'll keep it basic. I was just going to say that even bed wasn't that great. Not that there's anything wrong with her. She is gorgeous. But it just seemed – oh, I don't know – odd. When I woke up in the morning and she was there, it seemed so weird I jumped straight up and went and showered.' The pause was so long that Slider didn't think he was going to finish, though he had guessed what it was. 'It seemed weird because she wasn't Sue,' he said at last.

Slider kept silence. When people tell you their troubles they rarely want your advice, though the human urge is always to give it. And he didn't want to get into the position of agony aunt to Atherton, who was not only his friend but his colleague and subordinate, which complicated things. Atherton was staring at his feet again, his thoughts far away. At last he said, in a low voice, 'I miss her.'

Despite his noble resolve, Slider found he had said, 'Why don't you ring her?' before he could stop himself. He cursed inwardly.

Atherton looked up, the steel coming back into his face. 'She dumped me, if you remember. She was the dump-er, I was the dump-ee. I am not going to extend my rear for a second kicking, thank you.'

There was an awkward silence (and serve him right, Slider chastised himself, for opening his mouth), and then Atherton rose from the windowsill and said, 'I'll get off home, then, if that's all right?'

'Yes, okay. Nothing that can't wait until tomorrow.' He hesitated and then added, 'Do you want to come round later for supper, when Jo gets home?'

'No, thanks all the same. I might have an early night. I'll just clear my desk and be off.'

He went away into the CID room. Slider returned to his work. A short time later he heard the phone ringing through there, but it stopped quite quickly so Slider assumed someone had picked it up. A few minutes more, and Atherton appeared in the doorway. 'News,' he said.

'Good or bad?'

'Depends on your viewpoint. We've found Darren. He didn't get very far from Brixton, home and beauty. He's been staying with a friend in Coldharbour Lane, about five minutes from Ferndale Road. He and the friend went out in the friend's car this morning to get some more supplies, and got stopped for running a red light: the car's rather conspicuous, death's-head paint job, no silencer and no tax disc.'

'Dumb,' said Slider.

'And it gets dumber. The friend pulls over, and as soon as he stops, Darren's out and running for it. Of course, that's a hare to a greyhound as far as the Brixton officers are concerned. Suspicion circuits engage, they go after him and bring him down running. He manages to break loose and lands a punch on one of them. He gets nicked for assaulting a police officer, while the friend meanwhile takes the opportunity and scarpers.'

'A tale for our time.'

'The patrol takes him in, he refuses to give his name and has no ID on him, but the custody officer recognises him from the picture we circulated, takes his tenprint and runs it to confirm. So Darren is now sitting in a cell in Brixton nick waiting for us to go and interview him.'

'Well, that sounds like good news. Where's the bad news bit?'

'I only said it depended on your viewpoint. It's bad news for Darren.'

Slider stood up. 'I'd better get over there. This Sunday never seems to end.'

'I'll come with you,' said Atherton.

'I thought you were going home?'

'When all that awaits me is the cold hearth and the empty chair? I'll take a sweating villain any time.'

★ ★ ★

Darren was sweating. He was also sullen. There was a bump on his forehead, presumably where he had hit the pavement after the rugger tackle that brought him down. But he hadn't the look of a junkie, for which Slider was grateful. There might be more frustrating jobs than having to interview the chemically altered, but he hadn't come across one yet. Darren looked well fed and strong, he didn't twitch, his eyes didn't wander – on the contrary, they glared with full resentment and purpose. He looked like a dangerous animal. His hair hung round his head in matted dreadlocks, and he wore a tuft of beard between his lower lip and his chin. There were rings in his ears and eyebrows and a tattoo of a rearing cobra on one forearm – which must have been a bit of a handicap to a criminal wanting to avoid identification. He bared his teeth when Slider and Atherton came in.

'Darren Barnes?' Slider said. The reply was a profanity. 'Give it up, son,' Slider said. 'We know who you are. We want to ask you some questions. Don't make things worse for yourself.'

'What you want?' he snarled.

'I want to know about you and Chattie Cornfeld,' Slider said. He pushed a packet of cigarettes across the table. 'Smoke?'

Darren took one automatically, and then the action seemed to give him pause. He stared at Slider with sudden fear. In a moment of telepathy, Slider saw that the small piece of kindliness had made him realise this was something grave. It was like the consideration of the executioner. Darren, Slider concluded, was not as thick as he looked.

Darren lit the cigarette and dragged the smoke down. His eyes flitted once to Atherton, who was being a self-effacing stork, standing a little back from the table, but then returned to Slider as if drawn by strings.

'Let me help you along a bit,' Slider said. 'I'd hate you to waste your time denying things that are established beyond any doubt. A large stash of cocaine was found in Chattie's house, hidden there by you. This, as I'm sure you know, is too large an amount for a mere possession charge. This is dealing, and you know what that means.'

'You can't prove it's mine,' Darren said, his voice husky with smoke and fear.

'Don't be stupid, of course we can,' Slider said, in an offhand way.

Darren clenched his fist. 'Don't call me stupid!' he shouted, his eyes glaring.

'On the contrary, I don't think you're stupid at all, Darren,' Slider said calmly. 'You've done some stupid things, but you're not such a fool you think you can get away with them. How well did you know Chattie?'

'She's my bird's sister, that's all.'

'You knew her house well enough to know where to hide the charlie, didn't you?'

'I stayed there wiv Jass sometimes.'

'Were you and Chattie closer than that? Were you selling her stuff?'

'Fuck off.'

'That's no answer. Did you sleep with her, Darren?'

His nostrils flared. 'That snotty slag? I'd sooner shag a dog.'

'She turned you down, did she? That must have made you angry.'

'I never asked her. I told you, I wouldn't touch her wiv a bargepole. I just—'

'You just used her house to hide your stash until the

heat was off,' Slider supplied. 'Well, we know that bit. What I don't understand is why you killed her.'

Sweat jumped out of his pores almost visibly. 'I never! I never! Get outa here, you pig bastard! You ain't gonna stick that on me. I know what you're like, you fucking pigs.'

'But you were seen, Darren. You were seen talking to her in the park that morning, just before she died, right on the spot where we found her body.'

He stared for a moment, and then something quite visibly came to him. His mouth hung open for a moment as he thought something out, and then his hands relaxed. 'It wunt me. I gotta nalibi.'

'An alibi for what?' Slider asked.

'You never saw me in the park that morning. I was in Manchester.'

'Yes, so we were told. Unfortunately, your mate Dave didn't back you up. He said he'd not seen you in weeks. So I'm afraid that won't help you.'

'Not Dave. I wunt wiv Dave.' He looked at them triumphantly. 'I was in the nick.'

'Nice try, Darren, but not very convincing. We asked our colleagues in Manchester about you and they hadn't seen you either.'

'Yeah, well, they din't know it was me.' He grinned. 'I borrowed me mate's credit card. I went to see a bird I know down Moss Side, but we had a row so I dumped her and went and got legless. The coppers picked me up and shoved me in a lockup overnight and let me go in the morning. I told 'em I was Trevor Wishart. Well, he ain't got a record. You ask 'em. That's where I was Tuesd'y night.'

'We will ask them,' Slider warned, 'so you'd better not be wasting our time.'

255

'I never killed her,' he said with growing confidence. 'I hated her, but so what? She was nuffing, just a piece o' snobby trash. I wouldn't waste my time killing her.'

'So why did you run?' Slider said. 'You took off Wednesday night and you've been in hiding since. What was all that about?'

The self-satisfied grin faded and he looked sullen again. He shrugged, and smoked.

'The cocaine in Chattie's house? Was that why you ran?'

He muttered something, avoiding eyes.

'You're not such a big man after all, are you, Darren? You're just a chicken-shit little dealer, and we've been wasting our time on you. Brave enough to hit a woman, and leave her to take the fall, but that's as high as you go, isn't it?'

Darren threw him a quick glance, in which anger gleamed, but he held his tongue.

'Or *was* it just about the cocaine?' Slider said musingly. 'Maybe you wanted Chattie dead. Maybe she'd crossed you. Maybe it was about the money. Was it the money? She was pretty well off, wasn't she? If she was dead, maybe her money would go to her sister, your girlfriend.'

'There wasn't nuffing comin' to Jass from that cow. She told her, she leavin' everfing to charity, the stupid bitch!' He said it with deep contempt not unmingled with wonder that anyone could be so mad.

'Revenge, then. That's a good enough reason to want her dead. But you hadn't got the bottle to do it. So you got someone to do it for you – is that the way it was?'

'If I kill someone I do it myself, man,' Darren snarled. 'I don't need no-one to do my dirty work for me.'

'Oh, really? So what sort of work does Dennis do for you?' He slapped down the photograph of Dennis and shoved it across the table in one movement, his eyes on Darren's face.

But Darren looked at the picture with complete blankness. 'Who this piece o' shit little kid? I don' mix wiv the kiddie league. An' who the fuck is Dennis?'

Slider believed him. The whole Darren edifice had crumbled at a touch. He was not their man. He found space in his mind for relief that it looked as though Chattie was cleared of any suspicion of dealing drugs. But mostly he felt a weary anger that they had had to waste so much time and so many resources in trying to find this graceless, worthless crook. If the Manchester alibi stood, and he believed it would, at least they could still get him for the cocaine and for striking a police officer. That ought to add up to a spell inside for master Darren.

In the car on the way back to Shepherd's Bush he was silent, deep in thought. A phone call from Brixton to Moss Side had confirmed that a Trevor Wishart had been held drunk and incapable overnight on Tuesday, and a photograph of Darren sent through was identified as the same man. So Darren had not killed Chattie, however else he was connected with the case – and Slider was afraid it was turning out to be not at all. So much of police work was like that, following trails that petered out in the sand, unpicking lies that had nothing to do with anything and need never have been told.

But it left them with their work to do all over again. Running Man was a washout – it was impossible to believe now that Dennis Proctor had had anything to do with it, and it was very plain that Darren did not know him. And it seemed equally indisputable that Standing Man was not either of them. So who was he? Was he the murderer or had he merely stopped to ask the time or something? Was he Toby Harkness?

Atherton must have been thinking along similar lines, because he said now, 'So we're left with Toby.'

'If he was Standing Man, where are the clothes?'

'Yes, there weren't any tracksuit or jogging-type clothes in the flat at all. And in fact from what I know of him from his colleagues, he wasn't the exercise type – which is confirmed by his chubby, under-muscled bod.'

'Which is not to say he couldn't have bought them for the purpose,' Slider said, 'and chucked them away afterwards.'

'The knife, the knife,' Atherton muttered. 'It's all on the knife. I hope the lab gets on with it!'

'Does it occur to you,' Slider said, a mile further on, 'that there's no reason to think he'd use the same knife? He could equally have bought a new knife for the purpose, and thrown that away afterwards.'

'You do have these lovely thoughts,' Atherton complained, hunching deeper into his seat.

As they trudged upstairs from the yard, Slider realised he was hungry again. His late lunch seemed a long time ago. 'What about some nosh?' he asked Atherton. 'I don't think I can wait until Joanna gets home. Are you hungry?'

'Starving. I didn't get any lunch.'

'Oh, the glamour of police work! I'm just going to tidy my desk, and then I've had it for the day. How about a ruby? There won't be much else open around here this time of a Sunday.'

'Okay, I'm game.'

They reached the door of the CID room, just as Wendell, one of the loaners from uniform, came off the phone. He turned to Slider, his excitement palpable, and

Slider had a sinking feeling that Sunday had a few surprises left up its sleeve, and the chances of a curry were receding faster than a prime minister's hairline.

'What is it, lad?' he asked. 'Break it to me gently. I'm in a fragile state.'

'Someone's found some clothes, sir. Looks as if it could be what we're looking for.'

Monday was rubbish collection day in Ashchurch Grove, a side-street that cut off a bend of Askew Road, running between it and Goldhawk Road. The residents were accustomed to putting out their rubbish on Sunday night, because the bin men came early in the morning. Not that they were strictly bin men round there, since they would only pick up black plastic sacks.

Mrs Emerald O'Connor, who was elderly and rather wispy about the chin, nevertheless looked braced by the shock of her discovery rather than upset. Slider supposed that anyone who had lived through the war would be hard to shake; and besides, what old people like her often suffered from most was loneliness and boredom. Here was something new and different in her life, and something, moreover, which made her the centre of attention to all these nice young policemen.

She didn't waste a moment, and was off into a tirade about the garbage situation like an over-eager runner getting off the blocks before the gun fired. 'It's the cats, mostly. You can't keep a cat away from rubbish, not when it's only in a sack. You can see them hanging round on Sunday nights, dozens of 'em, just waiting for people to put the sacks out, and the minute the door's closed they're down there clawing the bags open. And then it's stuff everywhere, bones and packets of this and that and – well, I wouldn't like to say what! And people put their stuff out far too early. Sunday night, it's supposed to be, but I see them bringing it out Sunday morning, even Saturday. Some of 'em put a bag out any old day they like, just to get it out of the house, never mind anyone else's convenience! Oh, no. And there it sits, spreading rubbish about because of the cats, and smelling like the Dear knows what. And all because the bin men won't empty a bin! Have you ever heard the like? What's a bin man for if he won't lift a bin? Too dainty, that's what they are. Afraid of hurting themselves! So we all have to suffer. It'll be rats next, you mark my words. Where I lived before we had them, rats as big as cats, dirty things! And with all the food these restaurants throw out, it's a wonder we haven't all been bitten to death in our beds. It's a crime and a sin to waste food, that's what I've always said, but that one across the road throws out enough food to feed the five thousand every morning. And people passing by see the bags out and they just dump stuff on top. It's nothing but a temptation to bad habits and dirtiness.'

Shorn of the by-way perambulations, what her story amounted to was that she had brought her meagre black sack of rubbish ('Two sacks is supposed to be the maximum, but what some of them bring out – well, you'd think it was the whole contents of the house. It's a wonder they've anything left in there!') down the front garden to leave it in the approved spot by the front gate. As she put it down, she noticed that someone had thrown a plastic carrier-bag of rubbish over her hedge into her garden, something that happened not infrequently. She went to retrieve it and put it with the black sack for the bin men to take the next morning.

'And I picked it up carefully, I can tell you, because you never know what's in them things. Broken glass, needles, anything – and worse. But this one was squashy, like something soft, and one of the cats must have clawed at it because it was ripped down the side, like you see it. And naturally I have a look to see what's in there, and I can see it's something grey, and a dark stain on it. Well, of course, then I remembered that nasty business in the park with the poor girl that was murdered, and I remembered it said in the paper that the police were looking for bloodstained clothing. It must have been the smell of the blood that made the cats go after it. Nasty things, cats. I don't like 'em. Dogs, now – I always had a dog, up until a few years ago when my old Dandy died, and I didn't feel I could cope with starting again with a puppy, not at my age, but I often wish I had, because a dog's company, now, not like a cat, stand-offy creatures they are . . .'

She babbled like a running brook as they examined the immediate area. It was plainly only too easy to walk along with a carrier bag in your hand and simply lob it gently over a suitable fence or hedge when no-one was looking. And dumping rubbish in this way was clearly such a commonplace thing that even had someone seen you they would probably not remark it or remember it. Mrs O'Connor had no idea when the bag had been left there. She hadn't noticed it at all until she brought the rubbish down. It could have been there all week, or it could have been left this morning. She simply couldn't say.

The bag proved to contain a grey hoodie with blood-stains on its front – smears, Slider thought, that looked as though the knife might have been cleaned on it – and a pair of latex surgical gloves, also bloodied.

'Well,' said Slider, with satisfaction, 'we've got him now. He must be an amateur to have thrown out the gloves like this. Even if we couldn't get any DNA off the hoodie, we'd certainly find some cells inside the gloves. Thank heaven for the stupidity of criminals.'

'If it was Toby, I can see him being clever enough to think of wearing gloves and daft enough to dump them like this,' Atherton said. 'Definitely not firing on all cylinders. Well, this is better than a poke in the eye.'

'It's the best,' Slider said, much cheered. 'We get Chattie's DNA out of the bloodstain and the murderer's from the gloves or the clóthing, and we're home and dry.'

'More work for the lab. Can we fast-track this stuff as well?'

'Oh, definitely. If there was anything faster than fast track, I'd even pay for that.'

14

Aisle Altar Hymn

There are many sacrifices made on the altar of Hymen, but it probably doesn't matter as long as one is sure of the discretion of the spouse. And Slider had good reason, in his own opinion, for telling Joanna about Atherton's romantic difficulties. He didn't tell her that Marion Davies had rejected him, only what Atherton had said about finding he was unhappy with someone who wasn't Sue.

They were having boiled eggs for breakfast (folic acid in the yolks, prevents spina bifida, he thought automatically. Childbirth had become much more complicated since his son and daughter by his first marriage had been conceived). Joanna sat across the table from him, the sunshine in her tumbled bronze hair, the shadow of her breasts under her muslin robe both disturbing and comforting. She looked tired, he thought. Three long days of hard work were too much for her in her— He caught himself up, smiling inwardly. Women throughout space and time had worked long and hard in that condition and never thought twice about it. But there was such a fuss made these days about pregnancy that it was hard not to fall in with it. Joanna had more than once complained that the medical profession seemed to regard it as some kind of serious illness.

Joanna sipped her tea as he told her about Atherton, then put down her mug and said, 'I can see you want me to say something about it but I'm not sure what. He's missing Sue. I'm not surprised. They were very good together – better than I think he was ever willing to admit.'

Slider thought that was unfair. 'He did offer to marry her.'

She gave a faint smile. 'The ultimate sacrifice. How generous.'

'You know I don't think that,' he said, hurt.

'But I think you do – subconsciously. It's atavistic. For centuries men have regarded marriage as a trap in which the only beneficiaries are women, and you can't change that mindset in a minute.'

'Well, let's not forget that it was Sue who rejected him, and not vice versa.'

'I know, and I could kick her.'

'I thought you wanted to kick him?'

'Oh, yes, that too,' she said, as if she were not contradicting herself. The workings of a woman's mind were deep and mysterious, he thought. He remembered the old adage, that having female hormones was like drinking twenty-five cans of lager: you can't talk rationally or drive properly.

'He was an ass to take a huff and not pursue her,' Joanna went on. 'I mean, that's traditional too, isn't it, saying no the first time just to test your suitor's resolve? Read Jane Austen – and I know Jim has, so he ought to have recognised it. But, then, she was an idiot not to realise how fragile he is.'

'Fragile?' Slider exploded.

264

'Psychologically. Those serial womanisers always are. Low self-image. It's only by numerical conquest they can reassure themselves of their worth.'

'I think he just likes sex,' Slider suggested mildly.

She grinned. 'Who doesn't? But you must admit he was a bit crazy, the way he had to have anything that moved. But of course,' she went on, buttering more toast, 'Sue's fragile too. She had a rotten relationship with a man who knocked her about, and it's made it hard for her to trust. Jim ought to know *that*.'

'You do make things complicated,' he complained.

'*I* do?'

'You women. Why can't two people just like each other and get on with it?'

'Darling, you're so sweet,' she cooed.

'Well, *we*'re all right.'

'We're exceptional people. Intelligent, well adjusted.' She eyed him. 'What is it you want me to do? Talk to Sue? Talk to Jim?'

'I'm not sure that we ought to get involved. They're both adults, after all.'

'As the bird with the broken wing said, that's a matter of a pinion. But it's always difficult,' she added, 'with people who get to their age without being married. It takes adjustment and compromise for two people to live together, and the older you are, the more set in your ways, and the harder it is to change.'

'Hm,' said Slider.

'If I get a chance, I'll talk to Sue. And Jim, if the opportunity arises.'

'All right, but don't say I told you to. I'm having a hard enough time with this case without hurt feelings intruding.'

'Yes, it was awful about poor Jasper. It's terrible when

it happens to someone you know. Is he going to be all right, do you know?'

'Probably yes. Physically, anyway.'

Joanna knew he was thinking of Atherton, who had been stabbed in the course of an investigation a couple of years back and had taken a long time to recover his nerve – if, indeed, he had recovered it completely even now.

She said, 'A few people last night said they weren't hugely surprised that Toby went off the rails, because he's been in the balance for ages, only surprised about the level of violence. I didn't know him, but Stef Beaton, the clarinettist, said he's known Toby for years, and thought he was barmy. He had a total obsession with a girl some years ago and ended up practically stalking her. Her father had to warn him off in the end.'

'Pity we didn't know that earlier. So people were talking about the incident already last night?'

'Goss gets round the music world like grass through a goose. I was first told about it at lunchtime. It's a terrible shame for Baroque Solid as well, because I can't see how they can survive the loss of two of their members at this stage – not to mention the shock of what happened. If they were established, they could recruit replacements, but it will all be too personal and delicately balanced at the moment. And they were so talented. It's a great loss.'

Slider nodded absently. 'Did the gossip mention that Toby confessed to having killed Chattie Cornfeld?'

'No,' she said. 'Did he really? There was some loose talk that maybe he had done it – you know the way people speculate – but not that he'd confessed. But that's good, isn't it, from your point of view?'

'Yes,' said Slider, 'if he really did do it. He's so disturbed, it's possible it was a false confession.'

'Oh. But why do you think he didn't do it? I mean, passionate jealousy, a woman who'd rejected him, a rival – it makes sense, especially given this near-stalking thing in the past.'

'Well, of course, I didn't know about that. He had no police record.'

'No, the girl's father sorted it out. It does add a bit of flavour to the confession, though, doesn't it?'

'Yes,' said Slider.

'And doesn't trying to kill Jasper tend to prove it?'

'I'm keeping an open mind about it,' Slider said, 'but I can't help feeling if he was going to do it he'd have done them both more or less at the same time, not waited three days before attacking Jasper.'

'Maybe he didn't have an opportunity before.'

'But he saw him every day.'

'In company with the others, presumably. Maybe he couldn't get him alone before.'

'Hmm.'

'You're not convinced.'

'I wish I were. It just doesn't feel quite right to me. But I'd be happy to be convinced, if only we had some evidence apart from motive.'

'And a confession,' she reminded him. 'And if Toby didn't do it, who did?'

'Ah, that's the problem. We've eliminated the other suspects.'

'Maybe you'll find some more.'

'Thanks.'

There wasn't much to do but wait for the lab reports. Hart had managed to persuade Dennis Proctor to go home, and a phone call to the print shop found that he had gone in to work that morning, which was good.

Toby Harkness had been moved to a secure psychiatric bed, and Swilley had been to see him, but was unable to get anything useful from him.

'He's completely out of it, boss,' she said. 'He doesn't respond to questions, just sits rocking himself and staring at nothing. The shrink reckons it could be weeks before he comes back to planet Earth. If he really is off his kadooba,' she added glumly, 'even if we did have enough evidence against him, we'd never get him for it. It'd be diminished responsibility and a nice comfy bed in a psych hospital.'

'What's the news on Jasper?'

'The hospital says he's "comfortable".' She grimaced. 'I love the words they use. I should think that's the last thing he is. But it looks as if he'll recover all right. They said he can be interviewed this afternoon.'

'Right, Hart can do that.'

Swilley was leaving, and turned back to say, 'Toby's parents were flapping round this morning, making threatening noises. I couldn't make out what they thought we were guilty of. I suppose it's just habit with that sort of people, to try and do us down. I mean, there's no doubt he just about filleted poor old Jasper. Literally red-handed. But they're looking for something to complain about, so I thought I'd better warn you.'

Slider spent the time going through all the evidence again, trying to spot an anomaly, panning witness statements for previously unnoticed nuggets, studying the photos taken of the crowd at the scene in the hope of recognising a face.

It was late morning when the lab rang. The labs were all private now, with the police buying their services out of budget, and Tufnell – Tufty – Arceneaux had become head of the biology section under the new regime. Biology basically meant the human body, but the vast majority of their work now was DNA testing, for, with improvement in techniques, DNA could be retrieved from an amazing number of sources and from amazingly small samples. The old blood groups were as dead as phrenology, and it wouldn't be long before fingerprinting went the same way.

Tufty was a huge man with a huge voice, though his new responsibilities and being in the private sector had slightly muted him. It unnerved him to think of the police being 'customers'. But he and Slider were old friends, and in their palmy days, when Slider had been at Central, had enjoyed many a frolic, which always with Tufty involved ingesting large amounts of food and alcohol. Since Tufty had about twice the body mass of Slider, it was always Slider who had come off worse in these encounters.

'Bill! How are you, old fruitbat?' Tufty cried.

'Struggling along. How are you?'

'Fine, fine! Full of juice.'

'How's the family?' Tufty had two sons of whom he was immensely proud.

'Young Rupe's got a new girlfriend. She's a vegetarian,' Tufty mourned.

'Oh, bad luck,' said Slider. 'Are her parents cousins?'

'Wouldn't be surprised. But Triss is doing very well. He's up for a part in what they call a Major Motion Picture. Queer phrase. Always makes me think of an endoscopic examination of the large bowel.'

Slider laughed. 'And how come you never hear about a minor motion picture? Or a minor best-seller, come to that.'

'Beats me. But anyway, Triss reckons he's got a very good chance, and it could be the breakthrough for

269

him. One of those frightfully English pictures, set in the thirties, something about upper-class spies. He's very excited that someone called Ewan McGregor is going to be in it. I thought he was a footballer,' Tufty complained.

'The world is leaving you behind,' Slider sympathised.

'Ah, well, I never go to the flicks these days. Put me in a dark, warm place after a day's work and I either want to sleep or roger something. Or both.'

'But not necessarily in that order.'

'Not sure, these days. Anyway, talking of a day's work—'

'You've got a result on the knife for me?' Slider said hopefully.

'Pulled out all the stops, old bean. I hope you appreciate the fabulous velocity of our efforts, because you're not going to appreciate much else. There's only one sort of DNA on the knife, and it matches the sample you sent us of – let me see, sample number dum-de-dum-de-dum, here it is – Jasper Stalybrass. That's a nice old-fashioned name. I hope he lives to pass it on.'

'It seems probable,' Slider said.

'You sound glum, chum.'

'You've just told me I've got no evidence. Sometimes I wish I'd never left the uniformed division.'

'Ah, life isn't the same without a lump of wood down your trousers,' Tufty sympathised cheerily. 'Never mind, you'll get him some other way, whoever he is.'

'I didn't entirely believe it *was* him.'

'Well, what are you complaining about, then?'

'Just life in general. What about the clothing I sent you, the jacket and the gloves?'

'Plenty of stuff there for me to play with,' Tufty said. 'Blood, of course – presumably the victim's? What's the name – Charlotte Cornfeld? That's who you want us to match it to?'

'Yes, and Freddie sent you a swab and blood sample for that.'

'Yup, all in order. Then there's the wearer of said jacket and gloves, and we've got skin cells, sweat, dandruff and loose hair to work on there. No trouble at all. We'll get a nice profile out of that lot for you.'

'How long?'

'Fast track?'

'Top priority.'

'Thirty-six hours is the absolutely fastest we can do it,' Tufty said. Slider left him a pause, knowing him of old, and after a beat he continued, 'For you, maybe an hour or so sooner.'

'Thanks, Tufty. The ASAPer the better.'

'Well, after all, guv, it doesn't prove it wasn't Toby,' Hart said. 'It just doesn't prove it was.'

'I know that,' said Slider. 'We can only hope the lab tests come back with something. In the mean time, we have to try to find some other evidence.'

'How about we try all the people who've said they were in the park at the time with a photo of Toby?' Swilley suggested.

'The one on the website's a good one,' Hart said. 'We could use that.'

'Fine. And I want someone to follow up on this story that Harkness stalked another girl. Talk to his colleagues and friends, if any.'

'Jim's got the in on that little lot,' said Swilley.

Slider caught Atherton's horrified look and said, 'I think after the Toby-Jasper incident they may want a fresh face. You can do it, Norma. We know he didn't have a record, but there may have been more than one incident. Probably best not to bother his parents—'

'In spades,' Swilley agreed fervently.

'In any case, they'd probably deny it. But get everything you can, and especially if he became violent at any time, even if it was only a punch-up.'

'Righty-oh, boss.'

'And,' Slider said to the whole group, 'we have to consider the possibility that it wasn't Toby, hard though I know that is for you all to bear. We have to find some other lines to follow up, in the eventuality.'

'Well, like Jim always says,' said Hart, 'it always comes down to two motives – sex or money.'

Atherton gave her an ironic bow from across the room. 'So if Toby is sex, who's money?'

'Darren said Jassy knew about the will,' said Hart. 'So it can't be her.'

'There might have been other money that would've come to her if Chattie was dead,' Mackay said. 'What about other relatives? Did Granny have anything to leave? What about her old man?'

Swilley damped his fire. 'But Darren and Jassy have both got alibis.'

'An alibi's made for breaking,' McLaren said almost absently, as he licked the last melted chocolate off the inside of a Twix wrapper.

'Oh, and what does that mean, Food-face?'

McLaren obviously hadn't got as far as working out a meaning for his words. His expression went blank for a moment with effort, and then he said, 'Doesn't say she might not've got someone else to do the hit for her.'

'She hasn't got any money. How would she pay a hit man? They like to be paid up front, you know,' Swilley told him kindly.

'Darren had all that coke. He must have money. He could've given it her.'

'If we've got to look for a contract killer,' Hart said, 'we really are in the clarts.'

'It's too daft a killing for a contract killer,' Slider said. 'Let's not lose sight of the fact that whoever did it, they were dumb enough to try to make it look like the Park Killer's work, and to believe we wouldn't see through it. It's an amateur killing; a planned killing; a cowardly killing.'

'Which sounds,' Swilley said, meeting his eyes, 'more like money than sex.' He nodded agreement to her, but said nothing.

'Well, maybe it's something to do with her dad's business after all,' Hart said. 'Only what? If someone was trying to get at him, you'd think he'd know it.'

'Not blackmail,' said Atherton. 'But how about revenge? He loved her, and a businessman who's successful must have trodden on somebody's toes on the way up.'

'He upset enough people in his family,' Hollis said.

'That's certainly a line to follow up,' Slider said. 'Get on to your contacts on the papers, get everything you can from their morgues on Henry Cornfeld.'

'And keep hoping it turns out it was Toby after all,' said Hollis, 'because we lose the extra bodies tomorrow.'

It seemed strange to have enough time for lunch again. His body was so unused to being fed at the right time that he couldn't manage more than a few mouthfuls of the canteen liver and bacon, mash and peas, and, aware that he was being stared at by some of the uniform relief also lunching, he abandoned the effort and took a cup of tea back to his office. There he sat brooding over the photographs of Chattie, wrung by her smile, trying to make her tell him what had happened. Little Princess

Perfect, Hart had called her spitefully, but she had turned out to be pretty nice after all. She had had enough income to have been idle like Jassy, but she had preferred to set up her own business and work hard at it to prove she could make it alone, as her father had done. She was her father's favourite child. Her grandmother had adored her. She had had lots of lovers. Toby had been obsessed with her, Jasper a long-time admirer. Any number of people had come forward to say how much they liked her, how she was kind and cheerful and funny. Yet someone had killed her. Someone – presumably someone she knew – had beckoned her into the shrubbery for a private talk, and she had gone without a struggle, drunk poison and died. It was bizarre. But there had to be a reason. Passion, jealousy, money, what?

Something to do with her father's business? He remembered Joanna saying she had seen something in the paper recently about Cornfeld Chemicals, though she couldn't remember what, not having been interested in the story.

He rang Tufty Arceneaux.

'What is it this time? Asking me again won't get your results any sooner, y'know.'

'It's not that,' Slider said. 'You play the market a bit, don't you, Tufty?'

'Have to, old fruit, now I own shares in this place.'

'Seriously – you always have, haven't you? Do you have someone who advises you? Someone who understands the City, knows what's going on?'

'You mean not just a broker but a chap who knows. Finger on the pulse, head in the bucket, sort of thing?'

'That sort of thing.'

'Fellow you want is Colin Jenkins. Old drinking buddy of mine from way back. Used to be City editor of one of the broadsheets, still knows everybody in the Square

Mile. If Colin doesn't know about it, it ain't happening. Want me to give him a bell?'

'Would you? If he's willing, ask him to ring me. I need a bit of information.'

'Willco.'

'Oh, and, Tufty?'

'Still here, old cork.'

'Tell him it needs to be done discreetly.'

'Oh, it'll be discreet all right. Old Col's so discreet, if he had an affair, even he wouldn't know about it.'

The call came through about fifteen minutes later. Colin Jenkins had a rich-toned voice and an old-fashioned accent that would have done well in Tufty's son's new movie. Think Dennis Price playing a senior civil servant, Slider mused to himself.

'Tufty says you need information and that it's in a good cause,' he said.

'Yes. I'd rather not say too much about my thought processes at the moment, but—'

'Tufty's word's good enough for me. What can I do for you?'

'Cornfeld Chemicals,' Slider said. 'What can you tell me about them?'

'Ah,' said Jenkins. 'Well, now, it's a good little company, if anything slightly undervalued. Used to be a family business before it was floated and the family are still large shareholders. The founder, Henry Cornfeld, is the chief executive and chairman of the board, but he knows his business. I'd say it was a sound investment. If you get hold of any shares I'd hang on to them.'

'Yes, I see. But weren't they in the news a few weeks ago? Someone told me they saw them mentioned in the papers, but can't remember what the story was.'

'Oh, yes – there were rumours about a takeover, but

I don't think anything came of it in the end. There was a piece in the *Telegraph* City pages – perhaps that's where you saw it.'

'Takeover by whom?' Slider asked. Jenkins was having a good effect on his grammar.

'As I remember, GCC was sniffing around them – Global Chemicals – but I don't think it ever got as far as an offer. Just speculative stuff.'

'Why would they want them?'

'Well, Global's about number three in the pecking order, after Astra and Glaxo, so the thinking would be that an acquisition or two would allow them to punch the same weight,' said Jenkins. 'It's the main preoccupation of these very large companies. Rather like the eighteenth-century obsession with the balance of power. If France has Austria, Britain has to have Russia, you know the sort of thing.'

'I see. So there wasn't anything . . .' Slider paused, feeling for the right words . . . 'Contentious about it? Anything odd or underhand?'

'Not that I know of. Look here, would you like me to do a little sleuthing and come back to you? I'm speaking at present without the full facts.'

'Would you do that? I'd be most grateful.'

'No trouble at all. Anyone in particular you have your eye on?'

'No,' said Slider, frowning. 'I don't think so. I'm just grasping at shadows, really.'

'This is to do with Cornfeld's daughter being killed, is it?' Jenkins asked, with an air of lowering his voice and speaking without moving his lips.

'Yes,' Slider said, 'but I'd be obliged if—'

'Oh, quite, quite. Consider it under the hat. Keeping secrets is second nature in my line of business.'

'So Tufty told me,' Slider smiled, 'only he said it was a secret.'

Hart came back from her interview with Jasper a little less gung-ho than she had left for it. 'I'm beginning to think you could be right, guv,' she said, leaning on his door jamb and folding her arms under her bust to disturbing effect.

'Wonders will never cease,' Slider said, keeping his eyes elsewhere. 'Right about anything in particular, or just in general?'

'Particular. Well, you know I already think you're a total planet-brain,' she grinned. 'That's not a secret.'

'Is that a compliment or not?'

'Yeah. Brain the size of a planet.'

'I see. Well, what's the particular?'

'I talked to old Jasper. He's flat on his back and weak as water, but he was quite clear about what happened. I fought it would upset him to talk about it, but he seemed to want to, so I let him go on about it for as long as he liked. Anyway, he was quite clear old Tobes said he killed Chattie but – this is the duff bit – he said he stabbed her to death. He didn't say anything about any drugging first. Just went on about plunging the knife in and seeing her blood. So I'm thinking maybe you're right.'

Slider, with his often unwelcome trait of seeing both sides of everything, now found himself playing devil's advocate. 'Toby was very disturbed by then. A raving man doesn't give detailed accounts. And the plunging-and-blood bit would have been the part he really cared about, and so the only part worth talking about.'

'Yeah,' she said, somewhat comforted. 'I can see that. He wants to come out king of the jungle, the stalking tiger, not the weak-kneed wally who can't stab a girl unless she's unconscious.'

'Still,' said Slider, 'it doesn't help the case against him. And it's just what a man *would* say, making a false confession on the basis of what he's read in the papers.'

Hart opened her mouth and shut it again, then gave him a bright smile and took herself away. Now she thinks you're irrational, Slider told himself.

Jenkins was evidently enough intrigued to make Slider's enquiry his first priority, for he telephoned again later in the afternoon.

'Good of you to call back so soon,' he said.

'Oh, not at all. I assumed it was a matter of some urgency. Well, the *Telegraph* article was a piece of speculation, based on a rumour that Cornfeld himself was thinking of retiring. He *is* nearly seventy, and though he seems hale enough there was some talk, or rumour, of a heart condition, and a desire on his part to enjoy the sunsets or take up water-colours or something of the sort, before it was too late. Of course, if he did retire, it would mean a big change in the company, seeing as he really does run everything himself – and the old boy's very autocratic. Iron hand in the iron glove, so to speak.'

'Would his retirement mean the company failing?' Slider asked, on the tail of an idea.

'Oh, no. The business itself is pretty sound. But there would be an upheaval and inevitably some reorganisation. And given that GCC was thought to be looking for acquisitions, the article speculated that Cornfeld might be a suitable target.' Jenkins hesitated, and added, 'My chum on the *Telegraph* said that he heard a definite rumour that GCC *was* looking at Cornfeld, but it was all hush-hush, of course, and he couldn't reveal his source, but he says to tell you that you can take it as read that there was something in it. But he hasn't heard anything since, so he's assuming that the idea has gone away or been shelved.'

'Why would they go off the idea?'

'Oh, any number of reasons. I don't think it's because there's anything wrong with Cornfeld itself. It may be that Global is thinking, given Henry C's age, they could just wait until he dies and then pick the place up more cheaply in the aftermath. Or they might be looking at another company to buy. Or someone at Global might have been kite-flying, and it was never more than an idle thought.'

'But there was nothing – sinister about it? I mean, if it had gone ahead, would anybody stand to lose?'

'No, not really. Certainly all the shareholders would be likely to do well out of it. Global would offer them a good price, so they could cash in and do as they pleased with all that lovely lolly. Apart from the dividend, shares have no actual value until you sell them, you know. And given that Cornfeld is quite a tight ship, there wouldn't be likely to be many redundancies, so the employees would be happy. They'd probably expect better peripheral benefits from the larger parent company. The only difference would be that the Cornfeld name would probably be dropped – Global don't go in for that Glaxo Smith Kline Beecham business – but I can't see that anyone would do murder to preserve the company name,' he concluded shrewdly, 'which I suppose is what you're trying to get at.'

'That's the sort of thing I'm wondering,' Slider admitted.

'No, I can't see any reason anyone would be against it,' Jenkins said. 'And especially why anyone would kill the Cornfeld girl over it. I'm assuming she was a shareholder?'

'She was. She held ten per cent.'

'Really? That's quite a lot. But not enough for her to block the deal, so that can't be it.'

'Who could block the deal?'

'Well, Henry himself, I suppose. As I said, he's an autocrat. If he was against it, the board would go with him and not recommend it to the shareholders. But I can't see why anyone would want to block it. It's what they call nowadays a win-win situation.'

'Well, thank you,' Slider said. 'You've been most helpful. Just one more thing.' A thought had occurred to him. 'I'm a complete ignoramus when it comes to shares and stock markets and so on, so forgive me if it seems a stupid question to you—'

'No, no,' Jenkins murmured, impelled by his native politeness.

'But why would it have to be hush-hush if GCC did want to buy Cornfeld Chemicals?'

'Oh, well, because an impending offer by a big company like Global could affect the share price, and the FSA would be down like a ton of bricks on anything that looked like price-rigging or insider-dealing. My chum on the City desk had to go through the paper's lawyers for a pretty rigorous combing even to write what he did, which was a very innocent appraisal of the company and didn't mention Global by name. If Global really were going to make an offer the preliminaries would all be conducted very secretly, and the principals would have to be very careful what they said and who they said it to.'

'Thank you,' Slider said. 'I'm most grateful.'

'My pleasure. If I hear anything more, I'll be sure to let you know.'

Slider put down the telephone absently, and began to search through his papers for the transcript of his interview with Mrs Cornfeld senior. Yes, there it was. Cornfeld's eldest daughter Ruth had married a David Cockerell, who had won opprobrium from his father-in-law by leaving the family firm and going to GCC. Was he, Slider wondered, still there? That was definitely something worth finding out. Possibly there was nothing in it – and, as Jenkins had said, what reason would anyone have to kill Chattie over the supposed acquisition, which in any case hadn't come to anything?

But, as he ought to have realised before, or at least connected in his mind, David Cockerell's initials were DC. And wasn't it possible that 'DC10' meant David Cockerell, ten o'clock? If she had had a meeting with her brother-in-law on the last day of her life, it was possible he might know something of interest about her circumstances, or her state of mind – if not her death.

15

Who Thrilled Cock Robin?

The Global Chemical Company had its London office in Northumberland Avenue. Slider knew it, one of those huge anonymous buildings, part of a long block lining the street that always reminded him of the Hauptmanised part of Paris. Northumberland Avenue, just off Trafalgar Square. Trafalgar Square. He wrote the words down and stared at them. DC10 TFQ. But Trafalgar Square would be TS as initials. Yet someone jotting down a note while talking on the phone would not necessarily use strict logic, but write down what the mind picked out as significant. TF for Tra-Falgar. And though Square began with an S, the Q was the most significant letter in it. It was eccentric, but it was not unbelievable. Idiosyncratic, rather, was the word. And the whole point of a mnemonic was that it triggered a response in your own brain, not anyone else's.

He went to the door of his room, beckoned Atherton in, and tried it out on him.

'Trafalgar Square? Well, it's possible, I suppose. When I do that sort of thing in my diary I do a little square for Square, and a circle with a dot in it for Circus. We all have our own methods. Why would she meet her brother-in-law in Trafalgar Square?'

'Because his office is in Northumberland Avenue.'

'Yes, but I meant why would she meet him at all?'

'Because his company, GCC, was thinking about taking over Cornfeld Chemicals, and she was a large share-holder.'

'You think?'

'Well, I'd like to find out. Shall we go and see him?'

Atherton looked doubtful. 'Shouldn't we wait for the results on the clothes to come back? We'll look like fools if it turns out that Toby did it after all – which is still the most likely scenario.'

'I'd sooner try to keep ahead of the game than waste a day if Toby's innocent. And I'm curious, anyway. I didn't think there was any contact between those two parts of the family.'

'Curiosity I'm always willing to indulge,' said Atherton. 'Why not? Let's go.'

The GCC building was very old-fashioned inside. A lofty reception hall was lined with polished stone – granite, Slider thought – and at the far end was a wide, dark wooden desk behind which two elderly porters stood, wearing heavy navy uniforms and flat caps reminiscent of the defunct GLC. Was there such a thing as a GLC Surplus Store? Slider wouldn't have been at all surprised. There was a bank of lifts to one side and polished stone steps going up at the side of them, and in all the expanse of floor space there was not one potted plant, leather chair, glass coffee table or magazine. This was a stern, no-nonsense reception hall of the old school, where you stated your business and were admitted, or were firmly ejected with the coldest of cold eyes.

One of the porters examined both Slider's and Atherton's warrant card with almost offensive thoroughness, while the other telephoned 'upstairs', and carried on an inaudible conversation without ever taking his eyes from the visitors. At last he replaced the receiver, wrote laboriously in a visitors' book, produced two clip-on visitors' badges, and said, 'Seventh floor. You'll be met at the lift. Make sure you bring the badges back when you leave. They're numbered,' he concluded menacingly. Both porters watched Slider and Atherton walk to the lift with an air of being prepared to bring them down with a flying tackle if they veered towards the stairs. Neither of them had smiled at any time during the transaction.

Inside the lift, Atherton said, 'Whew! I thought there was going to be a blood test and a retinal scan before we got in.'

The lift was panelled on two sides, but mirrored, behind a decorative grille, on the third. Slider cast his eyes towards it and said, without moving his lips, 'Careful what you say. We may be being watched.'

Atherton smirked, but rode in silence the rest of the way.

Outside the lift doors was a corridor panelled in light oak, with grey carpet on the floor, filled with expensive silence. Whatever was going on behind the closed doors leading off it, no sound penetrated. A woman was waiting for them, a top-of-the-range middle-aged secretary in a fawn suit, silk blouse, knotted silk scarf round the neck, pearl earrings, and large, careful hair in a short bob held off the face with a velvet Alice band. It was like stepping back in time, Slider thought.

She didn't smile, either. 'I'm Mr Cockerell's personal assistant,' she said in a voice so cut-glass you could have sipped single malt from it in a gentlemen's club. 'Follow me, please.'

She led them down the corridor to an anonymous oak door in the oak wall, which led into what was obviously her room, for there was a desk with papers on it, a typewriter (really!) and a computer, filing cabinets and cupboards. It was windowless, which Slider thought horribly claustrophobic. She walked straight across to the door on the far side, tapped on it and opened it, saying, 'Detective Inspector Slider and Detective Sergeant Atherton, sir,' stepped aside to usher them through, and closed the door noiselessly behind them.

The room beyond was a different animal altogether. It was much larger, to begin with, and it had windows all along the far wall, though they were covered with venetian blinds and let in little natural light. The walls were wood-panelled, there was concealed lighting round the edges of the ceiling, and the carpet was thick and plush and blackberry-coloured. There was no office paraphernalia, only a vast oak desk, a sofa, coffee-table, and several chairs. On the left-hand wall was a unit, cupboards along the base, further cupboards up each side, and shelves across the middle, containing a few tooled-back leather-bound books and some photographs in heavy silver frames. The desk had on it only four telephones and a blotter. This was a man, said the office, so powerful he did not have to *appear* to work. Two of the chairs were pulled up to the near side of the desk, and Slider and Atherton trudged towards them, which was hard work given the depth of pile on the carpet. The man seated in a large, padded, leather executive chair on the other side, rose to welcome them.

He was a surprise to Slider too. He appeared to be about fifty, tall and well-built, immaculately suited and extremely good-looking. His thick dark hair was swept back from a lightly tanned face with even features, a straight nose, dark eyes and a firm chin with a slight cleft in it. The surprise, for this place, was that he was smiling. His teeth were white and even – perhaps a thought too white. Slider's rapid process of instant summing up had said here was a man who had relied on his looks and charm all his life, with the corollary that he didn't have many other abilities. He was aware that this was probably unfair, and also probably a reaction from all the stern inhospitality they had met up until this point. He summoned up a smile of his own, pushed away his judgement and prepared to meet the man with an open mind.

'David Cockerell,' said the man, extending his hand. His handshake was efficient, neither too hard nor too limp, and brief without being surly. Professional, Slider thought. 'How can I help you? Please sit down.'

Slider sat. 'I'd like to talk to you about your sister-in-law, Charlotte Cornfeld.'

The smile widened just a little. 'I suppose I was half expecting this,' said Cockerell. 'You fellows have to be thorough, I know that. But I'm afraid I won't be able to help you. I really didn't have much to do with Chattie. That was her nickname, by the way. You knew that?' Slider nodded. 'Can I offer you a drink?' As he said it, he crossed to the unit and opened one of the upper cupboards, which proved to contain decanters and glasses. 'Whisky, sherry, gin and tonic? Not too early, is it? The sun's over the yard-arm somewhere in the world, that's what I always say.' He laughed, a purely functional laugh that had nothing to do with humour but was a social signal: I'm a good guy, you're good guys, let's all be good guys together.

Slider smiled. 'I'm afraid we can't, but please don't let that stop you.'

'No! Really? I thought that was all bushwah, about you people not being allowed to drink on duty. Surely a small one?'

'I'm afraid not, but thank you,' Slider said.

Cockerell hesitated about the glasses, and then decided against solo drinking, closed the door and returned to the desk. He sat, folded his hands together, and placed them on the desk in front of him. 'So, what can I tell you?'

'What was your relationship with Miss Cornfeld?' Slider asked.

'Well, I can't say I really had one. The family wasn't all that close, you know. The occasional dutiful Christmas gathering, and that was that.' He looked straight at Slider, like a man about to reveal something painful. 'My wife and her father do not get on, I'm sorry to say, and so we aren't at the old man's house very often. I believe he and Chattie were very fond of each other, though.'

'Did Chattie visit you and your wife at home?'

'No, I don't think Chattie's ever been to our house. We only ever met at Frithsden – my father-in-law's house – and not very often there, as I've said. Ruth, my wife, doesn't approve of the way her father lives. His personal life. I don't know if you know . . . ?' A delicate pause and lift of the eyebrows.

'You mean Kylie?'

'Ah, you have seen her.' Cockerell leaned back with a faint man-to-man smile. 'She's one of a string of similar lovelies. In my humble opinion, the old man's entitled to take his pleasure where he likes at his age, but Ruth doesn't agree. So we don't visit very often.'

'So when did you last see Chattie?' Slider asked, still as if going through the motions.

Cockerell was quite relaxed. 'Oh, well, let me think. I suppose it must have been last Christmas. Did we go there at Christmas? Oh, yes, I remember there was some disaster in the kitchen and dinner was terribly late.' He smiled. 'One needs these signposts to remember one Christmas from another.'

'So you haven't seen her at all for six months?' Atherton asked, picking up the minute pause Slider left for him. They had worked together for so long they knew each other's rhythms without having to think about it.

'No, I suppose I haven't,' said Cockerell.

'Then last week's meeting must have been about something out of the ordinary,' said Atherton.

Cockerell's smile remained behind, like the Cheshire Cat's, though the rest of his face had abandoned it. 'I'm sorry?' he said.

'Your meeting last Tuesday with Chattie,' Slider took over. 'It was obviously important, as it was so unprecedented.'

Cockerell blinked rapidly several times, and cocked his head slightly. 'I'm afraid I don't follow you. I didn't have any meeting with Chattie last week. Or indeed any week.'

It was well done; it was very natural. But having had the interrogation split, Cockerell did not now know who to look at, and when he looked at Atherton, Slider looked at his hands. The truth, like blood, will out. Cockerell had his face and voice under control, but Slider had seen the small, convulsive clasp of the hands. He relaxed, and felt Atherton beside him feel it.

'Please, Mr Cockerell, don't waste time. We know that you had a meeting with Chattie at ten o'clock on Tuesday morning. Now it may have been – I expect it was – a perfectly innocent meeting, but as it happened on the last day of her life, we have to ask about it. You do see that?'

'I'm sorry, but you're mistaken,' Cockerell said. 'I had no meeting with Chattie. Why should I? And now I'm afraid I shall have to ask you to leave.' He half stood, admitting, though he was not aware of it, defeat.

Slider did not move. 'It is pointless to deny it. We know that you met her – in Trafalgar Square.' He waited a beat, and then said, gently, 'We have the evidence. If you won't tell us about it, we're bound to become suspicious.'

Cockerell, still in his half-risen crouch, seemed to consider. Then he sat down, slowly, leaned back in his chair and swivelled a little, passed a hand over his mouth in thought, and then said, 'Look.'

The word of capitulation. Slider looked.

'Look,' said Cockerell, 'I did meet her, but it has to be kept a secret. It – it wasn't exactly improper, but if it was known that we met, it could be thought that something was going on, that we were colluding. You've got to promise me this won't get out. There could be consequences. Serious consequences. It could ruin the whole deal, and a lot of jobs depend on it.'

'The deal – you mean the takeover?' Slider said. 'The takeover of Cornfeld Chemicals by GCC?'

His eyebrows shot up. 'You know about it?'

'It was in the papers,' Slider reminded him.

'Speculation only, several weeks ago. But we killed that. What made you think we were still interested?'

'We have our sources,' Slider said, 'just as you do. You are still interested, aren't you?'

'Well, yes. But that's not for public consumption. You see why Chattie and I had to keep the meeting secret. The way we were placed, if the reporters had got hold of the fact that we'd been seen together, it would have been disastrous.'

'And what was the purpose of the meeting?' Slider asked.

Cockerell hesitated. 'I wanted to find out how Henry felt about it. Chattie's the person closest to him in the world. I knew she'd know.'

'Why couldn't you ask him yourself?'

'I'm in negotiation with him. He's not going to tell me the truth, is he? That's not the way these things work. He takes a position and I take a position. We try not to give away anything to one another. And Henry's a master at the game.'

'So you thought you might cheat a little and ask Chattie what his real position was?' Atherton asked.

'That's right. But it wasn't really cheating. Just – trying to get an edge.'

'But it was a little shady, so you kept it a deep, dark secret,' Atherton led him on. 'Did your wife know about the meeting?'

'Yes, she knew, and Lucinda knew – my secretary.' In the heat of the moment he had forgotten to call her personal assistant. Lucky she wasn't listening. 'But they're both sound as bells. They would never tell a soul. I don't know how the hell you found out,' he complained. 'I would never have thought Chattie would be indiscreet.'

'You said you were afraid of being seen together,' Slider said blandly.

'Oh, so that was it, was it? Well, that was damnable bad luck. We took such precautions.'

'And what was the result of your meeting?' Slider asked. 'Did Chattie tell you how her father felt about the deal?'

'No, she didn't,' he said. He frowned angrily at the memory. 'She refused. I didn't get anything useful out of her at all, so it was really a waste of time.' He engaged

Slider's eyes and tried for lightness after the frowns. 'So, you see, there's no need to report it to anyone. Nothing improper happened, but if it was known we had met, people would assume, and rumours would spread.'

'Was anything else discussed between you?' Slider asked. 'You see, you were one of the last people to see her alive. Did she say anything that might help us? Did she talk of any worries she had? Did she tell you who else she was going to meet that day?'

'No,' he said. 'Nothing else was discussed. The meeting was very short. I wish I could help you,' he said, with a look of sincerity, 'but I knew nothing about her life and she didn't say anything about it then. I've no idea who killed her or why.'

Slider stood up. 'Well, thank you, sir,' he said. 'You've cleared up one little mystery for us. We're most grateful.'

Cockerell was all beams now. 'Oh, not at all, not at all. Glad to help. Anything else I can do for you, don't hesitate to ask.'

He was coming round the desk to usher them out. Slider veered across to the wall unit to look at the photographs on his way out. 'Your family?' he asked.

'Yes, that's my wife, and our son and two daughters.'

Granny Cornfeld was right, Slider thought – they did look dull. But the wife, Ruth, looked faintly familiar to Slider, though he couldn't place her. Perhaps there'd been a photo of her in Frithsden House?

They were shown back to the lift, rode down in silence, handed in their badges to the two Cerberuses, and made their way out of the heavy swing doors into the early-evening sunlight.

'He's lying,' Slider said.

'Yup,' Atherton concurred. 'But why?'

There was a pub at the end of the street, its doors

open on the pavement and, for a wonder, no piped music inside. 'Pint?' said Slider.

'Hm. Okay. Might help the little grey cells.'

It was cool and dark inside, one of those *faux*-traditional places with bare floorboards, dark wood everywhere, tall barrels for tables, the ceiling painted an authentic smoke-dimmed dirty cream. They ordered two pints of Director's, and Slider led the way to a couple of stools pulled up to one of the barrel tables just by the open door.

'All right,' said Atherton, having taken the top third off his pint. 'Cockerell's story.'

'It makes sense in its own terms. I just don't feel that's all there was to it. Both Jasper and Marion said Chattie was preoccupied that evening.'

'Wouldn't she be disturbed by Cockerell trying to pump her about the old man's feelings on the takeover?'

Slider shook his head. 'I'm not sure. If it was just Cockerell saying, is he pro or con, and her saying, mind your own business, would she really be that bothered? It surely wouldn't have been news to her – at least, judging by what Granny Cornfeld said – that he wasn't quite pukka.'

'Well,' Atherton said, as one stretching a point, 'you could be right. But she could have been preoccupied about anything – her business, her love-life, the state of the economy.'

'Of course. But what did she do with the rest of the day? She cancelled her appointments, but she must have been out of the house, because Marion Davies said she was just sorting the mail when she called round at a quarter past six, still in her business suit. So where was she, and with whom?'

'What's your theory?'

'I haven't got one,' Slider admitted, taking a long swallow. 'I'm just working out the pattern. Cockerell said something to her, she was disturbed by it, she – perhaps – went and saw somebody else about it, and the next day she was murdered.'

'You think Cockerell did it?' Atherton said. 'That's a very large size in assumptions. Although,' he allowed, 'I didn't like him, and he did seem to be just dumb enough to do the murder that way. And, perhaps more to the point, he's a senior executive in a drugs company that manufactures ultra-short-acting barbiturates.'

'It does?'

'I do my homework,' said Atherton. 'If anyone could work out how to get access to them, he could. But for all you know, he's got an alibi.'

'That's why we're sitting here – to catch his secretary on her way to the tube.'

'How do you know she goes home by tube?'

'I saw a tube ticket sticking out of one of the front pockets of her handbag.'

'Blimey, the eyes of the sleuth! What if she doesn't come this way to the station?'

'Then we're stuffed,' said Slider patiently, 'but at least we've had a pint.'

'The man's a genius.'

'Keep your eyes peeled.'

Atherton turned his stool so they were both facing the street; and indeed, half an hour later, the big hair and the suit went past, with the addition of a fine leather shoulder-bag and a rolled umbrella by way of accessories. Atherton and Slider left their seats and went after her. A little hampered by not knowing her surname, they fell in one on either side of her and almost got clobbered by the umbrella as her natural reactions were set off by being bracketed.

'I'm sorry to startle you,' Slider said. 'We just wanted a quiet word.'

'I thought you were bag-snatchers,' she said, very much annoyed. 'What are you doing here?'

'We've been waiting for you.'

She faced them, glaring. 'This is ridiculous. If you wanted to speak to me, why didn't you do it at the office?'

'I rather wanted to speak to you privately,' said Slider.

'Without Mr Cockerell knowing? I see. And why should you imagine for a moment that I would betray my employer to you?'

'Betray?' Atherton said. 'Now there's an interesting word for you to have used.'

'Betray his trust,' she said witheringly, 'by talking about him behind his back.'

'Oh, come on,' he coaxed. 'You don't *like* working for him. He's a jumped-up little turkey cock. You've got ten times his brains and character. And he called you his secretary.'

Her lips twitched, but she kept her countenance. 'Nothing would induce me to say anything behind his back that I would not say to his face.'

'Fine, then tell him to his face tomorrow. For now, come and have a drink – a gin and tonic to brace you for the tube journey home.'

Slider could only look on in admiration as Atherton worked his magic, and then followed them back to the pub like a younger brother tagging along. This time they took seats away from the door, round the corner. Lucinda Gaines-Harris, for such was her name, accepted the offer of a gin and tonic, and while Atherton chatted her up, Slider observed with interest her struggle to keep her face disapproving and not to show that she was rather enjoying the adventure of something that didn't happen every day or to everyone.

'I bet he's tried to get off with you,' Atherton said, with almost girlfriendish sympathy.

'Why do you say that?'

'I know the type. It must be galling for you. Where did you go to university?'

'Cambridge. Chemistry,' she said, flattered that he had guessed she was a graduate.

'So how did you end up here?'

'It was the best I could do,' she said. 'I get paid more this way than I could as a lowly researcher or a lab-rat, and I have my mother to support. Of course, if I were a man, I could go up the executive ladder. But I don't have back-scratching privileges, so that's out.' She had loosened up enough to swig back her G-and-T like a man, and Slider hastened to get her another before the mood was broken. When he returned with it, she said, 'I hope you aren't thinking of getting me drunk, because it won't work.'

'Absolutely not,' Atherton said. 'I bet you could drink me under the table. I was just being hospitable.'

'So, what do you want to know?' she asked, apparently abandoning pleasure for business. She glanced at a gold watch on a slim wrist. 'I can't be too long, because of Mother.'

Atherton got down to it. 'On Wednesday last week, what time did he get to the office?'

'Eight,' she said. 'He's always in at eight, when he's in the office. Of course, sometimes he goes to other offices, or to meetings elsewhere, or to one of the plants. But when he's here, he's in at eight.'

'Did you actually *see* him at eight that morning?'

'Oh, yes, certainly. In fact, he was already at his desk when I came in at eight.'

'When he comes and goes, does he have to go through your office?'

'No, there's another door to the corridor through his bathroom, which leads off his office. But in the morning he usually comes in through my office and I give him the mail and any messages.'

'I see.' Well, that knocked him out from being First Murderer, said Atherton's glance to Slider. Only Superman could have got from the park to the office, with a change of clothes thrown in, in the maximum possible allowance of ten minutes. Pity, really. It would have been nice to de-smug him. 'And can you cast your mind back to the day before, to last Tuesday? He said that you knew he had an appointment to meet Miss Cornfeld.'

'Yes. Well, he pretty well had to tell me, because I'd have to cover for his absence if anyone called.'

'Did he tell you what the meeting was about?'

'I'm not sure if I should tell you that.'

'He told us it was about the takeover – wanting her to find out how her father stood on it,' said Slider.

She looked relieved. 'Oh, well, that's what he told me, too. But it had to be a secret meeting. Rather dangerous if anyone found out and suspected collusion.'

'The meeting was at ten o'clock?'

'Yes. He left at five to. He said he was meeting her in Trafalgar Square.'

'Isn't that rather public for a private meeting?'

'That's what I said, but he said it was safer in the open because you could see people approaching – they couldn't creep up on you and overhear. I think he saw that in some spy film or other,' she added, with a sneer.

'And what time did he come back?'

'It was about ten to eleven.'

Slider was surprised. 'He told us it was only a brief meeting.'

She shrugged. 'I don't know about that. I suppose he may have gone somewhere else afterwards. All I know is that I heard him come in at that time. He went in through the bathroom and banged the door very noisily. I went straight in to give him his messages and he was stamping about in an absolute temper.'

'What about?'

'I don't know. I said, "Is everything all right?" and he said, "Not now, Lucinda. Leave me alone. I'll buzz when I want you." So I put the messages down on his desk and went out. When he buzzed for me I went in and he was quite calm again, and he didn't mention anything about it, so naturally I didn't ask. It wasn't my business.'

'So you've no idea what put him in a temper?'

'None at all.' She hesitated. 'All I can tell you is that when I went in – the first time – I heard him mutter something like, "Thank God there's a few days left" or "There's still a few days" – I can't swear to the exact words. But he never mentioned it again.'

'How did he react when he heard about Miss Cornfeld's death?'

'I'm not sure when he did first hear. I heard about it on Thursday evening on the news, when the name was first given. The next morning at the office I said something to him about how dreadful it was, and he seemed already to know then, because he said, "Yes, it's tragic," or something like that.'

'Did he seem very upset?'

She thought. 'Yes, I'd say he was. He was very quiet and thoughtful all morning, quite absent-minded. Brooding, almost, you might say. In the afternoon he went off to the plant in Bedford so I didn't see him again that day.'

'The plant — is that where the drugs are manufactured?'

'Some of them. Bedford's the secure plant for the restricted pharmaceuticals. It's only a small place.'

'Does he go there often?'

'Oh, from time to time. He was there last Monday, as it happens, but that was unusual. It was for the opening of the new lab block. Some local bigwig cutting the ribbon, and the press were there, and there were drinks and so on afterwards, with the Health Minister looking in.'

'A big do like that, that date must have been known well beforehand,' Slider said, the germ of an idea twitching in the depths of his brain.

'Of course,' she said. 'To get a cabinet minister you have to book months ahead.'

'Did you go with him?'

'Certainly not. A frightful waste of time, those things, but useful publicity, I suppose, which is why he had to go. In any case, his wife was there if he wanted his hand holding. I'm not obliged to do it, thank God. Oh, look at the time. Is there anything else, because I really ought to get going? Mother frets if I'm more than half an hour late.'

'Just one last question,' Slider said. 'The proposed acquisition of Cornfeld Chemicals. Is there anything — odd or unusual about it?'

'I don't think so. In what way?'

'I don't know,' Slider said ruefully. 'That's what I'm trying to find out.'

'Well, I haven't heard anything. It's all still very secret — has to be, until the offer's made public, or the shares would go haywire. But as far as I know, it's a simple purchase.'

'Thanks,' said Slider, and stood up to pull out her chair for her as she made getting-up movements.

She gathered her belongings, and at the last moment paused and said to Slider, 'You think she was killed because of something to do with the takeover?'

'I don't know,' he said. 'But all murders come down to money or passion in the end, don't they?'

'I don't know anything about it,' she said, 'and I hate gossip, but I suppose it is murder after all, so I ought to tell you. There was talk a couple of years ago that there was something between him and that girl.'

'He had an affair with Chattie?'

'I don't think it amounted to that. Just a brief fling. For a few weeks there were a lot of phone calls, and he went off for long lunches without saying where he was going, and – well, all the signs of an affair. He's had them before – and since – so I know the symptoms. It may not even have *been* her. I mean, the calls were, but maybe not the lunches and so on. I don't know. It was just what the rumours said. But if it was her, there's been nothing since. The calls stopped, and as far as I know he hasn't seen her until that meeting last week. So you see,' she looked from one to the other, 'it might not have been the takeover at all. I just thought you ought to know.'

They thanked her again, and escorted her to the door. When she had walked away, Atherton said, 'For someone who didn't want to betray her boss, she certainly let her hair down.'

'Chattie, an affair with Cockerell?' Slider mourned. 'I can't believe it.'

'Rather a lapse of taste,' Atherton agreed. 'But we know she liked to have it large, and he's not without his attractions. I fancy even Miss Gaines-Harris has yearned for a slice of that particular beefcake at some time in the past – and didn't get one, which is why she's so ready to shop him.'

'Stop with the psychology. You're making me dizzy.'

'Seriously, when I said I bet he made a pass at you, she didn't say he did and she didn't say he didn't. So I reckon he didn't. Hell hath no fury, et cetera. Anyway,' he went on, 'at least if Chattie did have a fling, it was a brief one. Presumably she fell in a weak moment and got out of it as quickly as possible.'

'I'm not comforted,' said Slider.

16

Can't Say Y

'It's me!' Slider called as he let himself into the narrow hall.

'Hi! I'm in the kitchen,' Joanna called back.

It was every man's dream, he supposed, to come home from work and find his beloved safely in the kitchen. He extended his sensitive nostrils and identified onions, garlic – tomatoes – some kind of herb. After a day of sensual deprivation he fancied something rich and tasty. And a good meal, too. He picked up his mail, which she had left for him in a pile on the edge of the hall table and went to find her.

She was at the stove, stirring a pot. Hallelujah! It was going to be Bolognese sauce.

'Yum,' he said, kissing the back of her neck.

'Me, or dinner?'

'Both. Always,' he said, opening envelopes. Bill, begging letter, you have been preselected to own one of our platinum credit cards (where were they going to go after platinum – titanium? Green kryptonite?), bill, bill . . .

'I'm doing a proper *ragù*, with chicken livers,' she said, 'since I have time. Do you want it over short pasta, spaghetti, or baked in the oven?'

'It would break Garibaldi's heart if we had it over anything but spaghetti.'

'Why Garibaldi?'

'Wasn't he the father of modern Italy?'

'Dunno,' she said. 'All I know is he made the biscuits run on time.'

He wasn't listening. He was reading the letter he'd just opened. He frowned. 'What's this about a scan?'

She turned and craned her neck to read it, and then snatched it from his hand. 'Don't read my letters!'

'It was in my pile,' he protested.

'Since when have you been "Dear Ms Marshall"?'

'I didn't read that bit. I opened it without looking. I assumed you'd sorted my stuff out from yours.'

'You've no right to read my letters.' Her face was a little flushed, though that might have been the heat of the stove.

He looked at her carefully. 'Jo, what is it? It says you're refusing to have a scan.'

'It's none of your business,' she said, stuffing the letter into her pocket with an angry, careless gesture.

'Well, it is, really,' he said gently, not to annoy her. 'It's my baby too.'

'You're not the one who has to carry it and bear it and feed it. Ultimately it's my responsibility.'

'I can't help being a man,' he said. 'I know you have the hardest part, but we're having this baby together, and it's my responsibility too. You both are. Why are you refusing a scan?'

She turned her face away, pretending to be concentrating on the sauce. 'They don't like it, you know. Babies. They try to get away from it. You can see on the monitor. I went with a friend a couple of times, and you can see the babies hate it.'

'But it doesn't harm them, does it?'

'How do we know? It doesn't do any immediate, obvious damage, but who knows what it's really doing to them?'

He took her arms and turned her to him, against resistance. 'Darling,' he said, 'what's wrong? What's really the problem? Surely this scan business is simply routine? Why are you so against it?'

'People managed perfectly well in the old days. My mother had ten children without ultrasound, or any of the other horrible machines they rig you up to these days.'

'People in the old days had their legs cut off without anaesthetic,' he said. 'What's the real reason?'

'You haven't thought it through. They scan to find out if the baby's defective.'

'Yes. Isn't that a good thing?'

She met his eyes with resolution. 'And if it is defective? You know what comes next. They offer you an abortion. Are you prepared to take that decision? Because I'm not. I hate abortion. I would *never* have an abortion. But what if they say the child's terribly damaged in some way, so that it wouldn't die, but live on in some terrible condition?'

He didn't answer for a moment. No, he hadn't thought about that before, and now he did, he saw the gravity of it. To choose life or death, death or tormented life, for your own child? And how much worse for the mother, with the child actually growing inside her, part of her in the way it could never be for the father?

'There are other reasons,' he said. 'They could find something that could be corrected in the womb. It could save the child from being born with a defect.'

'Do you think that makes it easier?'

He saw then that she was really afraid, and close to tears. He pulled her against him and held her close, cradling her head, and she pressed in, needing his strength.

'Darling,' he said, 'don't worry. There's nothing wrong with our baby. Everything will be all right. It's going to be healthy and normal.'

'You don't know that,' she said, muffled by her chest.

'I believe it,' he said firmly.

She pulled her head up and laughed, shakily. 'Oh, religion!'

'Well, what else is there at a time like this?' he reasoned.

'Don't you realise, you jughead,' she said kindly, 'that I'm not a sweet young thing any more? I'm what they call an elderly primipara. Biologically I'm an old lady doing what only young girls should do. It's an extremely risky business.'

'Rubbish,' he said. 'Women of your age and older have babies every day of the week – first babies,' he anticipated her interruption. 'You're perfectly healthy and so am I. Why should anything go wrong?'

'Things do.'

'Not as often as they don't, by a very long chalk. You're falling a victim to the very thing you despise: haven't you said how wrong it was that doctors treat pregnancy as a serious illness?'

'They do. That's what this is all about.'

'They try to, but you don't have to listen. You don't have to let them get to you. You're not ill, you're doing something natural that nearly every woman on the planet does at some point.'

'Easy for you to say.'

He put her back a little to look at her seriously. 'Do you really think that?'

'No,' she said, after a pause. 'No, not really. I know you love me.'

'It's a bit more than that,' he said. 'I think your sauce is sticking.'

'Blast,' she said, and twisted out of his arms to stir it. He saw she had relaxed a little, given him a little of the burden to carry, and he was glad. 'So what about this scan?' she asked, in a small voice, her back to him.

'I think you should have it,' he said, after consideration. 'Not because I think there's anything wrong with the baby, but because if you don't they'll keep on bugging you about it and drive you nuts. But if you really don't want to have it, then I'll support you. I'll write to them and tell them *we* don't want it, and that if they send you any more letters about it I'll come round and reprogram their computer with a very large axe.'

She laughed, turning her head to look at him adoringly. 'My hero! What would I do without you? D'you want to go and get changed? I'm going to put the water on so we're looking at fifteen minutes to eating.'

She said no more about it that evening, and he thought she had put it from her mind for the time being. But in bed, when they had made love and she was lying in his arms and he was drifting comfortably into sleep, she said suddenly out of the dark, 'If I have the scan, and there's something wrong, what then?'

'If that happened, we'd face it together and decide together. But it's not going to happen. So don't even think about it. Never trouble trouble till trouble troubles you.'

She turned on her side then, into her sleep position, and he turned too so that she could burrow into him backwards. He folded his hands round her, one on her breast and one on her belly, and felt her fall instantly into

305

sleep like someone tumbling off a cliff. He held her, wakeful now, thinking of the two lives that lay in his arms; and from there to a whole range of preoccupations, his thoughts knitting and spreading an invisible web into the darkness, stretching wider and wider, thinning and growing more tenuous as the world turned through the short summer night towards dawn. When the first bird sang tentatively outside in the blackness, he slept.

Cornfeld Chemicals had its headquarters in Hemel Hempstead, a neat, new-looking low-rise block set in nicely landscaped surroundings on the edge of the town. Slider was received by Henry Cornfeld at nine o'clock in an office that was as different as it could be from his son-in-law's. It was small, lit from unshaded windows, cluttered with the business of business, and devoid of the accoutrements of glamour and power.

Cornfeld himself seemed to have aged since Slider saw him last. His movements were less brisk, his face seemed to have sagged; even his hair did not spring from his forehead in so lively a fashion. But his mind still gripped. He offered Slider a chair and coffee, seated himself and said, 'Have you found out yet who killed my child?'

'Not yet, sir, but there are promising lines we are following up.'

'That sounds like a stock answer,' he said. 'Haven't you anything better for me than that? I am her father. I love her.'

'I'm sorry. It sounds hackneyed, but it is the truth. We don't know yet, but I think we are getting there. I can't be more specific than that at the moment.'

'But you promise you will tell me, as soon as you know.' His eyes became piercing. 'The moment you know.'

'If you promise you won't take the law into your own hands,' said Slider.

He sat back a little and spread his hands. 'I am an old man. What can I do?'

Neither had promised the other anything, and they both knew it.

'You have some more questions for me?' said Cornfeld.

'Yes, sir. I don't know whether they have any relevance or not, but I'm feeling my way at present. I wanted to ask you about the proposed takeover of your company by GCC.'

'Oh, you know about that?'

'Is it supposed to be a secret?'

'It's not meant to be public knowledge yet. However, these things always do get about, no-one knows how. Everyone swears they haven't told a soul, but somehow people know.'

'So it is still going on?'

'Oh, yes. I have been in negotiation for many weeks now. These things take time.'

'And how do you feel about it? Are you for it?'

He looked surprised. 'Certainly, or I should not be in negotiation.'

'Then – you've always been in favour? Forgive me, but has Chattie's death made any difference to your attitude?'

'No,' he said. 'From the beginning, when Global first contacted me, I felt it was the right thing to do. I am old, and it is time to pass on the baton. It was a good opportunity for me to leave my responsibilities behind while doing my best for my employees and the share-holders. The only difference Chattie's death has made is that it has forced me to realise how old and tired I really am. I want to be done with it now.' Steel entered his face again as he added, 'But I shall drive a hard bargain, you may be sure. I'm not too old and tired for that.' He eyed Slider. 'You seem puzzled.'

'It isn't quite fitting in with what I was thinking.'

'You thought I was unwilling to sell, and that killing Chattie was supposed to take the heart out of me and make me agree to it?'

'You're very shrewd,' Slider said. 'It was one of the lines I was working along. But obviously that's not it.'

'No,' said Cornfeld. He looked bleak. 'It's true that I don't want to go on now, but that hasn't affected this deal in any way. Mine is a healthy, profitable company, with a proud history. We have done valuable work in our time, and produced some important benefits for the human community. I can look back on my life with pride – though this tragedy takes away the joy.'

'That brings me to another question,' Slider said. 'Your mother mentioned, when I was talking to her at your house last week, that you have a new drug that's about to come out, and that you are very excited about it. Can you tell me about that?'

The animation came back. 'Yes, indeed! We have been working on it for a long time, and we've just completed the two years of statutory trials. All we have to do now is to secure the approval of the various regulatory bodies, and we can launch it on the world!'

'And what is it? What does it do?'

'It is something quite tremendous,' he said, his eyes bright. He leaned forward across the desk to emphasise the excitement. 'It is a treatment for acne.'

'Acne?' Slider said.

Cornfeld smiled and shook his head. 'I can tell you don't understand. Well, why should you? One can see you have never suffered from it. You think I'm talking about a few teenage spots. You have no idea of its ravages.

You don't know how many millions of lives are ruined by this disease. You can't imagine how many billions of pounds are spent year after year on remedies that don't work, or don't work well enough, or have hideous side effects. Our product, Codermatol, works. It *really* works! It will benefit more people than you can imagine, allow them to come out of the shadows and live full lives. It is one of the most exciting and important breakthroughs of the last twenty years, the most important, I believe, that I have ever been personally involved in.'

'I see,' Slider said.

'*Do* you?'

'I take your word for it, sir. You convince me. And this new drug – this is part of the sale, I take it? It goes with the company.'

'Yes,' said Cornfeld. 'Naturally. That is partly why I am demanding such a high price. GCC knows that once it goes on the market, the share price will jump, so that must be reflected in the offer.'

'And have you any idea when the deal will be concluded?'

'Soon,' he said. 'Very soon. I anticipate the announcement will be made at the end of this week. I am only hanging on to receive the regulatory approval. I want that to come to me, as the crowning moment of my business life. Then I shall go. I shall take the money, and Kylie, and go abroad. I haven't had a holiday in years. I intend,' he said, with a look that dared Slider to mock, 'to make a very expensive fool of myself in all the smartest resorts and casinos in the world. I intend to go out in a blaze of glory.'

Slider didn't mock. He hoped very much that the old man would enjoy it; but he felt it was a hollow ambition and was afraid Cornfeld would find it a disappointment – and, moreover, that he knew it would be, even now at the planning stage.

Slider stood at the door of the CID room, looking round the bent heads.

Hart noticed him. 'You're back,' she said.

'Plus ten for observation. Who had the list of Chattie's telephone calls?'

'Andy,' she said. 'Shall I get it for you?' She jumped up and went across to Mackay's desk.

Slider wandered off into his room. Atherton followed him there. 'I know that look,' he said. 'Did Daddy Cornfeld say something interesting?'

'He's *for* the takeover,' Slider said. 'He always was. Killing Chattie didn't make any difference to his decision. He's been in negotiation for weeks.'

'Another damn fine theory hits the dust,' said Atherton, scratching the back of his head. 'So what does that leave us with?'

'There's something burrowing away at the back of my mind,' said Slider.

'Yes, I know, I just had that feeling,' Atherton said, but Slider, frowning in thought, didn't hear.

Mackay came in with the list. 'You wanted this, guv? I was just getting a coffee.'

'Yes, give it here.' Slider sat at his desk and ran a finger up the list. Mackay had written against the numbers who the subscribers were. 'Here it is,' Slider said, tapping the paper. 'She phoned Cockerell on his mobile on the Monday before she died. Why didn't you mention this?'

'Well, guv, once I found he was a family member – you said anything unusual. I didn't think that counted.'

'Hm. I suppose so.'

Atherton leaned over and looked. 'You were expecting to find that call?'

'It was a hunch,' Slider said. 'Don't you see? *She* made the appointment with *him*.'

'And you can deduce that from the mere fact of a telephone number?' Atherton marvelled.

'Don't get cute. Why else would she call him?'

'Maybe she called him about something else, and he used the opportunity to make the appointment. Why would he pretend he made the running?' Atherton countered.

'Because whatever she wanted to see him for, he didn't want us to know about. We knew he was lying. This is what he was lying about.'

'Ah. Even so, where does that get us?'

'I don't know yet. I have to think.' He waved them away.

Mackay said kindly, 'Shall I get you a cuppa, guv?'

'Yes, that'll help. Thanks.' He turned to Atherton. 'Can you bring me the list you had of the drugs GCC makes?'

'Okay. Anything I should know about?'

'You'll know when I know,' said Slider.

Mackay was a long time getting the tea. He came in at last, saying, 'Sorry, guv. I got waylaid, and then there was a queue.'

'Thanks,' Slider said absently, with the look that told Mackay he probably wouldn't remember it was there until it was well cold. 'Can you do something for me? Track down Mrs Hammick and get her to come in. I want to ask her something. Don't alarm her.'

'Sure,' said Mackay. Slider's head went down again. 'Don't forget your tea, guv. I've put it just here for you.'

'Mm,' said Slider.

* * *

Despite anything Mackay could do, Mrs Hammick arrived in Slider's office in a state of tension; though she still had enough self-possession to look round very sharply, and with an absorbent capacity that would have given her a real edge in the CID.

'Thank you for coming in,' Slider said. 'I hope it wasn't too inconvenient. There was something I wanted to ask you.'

'Oh, no, it's all right. I don't mind. I do a lady in Devonport Road Tuesday afternoons, so it's only a step.' She looked at the mess of things on Slider's desk as though it could tell her something. 'I've never been in a police station before, not the upstairs bit, but it's just like you see on *The Bill*, isn't it? Have you found out who killed poor Chattie?'

'We're getting there,' said Slider. 'Mrs Hammick—'

'Maureen, please,' she said, as though this were a social visit.

He smiled distractedly. 'There's something you said to me when I last spoke to you – when you so helpfully came in to the station to tell us you knew Chattie.' She nodded. 'I can't remember exactly what it was, but you were telling me how kind she was—'

'Oh, yes, there never was anyone so kind. Gave loads of money to charity, you know, and always ready to listen to your troubles.'

'Yes, of course, but I think you said that when you were there one day she was talking to a young man with acne.'

'Oh, yes,' she said promptly. 'That was not long before – before that dreadful day. Was it Monday? Let me think. No, Monday was the day I caught Jassy in there, the little tramp, up to no good. I'd only just popped in with the croissants, and a good job I did, as it turns out. No, it

312

must have been the Friday, because it was when I was there cleaning. Yes, that's right. He rang the bell and I was nearest so I went and let him in. Poor young man! Nice-looking, he would have been, if it wasn't for the horrible spots.'

'Do you know if he had an appointment to see her?'

'Well, I think he must have, because as I opened the door, Chattie came out of her office behind me and she said, "Oh, you must be . . ." whatever his name was, and he said yes and she said, "Come in, then," and took him into her office.'

'So you think it was a business call?'

'I suppose so. She didn't seem to know him. I mean, if it was social, she wouldn't have had to ask, would she?'

'No, that's true. Did you hear what they talked about?'

She looked offended. 'Are you suggesting I eavesdrop?'

'Not at all. I'm sure you would never do anything like that. I just thought you might have caught a few words inadvertently when passing the door that would give you an idea of the general subject,' Slider said delicately.

'Well,' she said, giving herself away completely, 'I *was* cleaning the hall at the time, while they were having their meeting, which is how I knew how kind she was being to him, because whenever I went past the door, she was looking at him and listening to him so attentively, poor young man, like the kind person she was. But as to what he was saying, no, I can't say I heard anything that would help you.' Something occurred to her, and she looked alarmed. 'You don't think he was the murderer?'

'No, not at all.'

'Oh, well, that's a relief. I'd hate to think I'd been feel-ing sorry for him, let alone talking to him, if he was a murderer.'

'You talked to him?'

'Well, I happened to be in the hall when they finished their meeting, and as Chattie and him got to the door of her room, the phone rang, so I said to her, "You take your call, dear, I'll see the young man out." Which I did.'

'And you talked to him?' Slider was not hopeful, given that she had only had the length of the hall to work in. 'What did you find out?'

'Find out?' she bristled.

'I know you were only passing the time of day,' Slider soothed her, 'but did you find out his name, or where he came from?'

'As to his name, Chattie did say it when she saw him at the door, as I said, but what it was I can't remember.' She screwed up her brow. 'Was it Bill something? Or John? Quite a plain name, I think it was. No, I can't remember.'

'If it does come to you—'

'Oh, yes, of course, I'll let you know. But as to where he came from, well, he worked in Boots, that I did find out.'

'Boots?'

'Of course, it might have been one of the other chemists. You see, as I was showing him out, I asked him was Chattie going to do some work for him, because she was very good and very efficient, and he'd not be sorry he'd come to her. Just to help her business along, you understand. I always said that sort of thing when I had the chance.'

'Very good of you.'

'Well, she was good to me. Anyway, the young man said no, that wasn't why he'd come, and I asked him what line of business he was in, and he said he was a chemist. And I thought what a shame it was he should work in a shop all day surrounded by all those medicines and

314

everything, and not be able to do anything about his face, poor man. But I didn't say it aloud, of course.'

'Of course not.'

'And in any case I wouldn't have had the chance, because he was obviously in a hurry, because that's all he did say – "I'm a chemist," he said, and the next minute he was opening the door himself before I had a chance to and he said good morning, really quick, and away he went. Not running, but hurrying as fast as he could walk.' She paused and looked at Slider, head slightly cocked, waiting for his reaction.

'Thank you,' he said. 'You've been very helpful.'

'Is that all you wanted to know?'

'Yes, that was it. If you should remember the young man's name, or if you remember anything you might have heard of their conversation, even a single word, you'll let me know?'

'Of course I will. But I don't promise anything. I wasn't really listening, you know. But if I recall his name . . .' She thought of something. 'It wasn't in her diary?'

'No,' said Slider.

'Oh. Maybe a last-minute thing, then. She always wrote appointments in her diary, but if he just rang on the off-chance and said, "Can I come round?" maybe she wouldn't write it down.'

'I'm sure that was it,' said Slider.

It was lunchtime when Tufnell Arceneaux called.

'You're not going to like this,' he said, his roar muted with sympathy.

'I've been expecting bad news,' Slider said. 'Tell me the worst. The blood on the hoodie isn't Chattie's. It isn't even human blood. It's the wrong clothes, this is the wrong case, and I'm in the wrong job.'

'Dear me, you are depressed,' Tufty said. 'Time I took you out on the spree and showed you how to get the hang of life.'

'Every time I go out with you I get the hangover of life.'

'That's because you lack practice. No skill is acquired without dedicated, repeated practice.'

'Tell me what you've got to tell me and let me crawl away and die in peace.'

'Well, it's not as bad as all that. The blood on the grey top *is* human blood and the DNA profile matches that of your victim, so you've got the right clothes. There was also some of her blood on the outside of the gloves. On the inside of the gloves we found sweat containing skin cells, which we were able to profile. There was also a longish dark hair inside the hood, though there was no bulb to it so we could only get mitochondrial DNA from the shaft, but there were also skin cells inside the hood from the scalp, which we were able to process, to determine that the wearer of the grey top and the wearer of the gloves were the same person.'

'And?'

'It wasn't your suspect.'

'Toby Harkness?'

'That's the feller. Only he wasn't the feller. I didn't even need to do a comparison. It wasn't any feller at all.'

'What do you mean?'

'DNA, my old banana, is a wonderful thing, but as you know, all the profiles in the world won't help a smidge unless you've got something to compare them with. About the only useful thing you can learn from unmatched DNA is the sex – or, not to be invidious, the gender – of the person concerned.'

'You're saying the murderer was a woman?'

316

'Now, now, don't put words into my mouth. I'm saying the wearer of the grey top and the gloves was a woman.'

'Are you sure?'

'I'll pretend you didn't say that,' Tufty said kindly. 'I know you're under a lot of strain. X marks the spot, old bean. Or, rather, XX. If it was a man, there'd have been a Y – if not a wherefore.'

Slider gave a gasping laugh. 'Tufty, I love you and I want to have your babies.'

'You don't know how many times I've heard that today,' Tufty said gravely.

'Well, well,' said Porson. 'So your hunch was justified. You thought it wasn't Harkness, didn't you?'

'It was the manner of the killing. It didn't look like a passionate frenzy.'

'No,' Porson said thoughtfully, walking up and down the space between his desk and the window. 'Now you mention it, the MO was daft enough, it could only be a woman.'

Slider concealed a smile. It was lucky that remark would never get beyond these four walls.

'So, what have we got in the woman-suspect department? Henry Cornfeld left enough chaos behind him in his personal life.'

'Yes, there are two ex-wives still alive and two other daughters.'

'Not to mention, presumably, a scad of mistresses and outworn dolly birds. But then they'd surely try to murder him, not his daughter.'

'And there are possibilities in Chattie's life – jealous rivals, perhaps.'

'I suppose,' Porson said, pausing to tap his fingers on his desk – shave and a haircut, two bits, 'I suppose the

Brixton daughter is the best bet. She's a bit of a loose canyon.'

'Jassy and her mother are alibis for each other,' said Slider, 'and there's nothing to suggest the mother's anything but honest.'

'When it comes to protecting her own daughter, though,' Porson said wisely. 'It's best to take no chances. Better have a look at that alibi.'

'We could get a sample from her and check it against the DNA on the gloves.'

Porson tapped again, frowning. 'Better get some sort of idea first. All this testing is expensive. Any other lines to follow up?'

'Yes, there's something I've been thinking my way through, but there's a link missing in the chain.'

Porson nodded, eyebrows raised, receptive; but Slider didn't want to go through it yet, for fear of dislodging something delicate. He hadn't completely worked it out himself. When he didn't speak, Porson went on, 'By the way, how is Hart working out?'

'She's good, and she fits in well,' Slider said.

'But?'

'Oh, no buts.'

'You sounded a bit muted. Not chucking bokays about.'

'Only that I didn't see the point, as she's temporary.'

'Ah, well, that was rather the point. I was sounding out Mr Wetherspoon, and it looks as though Anderson might be kept on for another six months.'

'Oh, no!'

'Oh, yes, I'm afraid. Which would leave you two men down, seeing as you were a man short before Anderson got requisitioned. I told Mr Wetherspoon it wasn't acceptable, and he agreed with me. In a way.'

'In a way?'

'Said yes, but didn't offer any suggestions. I suppose everybody's ear'oling him for more staff, and he's only got so many bodies to go round. But then I heard a rumour that Hart might want to stay with us.'

He may look like something escaped from Mount Rushmore, Slider thought, but there wasn't much escaped him, one way and another. 'I think she'd jump at the chance, sir,' he said.

'In that case—'

Porson's phone rang. He lifted a finger – the conversational pause button – and picked up the receiver. 'Yes? Yes, he's here. Yes. All right, put her through.' He held out the receiver to Slider. 'Your Mrs Haddock wants a word. Says it's urgent.'

Slider took it. 'Slider here.'

'Oh, Mr Slider? It's Maureen Hammick. I thought you'd want to know straight away, seeing as you said it was important. I've remembered that young man's name, that came to see Chattie on the Friday. It was Simpson. Bill Simpson. I knew it was something plain. And I've been worrying my brain about it while I've been Hoovering, and it suddenly came to me, because there used to be an actor called Bill Simpson, didn't there? Or was that Bill Sikes?' she tripped herself, troubled. 'No, wait a minute, that was Oliver Reed, wasn't it?'

'Oliver Twist,' said Slider, unable to help himself.

'Yes, that's right. Nasty piece of work, he was, a drunk and a bully.'

Slider managed to stop himself asking if she meant Oliver Reed or Bill Sikes, and asked instead, 'The young man who visited Chattie was called Bill Simpson? Are you quite sure?'

'Yes, absolutely positive. I remember now. When I opened the door she came out behind me in the hall and said, "You must be Bill Simpson?" and he said, "That's right," and she took him straight into her room. Seemed very nervous, he did, but maybe it was just his spots, poor thing, knowing what he looked like. But she was wonderful with him, put him right at his ease, and the way she smiled at him and paid him attention, you'd never know he wasn't Pierce Brosnan.'

'Thank you very much,' Slider said, anxious to stem the flow. 'You've been wonderfully helpful, Mrs Hammick.' He near as damnit said Haddock. Porson was catching. 'Thank you and goodbye.'

He handed the receiver back to Porson, who dumped it, and said, 'Oliver Twist?'

Slider made a never-mind gesture. 'Mrs Haddock – Hammick – has just given me what I hope is the last link in the chain.'

'Well, go to it,' Porson said. 'Sic, boy. Let me know if it works out.'

Slider went, blessing Porson's restraint and trust in him in not asking him for an immediate exposition.

17

Cloaca and Dagger

Hart came to his door. 'You wanted me, sir?'

'Yes, a little job for you. I want you to find out if GCC has an employee called Bill Simpson. They must have a central personnel department.'

'Human resources, guv,' she said. 'You ain't allowed to call it personnel any more.'

'He's a chemist, so he'll probably work in one of the labs.'

'In this country?'

'Of course in this country. I'm not asking you to trawl the world. It'll probably be in south-east England, so if the personnel lists are divided by region, try that first. If you find him, I want his name, address and telephone.'

'Okey-doke. Anyfing else?'

'Yes, send Atherton in.'

To Atherton he said, 'You're good at financial stuff. I want you to find out who bought Jassy's shares. Is that a possibility?'

'If they were bought as a block, it's easy,' he said. 'Anyone who buys more than three per cent of a company's shares has to make a special declaration to the registrar. If they were bought by a number of people it will be more difficult. It'll be a matter of comparing all the transactions at the time and tracking them down.'

'Okay, see what you can do.'

Atherton hesitated. 'Can I know what, yet?'

'Soon,' said Slider.

Atherton was back first, and he looked at Slider with what was almost admiration. 'Bingo,' he said. 'Jassy's shares were bought in a block – or, rather, ownership was transferred. One presumes she got payment for them. They were transferred to an offshore holding company in Guernsey, called Mobius Holdings. And the owners and sole directors of Mobius are David and Ruth Cockerell.'

'Ah,' said Slider.

'How did you know?'

'I didn't know, I wanted to find out. I suppose she got into money trouble and approached him.'

'She seems to have begged from everyone else.'

'Yes. It might have been one of those times when the usual sources had got fed up and cut her off for a time. And he took the opportunity to get his hands on some more shares.'

'I wonder what he paid her for them?' Atherton mused. 'Be interesting to know if it was market value. I'd take a bet it wasn't. She may think she's smart, but Jassy's got the brains of a glass of water. So, that makes the Cockerells together the biggest shareholder after old man Henry, with twenty per cent between them. What's your thinking?'

'That timing is everything,' said Slider. 'But we've still got to find out what the meeting with Chattie was really about. Ah, this could be the missing link.'

Hart had appeared at the door. 'She doesn't look a bit like an ape,' Atherton said.

'Wossup?' she said, looking from one to the other. 'Have I missed anuvver racist remark?'

'Have you got it?' Slider asked, seeing badinage in his colleagues' eyes.

'Yeah, boss. Bill Simpson. Research chemist. Works at the unit at Bedford. But I've found out something more. He's been off work for a week.'

'Has he, indeed? You interest me strangely.'

'Yeah. He phoned in sick on Friday week past, and he hasn't been in since. Said he had the 'flu. The person I spoke to at Bedford said he'd been looking a bit queer for a day or two before, so they weren't surprised he'd gone sick.'

'I wonder if anyone's heard of him since?' Slider said thoughtfully.

'D'you want me to ask 'em?'

'No, I don't want to alert anyone. I'll go round and see him. Where does he live?'

'Luton,' said Hart.

'Well, I suppose somebody has to,' said Atherton. 'I hope you don't want me to come with you.'

'Can I come, guv?' Hart said. 'I ain't picky.'

'No,' Slider said. 'I'll take Swilley. If I'm right, this could take sensitive handling.' He got up and went briskly through to the CID room.

Hart and Atherton looked at each other. 'Well, that's two of us he's insulted at one go.'

Bill Simpson lived in a flat in a glum new block in one of the less appealing parts of Luton. Swilley was a good companion, and rode with Slider in silence all the way, where a lesser mortal would have troubled him with questions. Only when they got out of the car did she say, 'How d'you want to work it, boss?'

'If I'm right, he's holed up and terrified, so he prob-ably wouldn't open the door to me. I want you to knock and get us in. Reassure him.'

'Am I police?'

'Oh, yes. I don't think it's anyone in authority he's afraid of.'

'Right you are.'

The block was long and narrow rather than square, and four storeys high. Simpson's flat was on the top floor, and the lifts weren't working. They walked up the stairs, which smelt faintly of urine, but at least weren't littered with abandoned needles. Glum, but not that rough, fortu-nately, Slider concluded. When they reached the door, Slider stood back out of sight and Swilley positioned herself in front of the peephole and knocked and rang. After a while she put her ear to the door, and whispered to Slider, 'There's someone in there. I can hear him moving about.'

'Try again, and call out to him,' Slider whispered back.

She knocked again and called, 'Mr Simpson? Could you open the door, please, sir? It's the police, and we want to talk to you.'

As Slider had hoped, the female voice gave the occu-pant hope. Swilley saw the shadow on the peephole, held up her warrant card, and smiled.

'What do you want?' came a muffled voice from within.

'Just to talk to you,' Swilley said. 'It's not trouble for you, I promise you.'

'Let me see your ID,' the voice said. 'Put it through the letterbox.'

Slider nodded, and Swilley obeyed.

Eventually the voice said, 'All right, it looks genuine. What do you want?'

'I can't talk out here. Please open the door. No-one's

going to hurt you. We just want to ask you a few questions.'

'We?' There was quick alarm. 'Who's we?'

'I've got my boss, Inspector Slider, with me. He's really nice, honest.'

She moved aside and Slider moved out to where he could be seen, and held up his brief as well. That, too, had to be pushed through the letterbox before Simpson would consent to open the door a crack, with the chain on. Slider smiled gently at the portion of a face that appeared, and said, 'I know you're frightened, Mr Simpson. We're here to help you, but you must tell us what it's all about. Please let me in. I promise you, you're not in trouble, and no-one's going to hurt you.'

'You don't know,' the voice quavered, and the red-rimmed eyes filled with tears. 'They killed her, and they'll come for me next.'

'We'll protect you. Please open the door.'

He seemed convinced at last, or perhaps was simply too desperate for someone to talk to to resist. The door closed, the chain rattled off, and then it was opened again with great caution. Slider thought he was still expecting the sudden rush, the door kicked in and himself grabbed, so he stood quite still, until Simpson had examined his appearance fully. As to Simpson, he was unshaven, haggard, and exhausted-looking. His hair was matted and tousled, his eyes bloodshot and haunted, and his face was ravaged by that cruellest of diseases, adult acne. Slider found himself remembering Barrington again, his tortured former boss, who had ended up with a gun barrel in his mouth and half his head on the kitchen wall. Barrington's face had been scarred like a moonscape from acne. A huge pity washed through him.

'Don't be afraid,' he said again.

Simpson's lips quivered. He was close to breaking. 'They must have known I overheard them,' he said, almost in a whisper. 'They killed her. It was my fault for going to her, getting her involved. I should have gone to her father, but he was out of the country, and I was afraid to wait. It was my fault she was murdered.'

'No, no, it wasn't,' said Slider, edging in gently past him, Swilley following.

'They killed her and they'll come for me next. You've got to help me.'

'I will help you,' Slider said soothingly. 'Just tell me exactly what it was you overheard.'

Atherton put the phone down. 'The cock o' the walk's not come in to work. Skulking at home with a stomach bug, apparently.'

'It may be true,' Slider said. 'Fear does go to people's stomachs sometimes.'

'You think he knows what we — what you suspect?'

'His secretary may have told him we pumped her,' Slider said. 'I felt at the time she was suffering from a crisis of loyalties. Or he may just be worried because we turned up at all. He didn't strike me as a man of great resolution or great intellect.'

'He struck me as a pillock,' said Atherton.

'That's what I said. Well, it's good that he's at home. We can kill two birds with one stone.'

'We?'

'You can come this time,' Slider said. 'I may need you. I don't know quite how the conversation's going to go.'

'He needs me,' Atherton observed to the air, in a quavering voice.

'Stop clowning, and let's get going,' said Slider.

* * *

Cockerell's house was in a village called Buckland Common, in the green and delicious edges of the Chiltern Hills. It was modern, large, set in an acre or so of manicured lawn, and built in the presently fashionable mock-Tudor style, whose vernacular involved stuck-on beams, diamond-pane windows, gables, long sloping roofs, and fancy tile hanging, but omitted any chimneys. There was also a tennis court and a deeply authentic Tudor detached double garage. Given its size, position and acreage, Slider reckoned it would probably market at about a million and a half, which hardly put the Cockerells in the poor and needy bracket. Ruth's resentment of her father's wealth was obviously comparative.

It was she who opened the door. Slider recognised her from the photograph in Cockerell's office. She was of medium height, slender, with dark hair in a hairdresser's arrangement; she wore slacks and a short-sleeved jumper of expensive but dull knitwear; her face was expertly made-up, which went a long way to concealing that she was plain; but her expression was sullen and, at the sight of Slider and Atherton, became also alert and wary.

'We've come to see your husband, Mrs Cockerell,' Slider said.

'Well, you can't,' she snapped. 'He's ill.'

'I'm afraid I shall have to insist. It's very important. Will you tell him we're here, please?'

Calculations flitted about behind her eyes, but at last she stepped back and let them in. 'I'll tell him, but I don't know if he'll come,' she said ungraciously, and left them standing in the hall while she went upstairs.

Slider looked quickly around. The interior was different from both Henry's and Chattie's, in that everything was modern and expensive, but conventional, arranged without flair or taste. It was the wealthy man's equivalent of a room display in a Courts' showroom. The nearest room on the left was the living-room, on the right a dining-room. The house smelt of furniture polish and new carpet, and was silent, not even a ticking clock anywhere, only the sound of birdsong coming faintly from the garden, struggling through the Tudor double-glazing.

In the living-room, on the floor beside one of the sofas, was an expensive crocodile handbag. Slider gave Atherton a sharp look and quick jerk of the head. Atherton went in and picked it up, looked through it quickly. He held up a mobile phone, one of the new tiny Motorolas that would fit into the top pocket of a man's shirt. The same sort that Chattie had had. 'Just one. Switched on,' he said.

Slider nodded and Atherton came back to his side. 'Must be upstairs,' Slider said quietly. 'Probably in one of her drawers.' And he remembered Nutty Nicholls saying once that women always kept things of value, or things they wanted to hide, in their underwear drawer.

Slider took out his own mobile, tapped in the number of Atherton's, and replaced it in his pocket. Then they waited in silence until footsteps came back down the carpeted stairs, and David Cockerell appeared, looking much less *soigné* than the last time, in a pair of grey flannel bags, a blue checked shirt open at the neck, and carpet slippers. Slider had a deep horror of men's carpet slippers and an instinctive suspicion of anyone who would wear them. Cockerell was looking ill enough for his excuse to be true, but interestingly he did not seem to be worried by Slider's and Atherton's presence, only annoyed.

'I don't know what's so urgent that you couldn't wait until I was back at the office,' he opened proceedings. 'I'm not well, as my wife told you.'

'Yes, I'm sorry to hear that,' Slider said. 'But it's rather important. I have some things I want to talk to you about. Shall we sit down and be comfortable?'

'You're very free with my hospitality,' said Cockerell, with weak indignation.

'It might take a while,' Slider said. 'As you're not well, I thought you ought to sit down, but we'll talk standing up if you like.'

Put like that, Cockerell had to submit. He led the way into the living-room. Slider almost held his breath over whether Mrs C would come with them, but it seemed she did not want to be left out of anything – or perhaps needed to know what they knew – and she followed them in. They all took seats, and under cover of the general sitting down, Slider pushed the send button on his phone. Atherton's mobile rang.

Slider and Atherton both reached for their phones. It had become a universal gesture, these days. Even Cockerell looked about for his own, and Ruth made a half-rise gesture towards her handbag before Atherton said, 'It's me,' and answered it. Slider pressed the end button on his and returned it to his pocket. Atherton spoke a word or two into his phone, then rose and said to the company, 'Excuse me. I'll just take this outside,' and left the room.

Mrs Cockerell completed the movement towards her handbag, took it back with her to her seat, extracted a packet of cigarettes and lit one, without offering them to anyone else.

'Well,' Cockerell said impatiently to Slider, 'what have you got to say to me? It had better be important.'

'I think it is. You see, someone told me a story today, which I hadn't heard before. It was very interesting. It seems that many years ago an Australian doctor discovered that ulcers weren't caused by an excess of acid in

329

the stomach, as everyone had always thought, but by a bacterium.'

'*Helicobacter pyloris*,' Cockerell said impatiently. 'Everyone knows that.'

'Yes, I suppose most people do know it now. But the thing was, they didn't then. This doctor did all sorts of tests and controlled experiments, and he proved conclusively that it was the bacterium that was to blame, and that you could eliminate it and cure the ulcers with a simple dose of antibiotic. Well, you'd think everyone would be delighted, and I suppose his patients were. But when the doctor tried to go public with his findings, things got rather nasty. The Australian medical profession and the drugs companies banded together to rubbish his ideas and prevent him publishing his findings. They condemned him as a quack and a lunatic. Because, you see, they had been making a fortune for years out of selling antacids to ulcer sufferers, and this doctor's research was going to kill off the golden goose.'

'What the devil has all this rigmarole got to do with me?' Cockerell said testily, but there was consciousness in his eyes. Ruth Cockerell was watching Slider like a cat at a mouse-hole, her whole face and body intent and alert. Only one hand moved, lifting the cigarette to her mouth and away.

'I'm getting to that,' Slider said. 'Just let me finish my story my own way, if you will, or I shall lose my thread. Anyway, this doctor's life was made such a misery that he lost his practice, and he was hounded out of the country. He went to America, where eventually he managed to convince people that he wasn't mad, and his findings were published, and gradually the right treatment began to be offered to ulcer sufferers. Though I believe there are still some doctors who won't believe it

330

and go on prescribing antacids and special diets. And the thing is that it was more than twenty years ago that this doctor first tried to get his ideas into the public forum. Twenty years! Doesn't that astonish you?' His audience didn't answer. 'You see, it hadn't occurred to me before,' Slider said pleasantly, 'but of course there's more money to be made out of cures that don't work than cures that do, because the sufferers keep having to come back for more, and they will do anything and pay anything for relief. And this is especially true with common, non-life-threatening ailments which are, nevertheless, extremely unpleasant to put up with, like ulcers. And like acne.'

Ruth's expression did not change, and her body language gave nothing away, but Cockerell's shoulders seemed to slump a little, and he drew a breath like a sigh, as of one caught at last. Still, he seemed prepared to play the end game.

'I still don't see what this has to do with me.'

'Oh, I think you do, but I'm happy to spell it out for you. On Monday fortnight past, you were at the plant in Bedford for the opening of the new block. You were both there, in fact,' he said, gathering Ruth with his eyes. 'But you were not together the whole time. There was a rather good and rather liquid lunch, and just after it you separated for a very basic reason, and you, Mr Cockerell, went to the gents' lavatory with one of your fellow directors.'

'Is this really necessary?' Cockerell said, with great scorn.

'Yes, it is. Because while you were in there, perhaps fuelled by the champagne, you talked with rather too much frankness about Cornfeld's new drug, Codermatol. But in fact, you were not alone. Someone was in one of the stalls and, without intending to, overheard what you said.'

Cockerell looked startled. He stared at Slider in a

strained way. Interesting, Slider thought: Simpson's fears were quite unfounded. Cockerell had not known he was overheard, or, therefore, who had overheard him.

Slider went on: 'GCC makes a huge amount of money from selling acne treatments, none of which is really more than a palliative. But Codermatol really works. Obviously if it came out, it would kill off GCC's golden goose, just as the Australian doctor's findings about the *Helicobacter* would have. That was why GCC was so eager to buy Cornfeld Chemicals – so that it could suppress the new drug and make sure it never came on the market.'

'That's preposterous!' Cockerell said. 'It's total rubbish.'

'It's exactly what you said in the washroom that you were going to do. You had been in the forefront of the negotiations with Henry Cornfeld. You had to make him believe that you were interested in the new drug, and you had to make the offer for his company high enough to convince him that you were, because you knew that if *he* knew you never meant to let it reach the market, he would never have let you take over the company.

'Of course, you had no idea your plot had been uncovered until Chattie telephoned you on Monday last week. The person who overheard you had gone to her with the story, in the absence abroad of her father, knowing her reputation for liberal thinking and charitable actions.'

Ruth snorted at that point, apparently overcome by the praise of the deceased. Slider glanced at her curiously. She changed it to a cough, stubbed out her cigarette and lit another.

'You arranged to meet her on Tuesday, in the hope that you could persuade her to go along with the plot. Did you offer her money? I've been wondering what inducements you used. Well,' he dismissed the question with a wave of his hand as it was obvious it would not be answered, 'it doesn't matter. She refused absolutely to go along with it, and warned you, moreover, that she was going to tell her father as soon as he got back from the States exactly what was going on. And she knew, as you did, that Henry Cornfeld was a man of principle, in this if not in his private life, and that he was immensely proud of Codermatol. He would not allow you to bury it. The sale would not go through – and you had so much to lose, hadn't you, Mr Cockerell?'

Atherton came back in at that moment, and by nothing more than a blink told Slider that he had been successful. Slider felt a huge rush of relief. They were on the right track. A hideous embarrassment and a writ like a Rottweiler to the goolies were going to be avoided.

'Sorry,' Atherton said, sitting down. 'Have I missed much?'

'We were just about to calculate what Mr Cockerell stood to lose if the Cornfeld acquisition didn't go through,' said Slider. 'To begin with there were the shares in Cornfeld Chemicals. Mrs Cockerell's ten per cent, which had been given to her, and the ten per cent you bought very cheaply from Jassy would both show a very nice profit and net you a huge lump sum. And then there was your job at GCC, the promotion, share options and golden eggs you could expect from a company whose contin-ued prosperity you had assured. So Chattie had to be stopped. You were heard to say, when you got back from the meeting with her, thank God there were a few days left – which meant, of course, before Henry Cornfeld came home. Once she'd had a chance to tell him, all would be lost. She said she was going to wait and tell him face to face. But what if she changed her mind and telephoned him in the States? It wasn't safe to take the chance. And the next morning, Chattie was murdered.'

Cockerell made a strangled sound, and his eyes flew wide open. 'Good God! You don't think—? You can't possibly think *I* killed her? I'm not a murderer! I could never do a thing like that.' He stared at them wildly. Ruth was keeping very still, her whole body outlined in tension, still watching and waiting, but poised for sudden action. 'Come on!' Cockerell pleaded, almost groaned. 'I wouldn't hurt her, let alone kill her. I admit I felt a moment's relief when I heard she was dead, because – well, you were right about the other thing, and she was going to ruin it for all of us, the stupid girl. I said to her, you stand to gain as much as the rest of us. Everybody wins, you, me, your father, everyone. But she wouldn't listen. Went all pious and ethical on me, talking about the sufferings of millions. I said to her, it's only bloody acne, not cancer of the liver, but she wouldn't budge. I could have throttled her – oh, God, I don't mean that! That's just a figure of speech! Look, I know what we were doing about suppressing the drug was unethical, and I'm owning up to it, but murder's something different. I could never kill anyone, never. And certainly not for something like this. It's fantastic!'

Fascinating, Slider thought: he doesn't even think about his alibi. He wants to convince me that he *wouldn't* do it, rather than that he *couldn't*. He still wants to be a nice guy, despite all his greedy, sleazy plottings.

Still, he let him writhe a little bit longer before saying, 'As a matter of fact, I know you didn't do it.'

'You – you do?' Cockerell was sweating now, and licked his lips, looking at Slider in a slightly dazed way as he heard these words.

'What time did you leave for work that morning, sir?'

'That – that morning? I don't remember. But – wait – I was in the Northumberland Avenue office that day, wasn't I? So I would have left at half past six. I always leave at half past six, to be in at eight.'

'You were in the office by eight o'clock?'

'Yes. I mean, I don't remember exactly, but I must have been. I'd remember if I were late. My secretary—' he began to add, with a flash of inspiration.

'Yes, she says you were there at eight. And Chattie was killed somewhere around eight o'clock. So we know you couldn't have done it. Actually,' he added conversationally, 'I believe you when you say you wouldn't kill anyone just for money. But there is someone I think would.' He didn't look at Ruth. He kept his eyes on Cockerell as he said, 'When you went home that night, the day you met Chattie up in Town, you were angry. You told your wife all about it, how that damned girl was going to ruin things for everybody.'

'Yes, I suppose I did,' Cockerell said, pulling out a handkerchief to wipe his face, not following where this was going.

Slider turned to Ruth. 'You look very fit, Mrs Cockerell. Do you like to keep in trim – go jogging, go to a gym, anything like that?'

Her face was immobile. 'No,' she said. 'I don't.'

Cockerell, the dope, said, 'Yes, you do, darling. You're always exercising – I'm very proud of my wife's figure,' the poor goop went on, evidently pleased at this less threatening line of questioning. 'She goes out running most mornings.'

'Is that so?' Slider said, with interest. 'So you'll have jogging clothes, then. Training shoes, tracksuits, that sort of thing.'

Mrs Cockerell only glared, her face so tense he could

335

see the muscles of her jaw writhing under the skin, but she didn't answer him.

'I don't suppose,' he said gently, 'that you have an alibi for that morning, Mrs Cockerell?'

Cockerell stared at him in astonishment, and then gave his wife a quick, flashing glance. He opened his mouth to protest to Slider, but nothing emerged. A look of great sickness came over him, sickness and knowledge at the same time, and from the same source.

'Mrs Cockerell?' Slider pressed her.

'I was out running,' she answered, unclenching her jaws for just long enough to get the words out.

'How long had you been planning it? That's what I've been wondering,' Slider said, as if ruminatively. 'A long time, I would imagine. She'd been a thorn in your side for years – well, all her life, really. Your mother abandoned for her mother, and treated so badly in comparison with Stella Smart. And then the usurper's brat turns out to be pretty and clever and everybody loves her, while you – what do you get? Nothing! Your father dotes on Chattie, but he's got no time for you.' Mrs Cockerell's face was undergoing a reaction while he spoke, a look of boiling fury clenching it until he thought her teeth would shatter. 'And then, to crown it all, there were the rumours that she'd had an affair with your husband.'

'No!' Cockerell cried. 'That's not true. Good God, what are you saying?' He looked at Slider, seeming genuinely appalled. 'How can you say such a thing? There was nothing like that between us. We were friends, that's all.' He looked at his wife. 'I swear it was innocent! I never – we never—!'

'Shut up, you idiot!' Mrs Cockerell hissed. 'Don't you see what he's doing? For God's sake, shut up!'

Slider resumed, looking from one to the other with

apparent sympathy. 'Well, in practical terms, it doesn't really matter whether it happened or not. The fact was there were rumours. Had you brooded over it, Mrs Cockerell? Thought about murdering her, stroked and cherished the idea of it until it became a possibility, and then an inevitability? Until it was just a matter of how, and when. After all, you wanted her dead, but you didn't want to get caught. And then the Park Killer turned up, practically on Chattie's doorstep.'

'No,' Cockerell moaned. 'Oh, no!'

'Shut *up*, David!'

'The Park Killer kills joggers,' Slider continued to Ruth, not looking at him, 'and you know Chattie goes running every day in the park. But Chattie's younger than you, and she's strong. You don't think you'll be able just to stab her to death, the way the Park Killer does. You need some way to render her helpless first.'

Now the first chink appeared in Ruth's armour. She hadn't known he knew that, that the false stabbing had been detected. Her eyes widened and her nostrils flared, but she closed her lips tightly, as if to prevent anything escaping.

'You'd worked in a hospital pharmacy, so you knew what you needed. And you knew you'd have the chance to get hold of it at the opening of the new building at Bedford, which you were going to attend with your husband. They made the right sort of drugs there, and you knew your way around. No-one would ever wonder at your presence. You took what you needed, and then it was just a matter of waiting for the right opportunity. But when David came home and told you he had met Chattie that day, and what she had said, you knew you couldn't wait any longer. It would have to be done right away. You couldn't let her rob you again of what was your due. Kill her, be revenged for everything, and, as a bonus, break your father's heart, the way he had broken yours and your mother's. She deserved to die, she had to die.'

'Stop it!' Cockerell said. 'I order you to stop it! Get out of my house! I won't have you say those things to my wife!' He jumped to his feet, but Atherton was up too, and stood between him and Slider.

'Sit down, sir,' Atherton said. He could be amazingly menacing when he wanted to, Slider thought absently. 'Just sit. It has to be done. Sit down.'

Suddenly Ruth spoke, quite calmly. 'Yes, sit down, David. Don't make a fuss. This is all nonsense anyway. I didn't do it and they can't prove I did.'

'I'm afraid we can,' Slider said, with infinite, deadly kindness. He flickered a glance at Atherton, a signal between them. Somewhere upstairs, but just audibly, a telephone started to ring. Again Cockerell, the business-man, made the automatic gesture of looking for his mobile, but neither Slider nor Atherton moved. They were look-ing at Ruth. She looked faintly puzzled at first, and then her jaw dropped a little as understanding came to her.

'You know what that is, don't you?' Slider said. 'That's Chattie's mobile ringing. She had the same sort of mobile as you, the new, very dinky, pocket-sized Motorola. She dropped it while you were killing her, and you picked it up automatically, assuming it was yours. Perfectly under-standable, one of those things one does without think-ing – like stubbing out a cigarette. How long was it after you got home that you realised you had two mobiles in your pocket, yours and Chattie's?'

Ruth Cockerell gave an inarticulate cry of rage, leaped out of her chair and flung herself at Slider. 'I'll kill you!' she screamed, as she tried to claw his face.

Atherton jumped, and between them, though with

338

difficulty, they managed to subdue her, until she fell back into an armchair, hunched and panting. Cockerell remained motionless all through, his hands clasped together in his lap, his head turned away and his fixed eyes staring at nothing, at disaster and ruin.

'I'm glad I killed her,' Mrs Cockerell shrieked. She punched the upholstered arm of the chair repeatedly. 'She deserved it, the greedy, evil, man-grabbing little bitch. She deserved to die. She had everything, everything she ever wanted, she stole my father and my home, and still she had to have my husband and my money as well. I killed her and I'd kill her again if I could. Do what you like! You can't touch me for it. I hate you all!'

Cockerell moaned softly, closing his eyes, as if that would make it all go away. Slider stood over her, in case she tried to make a run for it, and said, 'Ruth Cockerell, I arrest you for the murder of Charlotte Cornfeld. You do not have to say anything . . .'

The firm's celebratory drink had to wait until Wednesday evening. They went to the Boscombe Arms, having had to abandon the Crown since it modernised itself, and Joanna joined them there. Everybody was hungry, and once they had settled themselves comfortably in the snug, Swilley was sent to operate her charm on Andy Barrett, the landlord, for the provision of snacks, which came in the end in the form of packets of crisps, pork pies and some hastily knocked together cheese and pickle sandwiches.

'A feast fit for a king,' Joanna said, observing McLaren savaging a sandwich with faint wonder. The sandwich didn't have a chance.

Swilley swung the plate her way. 'Have something,' she said, 'before Maurice scoffs the lot.'

It was the first time Joanna had been to one of these dos. She sat on the banquette beside Slider, and felt all the pleasure of being his woman, accepted, not exactly one of the group but a welcome honorary member. Pints were sunk, conversation blossomed, the noise level grew. She answered friendly questions from Swilley about her pregnancy and from Hollis about their plans for finding somewhere else to live. At one point Slider put his arm round her casually to balance himself as he leaned over for a piece of pork pie, and then left it there, warm and heavy and comfortable. She tried not to be aware of Hart watching the action, but noted in spite of herself that Hart looked at Slider a great deal more than she ever looked at Atherton. She saw Atherton watching her and Slider together, too, when he wasn't swapping barbed badinage with Swilley. She wondered whether he wished he had Sue there, as Bill had her.

'And there's something else to celebrate,' Hart said loudly, to catch attention. The noise level fell a notch as everyone looked at her. 'Least, *I* think it's good news,' Hart went on, looking round the group, but allowing her eyes to come to rest at last on Slider. Well, Joanna told herself, that's natural. He is the boss, and the heart of the group: she appreciated so much more, now, for having witnessed the drink-up, how that was true.

'Go on, then, Tone,' McLaren invited, gathering the crumbs from the otherwise empty sandwich plate with a wetted forefinger. 'Tell us.'

'Mr Porson's had a word wiv Mr Wevverspoon, and I'm not going back to the DAFT squad. I'm wiv you permanently. How about that?'

She beamed, and so did everyone else, and there were thumps of congratulation on her back and a tickly kiss on her cheek from Hollis's appalling moustache. Atherton took advantage of the precedent and said, 'Jolly good,' and kissed her too, only on the mouth. She let him, to a chorus of oy-oys, and even gave a show of wriggling her shoulders and lifting one foot behind in a Hollywood manner, but as soon as they broke apart she looked inevitably at Slider for his reaction. Joanna glanced up at him and saw he was smiling indulgently, and laughed at herself for a fool. There was nothing in that smile but fatherliness.

All the same, she thought, there's too much attention being paid to that girl, and she said, loudly enough to attract attention, 'I still don't know the end of the story. Who's going to tell it?'

'Go on, boss,' Hart urged, giving him her full attention. 'I think there's different bits all of us're wondering about.'

So Slider told the tale.

'The effect of theatricals on a weak mind,' he concluded, when he got to the bit about Chattie's mobile. 'I had the feeling that a parade of scientific evidence wouldn't move her – especially as we hadn't actually matched her DNA at that point to the stuff found on the clothes – but the entirely superficial ringing of the mobile got through her guard.'

'How did you know she had it?' Joanna asked.

'I didn't,' said Slider. 'But we couldn't find it anywhere, so it seemed likely that the murderer had taken it away, and when we checked and found Ruth's mobile was the same model, it seemed even more likely.'

'She might have thrown it away.'

'She might have, but if she had, I felt it was likely someone else would have found it, and either they'd have handed it in, if they were honest, or turned it on, if they weren't. As soon as it was turned on, we'd be able to

341

trace the signal. It never was, so it was a matter of Atherton slipping upstairs while I talked to them and seeing if he could find it.'

'It was in the drawer of her bedside table,' Atherton said, 'along with her pearls and her pills. Very traditional.'

'As to the actual murder,' Slider went on, 'Ruth had the perfect excuse to accost Chattie in the park, and persuade her to go into the shrubbery to talk. Chattie would believe it was about the suppression of the Codermatol again, and the secrecy, and Ruth wearing the hood of her top up would make sense and not make her suspicious.'

'You guessed from the beginning it was someone she knew, didn't you, boss,' Swilley said, 'because the CD Walkman had been turned off and she'd taken the earphones off. They were hanging round her neck. She wouldn't go to that trouble to talk to a stranger stopping to ask her for a light, or something.'

'The knife was an ordinary kitchen knife,' Slider went on, 'of the sort of which Ruth has a set in her kitchen. We'll test them all for blood, of course. It's surprising how often you can get enough even from a knife that's been washed several times. She'd have done better – from the Murderer's Manual point of view – to discard it with the clothes and replace it with a new one, but I suppose she didn't like the waste of the idea. She'd been brought up frugally. She wiped it on the grey top before she chucked it. Her biggest mistake, of course, was discarding the jacket and gloves so close to the scene. Otherwise we might never have found them.'

'Yes, why did she?' Joanna asked.

Atherton answered. 'Because she wanted to have a look at the scene of her crime, and admire the way she'd mis-directed us.'

'I guessed it when I saw the map in my mind's eye.

Ashchurch Grove makes a sort of D shape with Askew Road, Askew Road being the curved bit. When she left the park she went off up Askew Road, presumably heading back for her car; but then she passed the end of Ashchurch Grove and I suppose its direction tempted her and curiosity overcame her. There was no hue and cry after her, so she felt safe and thought she'd stroll back from a different direction and have a good laugh at how she'd fooled us. But she didn't quite like to bring the blood-stained clothes back, so she dropped them, in their carrier bag, over the fence of one of the gardens. There were bags of rubbish everywhere, so why should one more be noticed?'

'And in any case, she'd worn gloves, so no-one could bring it back to her – so she thought,' said Atherton.

'How do you know that's what she did? Did she tell you?' Joanna asked.

'No, I told her,' Slider said. 'At the very beginning, when I still thought it was the Park Killer, I had the faces in the crowd round the scene photographed, because it's amazing how often they will come back to see. Curiosity, I suppose. A very basic human instinct.'

'And she was there?'

'She was there,' Slider said. 'When I saw her photo in her husband's office, I thought she looked familiar. I'd spent so long staring at those damned crowd photos, her face had lodged in my brain.'

'One thing I don't understand,' Joanna said. 'How did she get Chattie to take the poison?'

'I worked that out,' Slider said, 'when I remembered something Bicycle Man, Phil Yerbury, did when he came in to be interviewed. Ruth was a runner too, so she knew the pattern. What's the first thing a runner or a jogger or whatever does when they stop for any reason?'

Joanna had followed him. 'Take a drink of water?'

'Right. And they don't just sip, they chuck it back in a couple of huge gulps. All Ruth had to do, as Chattie was feeling for her bottle, was to say, "Here, have some of mine." A little Lucozade or something in it to disguise any bitterness and – wallop.'

'Clever,' said Joanna.

'If she'd refused, Ruth would just have had to stab her cold, but it was worth a try. And evidently it worked. Chattie was so kind-hearted she probably wouldn't have refused what seemed like a friendly gesture, especially as I imagine Ruth had not been particularly friendly before. Maybe Ruth said it was a special energy drink or something. Anyway, she swallowed enough to put her into a coma within minutes.'

'And you still don't know what it was?'

'It doesn't matter, really. The tox lab will come back to us in its own good time, but we've got enough evidence to be going on with.' Even as he said it, a slight doubt was niggling the back of his mind. They could link Ruth to the stabbing, but in Freddie Cameron's opinion it wasn't the stabbing that killed Chattie. Unless they could link the drug to Ruth as well, a clever brief might still get her off. His brain began to worry over the possibility, and he pulled it back. Not here, not now.

'Anyone want another pint?' Hollis asked.

The order was taken, and under cover of the conversation that broke out around it, Slider said to Joanna, 'Well, we've got her, anyway, and a better example of where greed and self-pity can lead you, you wouldn't need to find. Her husband's a broken man. Poor Bill Simpson has been scared out of his wits, and still feels guilty about Chattie's death—'

'But at least the acne cure won't be suppressed. He'll be glad about that.'